THE ELECTRIC

EEL!

A Novel

BY CARSON PEAL

The Electric Eel!

Sunday June 1, 1919

ONE

Two A.M.

Julius stumbled downtown, pondering recent events. The gritty sights and aromas of High Street, near the state's capital, greeted him. The putrid smell of urine and unwashed humanity assailed him, buffeting his senses with noxious unpleasantries, constant reminders of the Grippe or something more commonly known as Spanish Flu. The article underneath a hobo screamed out from a disgusting newspaper in the near dark.

"...There is no need to worry as far as Columbus is concerned. The epidemic appears to be at its peak, and we are looking for a lessening number of cases within the next few days...October 8, 1918..."

But reports from his friends and family back east convinced him otherwise. His relatives in Boston and Philadelphia had written to him, begging him to stay away. For more than a year they had described the unimaginable horror of loved ones with hemorrhaging mucous membranes and bleeding from the eyes and nose...And the possibility of another wave coming back with G.I.s remained.

"It didn't originate in Spain..." a learned person had informed him... "It was just reported there in wartime as belligerent nations censored it..."

The vagrant rolled over in his partial slumber; his pants soiled light brown, breaking his train of thought. He gave Julius a look of displeasure, an inebriated sepia toned glare. The man blinked with indignance as if filled to the brim with stale beer and

The Electric Eel!

closed his eyes. His large tumescent belly vacillated against the newsprint like a shelf as he let out a painful, wheezy cough and rolled on his back like a beached whale.

Julius took two steps back as a hot stinky cloud exited the man's mouth... Was he now contaminated? He touched his face and recoiled. Quickly, he continued a few feet up High Street, his feet doing a makeshift drunken two-step.

As he walked up the main drag, a whoosh of warm early summer air blew over the backs of his arms and legs. Julius was now closer to the state capital where it was cleaner and more manicured. Across the street, a few vaudeville clubs were still boarded up from the recent quarantine. Many still refused to leave the house without something they called atomizers, water vapor sprays they believed kept the throat and nasal passages open.

To many, eating in large crowds was out of the question. During the past year tables were mandated to be twenty feet apart and restaurant workers were ordered to wear masks while serving or preparing food. He'd heard of ordinances where dishes were to be scalded with water to curb the flow of the disease. Schools were also closed, and teachers were ordered to conduct lessons via telephone.

As if on cue, an overwhelming nausea overtook his abdomen. Was it the effect of the alcohol or the dreaded flu? He couldn't be sure.

"How much did I drink?" he had asked his wife earlier that night.

"Not that much but those have some staying power..."

"*What* did I drink?"

"Something called an Electric Eel... Isn't it faboo?"

"Why is it green?" he had asked with much skepticism.

"Shhh... That's the Pernod Absinthe...Banned since 1912...The lemonade masks most of it anyway...But the crème de menthe makes it vibrant!"

"Where did *you* get it?"

But her usual, she walked away without answering. She had always had this

The Electric Eel!

fascination with mixology...Spirits as his father always called them...Though she rarely consumed alcohol herself... Why were women always so mysterious?

"Lately some women are feigning coughs to keep men at bay..." a male friend had whispered.

Up ahead on a side street stood an old, foreclosed restaurant. A casualty of the pandemic, most likely. A risky time to open an establishment, no doubt...

The structure was originally painted a bright white that had now turned to a dinghy grey. A decade of Central Ohio unpredictable inclement weather had sullied its exterior to its present state of decay.

"What a monstrosity!" Julius exclaimed as he walked the perimeter of the property.

A few scraggly Morning Glories climbed the remnants of a dilapidated chain fence, their spindly vines climbing haphazardly. Two purplish Victrola shaped blooms remained open despite the dark, hanging upside as if placed there intentionally. A rusty metal sign was secured crudely to one side. *Stay out!* Julius shuddered and walked away.

As he moved a gentle rain formed above. While it was unfamiliar, it was not unpleasant. Refreshing almost... Perhaps it would wash the alcohol out of his pores...

Once back on High Street, Julius caught his breath. It began to rain harder. He thought he'd heard footsteps.

"You're acting crazy... Get out of the rain...!" his mother's voice echoed in his head.

But he *wasn't* crazy! There was no time to think as two individuals emerged from the alley and appeared in the shadows, their faces stark in the dim light. Julius smiled briefly in recognition, but their expression belied any warmth.

Without hesitation one of them nodded to the other as a third individual appeared and then a fourth. All of them brandished something sharp and metallic. Julius began to panic and sprint. But soon they were on him...Stabbing at him from every angle. A second later Julius landed on the sidewalk, his chin hitting the concrete.

As Julius tried to catch his breath, the hobo from before began to run. One of his attackers sprinted after him and another landed on Julius's back like a jackal. Both were now bathed in blood. Rain began to pour down from above, mixing with Julius's hot, coppery blood.

Suddenly, an obnoxious *Aaoga* emanated from the blare of a Model T 's horn spooking his attackers. A spray of sidewalk runoff, warm rain and blood covered Julius as the jalopy whizzed by. Then Julius was left alone, face down in the rain to exsanguinate and expire.

TWO

June 28, 1919

Carlotta Alfonso was a big presence: She favored too much rouge on each cheek, giving her an angry, tempestuous appearance and a wavy, auburn, Edwardian hairdo that sat on her head like a dead squirrel, cinched severely with a beaded headband. A large, faceted, crimson semi-precious stone sat perched directly above her forehead like a circus performer.

"Drink up..." she said flashing amber eyes.

"Welcome to the Electric Eel..." someone else announced.

Carlotta pushed a curious cocktail down the bar. The bar patron looked at the concoction with suspicion and blinked. She burned a little at his indignance.

"No thanks...Looks like antifreeze..." he slurred. "I'll take a beer..."

"Take it on the house..." the other woman said. "Our signature cocktail...Then I'll get you a beer..."

The man at the bar turned to see everyone in the establishment was holding a bright green cocktail. He held it up to the light gingerly as if being peer pressured to do

The Electric Eel!

so. Heavily made-up women and men in three-piece suits looked up at him, hints of faceted, green glass reflecting in the light.

"Welcome to the grand opening of The Electric Eel!" Carlotta yelled. "Lobelia will serve you!"

She gestured to a full-figured black woman with unreadable eyes. A large white five-pointed flower dangled over her right ear like a nebula. Lobelia gave an obligatory nod and reached for a tray of minty cocktails.

Next, two handsome young men with sandy hair entered the establishment. The first, was slightly older with a substantial chin and light eyes. The second was taller and leaned on a crutch where his right leg should have been.

"Probably lost it in the war…" someone whispered.

"They just lost their father too-"

"Shh…"

"*Edgar!*" Lobelia exclaimed.

Someone attempted to help the young man on a bar stool, but he placed his hand up in protest. He sported a long sleeve shirt, tie, and silvery vest. He placed the crutch against his arm as his brother chose a seat close by.

"Looks like everyone's drinking the green stuff, Orville…" he said to him.

Orville Alfonso flashed him a disarming smile. As his mother poured her sons a cocktail the lace sleeve of her demure white Georgette blouse, dangled on the bar. His petite wife sat next to him; however, Carlotta pretended not to notice…

"Nice to see you, Carlotta…" she pressed.

"You too, Poppy…"

Carlotta turned and beamed at Orville, the clear favorite and examined him. *He looks like his brother…She pondered…But more handsome… And he thinks like his father…But smarter…And more pleasant than both of them put together! With my style and panache!* Lobelia caught her gaze as she giggled to herself.

The Electric Eel!

"Everything all right?"

"Oh, yes!" she said clapping her hands together. "Everything is...Just...Fine..."

And with that, Mrs. Alfonso turned to get the group's attention. Next, she lifted the signature cocktail and moved in a semi-circle. Her polished, well-manicured cranberry-colored nails shined in the dim light, the pointed edges of the fabric on her wrist drooping. Twenty pairs of eyes looked at her hypnotized.

"Wilson just announced the treaty has been signed! The Great War is over! What a glorious day to be alive! Today is the grand opening of The Electric Eel... My late husband Julius's, Lord rest his soul, and my dream..."

Carlotta looked up at the ceiling and paused for effect. A few in the room who knew Julius Alfonso found themselves waxing sentimental as well. Others who had lost sons in the war, remembered. She raised the emerald cocktail and beamed.

"Drink up! To new beginnings! To the end of the war! And to remembrance!"

"To remembrance!" someone shouted.

"To the end of the war!" someone else repeated.

"To Julius!"

"To us!" Carlotta said cutting them off. "While we have Electric Eels, of course, Lobelia has also made Punch a la Romaine... The same recipe that was on the Titanic...And Rum Cocktails... And Manhattans, the same way Jennie Churchill made them for the World's fair... And daiquiris...If you are feeling fancy...And of course wine and beer...And we have a few food items for purchase as well...Enjoy!"

"To Carlotta!" a stately older gentleman.

But Carlotta did not answer and instead gave a ladylike wave and disappeared behind the bar like an ingenue giving her final performance. Several of the bar patrons stood and applauded. Others were in tears. More than a few of the guests were already intoxicated.

"To family!" someone else yelled.

The Electric Eel!

"Without further ado, let me introduce our band…" Orville Alfonso said standing and taking the reign. "We have Jib on String Bass…Wallace on piano…And the beautiful songstress Iris on vocals…"

The group turned and clapped for the trio as they began: "Good Lucks to our Boys in Tan…"

"Where's Nani and Papi?" Edgar whispered to his brother.

"Shh…" Orville chided with brotherly condescension. "They wouldn't set foot in this place…"

"How's your sister?" someone else asked.

"Still on holiday…" Orville answered with much chagrin.

Iris's voice resonated throughout the din of the bar as people began to get served and chatter. Several small rectangular cakes in shades of light yellow were placed neatly on small plates.

"Victory cakes…" Lobelia informed the brothers. "Nice to finally be able to eat flour and sugar again!"

"And have a good steak!" one of the patrons yelled.

"Here! Here!"

In unison, they clinked their glasses and drank their green cocktails and then opted for more. Next, Lobelia reached for the collection of rocks glasses and pushed them on an aluminum tray. Carlotta ladled the Titanic era punch in crystalline cups as Orville took patrons' money…

A second later a commotion emanated from the front door. The brothers looked up, but Carlotta ordered them to remain quiet. She placed her cocktail on the bar and whispered.

"Let him handle it… That's what we hired him for…"

The bouncer, stood at the entrance like a wall and looked outside. The smell of sour hooch and body odor emanated under his nostrils. He sneered and called out into the night.

"Can't come in here!" he barked into the darkness.

"Murderers!" a hysterical voice shouted. "Bunch of no-good murderers!"

"Get outta here, you old sot..."

With hesitation, the bouncer took two steps forward underneath the midnight sky. *Where did he go?* He wondered.

Sensing trouble, Orville ignored his mother's direction and moved passed inebriated customers to the front of the building. He looked up at the doorman, who towered over him. The bouncer shrugged.

"Just a lush..."

The bouncer looked around as if he weren't sure... Orville forgot about the hub bub for the moment and turned to admire the establishment... *His* establishment... In a short period of time the building had been transformed from a dingy battleship grey to a crisp white with acidic green highlights. The words: "The Electric Eel" were written in a curly Art Nouveau script. He beamed with pride as the music concluded and walked inside.

"Where've you been, Orville?" a visibly intoxicated Iris called.

"Nowhere..."

"Let's celebrate..."

"You got it...!"

THREE

*A*s the night of the Twenty-Eighth of June turned into the morning of the Twenty-Ninth, a janitor pushed a mop across a sticky Electric Eel Bar floor...A newly invented wooden T-shaped groove sat atop the bucket allowing the mop head to slide easily in and out of the bucket without wringing the cleaning tool by hand. One of the cleaning crew put the mop head inside and pulled a large vertical lever downward to squeeze the excess filthy water and placed it back on the floor...Soon the water darkened.

"What a bunch of pigs..." one of them whispered to the other.

"Who says money buys class?"

"This sticky green stuff is everywhere..."

One of the crew stopped to examine it and sniffed. In the near dark, he couldn't place it... The woman, his partner, put her hands on her hips in indignation.

"Mint..." she said turning one of the bottles around and reading the label "Crème de menthe to be exact...And Absinthe..."

"Fancy..."

"Smells like toothpaste..."

"At least we're almost done..."

"Not so fast..." she responded handing him the cleaning tool. "There's more outside...And don't drip that mop across the clean floor! There's a broom on the porch!"

With reluctance the janitor placed the mop on the floor and wandered out onto the porch. The artificially sweet smell of liqueur was momentarily replaced by the smell of stale cigarettes, clove and burnt paper. Bent butts, or *coffin nails* as they were commonly known, stuck out in all directions from the outdoor seating and ashtrays, aptly named even though it would be decades before physicians would link smoking to cancer and early death. The words Muratti and Reynolds Camel were clearly imprinted on some of the more expensive ones.... Others such as Lucky Strike were simply unmarked and snuffed on the ground.

As he swept the discarded smokes into a pail, a noise caught his attention. *Perhaps a nocturnal rodent or opossum out searching for sustenance...*He thought. But something in his gut told him he was incorrect. He turned the broom on a shiny blue and white package of Muratti Ambassador Cigarettes with a gold band on the front and a small pile of tan dirt and discarded it. The smell was suffocating.

Next, another distinct sound resonated from somewhere outside. *Was this where*

The Electric Eel!

they offed the guy? He tried to picture the attack in his mind and then blocked it out as he emptied a tin ashtray.

He'd heard horror stories about the violence downtown, the spike in crime after the Great War. Some said it was returning G.I.s who had seen so much violence through battle fatigue coupled with their military training who turned it on their wives and children...Others said it was the influx of immigrants who were notoriously more violent than those who had lived here for generations...Others blamed it on the decrease of values amongst contemporary women particularly with the push for Suffrage and the consumption of alcohol. He couldn't be sure.

"Help me..." someone called barely above a whisper.

The custodian froze with broom in hand. For a second he thought it was over, but the voice called again. Gingerly he walked to its source. A coppery smell tickled his nostrils and then dissipated. *Blood!*

"What are you doing?" a stern voice yelled from inside.

"Nothing..." he stammered, realizing his own stupidity. "Just thought I heard something..."

"Well! Get this cleaned up out here and get in here! We don't have all night!"

"Sorry..."

But once she was gone he felt like a heel. Quickly, he swept the rest of the disgusting cigarette butts and straightened the chairs. Finally, he reached for the collection of used bar glasses and carried them inside to be washed. For a moment he thought he heard the cries again but this time he ignored it and closed the door.

Inside his partner was standing in a white dress and sensible shoes looking at him. He spotted something square and glass in the corner. He shook his head but couldn't place its intended purpose. She spoke to him without looking at him before he could inquire.

"Aquarium..." she informed him. "Mrs. Alfonso wants a live electric eel in a tank as a conversation piece...Says they can get up to eight feet long! No doubt we'll end up

The Electric Eel!

cleaning up after it!"

He shivered. *Where would someone even find something like that?* He wondered. A vision of being shocked filled his senses... A moment later, with no effort to hide her annoyance, his partner handed him the tray of glassware and pointed him in the direction of the small kitchen.

"And be careful with that stuff... Mr. Alfonso warned me that anything we break we pay for!"

A large Garis-Cochrane dishwashing machine sat in the middle of the kitchen, an ancient crude box with a motor and a pulley-driven pump that pumped water through the dishes. Carefully he placed the dishes on the top rack and closed the lid. Next he pulled the lever and forced the hot soapy water through the chamber.

A large cast iron, propane cookstove sat in the middle of the room alongside several stacks of already washed plates and saucers. Six tiny black burners sat on top of the appliance along with three compartments underneath that served as an oven and a warming drawer. His partner came in from the main room and began polishing the top as he stacked the bar glasses.

When satisfied the stove was clean, she moved onto the large white icebox in the corner. The appliance was white with a self-contained compressor and a large ominous, stainless-steel handle. She gave the door a push to make it sealed and stepped back.

"Looks good..." she complimented.

"Do we have to do this *every* night?"

"Three nights a week!" she said untying her apron and throwing it in a gunny sack. "But good steady work for now! All right! Almost morning! Let's get some shut eye!"

In the quiet of the night, he placed the key in the door and secured it. He paused in the dark and his partner looked at him with bemused curiosity. A voice called from somewhere in the night...He turned slightly as if trying not to appear daft.

"Did you hear that?"

"Hear what?"

"Nothing..."

FOUR

*N*ani and Papi, or Senor and Mrs. Alfonso, to most, sat on a small, China Blue loveseat in their modest home in Columbus, Ohio. Mrs. Alfonso stood and fiddled with a rag, polished a dish, and placed it back in a hutch. Her husband looked up at her with kind understanding eyes.

"Why are you so jumpy?" he asked.

"I'm not jumpy..."

But she looked down in the realization that she had wiped the same bowl off three times...Her hands shook slightly. She never could hide anything from him...*Ever*... A car horn honked outside. He gave her a meek smile.

"They're here!"

Once outside all his fears were quelled when a boy of about four in short pants ran into his great-grandfather's arms. Next, he turned and spotted his grandmother and ran to her. Orville, his father, seemed less sure about them as he got out of a reddish-orange convertible.

"Nice ride!" his father noticed.

"It's a 1919 6 Cylinder Buick Touring Car..." he bragged. "Bought it on credit..."

The vehicle's black carriage style wheels gleamed in the daylight in contrast to the white outer rim of the tires. A bright yellow highlight lined the perimeter of the center spoke of the wheel as if painted by hand. Orville pulled off a pair of pig skinned driving gloves and put them in his pocket.

"I thought you could only order black cars..." his grandfather pressed.

"Poor plebians can only get black..." he jeered under his breath with a haughty, blank stare. "But if you have money, you can order what you want..."

The Electric Eel!

Senor Alfonso's jaw dropped at this sentence. Orville, however, had already moved on. He turned to see his wife helping his disabled brother out of the car... Almost as an afterthought...

"Hi, Alastair!" Mrs. Alfonso beamed. "Hi, Poppy!"

She beamed with genuine affection for the young woman. Poppy was dressed in a creamy yellow bonnet that tied at the sternum and a gossamer sun dress. A pair of white summer sandals stuck out from the hem of the garment, the color of her painted toes peeping out slightly.

Edgar appeared next on the sidewalk as Poppy steadied his crutch. He gave his brother a wry look, years of frustration appearing briefly behind the whites of his eyes and then disappearing. He smiled at his grandparents as they led them inside.

"Beautiful day, Papi..." Orville said, forcing pleasantries.

"Mmm-hmm..." he said biting his lip.

"Oh! Mrs. Alfonso! Your plants are lovely!"

"Thank you, dear!"

Poppy reached for the door, but Alistair stepped in and held it for his uncle. The other adults looked at him with amusement. The house retained its Spanish influence... Black lace hung in every room like moss along with several gold crucifixes. Most of the home was decorated with waist high blue, yellow and white Merola tile. Poppy sniffed at the aroma of something distinctly floral that she couldn't place.

"Gardenia..." Mrs. Alfonso said answering her unspoken question. "Orville's sister brings it to me when she goes to Spain every year...

"How is she doing by the way?"

"Okay, I guess...Still on holiday..."

Edgar thought of his rarely seen baby sister Irene. *Funny how everyone talks about her even though they don't see her...* A small, framed picture of the three of them sat on the mantle.

The Electric Eel!

"It's a beautiful house!"

"We like it..." her husband chimed in.

"We have finger sandwiches and Gazpacho if you are hungry... Made with Manchego cheese...Can only do that when the cucumbers and tomatoes are fresh..."

Mrs. Alfonso motioned to a two-tiered tray in the middle of an inlaid tile table where several dainty sandwiches had been placed in a circle with the crusts removed. Poppy took one and balanced it precariously between her fingertips. Edgar leaned on his crutch and handed her a plate.

"Where are my manners? Do have a seat all of you..."

Edgar chose a heavy wooden armless chair that would be easiest to get in and out of without assistance while the others chose the more comfortable furniture around the sitting room. They sat for a moment in complete silence. Alistair looked around the room in childish boredom.

"How's your mother?" their grandmother asked.

Both brothers shifted in discomfort simultaneously as Poppy chewed on a mouthful of white bread and cream cheese. Senor Alfonso's eyes darted between his grandsons and great-grandson's similar faces. Poppy passed a piece of crusty bread to Alistair to chew on to keep him quiet.

"Mother is marvelous..." Orville piped up in her defense.

"Yes...Yes..." his brother added. "She just opened a restaurant and bar...It's called the Electric Eel after a bright green cocktail that she found out how to make and it's doing spectacular and-"

"Nope..." his grandfather said cutting him off.

"We just don't feel comfortable being in that area where your father died..." Mrs. Alfonso added.

"Understandable," Edgar said under his breath, caught completely off guard.

Senor Alfonso narrowed his eyes and looked at his wife in half-annoyance. She in turn pretended not to notice and stood to reach for a cucumber sandwich. Poppy noticed a large black and white photo of a young man in knickers and boots and a wide brimmed hat in a thick round silver frame.

"Is that Julius?" she asked.

"Yes," she answered trying not to tear up. "Right after he came back from the Spanish-American War...He wasn't very old then...All of about nineteen... Had to go against his own father's countrymen to do it..." she trailed off.

"My family practically disowned us..."

"I never knew that..." Edgar said.

"We were so proud!"

Then an awkward pause ensued. Alistair walked and sat between his great-grandparents but said nothing. Mrs. Alfonso reached for the young boy and held him close to her bosom as if she may never see him again. Alistair looked around, not comprehending the obvious tension between the adults.

"My sweet boy..." she whispered.

With that, the older man pushed past them and reached for something in a small drawer. He turned to Alistair and smiled. He held a hollow, brightly painted, leaden figurine in his palm and handed it to the boy.

"It was your grandfather's..." he announced. "I think we have a few more around here somewhere...I know there was a horse and a carriage and a cannon...Might be worth a fortune as an antique someday..."

Alistair looked at the toy with elation. He held it up to the light and zoomed it around the room. They softened a bit at his joy.

"That other picture..." Mrs. Alfonso said pointing to a teenage boy and a girl in a communion dress. "Was your dad and Virginia right after she was confirmed... They were so close... Even though they were twelve years apart, they were close..."

"How is Aunt Gin?" Edgar asked, as he always thought fondly of his aunt.

"Not the same since your dad died..." she trailed off. "But none of us are... Never did get married... Beautiful girl like that...It's a crying shame..."

"She stops in occasionally..." her husband added. "But we understand she's busy..."

"Well..." Orville said, growing bored with the conversation. "We'd better be going..."

"But you just got here..." his grandmother tried to protest.

But her husband stopped her as if glad that the meeting was ending. They stood in unison like a choir or a jury as Edgar leaned on his crutch and found his center of gravity. Alistair gripped the toy soldier in his fist like a prize.

"Your grandmother is pro-temperance..." Senor Alfonso whispered in Edgar's ear. "I personally prefer a glass of wine with dinner..."

Slowly, they processed outside into the bright June light. Mrs. Alfonso shielded her eyes and squinted. The hot sun had moved directly above the house, its yellow-white rays bouncing off the tile roof in all directions. Orville jumped in the car in impatience and started it.

To everyone's surprise, Alistair turned and clung to his grandfather's pantleg. A catch rose in the bottom of Senor Alfonso's esophagus as he placed the boy on the ground. Poppy lollygagged and waved to her husband's grandparents as she helped Edgar and the boy into the front seat of the car.

"If you change your mind..." Orville called to his grandfather from the front seat.

"If you change yours..."

FIVE

Virginia Alfonso slipped quietly into the Electric Eel at nine o'clock that following Friday. Despite societal rules lessening for women to imbibe, the bar scene in the late teens was still overwhelmingly male. And women who *did* chose to frequent establishments that served alcohol were often looked down on.

"Have you seen some of those homely bar flies who come out of those places downtown?" her father had told her with a grimace as if sucking a lemon.

But Virginia was *not* one of those undesirable women...Instead she was comely with a symmetrical face, wide silvery eyes, and wavy platinum blond hair...She was slender and in heels stood taller than most of her potential dance partners. On this particular night she had chosen a pale blue knee length silk dress and chunky shoes that laced up the vamp.

An equally attractive man waved to her from his place at the bar. Despite the heat, he was dressed in a tan tweed suit and matching hat with a dark band. As Virginia pulled up a seat, a chatty, tipsy man began talking to them from his hunched over position at the bar.

"Thank God that dreadful 1917 prohibition is over...Eh?"

"That was only supposed to be temporary..." Virginia's male friend answered. "Wilson wanted all the grain to go toward the war...And it was originally only in grain-producing states!"

"Temporary, my foot!" he rebutted.

"Now if the Volstead Act passes Congress, and alcohol is made illegal...We're in trouble!" Virginia found herself shouting over the din of the crowded bar.

"Never happen..." he said. "Name's Talbert... But everyone calls me Tal..."

The man nodded to him politely. He leaned over verdant green cocktail now partially watered down from melting ice. Virginia pointed to it.

"Said it was their signature cocktail..." he said dryly. "Personally, I don't care for it..."

"Yea give me a beer any day..."

"Here's your gin and tonic..."

The man held the amber drink up to the light and smiled at its familiarity. He looked at both of them as if he were done talking. A black woman with dark eyes examined him.

"All good, there, Phil?"

The Electric Eel!

"Perfect..."

"And what can I get for you two?" she asked turning to them.

"I'll have a white wine spritzer..." she informed her without hesitation.

"And I'll have whatever you have on tap..."

"What kind of hors oeuvres do you have?"

"I'll get you a menu..." she said with a bright smile, turning toward the back.

Just then a loud voice bellowed behind her. Talbert felt himself being slapped on the back by a considerable hand and for a moment he felt the urge to fight. Virginia turned to see her nephew, Orville, who was closer to her age than her own sibling.

"*Aunt Gin!!*" he yelled with much more manic volume than intended.

"Well, hello there Orville..." she said trying to hide her disdain for him. *Don't embarrass me!* "This is my friend Talbert..."

"Tal..." he corrected.

"Tal...Got it..."

Is he drunk? Talbert wondered. He swiveled on his barstool and looked at him. The young man reeked of alcohol and too much cologne...Shalimar or Jockey Club...Virginia held her breath and gagged.

"Here's your white wine spritzer..." Lobelia said with genuine pleasure.

Virginia was relieved to focus on her drink...On *anything* other than her intoxicated nephew... She reached for a rye grass straw and fiddled with it.

"Well! The band is starting! You should take a gander...That Iris is quite a dish..."

Orville made an hourglass shape with his hands and gave a wolfy smile. Then his mother appeared behind him, paying no mind to her sister-in-law or the man with her. The band began to play Marion Harris's contemporary tune as she pulled him out of earshot.

"My heart's sad and I am forlorn,

My man's treating me mean,

The Electric Eel!

I regret the day that I was born

And that man of mine I've never seen,

My happiness, it never lasts a day,

My heart is almost breaking while I say:

A good man is hard to find..."

Orville's gaze shifted to where Iris sang in front of a large grey and black microphone on a stand. Her alabaster legs peeked out from a slit in her low-cut black dress as she sang the mournful ballad. Iris's equally pallid hair moved in time with the music. Orville swooned.

"Focus, Orville...*Focus!*"

"Sorry..."

"Why is your aunt here?" his mother hissed.

"Darned if I know..." he said turning from her. "Maybe she wants a drink?"

Not to be patronized, Carlotta grabbed her eldest son by the shoulders and spun him like a top which, in his inebriated state, made him feel a little queasy. Next, he grabbed his abdomen and doubled over for a second as if he had been sucker-punched. She forced eye contact with him the way one might confront an aggressive dog.

"And who is that guy she is with? Why is *he* here?"

"Maybe she finally got a beau... Papi will be so happy!"

Carlotta looked at him with incredulity. Her face was painted heavily in shades of pink and red like the villainess in a campy opera. Strands of her coppery hair fell forward into her eyes.

"She hasn't had a *beau* in forever..." she hissed like a copperhead. "What'd he say his name was?"

"Tallmadge...Talman... Something like that...Goes by Tal..."

"Talbert?" she said cutting him off.

"Yea! That's it!" he said brightening.

The Electric Eel!

"He's a detective you twit!"

His light eyes darkened like a bathtub suddenly filled with polluted water and soon the apples of his cheeks burned with some unknown internal fire. A second later Lobelia appeared in the doorway with a tray. Her eyes looked at them as if she were interrupting.

"We were just passing through..." Carlotta promised forcing a calm bravado.

"Was there something you needed, Lobelia?" Orville asked.

"Ummm... Miss Dupeon brought her dog with her..."

Carlotta blinked as if not fully understanding what was being asked of her. Orville narrowed his eyes. Lobelia smiled awkwardly awaiting her next move.

"Iris Dupeon... The singer..." he explained.

"What do I care?" the look on Carlotta's pinched face said.

"She brings it everywhere..."

"Is it hurting anyone?" his mother asked.

"No... It's backstage... She brings in quite a crowd...And she sings beautifully," he offered.

"Keep it away from the food..."

Orville walked out of the kitchen away from the bar to where the band was taking a break. A statuesque wheat-colored Afghan Hound with a black mask and a tail like a question mark acknowledged him cordially. The dog's aloof demeanor changed at the sight of Iris, and it mustered a happy, dopey expression.

"The dog can stay..." Orville informed her. "As long as it doesn't cause problems...Any complaints and it's out!"

"Oh, thank you, Mr. Alfonso!" she called in a speaking voice that was much higher and girly than he expected.

"You're welcome!"

And then to his surprise, she dropped to her knees in front of the dog and wrapped her twiggy arms around its neck. The dog straightened and panted slightly as she pressed her nose into its fur. Then she kissed the dog on the head the way one might a child.

"Did you hear that, Peaches? You can stay! You won't have to be locked up in that apartment of ours all day!"

Next, she stood and kissed Orville in the same way that she had the cherished pet. He blushed slightly. His mother caught his eye from across the room and he was forced to release her.

"Are you done carousing with the band?" Carlotta barked from her place near the bar.

"She promises to keep the dog quiet..."

"Your aunt and I were just talking..."

"Well, Tal and I'd better be going..." Virginia said standing from the bar, more than a little tipsy.

"Don't you mean *Detective* Talbert?" Carlotta shrieked.

Virginia blanched. Tal steadied her by placing his hand in the middle of her back. Both sought out the nearest exit.

"Easy now... Those Electric Eels will throw you for a loop!" someone from the bar offered.

"She never could hold her liquor..."

With that Orville led his Aunt Virginia and Tal to the front door. From the bar his mother gave them a searing glare. She motioned to the bouncer, but Orville put his hand up.

"That won't be necessary, mother..."

"This establishment and everyone who works here is under investigation for the murder of Julius Alfonso..." he informed them with the flash of a badge.

"Please don't return without a warrant..." Carlotta said.

SIX

*E*dgar Alfonso learned separately of the family drama from his mother, brother and then aunt; however, like always, he remained neutral. After a long day of managing books for the bar, he lay prostrate on his back on his mattress in his ground floor apartment behind his brother's home. His nephew Alistair played with his toys on the hardwood floor.

"Pow! Pow!"

"How are you going to get up to catch him?" Orville barked at him as he tied his necktie.

"Leave your brother alone!" Poppy said in defense.

"I wasn't being ugly... Alistair is fast and can get into things..."

"We'll be fine..."

"He has a phone..." Poppy whispered to Orville as she reached for a ruana to wrap around her shoulders. "And Alistair can get into bed and in and out of the tub by himself with little help..."

"I'll be fine..." Alistair answered.

"Can we go now?"

"Gladly...!"

Edgar sighed and looked over at the shoe black candlestick style phone on the end table. A flared morning glory shaped receiver hung from a clip on the end alongside the small circular rotary dial. A year or so earlier, his father had paid someone from Ma Bell to install it and connect it to a local switchboard.

"Luckily, the state capital has tons of local switchboards..." he remembered the repairman saying.

Despite all the worry about his safety, the phone was rarely, if ever, used. He had long ago come to terms with the fact that he was a single man who didn't get social calls. *No*

The Electric Eel!

decent woman wants to be saddled with a cripple... He thought.

And all the women who are interested in me want to baby me... He thought sitting up slightly, looking around the small bedroom. *And I don't need a mommy...My own mother doesn't want to mother me!*

Edgar looked down at his right side where his right leg had been. A chunk of his body was now cut off at the hip, the end of his pants leg squishy like an empty sleeping bag. Occasionally he favored a short pant while home alone but with his nephew around he got tired of being asked about his amputation.

"What time do you go to bed there kid?"

"Nine..." Alistair answered without looking at him.

"It's ten till..." he said looking up at the clock. "A few more minutes...Then go get washed up..."

"Okay, Uncle Edgar..."

What's my brother talking about with this kid? He's a gem... Edgar pictured his friends other children who acted like brats...*But I've never seen it with this one...*

"And he's smart..." he had told his sister-in-law earlier.

"Oh, I know..."

"All right, Alistair! Go get ready and get in your bed clothes..."

The boy gave an exasperated sigh but did as he was instructed. Carefully he picked up the figurines and placed them in a small toybox that had been set up for him to use when he was visiting. Edgar reached for the crutch on the right side of the bed and hoisted himself upright and walked to the door. Alistair disappeared and a moment later he heard the tap groan.

"Don't let get it too hot..." he instructed from the hall.

"I won't..."

"And use soap behind your ears..."

"I promise..."

The Electric Eel!

Alistair emerged a second later drying himself with a linen towel. His uncle nodded in approval and pointed to the small wooden four post bed that had been set up in the next room. He watched as his nephew pulled on a pair of night clothes.

"He's so grown up..."

Soon Alistair climbed into bed and closed his eyes. A minute later, Edgar climbed back onto his own mattress to rest. Since he'd become disabled, sleeping had become precarious. Sleeping on his right side, his preference, was now out of the question as the weight of his existent left leg crushed his waist. Sleeping on his left side was okay until the feeling of his heart beating against the mattress grew tiresome, then he'd have to move on his back. Soon he began to dream.

It always amazed him how in his waking life he was very immobile; however, in his dreams he *soared*...Often he found himself sprinting like a Cheetah or leaping like a gazelle...The way he had done as a kid...

As he dozed, he found himself in the yard behind their family home...The bright sun warmed his face and he smiled genuinely, the last time he could remember. His grandfather's car lay parked in the field, beckoning them.

"No! Papi said to stay away from it!"

"Ah, c'mon! Don't be a baby!" one of Orville's friends jeered.

And then, as often happened, the dream began to speed up like a record on a turntable. And, like always, he was begging his brother to slow down...Playfully at first...

"Please...Orville... Slow down..."

But then he began to panic...*Pleading* with his brother...His friends laughing at his terror...

But before he could get his brother's attention, a huge weight landed on his right side... Crippling his life forever...And like always...Edgar woke up in a cold sweat... Crying...

SEVEN

*I*rene Alfonso-Wright arrived in her Cadillac Type 57 to make an appearance in Columbus, Ohio... The kind of status symbol seen in silent films where the driver sits in a separate compartment from the passengers in the back. She'd make a *cameo* as her mother would call it...A pre-planned guest appearance in her own life...

Because of her husband's political motives...*Mr. Wright* as everyone called him...It behooved her to keep up the appearance of maintaining connections with her small-town roots... But Irene walked a fine line with them as well...She didn't want to appear *too* close... No sense in being too chummy either... With a recently murdered father... A foul-mouthed powder keg of a mother...A sleazy bar purchased under questionable means... And one brother a philanderer and the other a cripple... All *potential* liabilities to the aspirations of a budding socialite...

If she had it her way, she'd never look back...She was more comfortable in her world anyway, amongst the glitterati and the movers and shakers then in the world she had been born into. Gently she kissed Mr. Wright on the cheek and stepped out of the fancy car.

"I'll see you tonight..." she whispered.

"Thank you, dear..."

*He always bought into it...*She observed. *Men are so easy...* Touch their hand... Stroke their ego...Tell them how smart they are...

Up ahead the lights and sounds of a now happening club pulsed. She nearly gagged at the smell of hops and stale cigarettes. *The Electric Eel* was written in a gaudy brightly colored font against an equally bright background. *Hold it together, Irene!* She told herself, her curiosity getting the best of her. In silence she slipped inside.

At first no one noticed her...Every time she came to a bar she was surprised to see the number of women drinking...Used to be no woman would be caught *dead* in a bar...

The Electric Eel!

Perhaps her grandmother was right… Alcoholism was taking over men *and* women…

Unlike most of the other ladies in the establishment, she was dressed in conservative attire. Others sported short cocktail dresses, beads, headbands, and fringe but she had chosen an expensive suit jacket, wide brimmed hat, gloves, and pumps. *Most of these women I suspect are single and on the prowl…*

Unlike most other women in the place her hair was a dark sable brown…They'd all seen silent films with blond vamps stealing handsome suitors away. She looked around the room, unimpressed.

"A natural brunette in a sea of wanna be platinum blonds…"

Then a familiar bawdy voice called to her. The only redhead in the club…She cringed for a moment and then turned to acknowledge her mother.

"There's my youngest child!"

*She's drunk…*Irene observed…Orville approached next…*He's drunk…*

"Relax…" she called drawing the word into two equally irritating syllables. "I've just had wine…"

*That's right…She gets mean on whiskey…*Irene remembered. *She's pleasant and friendly on wine and beer…*

"I didn't think you slummed it with the likes of us anymore…" Orville shouted.

"Well, Mr. Wright was going to pick me up for that new Rudolph Valentino picture…They have a nine o'clock showing. "The Delicious Little Devil…" Maybe you've heard of it?"

"Oh, I've heard of that…" a woman with a squeaky voice and too much makeup butted in. "With Mae Murray but who's gonna notice it with him in the picture?"

"Sister dear, this is Iris…The blues singer in our house band… Iris this is my sister Irene…"

"Charmed, I'm sure…"

Both her voice and accent were distinct. Irene narrowed her eyes as it grated on her a

The Electric Eel!

bit. *New York maybe? New Jersey?*

"She has a beautiful singing voice…" her brother assured her.

"Where are you from?" Irene asked.

As was her custom she self-elocuted, intentionally choosing the sounds and shapes of her words before she uttered them. Many around her, especially those who were intoxicated, spoke sloppily allowing the words to just fall as they may instead of putting any classy forethought to them. She sensed Iris was in the latter.

"I live here…" she hesitated.

"Where are you *from*?" she repeated.

"Brooklyn originally…"

"Ah…" she said as if uncovering a gruesome clue.

Iris paused in awkward silence. Her cupid bow mouth pursed together as if afraid to say anything else for fear of being judged. Irene could see she was young…Maybe not even twenty-five.

"My sister has a habit of doing that to people…" he whispered in her ear loud enough for everyone to hear.

In the background the piano player began playing Gershwin's "The Love of a Wife…" Iris's ears perked up like a Spaniel and she headed toward it as if in a sudden fugue state. Orville straightened his body and gave a forlorn look.

"You're married…" Irene mouthed.

Orville turned and shot her a look as if caught off guard. His cheeks reddened in an embarrassment obvious to all around him at the bar. A few feet away his brother sat taking it all in.

"Nice to see you too, Irene…" Edgar called over an orangish cocktail.

As if on cue Irene walked to where he sat. He gave her a half smile. *He's at least sober…*She observed.

"Pull up a seat…"he offered.

The Electric Eel!

"Oh, I can't stay... I'm being picked up for a film..."

*Can't say that I'm surprised...*He thought. From a distance, he too watched Iris as she began to perform.

"I saw Aunt Virginia yesterday..." Irene started.

But before the words left her mouth she knew that she had misspoke. Her mother flew at her like a panther and the normally placid Irene shrunk. Edgar raised an eyebrow at the spectacle but said nothing, fearing she'd turn on him next.

"Don't *ever* mention her name in my presence again!" she shouted. "Did you hear what she did? She came in here with a detective...*A detective!*"

"Keep it down..." Orville attempted.

"I will not keep it down! Not in my bar! And I won't be talked to that way by my own son! Or by anybody for that matter! Sorry to fly off the handle at you, Irene, but that woman is dead to me...Dirt under my feet! In my day you didn't turn on family...And she *did*!"

"Well, I'd better be going..." Irene said with feigned, forced politeness.

"So *soon*?" her mother asked with pathetic inebriated eyes.

*They hate me...*She thought. *I'm an outsider amongst my own family...Maybe I should stick with just visiting my grandparents...They seem to get me...*

"I may stop in tomorrow night..." she informed her mother.

"Whatever you like, dear..."

"Nice to see you, Irene..." Edgar called.

"You too... Nice to meet you all..."

A second later, Irene was relieved to be away from them in the steamy night air. *Like throwing pearls before swine...*She told herself. Then she spotted it: the black Cadillac that would take her to her castle, her husband in the backseat waiting to shower her with gifts and affection... A chauffeur in a brown cap opened the door.

Once inside, Irene turned to look at Mr. Wright. He was older than she would have preferred, with a receding hairline, but he was epitome of class and had the connections she so desired. *And he adores me...*She thought. *Of course...What's not to love?*

She looked around the car's decadent leopard skinned interior and felt relieved. Quickly, Irene caught a glimpse of the seedy "Electric Eel Bar" as it passed in her periphery and then she turned and looked at her own, perfect, opulent world...And she was grateful to be away for the night...

EIGHT

Carlotta Alfonso decided to have one of her "spells" as she lay on the fainting couch in the parlor. As usual, her newly hired servants bought into it at her disposal. One of them placed a cool compress on her forehead and touched her temples.

*The new found joys of being nouveau-riche...*She thought. *Unlike my daughter who married into old money...*Carlotta surmised. *Who did she think she was coming in that Cadillac? Cecil B. DeMille?* Well, two can play at that game, Irene...

"You better call your son, Miss Alfonso, and tell them you won't be there..." the older more matronly of the two servants beckoned.

"I'll try..." she said meekly. "But I'm needed..."

"Shh... Just rest...I'll call..."

The first couple of weeks of owning a successful bar had been new and exciting; however, truth be told she had grown bored with it, night after night. While she loved the new found wealth, she found the work gritty and beneath her. When she has initially envisioned owning a restaurant she had pictured glamorous partygoers but instead she found mostly banal drunkards and ne'er do wells.

"How are you feeling?" one of the help asked with genuine concern.

She opened one eye like a sleeping dolphin and chose her words carefully and then peered at her with suspicion. The girl's brown eyes were wide and luminous. Carlotta smiled in spite of herself.

The Electric Eel!

"This ache is taxing..."

"I'll call Mr. Orville..." the older one sighed. "You best be gettin to bed..."

"I s'pose..." she said forcing the words out as it were an arduous task.

She allowed the young maidservant to help her up. *From one position of rest to another...*She observed.

"Mother pressed your nightgown... Do you want me to help you out of your day clothes?"

"She's a gem...But that won't be necessary..." she said looking at her with wide eyes.

As Carlotta lay, she spotted something that made her wince: a newspaper article about her husband's untimely demise. A salacious picture of Julius face down on the pavement with his eyes and mouth open in death. She pointed to it and let out a mouthy scream.

"*Noooooo! Make it stop!*"

Carlotta shrieked like a banshee. The other woman rushed into the bedroom and looked at her young daughter and then at the woman on the bed. *Was she possessed?*

"What is it, Ms. Alfonso?"

"I can't talk about it... It's too painful.."

"Come now... You can tell me...Did you see a rat?"

Carlotta let out an indecipherable yell and pointed. One of the women turned to see where she was gesturing. A crisp folded newspaper lay on the bedside table.

"Where did *that* come from?" the girl asked.

"Get it out of here!" Carlotta screamed. "Does William Randolph Hearst have no soul?"

The woman folded it under her arm and handed it to her daughter. Next, she reached for the cold rag from before and placed it on Carlotta's forehead as she took in a belabored breath. She placed the cloth over her eyes to calm her like a bird in a cage.

"Poor Julius... Poor, poor Julius..."

The Electric Eel!

"Try not to think about it and just rest…"

As Carlotta rested the other servants sat in the room and waited…Like a hospital room…Or a wake…

"Should we call a doctor?" the young servant girl asked her mother.

"I'll be okay…" Carlotta uttered barely above a whisper. "It's just been so traumatic these past few weeks and then seeing Julius splayed out on the concrete that way… It's all such a shock…"

"We tried to get a hold of Mr. Orville…" the other woman informed her. "We left a message for him at the club…"

"Thank you… Thank you all…But I just want to rest for a few is all…"

"We understand…"

The bedroom was what one might expect from a woman like Carlotta; loud, floral, and feminine in shades of warm reds and golds. Little did the servants know she had recently redecorated immediately after her husband's demise. The more masculine den-like appearance was now her own private sanctuary. One of the women pulled up a lacy Louis XIV chair and began mending.

A half an hour later Carlotta Alfonso's eyes opened with a shot. The servants stood over her as if she had woken from the dead. Next, she flung the comforter off the bed and placed both feet on the floor like the Bride of Frankenstein.

"Hand me my favorite red dress…"

"Where are you going? You need to rest…"

"The Electric Eel. My sons need me…" she mustered.

"She's so strong…" one of them whispered to the other.

An hour later than planned, a taxi arrived in front of Carlotta's home on East Broad Street. As she waited, her mood soured to contemptuous at best. To show her

The Electric Eel!

impatience and displeasure, she tapped her foot and touched the face of her filigreed ladies' timer wrist watch with the tip of her index finger as he pulled into the drive. To further her annoyance, the cabbie ignored her.

"Maybe you should just stay home, Miss Alfonso...?" one of the servants advised her with great caution.

"I'm going!" she snapped, turning to the cab driver. "You're late! Don't you know it's not safe out there for a lady after dark?" she barked over the side of the porch.

"Easy, lady! We'll get there..." he muttered.

"What did you say?" she responded.

"Nothing... Are you coming or not?"

"Such insolence!" she snorted as she walked to the cab. "It's filthy! And there's rust everywhere! I'd do better on the Lusitania! And it stinks!"

Per the custom of the decade, he opened the back door to the car so she could step up as if entering a stagecoach. A small black and white checkerboard pattern ran alongside the perimeter of the windows. Reluctantly she climbed in and began flicking specks of the detritus of cigarette butts and dirt off the car's interior.

Next, as if to let him know further about the malodor, she brandished a small black lace fan and pinched her nose slightly. The cab driver burned with ire. A second later they began their tense five-minute ride.

"Electric Eel bar, please!"

He raised his eyebrows in shock in the rearview mirror at the mention of the establishment. She narrowed her eyes like a bull preparing to charge. He gave a smug smile of satisfaction.

"Electric Eel, it is..."

"Don't be so quick to judge! I own it!" she snapped.

Up ahead the sky was beginning to darken to grey. A few small clouds formed nearby. The cab driver attempted small talk, hoping to salvage his gratuity for the ride...

The Electric Eel!

Carlotta, however, was having none of it.

"Rain's coming... Don't worry... It's summer. I think there's an umbrella back there if you need one..."

"Keep your eyes on the road! I swear! Is this road *this* bumpy or do you just not know how to maneuver a car? You are transporting a lady! Do you have a license to operate a motor vehicle in the State of Ohio?"

"Yes, ma'am!"

"If so, I'd like to see it!"

"Can do... Almost there!"

*Thank God...*He thought. The establishment glowed to the left; the melancholy wail of a clarinet hung in the air somewhere. He hopped out to help her. Begrudgingly, she paid him his fare and walked inside. A second later the tires squealed as he if were gunning it before she changed her mind.

"Carlotta!" someone yelled.

"Mother! You're supposed to be resting!" Edgar said from his place at the barstool.

I should have stayed home! She thought. *They don't appreciate the hard work I do, anyway...* She nodded.

"How are you feeling, Carlotta?" Poppy asked.

"Better thank you..."

All of a sudden Orville approached his mother and leaned in to say something. For once he appeared sober and collected. He was wearing a tan linen suit and polished wingtips.

"Don't you look handsome!" she yelled loud enough for everyone in the bar to hear.

"Aunt Virginia and Irene are here..."

Like a storm cloud, Carlotta's less than pleasant mood returned. As if on cue, the two attractive women emerged at the bar. Virginia suddenly became quiet at the sight of her former sister-in-law. Irene was unfazed by her mother's glare.

The Electric Eel!

"I feel my headache returning..."

"Nice to see you again, Carlotta..." Virginia offered.

"Did my son *allow* you in here?"

"You only banned the detective unless he had a warrant..." he whispered, walking between them.

"Fair enough...But keep your voice down..." she said with a dismissive wave of her left hand. "But if she tries anything she's out!"

"Understood."

"Pour me a scotch and soda, would you?" she asked.

"Sure..."

"Isn't the clarinet lovely, Carlotta?" Poppy asked.

"I was just thinking the same thing... Very now..." Irene said pulling up a chair enjoying the instrument's melodious whine.

"What's that dog still doing here?" Carlotta whispered to her eldest son.

"You told her the dog could stay..."

"I changed my mind..." she said caught off guard.

"It'll break her heart," Edgar piped in. *"You* tell her!"

Seeing she was outnumbered Carlotta acquiesced. *They're all against me...*She watched as the men swooned over the singer as she exited the stage. Her deep blue scope neck dress a dark contrast to her light hair and skin. Someone handed her a drink.

Soon Wallace the piano player and Jib joined her along with the new addition, Freddy the man with the clarinet. Iris sniffed the fizzy deep brown concoction carbonated concoction with suspicion   "What's this?" she asked.

"Coca-Cola..."

"What's *in* it?"

"Why! Cocaine silly! Didn't you know that's where it got its name? Coca leaves!"

Iris sipped it and nodded. The taste of sugar lingered on her palette for a second. And soon they were tasting it. Her sinuses cleared a bit as it went down, her heart raced a little.

A second later Orville joined the group of musicians. One of them poured a little more in each glass and offered him some. But Wallace hesitated for fear he'd rat them out. Orville sipped it with glee.

"It's not *illegal*..." one of them quipped.

"Just don't tell mother..." he made them promise.

October 28, 1919

"*T*he day that launched a million speakeasies..." one of the newspapers famously wrote, began on a chilly, banal Tuesday at the end of October.

A few regulars at the Electric Eel gathered around in a semi-circle around the bar. Despite the small group, it was *all* anyone could talk about... Carlotta became annoyed as they continued to talk about it ad nauseam.

"The government already banned it on Indian reservations..." one of the regulars informed them over his Jack Daniels. "Not their fault, they just can't handle it like we can..."

"I thought Wilson said that was just a war time thing..."

"Russia tried that too... Can you imagine banning booze in *Russia*?"

"Can we talk about something else?" Orville asked, sensing his mother's aggravation with the topic.

But truth be told, he was more than a little bit curious. *What would happen to their business? Their livelihood depended on the sale of alcohol... Their food sales were marginal at best...* Another customer persisted with the topic.

"And to think most of those Protestant tee-totallers are from Ohio... That LaGuardia fellow even called it a war on New York! Can you beat that?"

"Does that mean we can't drink?" Edgar asked.

Carlotta shot her youngest son a look. He shrugged and nursed his cocktail. A second later she disappeared behind the bar.

"I don't think so…They're just making it illegal to sell or transport it…" Lobelia informed them.

"Makes no sense…"

"And I heard you can still make up to 200 gallons for home consumption a month!"

"Is that true? I could do that in my bathtub!"

Together the group chortled, save for one. Carlotta poured herself a nip in the kitchen, downed it and returned a second later. It warmed the center of her chest in an instant and she regained her confidence momentarily. Lobelia pretended not to notice the immediate change.

Next Poppy walked in with Alistair. Now five years old, he looked up at his grandmother and uncle at the bar. With adult suspicion A few men at the bar straightened in unease at the sight of a child in a bar.

"He isn't staying…" Poppy informed them.

"If the Feds saw him in here we'd be shut down…As we *should* be…" Carlotta whispered.

"He just wanted to see his grandmother and uncles…"

Carlotta winced at the first word. If she hated being called a mother, she *loathed* being labelled a grandmother…Grandmothers knitted doilies and gave out hard candy and moms kissed boo boos and made lunches… She was neither of those things… At times even waiting on people in a bar was too much for her…

"Hi, grandma!" Alistair called.

"Oh, hello!" she called with much bravado.

To Carlotta's further annoyance, her daughter Irene walked into the bar. Per usual her youngest child was dressed impeccably. *Going to run a white glove over my bar, dear?* She wanted to ask but refrained.

"What are you doing in town?" Edgar asked with genuine affection for his sister.

Irene brightened. She straightened the hem of her cream-colored suit and touched his shoulder. *I never want to make him stand unless he has too...*

"Mr. Wright is in Columbus for a vote on ratifying..."

But as soon as she said it, she regretted it. What had started out as a brag had now become a point of shame. Ten pairs of eyes zoomed in on her in a sizzling glare. *They know where my husband stands on the political aisle... And they know I encouraged him to do so...*

"Will The Electric Eel still be able to stay open, grandma?" Alistair asked politely.

Carlotta burned with uncomfortable rage and looked away as if slapped. Taking her cue, Poppy touched her son's shoulders and led him toward the door. Alistair gave a confused look that children sometimes do when they say the right thing at the wrong time...

"We don't know if we'll be able to stay open, dear..." Carlotta began speaking to Alistair. She began to squeeze out big crocodile tears. "Some people don't think we should have the right to make a living..."

One of the male bar goers handed her a handkerchief. Carlotta blotted her eyes, careful not to swear her eye makeup. Irene drew in a breath and held it captive in her chest and then exhaled slowly. *Thank you...*She mouthed.

"Well, I should be going..." she said reaching for her handbag.

Her mother stood a few feet in painful silence. As always, Irene could not tell if her mother's hurt was genuine or if she was just trying to be manipulative. *I can't take the chance either way...* She approached her with caution, grateful that there was thirteen feet of bar between them.

*No one would ever know we were related...*Irene thought looking straight at her mother. *I am petite, svelte, and classy, and I have success… Everything she's ever dreamed of… She is brash and loud…Besides, I resemble father anyway…*

"I hope you're happy with yourself…" Carlotta uttered in her direction.

Her mother reached for a red dishrag and began polishing champagne flutes hanging nearby. Sensing tension, Orville looked first at Carlotta and then at his sister. Just then another bar patron piped up in Irene's defense.

"Wait a minute! We don't even know how Irene's husband voted or if he had anything to do with the Volstead Act…Our own president vetoed it!"

But they *did* know…The look on her family's face said. Even Edgar, her closest ally, had grown suspiciously quiet. He mustered an awkward boyish smile and reached for a highball.

At the front of the bar, the musicians were warming up; however, something seemed off with them too. The normally upbeat timbre of their tunes seemed somber somehow as if they were playing a hymn on the Titanic. One of them fiddled with a clarinet case while the other wrestled with a giant Bass Fiddle.

What's the point? The look on their faces said. They barely noticed Irene watching them.

The long muzzle of a large blonde sight hound peeked out from behind a small Shoji screen, but the singer beckoned the dog back from view. The dog's dark almond shaped eyes blinked, not revealing its mysteries as she coaxed it back again. She kissed the hound gently on the top of its skull and put her finger up to order the canine to remain quiet.

A second later Iris walked to the front of the stage and began warming up. The bass player ad-libbed, followed by Wallace on the piano. Irene heard the clarinet wailing its mournful tune as she walked outside.

While Irene was normally detached from all things spiritual and emotional, something hit her on the sidewalk. Perhaps it was the temperature dropping or the shunning of her immediate family...Or maybe it was something else? As she stepped onto the concrete she realized: *Father was killed here...*

From both numerous newspaper articles and having to identify her father, Irene shuddered. She knelt down, careful not to snag her hose. A small rusty stain streaked the storm drain. *Is that blood? Surely it wouldn't still be here after all those months...*

*When did he die? June? July? It was definitely summer...*She settled on. *Right here on this sidewalk...*

But something else caught her attention before she could inspect it further. A scraping, shuffling sound in the alley commenced from someone who did not wish to be seen. *It can't be a bar patron...*

"Stay away!" a figure with watery, orangish-brown eyes yelled from a distance.

"Who are you?" she called.

The bum turned to look at the sophisticated woman standing in front of her. Irene could see he was filthy and as shocked as she was to have this impromptu interaction. Like a sewer rat wishing to disappear into the shadows, he lay against the brick wall, trapped in an intense gaze. For a second she was afraid of him. Then he turned and looked up at the Electric Eel Bar, the neon green sign reflecting on the other side in the dim light of the alley.

"Murderers!" he screamed.

"Did you kill my father?"

He looked at her in surprise and shook his head no. Irene maintained her watch on the man as if afraid he might jump her. She spoke to him again in a calm voice.

"Did you see who killed my father?"

He paused and looked away. All of a sudden a familiar black Cadillac limousine pulled up to the front of the establishment. The driver looked around.

"Yes..." the disenfranchised man said.

"I'm over here!" she turned to call to the driver.

By the time she looked back the vagrant had disappeared. Irene blinked as if it had never happened and walked over to the car... A figment of her imagination...

"There you are!" her husband called as the driver opened the back door to let her in. "Where *were* you?"

"I thought I saw something in the alley..." she lied.

"Well, be careful..." her husband warned with serious eyes.

"Thank you for your concern..."

Together they pulled away in silence. Irene reached over and grabbed Mr. Wright's left hand. He looked at her inquisitively.

"What is it?" he asked.

Irene turned to look at her family's establishment in her peripheral vision. Then she looked back at her husband, pensively. She chose her words carefully.

"Do you think we did the right thing voting for Prohibition?" she asked.

"Of course, dear..."

ELEVEN

Unlike the way policework was romanticized in the early decades of the twentieth century, the actuality was anything but glamorous. Black and white films and the media portrayed the jobs of police as smart and snazzy, with overly made-up buxom women who hung on their every word of detectives. In the end they always captured the bad guy.

The original Columbus, Ohio Police building was an offshoot of the Central Market, the geographic center of the state, till a second location was opened in Franklinton; A large nondescript monochromatic grey and black building with high stonework. A row of matte black Model Ts with rudimentary police identification printed on each door were parked in a line out front.

The Electric Eel!

Before Detective Talbert had arrived for work, someone had poured an array of paperwork he had requested in front of his chair. *You'd think they'd place it neatly on my desk...* He thought. *Instead they throw it in a heap...* He let out a sigh of exasperation.

"Knock, knock!" a now familiar female voice called.

"Come in, Virginia..." he said without looking at her. "Can you believe they just tossed this here?" He held up a manila folder containing graphic photos taken on 35 mm film. "Criminitly! What if we needed to use these in court?"

Virginia reached for the file, but he stopped her. She knitted her brows together in frustration. He craned his neck and looked at her.

"You may not want to look at those..." he warned.

"Why?"

"Cause it's your brother..."

"Ah. I keep forgetting."

"We've been over this and over this... There has to be something we missed..."

"Let's try one more time..."

"Julius was wandering High Street at two o'clock in the morning... No one knows why... Most likely drunk before he got there..."

"And he lives on East Broad..."

"Right. But that doesn't mean he didn't patronize a bar in the Short North..."

"But you interviewed all of them downtown, right? And they didn't remember him..." Virginia remembered.

"Most of them but it was busy since people were celebrating the treaty so he could have been served without anybody remembering...Just another middle-aged white man who had too much to drink...And there's no evidence he drove anywhere..."

"You think he was dropped off?"

"Yes."

"Well Carlotta doesn't drive that I know of..."

"No, but that doesn't mean she didn't serve him alcohol beforehand."

Virginia gulped. She pictured her disdain for her sister-in-law and wondered if it was possible. The detective sipped his coffee and read her mind.

"So you think Carlotta set him up...?"

"It's possible..."

"*Anything's* possible...But why?

"Cause right after he is dropped off, he mysteriously gets attacked right in front of the property she ends up buying with his money...That's why! Too much of a coincidence for me..."

"But it's not just Carlotta who got the Electric Eel..." she began. "So did Orville and Edgar and Poppy...And Alistair by default..."

"Well, we can rule out Alistair and most likely Poppy... And the sister... What's her name...?"

"Irene... But she didn't want it...She has her own money...She told them to run it themselves... Probably cause of her stance on temperance, she didn't want to be associated with it..."

"Ok. So Irene's out..."

"And my parents didn't want it either...They won't set foot in that place..."

"Right."

"Did anyone *see* the attacker?"

"Attackers...Plural..."

"How can you be sure?"

"Different sized knife wounds on the body...Highly unlikely that one attacker brought two different knives to the scene..."

She winced and put the fact that they were talking about her brother's homicide out of her mind...*Poor Julius!* Virginia thought.

"But doesn't bringing a knife or knives to the scene go to premeditation?"

"Not always... Lots of people carry knives... But in this case, yes..."

Tal reached for the pictures and Virginia looked away. The slain body of Julius Alfonso in black and white photographs was chilling. *His eyes are open which means he was awake and conscious at the time...*His mouth hung open in surprise as if suddenly betrayed...

"Et Tu Brute...?" he whispered.

"Julius Caesar..." she said, catching his reference. "Beware the Ides of March..."

"I'm sorry about your brother..." he said turning to her in a rare display of empathy.

Virginia nodded in gratitude, lit a cigarette, and passed him one. The smoke tasted good and refreshing. She tapped his desk with the tip of her fingers and blew a smoke ring across the room.

"Getting back to the matter at hand...We don't think any of them actually killed my brother themselves do we?"

"Probably not..."

"Well, we know Edgar *can't*..."

"And Carlotta was home all night...The neighbors saw her...And Poppy was with Alistair all night..."

"Which means they hired someone..."

"But why?"

For this Detective Talbert had no answer...He tapped the end of the cigarette on the end of a ubiquitous tin ashtray. The room filled with smoke momentarily.

Tal's light brown eyes looked at her with suspicion. The hem of his wide-shouldered tweed jacket moved slightly as he took a final drag on the smoke and snuffed it out. Next, he placed the tips of his fingers in the middle of his forehead as if coming on with some unknown malady.

As always, Virginia was dressed impeccably, today in a royal blue dress and chunky Oxford heels. A long grey and brown mink stole was wrapped around her neck and shoulders. Tal found himself staring at her and then he looked away.

"What did your brother do for a living?"

"He worked for the railroads off and on... Then with the shipping industry...*Why?*"

Virginia looked into his eyes and realized where he was going with this. She had heard rumors of crime syndicates amongst these industries, but she'd never had believed it before now...Surely never as far as her brother was concerned...And no one he associated with...

"But my brother hadn't worked in *years*...He didn't need to... And everyone liked him..."

"Okay! Okay! So it probably had nothing to do with his career... But we have to check..."

"Could it be a random attack?" she asked next. "He stumbled in on something he shouldn't've..."

"Could be but I doubt it... What is the coincidence that he'd walk in on something untoward happening *there?*"

"I know it was two o'clock in the morning, but someone *had* to witness this... Did you speak to anyone? Did anyone *see* someone?"

"You'd be a great police woman, my dear," he said causing her to blush. "A hobo... But he won't speak to anyone as of yet..."

"Do you think we'll solve it?" she said placing her hand on top of his.

Tal turned his palm and squeezed her fingers in his. His hands were strong and well worn, hers were soft and manicured. Gently he kissed the top of her palm.

"I hope so..."

TWELVE

December 1, 1919

𝒯ensions continue to rise for all in the restaurant and beverage industry as the days ticked down to Prohibition. Carlotta acted like it didn't exist, going about her days as if this worldwide shift, wasn't coming…The others gave her wide berth, their own concerns for employment weighing on their minds heavily.

"She's in denial…" Edgar informed his brother as they started to close down for the night.

"She'll come around…" Orville promised.

But he wasn't so sure. And the business seemed to be suffering as well. One might think that before the country had gone dry people would be storming the bar; however, many seemed to be staying away intentionally.

"They're all stockpiling hooch at home…That's why. Even President Wilson has a private wine cellar…Fools all think they are going to get arrested…"

"They're already trying it in Canada… The women's groups think it will end domestic violence…"

"Sure cause everyone will be in jail away from the families!"

"No alcohol? Might increase violence at my home!" one of the regulars said making a fist.

"Bad enough we have to have a Sunday Liquor license…"

"I heard they're going to be pouring it down the drains…"

"Poor Milwaukee will probably go under! The paper said that seventy-five percent of their downtown labor is in the breweries!"

"Well! We might as well just close up shop now!" Carlotta barked, storming out of the kitchen.

Suddenly, everyone around her grew silent which irritated her more. Lobelia had long grown used to her boss's antics. She reached for a tray of mint juleps. *I need to look for work elsewhere… But how do I tell Carlotta?*

Instead she remained quiet. *I know everybody's secrets in this place…*She mused. *They couldn't fire me if they wanted to…They'd have to buy me off…*

The Electric Eel!

"Lobelia!" Carlotta bellowed. "Where are those mint juleps?"

"Right here…" she said hurrying to pass them out.

"What took you so long?" Carlotta hissed. "This may be the only income we ever get…"

But before Lobelia could respond, Carlotta had sauntered away. *Almost time for last call…Thank goodness!*

"Well! No point in staying here!" Carlotta announced reaching for her shawl and handbag.

"You can go with me…" Edgar offered. "Poppy is picking me up…"

"Does he drive?" one of the bar patrons asked.

"I don't think he can…" another responded. "Poor guy is so handsome too…"

Edgar shifted and lifted himself up on his crutches. He had heard it all before…*At least they are interested in me…*He thought. But then the conversation turned cruel.

"Imagine being a cripple like that…Having to have his sister-in-law drive him," she whispered. "Does he only use one crutch? I thought he used two?" an old bar fly asked her boyfriend with a chuckle. "Where's the other one?"

"Sometimes I use two… Today I only used one…Thank you," Edgar said not letting this comment slide as he passed.

The haggard old woman reddened in embarrassment. His mother approached him a second later and touched his shoulder. Expecting comfort, he looked up at her.

"I can't believe you talked to her like that! She's a paying customer and old enough to be your grandmother!"

"But…"

"Apologize!"

Edgar burned. The elderly couple exchanged glances at this interaction between mother and son. The old woman stifled a chuckle and sipped her drink. But he refused to budge.

The Electric Eel!

"He's sorry..." she said to them. "There! Let's go..."

As if on cue, Poppy stood in the doorway with Alistair. *You can cut the tension with a knife...* She noticed. Alistair beamed and ran to his uncle in an instant. Edgar softened a bit at the sight of the boy.

"Easy! You saw me this morning!"

Carlotta breezed past them and headed for the car. Poppy turned as if witnessing a trainwreck. Orville approached his wife with a kiss on the cheek.

"At least *somebody* can drive around here!" his mother snapped.

"I have no idea what's gotten into her..." he admitted.

"See you later tonight..." he promised. "Bye, Alistair!"

Orville waved his family goodbye and once he was sure they were out of sight, he walked to where the musicians were practicing. The polish on the beautiful well-worn stage glowed in the artificial light. The gentleman with the string bass was applying rosin to his bow and putting the instrument back inside its case and the clarinetist was changing the reed.

"You can all go home early...There's no one here. I'll make sure you get paid..." Orville told them.

"Thank you, Mr. Alfonso," the piano player said.

When the other musicians left, Orville walked to where Iris and her dog stood at the back. She was dressed in a stunning black cocktail dress with a seductive slit up the slide... *All these musicians wear black for some reason...*He noticed.

"You can head home, Miss Dupeon..."

"Thank you..."

"I can give you a ride if you like..."

"Oh! That's not necessary! It's just right across town! And I have to get Peaches home..."

"It's not safe out there for a young girl at night... Peaches can come too!"

"Are you sure?"

"Positive...Does she ride in the car?"

"*He*..." she corrected. "And yes he does..."

"Good! Then he can come with us..."

She thought of his father expiring on the sidewalk a few feet from the establishment. *Maybe he was right...It isn't safe...*Iris surmised.

And to let her know how serious he was, Orville reached forward and touched the soft skin on her forearm. Her eyes widened but did not pull her arm away. He smiled, showing he was unfazed by her anxiety and reached over to stroke the dog's silky fur.

"Are you ready?" he whispered.

Iris nodded.

THIRTEEN

𝒫oppy Alfonso went about her day as a wife and mother, while everyone else in her life focused on their classy lives at the Electric Eel. In those days, most women opted to stay home with the children...The few who did were forced to work menial jobs or were independently wealthy and could afford nannies or au pairs...

We thought when the Great War hit that women being allowed in the workplace would become common place cause so many of us were filling up those jobs in the men's place...But sadly after the men returned from overseas, the women were sent back home to be homemakers...No rest for the weary...

"Still I wouldn't change raising Alistair for the world..." she whispered to herself.

Poppy reached for a jar of orangish-brown peanut butter and a knife and spread some on two pieces of bread. The spread was sticky like glue and clung to the tips of her fingers. *Both luxuries that were rationed during the war...Thank God, that's over...*

"Mommy..." he asked as she placed the sandwich in front of him.

The Electric Eel!

"Yes, dear?"

"Grandma Carlotta says that once the alcohol is banned we are going to be in the poor house..."

Poppy gulped. *Out of the mouth of babes...*She thought, pondering what she should say next. He looked at her with wide, innocent, heavily lashed eyes. But to her dismay, the boy continued on the topic.

"And she says her and us and daddy and Uncle Edgar are all going to be living together...I love Uncle Edgar, but I don't wanna live with grandma..."

*Me either, sweetie...Me either...*She touched the side of his face gently.

"Well, that isn't happening just yet, baby..." Poppy said. "So don't you worry..."

"You promise?"

"Promise..." she said leaning in touching his forehead to hers. "Now go play..."

"Okay..." he said wondering outside. "Where's daddy?"

"Sleeping..." she said following him into the daylight. "Put on your coat."

Poppy handed her son a long, heavily starched, wool Russian-style coat in shades of walnut with tan patches on the sleeves and put on her own. His knee-high white socks stuck up out his chunky black winter shoes... *I love those...*His mother thought. *They remind me of Benjamin Franklin...*

"We can't stay out too long... It's pretty cold out here..."

"Wish there was snow!"

Even though it was winter, the sun made a cameo for a moment and heated the grass and sidewalk behind their house and for a minute she was afraid it was going to rain. The paint on Orville's red Buick radiated in the daylight. Poppy walked to the car to check the convertible top.

She studied the car. Its patent leather interior shined on all four sides like a Chesterfield. A small brown wooden steering wheel with a squeezable horn sat on the left side of the car. Suddenly, Poppy spotted something wispy.

The Electric Eel!

"Whose is that...?" she asked pulling something off the passenger side of the car and examining it.

Poppy leaned over the seat and found several more. Soon she was covered in long, ashy hair. She began to blush in anger as she couldn't immediately place its origin.

A second later the apartment door behind the house opened and Edgar emerged, breaking her train of thought. The hollow sound of his crutches echoed on the concrete. *Always be careful of ice...* He learned early on in this process...

"Where's your mom, Alistair?" he called to his nephew as he found his place on a bench.

"Over there..." the boy pointed.

"What's going on, Poppy?" he called.

"Nothing..." she called curtly.

She emerged from the car with a sullen look. Edgar craned his neck and looked over his shoulder at her. Poppy held something wispy and blond between her thumb and forefinger.

"What is that?"

"More importantly *whose* is that?"

Edgar shrugged. Alistair wondered over to his uncle and mother. Poppy dropped the hair, allowing it to fall in the slight breeze. It drifted for a second and floated to the ground before it blew away.

"Dog hair..." Alistair said finally.

"*Dog hair?*" she repeated in disbelief.

"That lady with the dog..." he answered.

Before she could answer with: *"What lady with a dog?"* Alistair had walked away.

"You mean Iris?" Edgar asked leaning over the bench toward his nephew.

"Uh-huh..." he answered.

The Electric Eel!

FOURTEEN

Workers showed up precisely at six p.m. on the evening of January 2, 1920 with a flatbed truck in front of the Electric Eel. Orville Alfonso greeted them outside in the cool air and examined their fare. Something enormous and fragile was wrapped in cloth and tethered to the back.

"We would've been here on the first, but it was a holiday..." one of the men informed him handing him a clipboard.

"Understandable..."

"Where do you want the tank?"

"On the far well inside..."

"How many gallons is it?" Edgar asked, standing on his crutches.

"Over a hundred gallons... Fifty gallons for each eel!" his brother announced proudly. "They get to be eight feet long in the wild!"

"Where *are* the eels?" someone else asked with a shudder.

"In the cab of the truck..." one of the workers informed him. "Too cold to be transporting them outside..."

Carlotta approached her eldest son with caution and tapped him on the shoulder. Orville looked at his mother and then brushed her off. She continued as he walked away.

"Maybe we should rethink this...What if we have to close down?"

Orville looked at her in frustration. They watched as a giant aquarium came in. Someone pointed to a carved heavily ornate stand, and they pushed it up until it was flesh with the wall.

"I guarantee no gig in town will have what *we* have!" he barked.

"Eels?" his mother asked.

"We *are* the electric eel..." he said opening his arms like a masters of ceremony.

The Electric Eel!

"But that's just the name of a drink!" she shrieked. "We serve Manhattans too and we aren't bringing bloody Rockefeller Center in here!"

She has a point... Poppy thought. She hesitated for fear of setting her off. Her mother-in-law spoke with as much calm as she could muster.

"How do we take care of them?"

"They eat fish..." Orville said grinning. "We have fish...And they promised to send someone once a week to clean it..."

"That's good..." his wife offered.

Before his mother could protest further, a partially filled oblong glass tube came in with something that looked like black snakes swimming at the bottom. Carlotta gasped and stepped backward. A few other women winced as well.

"Do they...*Bite*?"

"No but they can shock you..." one of the drivers informed them. "Not enough to kill you... But full-grown ones can give you about six hundred volts!"

"That's it! Get it outta here!"

"We can't... We paid up front..."

One of the men emerged with a long, curled hose under his arm like a fireman. Carlotta threw her hands up in the air. Another man emerged with a long rectangular heater on a cord.

"Spigot's in the bathroom and there's one in the kitchen..." he said reading his mind.

"Gotta be kept at about seventy-six degrees!" he said holding up a thermometer.

In unison they watched as they attached the long hose to the tap. Slowly the tank began to fill. One of them men stood on a step stool and dumped the fish in gently. The fish looked around for a second intertwining their tails together in protection, their deep-set eyes vacant with surprise.

"Why not pick something pretty like angelfish?" one of the regulars whispered.

"Cause we aren't the angelfish bar! Now enough talk about this! They're here! And they need names...Think of them as pets!"

*Some pets...*Carlotta thought. *But there's no point in telling Orville anything when he's got his mind set on something...He's just like me...*

"Now! A round of electric eels cocktails for everyone!" he announced. "On the house!"

"One other thing..." the worker said handing Orville a clipboard with a piece of paper to sign.

"Yes?"

"Feed them each separately or they'll fight..."

Orville gulped.

FIFTEEN

January 17, 1920

*I*rene had not seen her family in *months*. She'd heard rumors around her hometown that they were avoiding her. Anyone who had dared support the prohibition on alcohol that had shook the country was *out*...And it was *all* anyone could talk about...

"Extra! Extra! Read all about it!" a young man in a newsboy cap shouted in her direction. "Six bad guys rob Chicago freight train and make off with thousands of dollars' worth of whiskey! The 18th Amendment goes into effect! Prohibition begins as the country goes dry! Read all about it!"

The normally bustling streets of downtown Columbus, Ohio had changed too. Police officers in black uniforms and ridiculous hats were posted everywhere...Near where the row of bars in the Short North had been... A large man swung a baton and watched the sidewalk like a prison guard.

"All right, boys!" a burly man yelled. "Roll out the barrel!"

Just then the young men rolled a few dozen oak barrels off a flatbed truck and laid

The Electric Eel!

them on their side. Irene stood across the street as a group of onlookers began to watch history enfold. The same officer stepped forward and placed a silver whistle on a chain up to his mouth.

"Stay back!" he yelled. "Let her rip!"

The young men did as instructed and looked up as if posing for a picture. Then they opened the casks, allowing the brown liquid to flow into the sewers and drains. They opened several more barrels next, except this time the liquid was clear.

Is this all theater? Irene wondered. She shivered in the winter air as a few women in shawls and men in overcoats gathered to watch as the authorities released the hooch down the storm drains. A familiar sign loomed on the corner...*Electric Eel!*

What would become of it? She wondered. *It hadn't been open that long...When the world shifted... And it's not like they didn't know it was coming...*

"It's a small café now," a middle-aged woman whispered to her. "Little mom and pop bakery..."

"It's a strange name though for a pastry place..." the man walked away with a wink.

When the man was out of earshot, the woman pointed to a red brick building marked *RX Drugs...*With nonchalance, she motioned to the front door. Irene took it all in.

"If you want alcohol, you'll need to try the pharmacy next door with a prescription or get it from Father McMurray. Tell him you want it for Sunday mass... It's those damned Protestants who started this whole thing anyway!"

But the other woman wasn't finished yet. Irene looked closely at the rear entrance where a gaggle of twenty-something women in cloche hats and chunky shoes gathered. The old woman pointed.

"Why are they all going in the back?" Irene asked. "Are they getting booze?"

"No, silly..." the learned woman looked at her with narrow eyes. "Cosmetics..."

"*Cosmetics?*" she repeated in disbelief.

"They all wanna be flappers..."

The Electric Eel!

"Why not get their makeup at the pharmacy?" she said not understanding.

"Cause it's for women of ill repute and girls of loose character who don't favor their reputation...Or circus clowns!" she laughed. "No reputable vendor would sell it to them! So they get it on the down low..."

But Irene was confused. *Someone had to be selling it to them! Every one of those girls is painted!*

"They're getting it from somewhere! And they're all smoking! And what's with that short hair?"

Irene looked at two women barely out of their teens with blood red painted lips and wide mascaraed eyes. Both women had severe haircuts bobbed at their cheekbones. *How did the world change so quickly?*

"And look at the hem on those skirts...Rumor has it no tailor in town will cut them that short, so they grab the pinking shears and do it themselves..."

She made a motion with two fingers as if she were cutting fabric. *It's a lot to take in...*Irene looked at her family's business again.

"Well, I must be going..." the older woman informed her looking away at the pharmacy.

Has everyone lost their minds? Irene nodded in gratitude and walked toward the Electric Eel. *What time was it?*

"Hello?" she asked opening the door.

A brass bell on the door dinged announcing her presence. Irene blinked in disbelief. *Is this the same place?*

"Welcome to the Electric Eel!" a chipper voice yelled.

An attractive black woman in a red dress with a matching carnation on her lapel appeared. The two women examined each other, not fully processing the recognition. Irene smiled and spoke first.

"Lobelia?" Irene said finally placing her name.

The Electric Eel!

Lobelia narrowed her eyes and straightened her spine. A large freshly polished bakery case sat underneath her elbows, filled with delicate pastries on crisp white doilies. Two wrought iron tables spray painted white were placing in the lobby.

"Would you like something? They come in fresh daily!"

"Where is the Electric Eel?"

"This *is* the Electric Eel...The Eel Electric Café," the woman answered politely as if Irene were speaking a foreign tongue.

"No..." she said. "The bar...Everything..."

"Oh... We only sell food now...Wholesome, healthy products...Flour, sugar, and lard..."

"Where are the tanks?"

"Tanks?"

"You know with the eels... Never mind...How late are you open?" she said squinting in disbelief.

"Till seven... But sometimes we keep the doors open later on weekends..."

"Where is my mother Carlotta and my brothers?"

"They're out for the day...Do I know you?"

"It's me...*Irene*...Where is the rest of it?" she asked, it dawning on her that the place was now half the size. "Where's the bar and the stage?"

But Lobelia played it cagey and turned from her to focus on polishing the stainless steel. *Maybe if I buy something...*Irene thought. *They do look tempting...*

"I'll take a few of those Madeliene cookies..." she said pointing to a several finger-shaped biscuits on frilly paper now stained with melted butter and grease.

"Perfect..." Lobelia said with a sudden smile. "I'll get them wrapped for you..."

The now Electric Eel Café was decorated in ladylike shades of pale yellow and white. Intricate Irish lace curtains hung from the windows. *How did this transition so fast? No one told me...Anything...*

"How many did you say you want, Ma'am?"

The Electric Eel!

"Half a dozen... Er...Make it a dozen..." she said flashing her politician's wife smile.

But Lobelia was unfazed and handed her the baked goods in a waxed paper bag. She nodded cordially and headed back to the back, revealing nothing. Irene took it and walked outside in confusion. The smell of sugar and lemon zest hung in the air for a second.

Outside the establishment the air was chilly again. Irene fiddled with her bolero and pressed it under her chin, a buffer from the cold. She debated eating a cookie but decided instead to walk across the street to her husband's office.

"Psst..." an old man's voice whispered.

Figuring it was a come on, Irene ignored it. Men always cat-called her, especially downtown. She pretended not to notice. But the old codger persisted.

"Can't get hooch in there till dark..." he yelled across the street.

"Excuse me?" she yelled keeping her distance.

"Go in after dark... They'll let a classy dame like you...I *guarantee* it..."

And without saying anything further, he walked away...

SIXTEEN

January 30, 1920

a group of Electric Eel regulars stood on the street outside their former favorite watering hole like drifters. They seemed to recognize each other in passing, their only connection being the place where they stood. The old woman blinked in the frigid night air as if her eyes would freeze shut if she didn't move them.

"I'm Rufus and this is my best girl Annamary..."

"Phil..."

While they exchanged pleasantries, truth be told they were afraid. *Could they trust anyone now that Prohibition had gone into effect? Were they going to be arrested?*

The Electric Eel!

"It's only illegal to sell and transport it…" they kept reminding themselves. "*Not* to consume it…Only the businesses run afoul of the law…"

Phil smoked nervously and offered the others one. Annamary took it, her hands quaking slightly with an unknown palsy. *She's one of those broads who looks ninety but could be fifty…*He noted.

"Looks like it's a bakery now…" Annamary said.

She grabbed Rufus's hand and turned to walk away but suddenly someone opened the door. A large man they vaguely recognized from his time at the bar. *The bouncer…!* He motioned his with his head to the second door in the middle of the establishment.

"Mr. Alfonso recognized you…" he informed them. "Speak *easy*…And knock twice! The name's Tiny!"

To their surprise, a small window at eye level opened in the middle door and a hazel iris with a dark pupil appeared. They walked curiously like Alice falling through the rabbit hole. Phil blinked.

"I'm underdressed…" Annamary said turning to Rufus.

She looked down at the basic brown dress and matching pumps she was wearing and then at the everyone else in the room. Orville Alfonso put his hand up to tell her it was okay. She blushed a little in embarrassment.

"Everyone is welcome here… Anything goes…" he announced repeating the mantra he'd been hearing since the decade started.

Phil stared at the room that had been condensed into a smaller, more ostentatious space. Multiple wine glasses hung upside down from the center of the room in the shape of an elongated starfish and cascaded close to the front. The original bar had been moved backward in a semicircle.

"How about a beer?" Phil asked.

A new bartender he did not recognize pressed her lips together in a pout. She was chunky with a henna rinse and caked on makeup. The fringe on her truncated teal dress

The Electric Eel!

dangled diagonally toward her black fishnet stockings. Her chest heaved forward toward him.

"I'm Eugenia...How bout a rumrunner?"

"Phil..." he said hesitating. "I'll try it..."

"Three rumrunners..." Rufus informed her.

Edgar spotted Annamary and Rufus as they took a seat and looked around. He glared slightly remembering their cruelty and motioned to his brother. Orville was standing in an expensive embellished suit and matching vest. He leaned over Edgar and forced a smile in the old couple's direction.

"What are *they* doing here?"

"They were regulars at the old place..." he said not fully comprehending what was being asked.

"They insulted me..."

"Well, they're here now and they're mom's friends and we can't have them going to the feds..."

"Orville-"

But Orville walked away before his brother could respond. *A trait he picked up from mother...* He turned to look at the front...*Speak of the Devil...!*

Carlotta Alfonso was dressed in head to toe red, gold, and black...*Ala Mephistopheles!* Gold beads synched the garment in at the wrists, causing the garment to balloon at the sleeves. She gave a theatrical flair of the arms and gestured to those sitting around the room.

"Welcome to the Electric Eel! Where anything goes!" she said repeating her son's chant. "Where we have the lovely Iris on vocals..." she announced.

The onlookers blinked as if seeing a different woman. Where was the shy blond in black that they remembered only a few weeks ago? Instead a vamp in an abbreviated bright blue skirt stood with fringe trailing down the backs of her thighs like a horse's

The Electric Eel!

mane, the scoop neck of the bodice of her dress accentuated by a sundry of beads. Her demure long hair was now cropped at the ear and finger waved. She stood on too high heels giving her the appearance of a little girl playing dress-up in her mother's clothes...Her cupid bow mouth was stained crimson as she blew a kiss to the audience...

The men swooned...

"And she even brought her beautiful show dog Peaches!"

They looked to the far corner where the stately Afghan Hound stood in a diamond studded collar. The dog's monkey-like prehensile tail was curled like a question mark. Its expression was as it always been, flat and nonplussed.

"Next we have the talented Wallace on piano..."

The once goofy piano player had transformed into a debonair musician in a crisp white tuxedo and contrasting red bow tie. His hands flew across the keys in a pentatonic scale. And Carlotta motioned to a swarthy man on the string bass... The women swooned...

"And we even have live electric eels!" she gesticulated with heavily ringed fingers. "Eugenia will demonstrate the beasts for which our signature cocktail and bar are named!"

Those in audience watched as the stout Eugenia wandered over to where both eels intertwined in the dim light. The fish's deep-set eyes watched in suspicion as they backed their red-orange bellies in the aquarium as if getting away from the glare of the crowd.

"600 volts!" Orville announced like a sideshow barker. "*Each!*"

And to their amazement and horror, Eugenia placed her hands palm up in the tank, first the right and then the left. The tank buzzed angrily as the tail of one of the beasts quivered as the volts flowed through her. Eugenia pulled her hand out of the water unscathed and showed it to them.

"Electric eel cocktails...On the house!!!" she roared. "1920 is here! *ANYTHING GOES!!*"

The Electric Eel!

SEVENTEEN

Two women who rarely found common ground, gathered outside the Electric Eel one frigid February night with a common goal. While they were closer in age as sisters, they were aunt and niece... Connected by a family establishment with a growing continual raucous reputation in the community...

Virginia Alfonso rubbed her gloved palms together in the cold air as if trying to start a fire. Despite her reservations about the place, she was dressed in full makeup and a fringed shawl. *I can't believe she called me...* She thought.

While Irene saw the girls in short skirts darting in and out of the buildings on High Street, she still felt hidebound to her traditions and had chosen a more conservative attire. *You're barely thirty...* The look on her aunt's face said.

"It's a bakery..." Virginia said to her niece.

"Mmmm-hmmm," she responded pushing in the door. "Just you wait..."

"Welcome to the Electric Eel!" a large woman announced. "Happy Valentine's Day! Would you like a cupcake?"

"We're here for the bar..." Irene said cutting her off and breaking the invisible wall between them.

Lobelia blinked and pointed to the middle door silently as if speaking it out loud would jinx it. A sundry of rosy, red, and pink baked goods lined the top shelf of the pastry case. She was wearing a frilly pink and white apron. A small hole opened in the door with a slide.

"May I help you?" a booming male voice echoed through the large peephole.

"It's Virginia and Irene..." Irene shouted.

"Keep your voice down..." he chided.

"Sorry..." she corrected herself.

"Who is it?" they heard another male voice call on the other side of the door.

The Electric Eel!

"Virginia and Irene..." the larger voice answered.

"Tell them no feds...And no Mr. Wright...And we're watching them..."

"No feds..." he repeated. "And no Mr. Wright..." Tiny said slightly confused.

*They know my husband voted for the Volstead Act...*Irene thought wryly. The people on both sides of the room held their breath and waited. She proceeded.

"Just us women..." she called.

A nanosecond later the door opened, and they were quickly herded in like cattle. The large man who had greeted them closed the door swiftly so as if not to allow any further light in. He paused and put his hand out the door before they could enter.

"Ten-dollar cover...*Each!*"

Everyone looked to Irene...*Highway robbery...*She mouthed. A second later Irene shrugged and fished in her clutch for two bills and handed it to him. Alexander Hamilton's picture loomed in shades of grey and green in his gargantuan palm.

"She can afford it..." they heard Orville whisper. "Welcome sister and aunt!" he called taking the money.

"Thank you..."

"I see you've met our newest staff member Tiny..."

*An oxymoron if ever there was one...*Virginia thought looking up and down the skyscraper sized man. He spilled out of his three-piece suit like a toddler who had had a growth spurt and outgrown his clothes. His lips were huge and pressed together as if they were constructed of wax.

Then to their surprise, Tiny sucked in his stomach and backed up to let them through. He smelled of perspiration, they noticed, as he stood with his hands at his side. *Like he's afraid to raise his arms...*

Virginia and Irene looked around the room agog as if watching the first act of an opera. Low tables and benches sat in the middle of the room alongside long drooping white cloth suspended from the walls and ceiling. The rest of the small space was

The Electric Eel!

covered in beads and crystals.

"Welcome to the new Electric Eel!" Orville motioned.

In front of them they spotted Carlotta. She mustered a spooked, uncomfortable smile. Every part of her body dripped in jewelry and rhinestones like a parade float as she waved.

"Hello, mother..." Irene commented.

"Hi, Carlotta..."

"Hello..." she said coolly turning. "Orville, may I see you for a moment?"

"Yes..." he said without looking away, maintaining his ever present too white smile.

"Who let them in...?" she hissed drawing each word out as if each were a sentence.

"I did..." Orville said moving closer to his mother. "They're family..."

"They *were* family... Till Irene voted against us and *she*..." she said looking at her sister-in-law. "Brought that detective in here..."

"That was over my brother's death..." Virginia piped up. "*Not* alcohol..."

"She has a point..." her brother whispered.

She thinks we're murderers! The look on her face said. She put her hand up as if directing traffic.

"You can stay..." Carlotta snapped. "But anything fishy and you're finito!"

She made a garroting motion across her neck with her finger. Virginia gulped. Irene was unfazed and moved closer.

"All the politicians still need their booze..." she whispered. "They all know it's not illegal to drink it... Everyone sees them going in here without trouble...It's all ceremonial..."

They nodded, not wanting to discuss this further around patrons. Carlotta motioned into her eyes with both fingers. *Watch them!*

"Just in time for the show..." another male voice called from across the room.

"Hi, Edgar!" they called with fondness they did not have for Carlotta or Orville.

The Electric Eel!

"Sit down!"

"What *is* this place?" Virginia asked looking around.

"It's a speak-easy..." Edgar told his aunt. "Welcome to the Twenties..."

"What is *that*?!" Irene pointed wrinkling up her nose.

"That is our electric eel tank... Eugenia has been taking care of them..."

"*Eels?*" she said in disbelief.

"Yep..."

"Aren't they dangerous?" Virginia asked Irene.

"Not especially..." Eugenia said overhearing. "Just a mild shock... With my neuropathy I can't feel anything..."

All of a sudden someone motioned to the band, and someone began singing impromptu. Edgar noticed the tune immediately. Orville and the others took heed as well. Soon the employees were stashing bottles of contraband under the counter. A small trap door opened a minute later.

"Now won't you listen, honey while I say... How could you tell me that you're going away? Don't tell me that we must part... Don't break your baby's heart..." Iris began in the style of Marion Harris.

Next they scrambled and grabbed all of the drinks on the bar and dumped them down the drain. Virginia recoiled as others stepped back from their cocktails as they would be scalded.

"After you've gone and left me crying...After you've gone, there's no denying...You'll feel blue, you'll feel sad...You'll miss the only pal you've ever had...There'll come a time, now don't forget it. There'll come a time when you regret it..."

Eugenia dashed to the windows and peered through the scant curtains. She motioned to Tiny to lock the center door. *Is this any air raid siren?* Virginia wondered. *I thought the war was over...*

"The feds..." someone whispered.

"All clear…" Lobelia called through the center door.

And the music stopped as suddenly as it came without finishing. Iris stepped away from the microphone with nonchalance. The rest of the staff breathed in relief.

"Sorry, everyone!" Orville called. "We'll repour your drinks, no charge!"

Iris had long lost interest in the Marion Harris… Or music in general… *Or this place*…She thought. Someone handed her a pipe and a paste of something, and they passed a candle, spoon, and ceramic bowl around behind the Shoji screen to sample the drugs. She thought she heard someone coming as the dog wagged its tail in the hazy din, mellowing from the contact high.

"False alarm…" the bassist giggled.

"Happy Valentine's Day!" Iris wished taking the spoon and lighting it.

EIGHTEEN

*A*round March of that year, a different group of spectators gathered around the front of the Electric Eel bar. Unlike other visitors, who sought out illegal liquor, this group had little interest in imbibing. Nor were they like the temperance movement, who gathered occasionally across the street to ferret out places of potential drinking with their signs of protest.

These individuals, mostly women, were dressed in dark clothing. Two humorless ladies in long earthen-hued dresses shouted from a safe distance, their scuffed, black, sensible, shoes pressed firmly against the curb. Carlotta rolled her eyes.

"No alcohol here…Just a respectable bakery…" Orville had called to them out of habit. "Go picket elsewhere!"

Like Carlotta, their leader was flamboyant and strong. Madame Beulah, a diminutive woman with a booming voice, gestured to a spot in front of the bar. She was dressed, as usual, in shades of blue and indigo. Her hair was jet black with a white strip like a skunk down the front. Her followers gathered around her in a semi-circle.

The Electric Eel!

"What is all this?" Edgar asked as he made his way inside.

"Séance!" one of Madame Beulah's sycophants called with girlish glee.

"Don't you normally do those things *inside?*" his brother retorted.

"Not when a murder has occurred *outside!*" she retaliated.

Edgar winced and walked inside. Orville reddened. Madame Beulah pointed to the curb without noticing their unease.

"Our father was killed by an unknown attacker…" Orville informed them, trying to be discreet. "Please let us grieve in peace!"

"That's not what the police report says!" one of the followers shouted waving a typed piece of paper.

"Or what the spirits say!" Beulah said with a chuckle. "And how did you know I was referring to your father's murder?"

"Stay off our property!" Orville warned closing the door. "Or I'll call the cops!"

"Like you want the coppers here!" she shouted. "We have the right to assemble…"

"So do it from a distance like those zany, temperance dames…And let our father rest in peace!" he said. "I have a bakery to run…"

"Don't you mean a speakeasy?"

"Shh…" Madame Beulah chided. "We promise to be respectful."

"Fine."

And with that, Orville turned and walked inside. The group of supernatural onlookers began speaking as if he had never even been there. One of the women began to give a testimonial of their leader.

"Last time Beulah channeled, she oozed ectoplasm…"

"Ectoplasm?" one of the others asked unfamiliar with this term.

"Yes… The physical embodiment of spirit…" she said repeating verbatim what she'd heard from the medium.

"Are we going to do this or not?" a skeptical old man who had been coaxed here by his wife asked.

"Yes…" Beulah said finally, putting her hands under her cape. "Oh great spirit guides! Where is Julius Alfonso?!"

She warmed her voice up like an opera singer. The spot where Julius had fallen, evident to all. A small quarter-sized rust stained lingered on the concrete. *How long had that been there?*

The group of spiritualists looked up at the full moon, some of them holding hands. Edgar watched intently from the bakery's small window. *Had any of them even known my father?* He wondered, looking away.

"Julius are you there?" the soothsayer called a few minutes later.

*Opportunists…All of them…*Orville thought. But both men were intrigued.

"Julius, how many knives *were* there?" she called out loud enough for all to hear. "Or should I say: How many assailants?"

And then, to their horror, Beulah's voice changed. The voice of a middle-aged man bellowed a second, replacing her normal smooth alto timbre. The rest of the group watched around her like spectators at the Colosseum.

"I died…" the man's voice inside her called as she moved, "…right here…"

And then Madame Beulah returned a second as if giving them an update. Her dark eyes shot open in some strange hue between brown, black and green; her heavily mascaraed lids framed her eyes like two tarantula legs. She stared up at the dark sky.

"It was a brutal death…" she said with much hesitation.

"Who killed you, Julius?" one of them called as if talking to a live person in front of them.

"Unclear…But someone very close…"

"*Why* did they kill you, Julius?"

"Not clear…But they made a lot of money…"

Meanwhile Carlotta, Orville and Edgar watched the spectacle from their vantage point in the building. *These woman did put on quite a show...* They had to admit... Edgar continued to burn with rage, thinking of his father. He hobbled away from the window, not wanting to see anymore.

"Want me to stop them?" Orville asked his mother.

"Not yet..."

Outside Madame Beulah continued to prognosticate in the spot where Julius was slain. Then she began to make a horrendous gurgling noise as if choking...*Like a cat with a hairball...*Edgar noticed.

"She's choking..."

"On my own blood..." Beulah sputtered in a man's voice catching her breath.

They stepped back as if realizing that this may be real and not some childish party game and then she began to sputter again. A horrible strangling noise came next. She grabbed her neck as if giving the universal sign of choking.

"Make it stop!" Edgar yelled.

Orville and Carlotta walked outside just in time to see the madame regurgitate something. She leaned over the concrete and spit out the object *hard*...She stood and wiped her mouth as a puddle of spittle dripped down the corners of her mouth.

"What *is* that?"

The familiar profile of their loved one came into focus. It was slippery like lard but held an imprint like a newspaper clipping. Beulah twirled on the balls of her feet like a ballerina and swooned as if coming back down from spinning around in circles. She placed her palms in the air.

"Looks like a newspaper clipping..."

"It's Julius!" Carlotta noticed.

"He was here..." she said calling to all of them. "Julius was here..."

They stood enrapt for a moment. Carlotta raised an eyebrow, impressed. Edgar watched in anger as the three of them entered the establishment a second later. *Good!*

The Electric Eel!

Maybe mother and Orville will tell them to get the Hell out!

"Would you like some water, Miss Beulah, is it?"

The rest of the group stood outside the Electric Eel, in moderate confusion. *Was she okay? Would they scold her? Or worse, would they be arrested?*

"Julius was out there..." she repeated, sipping the water.

Beulah stared up at her like a naughty child in the principal's office. She, too, had been thinking the same thing as her followers. Carlotta's fiery hair and makeup glowed like embers against the fabric of her salmon-colored evening gown.

"You put on quite a show..."

Beulah said nothing, as always, not revealing her true intentions. Carlotta blinked. The madame took another sip of the cool water.

"Would you like to come back here on Thursday?" Carlotta asked finally.

"Come back?" Edgar barked in insolence. "Why would you want her to come back?"

But Carlotta ignored her second son's protestations. She put her hand out as he tried to speak again. The two women stared at each other a moment.

"You gave us quite a show..." she reiterated.

"Thank you...But I just channel the spirits...It's from Jubal, my spirit guide..."

"Save it!" she snapped, not buying it. "We could make a lot of money, you and I!"

"We *could?*" Madame Beulah asked with feigned innocence.

"On one condition..."

"What's that?"

"On the condition that you never mention my husband Julius ever again..."

"Deal..." she said her voice returning to normal.

NINETEEN

$\mathcal{J}$ris Dupeon's days were mundane compared to the raucous nights at the Electric Eel. A lot of her mornings now came with nausea and sickness. *Am I pregnant or just*

The Electric Eel!

hungover? She wondered. *I can't tell anymore...*

"Ugh... I shouldn't drink so much..."

*And they hide alcohol in everything now...Where are the days when you could drink a drink neat or on the rocks? Edgar kept telling me to drink those Bloody Marys... I don't even like tomato juice...*She thought.

To tell the truth, Iris was getting tired of drinking...She was a petite woman whose small frame could not handle that much alcohol...Night after night...*And it makes me gain weight...*

But despite the prohibition it was *everywhere*...Even for people who didn't *want* it... The whole world had turned in one big fraternity house... She noted. *A cigarette in one hand and a cocktail in the other...*

*If I never drank again...*I'd be okay with it...*The other stuff I crave all the time now...*Jib had been first to give it to her. He was always so suave, handing the huge string bass expertly. And the clarinet player who always put cocaine in the Coca-Cola... *He was cute too... What was his name?*

At first, she pictured bums on High Street with hypodermic needles shooting up. Down on their luck derelicts who overdosed with no other options in life... *But I am no derelict...*She thought looking around her luxurious apartment.

A heavy-toothed silver and green wallpaper lined much of the top of the space. Two large black marble Corinthian columns lined either side of the doorway that separated the main space along with an expensive inlaid parquet floor. A large multi-tiered chandelier with spaces for long tapered candles hung over a tile dining room table that she rarely used. Several Greco-Roman busts of famous people dotted the apartment along with two heavy candelabras.

*A museum tucked away from the world on High Street...*She thought. *And no one ever comes here except to clean...*She pulled out a white Queen Anne chair to sit down and reached for Peaches, her beloved Afghan Hound. The dog hesitated at first and then

The Electric Eel!

wagged his tail and gave in to her beckoning. She held him against her, his hair mingling with her own.

Her parents were rich. *Filthy* rich as people called it. Though she kept this a secret from most. People treated you differently when they found out. Her father, a silk magnate who rubbed elbows with the likes of J. Paul Getty, Henry Ford, King George and the recently deceased Andrew Carnegie and her mother, a Manhattan socialite with lineage dating back to the Mayflower...*And before that back to Marie Antoinette...*

She lit a cigarette and looked around her apartment again and thought of their three-story palatial estate in the Hamptons, their summer home in Tuscany and Coral Gables and their recently acquired property in Bexley with the indoor swimming pool...*It's the least they can do...*She thought dryly.

"Veronica..." her mother always called her, using her given first name.

"I go by Iris professionally now..."

"But we will always know you as Veronica..."

"Veronica Iris..." she corrected her.

"And what's with this singing thing, darling...?" her father mused over his cigar and snifter of Brandy.

"It's what I do now..."

"But you don't need to work...None of us Dupeons do... Especially in a seedy speakeasy like that! At least try Classical music like a debutante...We *paid* for music lessons..."

"Classical music is *boring*..."

"I'm not a fan of this new Bohemian lifestyle either!" her mother answered, buttressing her father's argument as always.

So most days she chose to be alone. They had their world and she had hers. *If only they knew...*Iris thought. *They'd pull my trust fund for sure!*

Last night I danced on a taxi with two men! She recalled fondly as if in a dream. Her sinewy body had been tucked neatly between their two muscular physiques; the smell of their colognes intermingled with her perfume and cigarettes. The three of them double fisted cocktails in rocks glasses on the car's roof car as they danced to an inaudible tune.

"Get her down from there!" that nasty Carlotta Alfonso had barked at her son. "What if the cops come by?"

"No one cares..." they taunted.

"I don't care what she does inside the facility..." Carlotta said, her annoying habit of talking *about* her instead of *to* her. "But if we get the feds in here because of her...I'm gonna be furious!"

"She's our biggest money draw!" she'd heard Orville say as he followed his mother like a sycophant.

"She won't be if we get closed down!"

But they were all amazed at how little law enforcement presence there had been since Prohibition started. As time went on, it actually became evident that most of the police were on the take, wanting to party like the rest of the world.

"All it takes is one with an axe to grind!" Carlotta shouted at her.

Reluctantly Iris climbed down from the cab, her gold fringed skirt blowing in the wind like the girl in an Erté print. The two gentlemen, whom she'd probably never see again, kissed her on each cheek as if posing for a photo. One of them paid the cab driver who owned the vehicle and gave him a polite nod and they parted.

"They were nice..." Iris said to the hound.

But like everything in this new decade, it was a temporary high. And like always, she was left with only her memories to fall back on. This flapper lifestyle was only even a small portion of her day... A bravado for a few hours till she returned home each night.

Iris opened the bureau and peered at the outfit she would wear for the night. As always, her clothes had been freshly prepared along with her meals which were freshly

The Electric Eel!

put in the refrigerator by some unknown hired hand. She stared at the grape shimmery number that had been pressed and laid out for her.

*It is beautiful...*She had to admit. *All those beads and sequins have to be washed and sewn on by hand.* She looked at the sapphire blue dress that she'd worn the day before as it lay on top the hamper.

*Orville Alfonso practically ripped it off me one night...*She recalled. *He'd never fire me...I know too much...*She thought smiling. *And his brother likes me too...*

"What time is it?" she asked out loud. "Almost six o'clock..."

And without another thought, Iris dressed and headed for another night at the Electric Eel...

"My taxi awaits..."

TWENTY

Somewhere around the time Madame Beulah arrived at the Electric Eel, ghost sightings began to be reported around the property. Whether it was the result of the suggestion being planted in patrons or whether she had actually *opened* up something on her first visit, was unclear... What was clear; however, was that the whole place went spirit crazy in anticipation.

On her first trip inside, Madame Beulah scanned every inch of the space like a detective. Her head craned the wains coating, looking up and down in examination. She stared at the dirt on a brassy ceiling fan and soured.

"Dust is a haven for negative energy..." she informed them. "Dead human skin cells..."

"Get it cleaned!" Carlotta shrieked at one of the employees.

Madame Beulah stared into the ladies restroom without entering. The green marble tiles floors glowed with a fresh polish. The smell of antiseptic lingered in their nostrils. Then she moved onto the men's.

"Keep the toilet lids closed!"

The Electric Eel!

"Why?" Orville asked, thinking of the momentous tasking of keeping the lids down in a crowded place such as this. *Especially* in the men's room!

"Evil spirits come right up them! Along with rats!"

"*Rats?*"

"Yes, rats...Rodents follow the diablerie..."

He paused a second, having never heard this word and looked at his mother, who seemed to be buying into the medium's instructions. Orville put his palms out as if to say: I have no idea...!

Slowly, he turned to Beulah, but she had already moved on to her next fleeting fancy. A large table had been set up in the center. She touched the table cloth with hesitation.

"As you requested, Madame Beulah..."

"White won't do..." she snapped.

"Why?"

"White is the color of death..."

"It will have to do for tonight till we get another color..." he said growing exasperated with her antics.

Doesn't she want death? He thought, knitting his brows together in confusion. Makes no sense.

"I s'pose..."

"Get her a black tablecloth!" the older woman barked at Lobelia. "Here's your crystal ball..." Carlotta informed her sweetly. "Baccarat as you asked..."

Why is my mother catering to this? Edgar thought, watching the spectacle. *She never cow tows to anyone...*

"Is she afraid of her?" he started to say under his breath.

But Carlotta shot him a searing look, overhearing. Edgar looked down over his libation and swirled the ice. Madame Beulah touched the crystal with the back of her hand and nodded in approval. *Finally!* Orville thought.

The Electric Eel!

"We start at nine...You are our Thursday night show..."

"Good...After the sun goes down is better..." she said her voice morphing into a different indecipherable accent. "The spirits always become more active at dusk..."

She looked up and down the table... Orville knitted his brows together in confusion. Beulah was unfazed.

"I hope these boards are secured together with screws... Nails are bad luck!"

"Bad luck?"

"Yes they bind everything together and then tear when you try to rip them apart... Replace them with wood screws! Ever hear of coffins! And get glasses of water and sea salt in the window sills to get rid of bad energy... Then dump it away from the property in a week! Not table salt!"

Suddenly, Beulah's short attention span shifted again to something else. She put both palms out in front of the eel tank. The fish's eyes glowed in suspicion.

"I'm showing them I mean no harm..." she whispered. "Eels are symbols of strength and healing...A serpent *and* a fish!"

Then she met Eugenia's gaze. Eugenia bit her lower lip and tasted waxy pink lipstick. Beulah waved her hand in dismission. Orville put his hand on Eugenia's shoulders.

"This is Eugenia... She has the arduous task of caring for our namesake eels..."

The eels looked up at the people, their tails intertwined in a makeshift heart shape. Eugenia tossed a bit of something pinkish in the tank and then another. *No sense in having them fight...* A second later they pounced on it.

"They love shrimp..." Orville said. "Shame we have to have it shipped in from New York..."

Eugenia looked at Beulah nonplussed as if realizing she was no longer their featured act. The eels swam behind her in search of more crustacean. Orville stepped forward and piped in.

"Madame Beulah will only be here on Thursdays..." he informed her.

The Electric Eel!

"Not that we wouldn't *take* her the rest of the week..." Carlotta offered.

"Almost showtime..." Lobelia called breaking the tension.

Tiny and members of the band appeared next in the doorway. A few bartenders and servers had been added for Madame Beulah's opening night that they did not recognize. Lobelia took a silver tray of glassware and hung it upside from the ceiling like sleeping fruit bats as patrons began filing in.

"Tonight we welcome the mysterious Madame Beulah..." Carlotta informed them. "Soothsayer extraordinaire...!"

Beulah pulled a chair up to the table and paid the other people no mind. Next, she stretched her hands out and waved each finger individually over the crystal ball. To their amazement, the ball began to get cloudy.

"The spirits are active tonight..." she said finally.

Tonight she was wearing an electric blue turban with a giant ruby perched over her the center of her forehead... *On my third eye...*She mused. A sundry of enormous costume jewelry decorated each finger like small boulders in the order of a rainbow. Her long fingernails were sharp like a falcon's talons and painted the color of fresh blood.

"Who here has recently lost a loved one?" she called without looking at any of them.

Edgar and Orville exchanged glances with their mother who looked away. *Surely she can't mean us...*Orville thought. *She promised mother she'd never mention father's name again...*

To their relief, a woman in the audience raised her hand slightly with great hesitation instead. She was of small build with round, gold pince-nez eyeglasses that pinched the nostrils instead of going over the ear; a style en vogue at the time. A pale purple cloche hat flared out at her ears like a small bell. *Is she part of the act or is this impromptu?* Orville wondered. *I can't tell...*

"Come over..." Beulah said in a man's voice.

"I recently lost my mother..."

The Electric Eel!

"Your father is with the spirits too..." she said changing horses mid-stream.

"Yes..."

"He is here..." she said cutting her off, her voice deepening more this time.

"He *is*?"

"And he isn't happy..."

The woman blinked, processing. But instead of protesting, she nodded in agreement with the prophesier. Madame Beulah raised both hands in the air above the crystal ball like the sorcerer's apprentice. The mousy woman stood with her hands over her naval as if accepting an award at a small-town pageant.

Suddenly, the seer began to twitch and rock back and forth like a coiled serpent wakening from its slumber. Next, her head and neck began to contort and move as well, but not in sync with the rest of her body. And then she fell off her chair in a heap.

Without hesitation, Orville sprinted to her. *She's stiff as a board...*! He noticed, slapping her on the cheek. Finally, she roused, her body still twirling like a whirling dervish. Unceremoniously, she coughed and spat something on the floor.

"Ectoplasm..." she whispered. "The physical embodiment of her father..."

"Someone get her a fan and a cup of water!" he yelled.

The room turned to look at what she had regurgitated: A clear mucous-y slime formed near the tips of Orville's brown shoes. He recoiled. The imprint of a man's face with a dominant profile was in the center of the blob. The woman with the eyeglasses shrieked and covered her eyes in surprise.

"That's him!"

"He died suddenly..." Madame Beulah sputtered taking a sip of water from a busboy.

"Yes of a heart attack..."

The audience gasped. Lobelia touched a small tray gingerly as if hiding it from the feds. The madame swooned a second as they helped her back on the chair.

"He went to the light...But not without a fight..." she informed them. "Let me catch my breath and Jubal, my spirit guide, will help another lost soul who has been sent here tonight by the dearly departed…"

"Let's give Madame Beulah a round of applause…" Orville shouted.

As the room broke out in thunderous ovation, Edgar watched as the woman with the glasses moved away from Beulah awkwardly. Someone fanned Beulah. He kept his eyes on the young woman and whispered to his sister-in-law.

"Do you think she Is part of the act?"

"I'm not sure…" she answered, still partway entranced by it all.

"That Madame Beulah puts on one helluva show, doesn't she?!" Orville broke in.

"She sure does!"

TWENTY-ONE

*O*rville Alfonso closed the bar for the night. As instructed by Madame Beulah he left the money on the table beside the crystal ball; however, he didn't see her leave. *What an odd individual!* The look on his face said.

"Did you expect a psychic to be normal?" his mother said exiting for the night. "I told you she'd make us millions…People will pay through nose for that!"

"Night, ma…"

Per his usual, he was the last family member to leave the Electric Eel along with the band. He watched as the bus boy, a young man who was barely twenty but looked sixteen walked around picking up empty glassware and bottles and putting them in a tub. *He looks like a teenager but has a receding hairline like a middle-aged man.* He noticed.

"Almost finished, Mr. Alfonso…" the young man said with quiet reverence.

"Thank you, Rory…" he said examining him.

Rory shrugged and spotted Iris's dog hiding carefully behind a red and black Shoji screen. The dog's tail was more primate than canine...He observed. Iris spotted him, wary at first of anyone who approached her dog. Rory put his palm out to allow the dog to sniff.

"Nice dog..." he said politely.

"Thank you..." she said warming.

The pooch gave an aloof wag of the tail and pushed his nose close to Rory's middle. The Afghan Hound allowed him to embrace him for a second and then moved toward Iris. Iris stepped back impressed.

"His name's Peaches..." she said, her speaking voice considerably higher than her singing voice.

"Name's Rory...Rory Childs..."

"Iris Dupeon..."

Why did that last name sound familiar? He thought. She read his thoughts.

"My father is involved with textiles..."

He blushed, not used to being read. Orville approached them next and touched them each on the shoulder. Rory felt his hand in the middle of his back and squirmed a little.

"It's pouring outside, Iris... I'll give you and the pooch a ride..."

Rory looked up to the ceiling. The rain pelted the roof as if being thrown by some unseen hand. *Perhaps Madame Beulah had made the spirits angry...?* They thought.

"Do you need a ride too?" Iris said fishing for his name.

"Rory..."

"Rory...Do you need a ride?"

"I think we can squeeze you in..." he said smiling like a hammerhead. "Hope Poppy put the top down..."

Normally, Rory preferred to walk home but the rain intensified...And it was getting colder. He pressed his lips together, fearing he had no choice.

Orville gave him an indiscernible look. Iris noticed the bus boy now too in the light...*He's cute...*She mused. *Normally I prefer more masculine men...But he has adorable innocent boyish quality that I find attractive but can't put my finger on as to why...*

Iris exchanged a glance with Orville. *Was he noticing too?* She couldn't tell. *There are rumors he's a switch hitter...*She thought, putting it out of her mind.

A second later Rory spotted a heavyset woman in red and black fishnet stockings and thick t-strapped heels near the giant aquarium. The large eels swam in a circle in nervous angst. She looked at him with a flat expression and explained.

"Storms always make them anxious. Must be the electricity..."

"Makes sense..." he said to himself.

He turned to introduce himself, but the portly woman was gone. Rory knitted his brows together at this slight as Orville approached. He put his arms out as if comforting him.

"That's Eugenia... Don't mind her. She's an odd duck..." he explained, feeling the need to apologize for his employee.

Iris came up to him next with dog in tow. Rory noticed her sparkly short black cocktail dress and shawl. She smiled.

"I like your dress..."

"Thanks..." she said. "My mother hates that I had it shortened..."

She rolled her eyes and turned from him. In unison they walked to Madame Beulah's table which had been pushed in the corner and neatly covered with a white ubiquitous sheet like a cadaver in a morgue. *Do not touch!* A handmade sign warned.

"It's the closest we could get to moving it without touching it..." Orville said with wry indignation.

"Did you see the look on that dame with the glasses' face when she contacted her father?" Iris asked with wide eyes.

"*Did* I?" Rory asked.

The Electric Eel!

"And then she spit out that...*slime*..."

She made an unladylike gagging noise and soon they were laughing together in an inside joke that Orville was not in on. Orville winced at the sound of her regurgitation again. *What did she call it? Ectoplasm?*

"My father says it's all fake..." Iris informed him.

"I hope it's *not*..." Rory said.

And at that moment, they bonded; an instantaneous liking for each other. *She's pretty...*Rory thought. *Like one of those classy girls he saw in print ads...*

"Well? You ready?" Orville asked slinging his slicker over his shoulders.

Eugenia exited first into the rainy night, followed by Lobelia, Tiny and then Orville, Iris, Peaches, and Rory. Iris shielded the dog's freshly groomed coat with an umbrella and then her new friend Rory. *He's not much taller than I am...*She observed. *Of course neither is Orville...*

"I'm parked right over here..." he informed them.

"Night, Orville..."Lobelia called somewhere in the darkness.

Despite the inclement weather, Orville's car was slick and shiny. Tiny particles of ice pelted the metal wheel well and leapt onto the pavement. *Is that hail?* They wondered.

Iris felt the ice hit her scalp as she and the dog climbed into the front passenger seat. Orville picked at her blond hair and brushed it off her face. She blushed in Rory's presence as Orville climbed inside and drove in silence.

"I don't live far..." the young man called from the backseat.

"Oh, we're not going there just yet..." Iris said, looking back at him.

Rory looked at her in confusion. Neither of the others commented further. The rain let up for a moment, slapping the windshield gently.

"What was that song you sang tonight, Iris?" Orville pondered.

"Whispering..."

Fifteen minutes later Orville stopped the car in front of her Olde Towne East building and reached over to kiss her. To Rory's surprise they looked back at him seductively. He waited patiently as Orville got out to open Iris's car door...The wind howled somewhere.

"You comin?" Iris cooed.

Rory nodded silently. Orville gave Iris a rakish half-grin. A large awning dripped against an expensive marble encrusted building. *Whoa!* He thought.

"Wait till you see the inside!" Orville called.

Thunder clapped again as they climbed the stairs to her penthouse. From floor to ceiling the building was decorated in shades of gold and brown in luxurious material. A few recessed areas lined the hallway in the shape of open seashells.

"We're here..."

Rory's eyes widened at the sight of her pad. *Is all this hers?* She blushed a little, embarrassed. Orville meanwhile reached for a globe on an expensive stand and flipped it open to reveal six tiny amber colored shot glasses and a crystal decanter. He poured a small amount of liquid out for the three of them.

"Remy Martin..." he informed the young man. "Brandy..."

"*Cognac*..." she corrected. "But I do have brandy here somewhere if you prefer..."

Orville took a sip and kissed Iris again. Rory stepped away and looked out at the sheer lace curtains. *It's raining again...* He thought. Iris stretched her arm out to him, but he remained out of reach. The brown liquor warmed their esophagus.

"Don't be shy..."

"I've just never done anything like this..."

"With a man or woman?" she asked without hesitation.

*Either...*He thought but instead said nothing. Finally, he allowed her to embrace him. She smelled of something sweet and expensive. Next, Orville reached for three long cigarettes and passed them out like a proud new father as Iris brandished a silver cigarette case and lighter with the letters I. V. D embossed in gold leaf on the side.. They smoked in silence for a moment.

The Electric Eel!

In nervous angst, Rory looked up at the wall to study a piece of art he'd never noticed before. The woman in the frame was wearing a large, wide brimmed hat with a faceted face like a sculpture. Her long neck was stylized and unnatural. Her eyes were almond-shaped and filled in completely with a pale pigment giving her a hollow, haunted look.

"Modigliani..." Iris said dryly. "Just died not too long ago from alcohol poisoning... Italian Jew... My parents know all those European artists..." she said trailing off. "That's his girl Jeanne Hebuterne...Jumped out the window after they found him dead and offed herself...She was about my age...A couple months pregnant if I remember..."

"You ready?" Rory asked mustering up courage, snuffing out the butt in the ashtray. "I do have to get home soon..."

"Are *you* ready is the question?" Orville asked.

Orville and Iris laughed at a joke that he was no longer in on. Her black dress was partially open at the neck. Rory peered down at her chest and gulped. Quietly, she undo Rory's tie and laid it on the hearth.

Up ahead Iris's bedroom peeked around the corner, lacy and expensive, with an intricate silken bedspread and matching shiny pale pink satin pillows. Four hand carved spiral wooden posts dotted each corner of the substantial king-sized mattress along with an antique gold Chinese chest of drawers and two Egyptian inspired nightstands and a heavy silk Persian rug.

Without further ado, Iris took both men by the hand and led them inside...

TWENTY-TWO

"*I* gave her a ride home...What's the big deal?"

"You've been giving her rides for *months*..." Poppy answered with hands on hips blocking him in the doorway.

"*Exactly!* It was raining, and she had a dog with her... I gave the bus boy a ride too...Should I let my employees get drenched?"

The Electric Eel!

"Plenty of times you've given her rides when it *wasn't* raining..."

*She has more money than all of us put together...She can afford a car...Or at least her own driver...*Poppy thought. *Why she chooses to work there I'll never know...*

"You get rides with my brother all the time!"

"There aren't rumors flying around the bar about me and your brother!"

Maybe there should be... The look on his face said. She returned his exchange with incredulity. With surprising anger, she pushed past him.

"Edgar's family..." she called with the slam of a door.

"I have a bar to run! Are you coming?" he called to the other room.

*Some job...*She thought emerging. *An illegal speakeasy...*He put his hands up and smiled. But it didn't seem to work this time...*I'll have to switch tactics...*Orville thought.

"I love you..." he mouthed, leaning over to kiss her forehead.

She allowed it for a moment, freezing and biting her lip. When he was sure she was convinced, he released her. Alastair bounded into his father's arms ten seconds later.

"Hey!" Orville yelled at his son.

"Are you gonna leave mommy for that blond lady?" Alastair asked with childlike naivete.

Orville shot his wife a glare. She put both palms up as if to absolve herself of blame. She spun around on her heels in a pirouette.

"No...I promise we'll be together forever," he said kneeling over the boy. "Would you like to come tonight?"

Poppy looked at him in abject horror. She narrowed her eyes like a bull. He had gone too far...

"Are you out of your mind?"

"What?"

"Inviting our child into a bar...*A speakeasy!* And it's a school night!"

"He's my child and I'm proud of him and I'm his father and I can take him wherever I

The Electric Eel!

want...!"

"Then I'm going with you!" she piped up, straightening her spine and neck like an ostrich.

Orville's face burned with a little hurt. *Does she really think I need a chaperone for my own son?* Poppy put a coat on Alastair and then pulled on her own. Their son looked at both of them in confusion as he was shuttled into the family convertible. An awkward quiet tension ensued.

"Will I still go to school tomorrow?" the child asked, looking first at his mother in the passenger seat and then at his father in the driver's seat.

Orville straightened his tan tweed newsboy cap but said nothing. In frustration he pushed his foot on the pedal and flew through the streets of downtown Columbus, Ohio. Poppy's eyes widened as he accidentally turned down a one-way street. A horn buzzed like slapstick in a Charlie Chaplin film, and he barely avoided hitting its source head on.

"Orville slow down!"

But her husband ignored her. She touched his shoulder. The car rattled beneath him like the deck on a rickety ship. He pushed his foot down further and barreled down High Street.

"Orville! I'm sorry! Slow down!"

But he grimaced like a hyena as another car buzzed around him; Poppy held her breath and gripped the car's door panel. Alastair looked around in fear as his mother began to panic. *Is he trying to kill us?* She thought.

To her relief, the corner where the Electric Eel resided came into view. But Orville still didn't decelerate and gave the wheel a sharp turn to the right....But it was too late...

A second later, Poppy felt herself catapulting forward as they went headfirst into a light post. The Buick sizzled as a large plume of steam belched out the car's radiator, emitting a hot, horrific sulfuric stink that permeated the air above. The light above

The Electric Eel!

flickered a second and died.

"Alaistair! My baby!" she cried. "Are you okay? Everybody okay?"

"Yes, mommy!" he called in the near dark of the car.

But his father snatched him up before she could inspect her son further. Without looking at his wife, he placed his son on his shoulders and bounded into the Electric Eel. A large eye peered through the peephole in the door, shocked to see a kid on a man's shoulders.

"Let us in, Tiny! It's me!" he called with more joy than was called for.

With much reluctance Tiny opened the door. Orville paraded his son around the space like he'd just won the World Series. Everyone in the establishment froze in confusion. Carlotta shot Orville a glare as Poppy entered next.

"What's *he* doing here?" Carlotta blinked.

"We were just in an accident!" Poppy bellowed reaching for Alastair.

"Oh my goodness! Are you okay?"

"Seems to be! *Everyone*! This is my son Alastair Alfonso!"

Poppy and Lobelia reached for the boy and lifted him down to inspect him. Lobelia moved her finger in front of his eyes checking him for concussion. They felt relieved and placed Alistair on the floor.

"Now...Now... Stop babying him..." Orville called.

Iris and Peaches wondered over to him next followed by Rory. The hound pressed his long, tapered snout in the boy's direction. Iris nodded that the dog was safe as Alastair touched the dog's silky feathered flaxen hair.

"We're so glad you all are okay..." one of the regulars called.

"Everything's fine cept my car..." he said frowning. "But that's what insurance is for..."

Edgar stood and leaned on his crutch and walked to his nephew. As always, Alastair hugged his uncle. Edgar closed his eyes in relief.

*My brother is so reckless...*He thought allowing the boy to hold onto him. Poppy approached them next, her face red with ire.

"Are you all right?" Edgar asked his sister-in-law.

"I'll live..." she said trying to find the words to describe what she'd been through.

Rory exchanged a glance with Iris when they were out of earshot. Iris shrugged him off as he took her aside. She put her finger out instructing the bassist, clarinetist, and piano player to warm up without her.

"What?" she asked making no effort to hide her annoyance.

"He's *married*?" he asked looking over his shoulder. "And he has a *kid*?"

"Yea..." she said walking away without giving it a second thought.

"Well I better go call the city before they give me a fine..." Orville said with a chuckle that made everyone else uncomfortable.

Rory followed him to the bakery in time to see his boss holding a black stick phone. He waited and tapped his foot as the young man picked up the used doilies for the evening...*Part of my duties anyway...* Orville smiled, trying to appear placid as a nondescript feminine voice came on the line.

"Yes, this is Orville Alfonso at the Electric Eel Bakery off High Street...I was just in an accident... Yes? Everyone is okay...Thank you... But unfortunately, my car isn't... Yea... A bunny rabbit ran in front of us, and my son grabbed the wheel..." he lied. "He has this thing for animals...You know how kids are..."

Then, he spotted Rory again and placed his hand over the receiver, his eyes darkening. *May I help you?* He mouthed.

"Nothing, I was just cleaning up..." he mumbled.

"Oh..." he said turning his attention back to the phone. "Anyway...How old is he? Five...Six...?" he tried to remember. "He just had a birthday...Time goes so fast...So he grabbed the wheel...And yes... I'll have a stern talking to him, ma'am. No his mother doesn't correct him often enough...You're right, I'll have to have a talking with her too... No we don't need an ambulance but if something changes I'll call you...Just a wrecker..."

And with that, he put the phone back on its clip and flashed Rory an electric white smile... *An electric eel smile...* Orville thought to himself with a chuckle.

"Orville!" someone called.

"Coming!" he yelled.

TWENTY-THREE

$\mathcal{R}$ory and Iris arrived after work at her penthouse apartment. Her driver stopped the car precisely at midnight beside the crisp white awning at the entrance of her building. Orville had informed them earlier in the week that he could no longer give them rides, per his wife's instruction.

"Cheer up," he told Rory. "Poppy just gets jealous..." he informed them. "And we'll still see each other at work...And besides, I won't have a car for at least another week...Who knows? Maybe once she cools off we can do it again!"

But Iris knew what *this* meant...Their relationship, however shallow and tenuous, was over. Rory climbed out of the immense black car like Jonah stepping out of the belly of the whale and onto the curb. An effulgent moon radiated above like a hubcap as the driver opened the back door of the automobile. Peaches hoped out, his luxurious parted hair shimmering.

"Thank you..." Rory said grabbing the dog's leash.

Ever since I saw Irene with a driver...I had to have one... She thought. *I have more money than she does... Why does she get a driver and I don't?*

And I have no interest in driving myself... Her train of thought continued. *As mother says: "No respectable woman drives anyway...They are whisked away like Cinderella's carriage to their destination..."*

"Did you see Orville's wreck?" she asked her friend. "Egad!"

And that preposterous story he told! Rory remembered. But he said nothing, not knowing how much she would repeat to his boss.

The Electric Eel!

Iris lit a long cigarette in contraption and reached down to twirl her fingers in front of the dog's muzzle. The smell of her expensive tobacco and perfume hung in the air for a second. The night doorman recognized them and opened the door.

"He needs to pee…" she informed him turning her back slightly.

"Evening, Miss Dupeon…" the man said. "And the stately Peaches…"

"Evening…" she repeated with only slight interest.

Rory allowed the dog to do his business and walked to the foyer. Like most of the building, the entryway was bedight in shades of gold and marble. A series of glyphs and swirls lined the top of a brassy, waist high ashtray. Iris snuffed out the Montclair twenty-two cigarette in contrast to the shorter, less expensive smokes in the sand.

"You coming?" she called.

This whole place is like a museum… Rory noted as she opened the door to her place. *Antiquities are everywhere! Porcelain from the Far East…Turkish and Persian rugs… French silks and Irish lace…Fine English wooden furniture…Red and black Japanese woodblock prints of stylized Geisha girls with white faces and black wigs hung above him…*

"It all works…" he mumbled to himself leaning on a Greco-Roman column.

"What all works?" she asked placing her shawl on a chaise lounge.

"Your apartment…"

"Oh…*That*…" she said as if none of it was a big deal. "I guess…"

He gestured to a giant blue and white menorah with something written in Hebrew at the bottom. She looked away. With the tip of his finger he touched the writing gently on the piece.

"My parents sent that over…It's a family heirloom," she said with a shrug. "Apparently, they don't want me to do a Hannukah alone again…" she said turning to the dog. "But I'm never alone with Peachy Poo Poo here!"

She leaned over and pushed her face against the dog's nose. *The dog seems to be the* *only thing that makes her happy…*He thought with more than a touch of sadness…*That and her music…*

"Want some wine or something? I normally just eat brie and crackers…"

He nodded, not wanting to be rude. Her eyes were glazed now as she stumbled to where he sat on a red brocaded love seat. *Is she drunk?* She placed her small clutch on the end table beside him. A small vial toppled onto the floor, and he handed it to her.

"Oh thank you…" she said with slight embarrassment. "Just a little pick me up that Jib the bass player gave me…But I think it takes the edge off…Want some?"

"No, thank you…"

Quickly she stuffed it back in her purse and reached for the bottle of something dark and luxurious. She motioned to the icebox and pulled out two squatty red wine glasses from a holder above.

"The stuff on top my mother sent over…Bor-ing…Kosher… Unless you want a macaroon," she said turning and looking at him. "The good stuff's on the bottom…There may even be some weed down there…"

She motioned to a tray of salami and Capicola ham on a white porcelain platter along with a sundry of assorted exotic cheeses. Rory looked for the marijuana out of curiosity but found only some yellowed slimy lettuce.

"Guess I smoked it all…Lucky me!" she said smiling. "Don't eat the salmon that's for Peachy…You can give some of it to him if you like."

He placed the small bowl of fresh fish on the floor and called to the hound. Peaches bounded over with surprising speed, his long hair flying like a racehorse. Soon the sounds of his munching came, his sharp perfectly white teeth and pink tongue scraping the bowl.

"I usually clip his hair back before I feed him something messy…" she said. "He's *sooo* high maintenance…""

When satisfied that the dog was satiated, Rory sat on the couch as Iris grabbed a glass of wine and a piece of brie and crackers and landed beside him. She leaned in close to him and thought of the night they had spent with Orville. She grabbed his hand and asked.

"How old are you?"

"Twenty-one..." he answered, allowing her to hold his hand. "Carlotta wouldn't let me work there till I was twenty-one anyway..."

Funny how she wants an age restriction considering the whole setup is illegal anyway... Well, to distribute and sell alcohol anyway... He reached for the glass of wine.

"How about you?" he asked in return.

"I'll be twenty-six in August..." she said leaning closer to him.

Rory stood and paced. He eyes narrowed. She looked up at him, the hem on her short dress coming forward.

"Come sit with me..." she whined.

He hesitated. Iris put her lip out in a little pout. But he turned. *Funny how that always worked with men before...*

"Oh my God..." she said realizing.

"What?" he asked a little self-conscious.

"You don't like girls, do you?"

He held his hands behind his back, pondering it. But Iris was already convinced and laid back on the couch with a laugh. The wine warmed his esophagus a bit as he walked.

"I'm not sure, but I know I care for you..."

And without saying anything further on the subject, Rory sat back on the sofa and held her. Her eyes were surprisingly dark and cloudy with intoxication in contrast to her platinum hair and light skin. He patted the soft skin on the top of her hand.

"I love you..." she informed him.

"That's the first time anyone's ever said that to me and meant it..." Rory admitted.

She reached for another bite of brie and handed him some. He took it and chewed it,

The Electric Eel!

the rind curious at its contrast in texture. *She obviously adores it...*

"Oh! I love French food! There's Camembert in there too! And pate! I give bites to Peachy, but it gives him gas..." she giggled. "Have you been to France? My father's a French textile magnate...We used to go to yachting on the Riviera all the time... Have you been to the Riviera?"

He shook his head. She, in turn, looked at him in disbelief as if surprised that most people did not go *yachting* in the South of France...He sensed she wasn't a braggart...Just oblivious...

"Since we're asking questions..." he stammered.

"Yes?" she said craning her neck over her armpit to look at him.

"Why is such a classy dame like you, who could have any man she wants, working as a lounge singer in a place like the Electric Eel?"

Iris looked at him with a little hurt. But he blinked, standing by what he said. She thought about it for a second.

"Cause life here is *boring*..." she said with that nervous chuckle of hers again. "And music is my life..."

"What about with your family?"

"Even *more* boring!" she said standing. "So here we are, Rory Childs... Two fabulous schlubs in a boring, mundane world!"

And to his surprise, she began to sing: A soulful ballad he didn't know all the words to. Her voice was clear and perfect like a woman much wiser and older than herself.

"I can't sleep at night.

I can't eat a bite

'Cause the man I love

He don't treat me right.

He makes me feel so blue,

I don't know what to do

Sometime I sit and sigh

And then begin to cry

'Cause my best friend,

Said his last goodbye..."

And to her surprise, he began to sing along with her, perfectly in tune. Iris pivoted on the couch in admiration as if she weren't used to people singing on key as she did and listened. *I think I found my soulmate*...She thought.

TWENTY-FOUR

1921

*I*rene and Mr. Wright waited in their Cadillac outside her family's bar, patiently. He looked at his wife with nervous angst and placed his palms in his lap. *This place and Prohibition have been the white elephant in our marriage...*

"I don't think they'll let me in, dear..."

"Nonsense!" she said trying to hide her own anxiety. "They let Aunt Virginia in and she's dating a *cop!* As long as we pay a cover..."

"A *cover*! They charge their own family a *cover?*! How much do they charge?"

"Ten dollars..." she whispered.

"*Ten dollars apiece?!* That's criminal..."

"Let's just see if they let us in..." she said with a patronizing sympathetic pat to his thigh as she exited the car.

Lobelia was standing at her usual place behind the bakery counter when they entered. She was dressed in pink and white, her dark face warming in recognition. Irene, in contrast, was in an ivory suit, matching gloves, and pumps. She reached for her pocketbook and withdrew two ten-dollar bills.

"That won't be necessary!" a booming male voice echoed.

Are we being watched? Her husband wondered looking up at the ceiling. The door

The Electric Eel!

opened with a groan like a b horror movie.

"Hey!" a group of people yelled in unison.

The room was packed. Several people raised glasses in celebration. Orville Alfonso greeted them with hands folded over his navel. He looked at his brother-in-law with muted suspicion.

"Welcome, sister!"

"I keep trying to get Mr. Wright to come here…"

"Well, it's Thursday so you're in luck… The legendary Madame Beulah will be performing soon…Along with the band…"

Despite the warm welcome, Mr. Wright felt the chill in Orville's tone. *He's such a liar I can never tell…*He thought. Someone handed him an electric green cocktail a second later.

"Our signature drink…" his brother-in-law informed him, answering the unspoken question.

"I've had the electric eel…" she refused. "I'll have white wine…"

She sipped the drink and wriggled her nose. *Ever since alcohol has become scarce people say the drinks are getting watered down…*She thought. *I never believed it till now!*

"How's your drink, dear?" she asked her husband.

"I've had better…"

"We'll have gin…" Rufus said putting up two fingers.

Orville feigned a smile but inside he felt the need to wretch. It wasn't like the old gin they *used* to sell before this whole craziness started. He thought of it coming in homemade, from God knows where, sometimes with wood alcohol added. *Bathtub gin as the locals called it…*Made crudely anyway they could and transported to and from Canada by opportunistic gangsters.

Grocery and hardware stores have been out of corn syrup, sugar, and hops for

The Electric Eel!

months... He thought. *Pharmacies are even out of cough syrup which could contain a small amount of whiskey...* He smiled and placed two of the wretched concoctions on the bar.

"I don't see how anyone can get that down their gullet..." he informed his mother. "It has to taste like turpentine..."

"Shh..." she chided not wanting to dissuade a sale.

Annamary took a sip of hers and grimaced. The taste lingered on her tongue for a second like battery acid. She looked at Carlotta and requested something unusual for a speakeasy in in the Twenties...

"May I have a glass of water?"

Carlotta looked at her son and he shrugged. The old woman thanked him as he placed the glass in front of her and sipped it. But the taste of rotgut liquor persisted in her mouth. She looked at her boyfriend who sipped his without compunction. Orville looked at him in shock.

"He can drink anything..."

"I got worse in the Navy..." he said placing the glass on the counter with a thud.

But Edgar sensed it was all for show. *No one* could drink that stuff. He exchanged an incredulous glance with his brother across the bar. *What could be worse?*

"Now without further ado! We bring the talented Madame Beulah!" Orville shouted.

Madame Beulah walked to the table without looking at them. Next, she walked to Orville and whispered something in his ear. He nodded, already in on the act.

Several people began to raise their hand and she picked a few and ordered them to sit at various intervals around the table. Eugenia handed her a long white skinny cone that tapered at the mouthpiece and flared in three pieces at the end like a morning glory.

"May I have the lights dimmed, please? This spirit trumpet is designed to amplify the voices of the dead so we all can hear..." she said holding it up.

Orville motioned to Tiny to turn the lights down. Rory lit a white candle with a long match. The smell of sulfur hovered for a second. The onlookers around the table looked on with morbid fascination, their eyes flickering in the orange flame.

"Hearing aids to the dead!" Orville informed them.

"May I have complete quiet?" she beckoned in a sonorous voice. "Sometimes the voices may be faint whispers or deep resonating booms...But you never can tell...Sometimes the spirit ear piece may actually float... Now! Let's all hold hands in the circle.... Great spirits of the beyond..." she called through the piece.

The whole room watched as Beulah raised the trumpet up in the air as if hitting a high note. Those at the table held hands as she began to cantillate something in Latin...A hymn perhaps? She motioned for them to join in on the singing...

"Ooooo..."

And then a loud knocking voice came on the floor. Peaches the dog's ears perked up across the room. Beulah put her hand up instructing them to move on. The eels backed up with caution in their tank behind where Eugenia stood.

"Animals always pick up on the spirits first...These animals be it living *or* dead..."

Peaches barked again. Iris touched his collar and pushed him behind the Shoji screen. The dog, however, was undaunted and remained fixated on the table at the back of the room. Rory leaned down to comfort the canine.

"The spirits are here..." she announced through the trumpet.

All of a sudden the table began to lift off the ground. Beulah raised both of her hands above to show that she wasn't hefting it; others at the table did the same. The table hovered a second and dropped with a thud.

Then Beulah fell into a trance, still holding the spirit amplifier between her knees. All of a sudden the candle blew out and the trumpet crashed to the floor, and she awoke with a shot. Her eyes remained open for a second as if she herself were deceased.

"The spirits have exited..." she announced. "But they mumbled something to me whilst they were here about the great beyond...We are all here in life, but death and the dead are all around...That was their message...Now all of you hold hands and resonate with that message..."

How could anyone buy this? Mr. Wright wondered holding his wife's hand. But they did as instructed for a second. Beulah raised her hands above the crystal ball as it darked from its normal clear to opaque. And the room went completely dark.

*All part of the show...*Orville thought. Rufus stood but no one seemed to notice save for his significant other Annamary. He stumbled in the scant light of the bar and headed for the men's room and vomited in the commode with as much discretion as he could muster and stood on wobbly legs.

"Ruf..." she called her pet name for him coming out like roof.

Rufus's vision was blurry and once the lights came back on he was nearly blind. Annamary walked to him and led him outside. Orville ran in their direction to do damage control.

"He's really sick..." she said to the man she considered a family friend. "We gotta get him home... He can't drink like he did when he was a teenager..."

Despite his normal lack of concern for others, Orville felt bad for them. *It's the rotgut shit...*He thought. He walked to his mother and took her aside.

"Rufus is nearly blind... "

"Well, he's old," she said lessening.

"It's that bathtub gin..."

"Oh," she said quietly. "Keep your voice down..."

Edgar joined in on the conversation. Carlotta shot her middle son an apoplectic glare. *This doesn't concern you!*

"You have to call an ambulance...Is she sick too?"

"No, she spit hers out..."

"We'll be sued! Get rid of that shit *first* and then call them..."

They looked at their mother with horror. Carlotta sensed she had overstepped.

Annamary appeared in the door again, confused.

"Be right with you..."

"Then have Lobelia get rid of it, and you call...You knew what I meant!"

"Someone's on their way, Annamary..." Orville lied.

Annamary nodded and walked back outside into the night. Rufus leaned alongside the building in a nearby alley. Quickly, Orville followed them outside. The elderly couple barely noticed the large woman behind them exiting with several barrels. A sea of amber-colored liquid began to flow behind him like motor oil into the storm drain. A second later Rufus let on a ragged, uncomfortable breath and collapsed to the ground.

*He's gone...*Orville thought. Annamary let out a shriek of despair.

TWENTY-FIVE

Edgar mulled over what had transpired with Annamary and Rufus as he stood outside. After the old man's death his mother had taken all the employees aside to give them clear instructions before they left for the night. Their *first* and *only* staff meeting.

Tiny, Eugenia, Lobelia, Rory, and the rest of the staff gathered near where Rufus had fallen. The band was noticeably absent, choosing to go to whatever after-party they had been invited to.

"We have to find a new source of hooch," Carlotta told her sons. "There's a rumor that they're going to be adding *kerosene* to it..."

"*Kerosene? Why?*" Edgar asked.

"To make it even less palatable..." Orville said, having heard his mother repeat this rumor before.

"This can never happen again...We'll lose everything..."

*Not to mention you'll kill someone...*Edgar thought. Lobelia blinked. *Money is her only concern...*

"What source are you talking about?" Edgar asked and then regretted it.

The Electric Eel!

Carlotta smiled but did not expand further. The feeling of icicles ran up and down Lobelia's spine. But she didn't have to say anything...They had seen the kind lurking around the pharmacy...Thugs in expensive tailor pinstriped suits and hats. The kind who were all over the news and silent films. It was only a matter of time...

"Now! No more of this unpleasantness!" Orville said with a clap of the hands. "We must'nt dwell on the past..."

"What he means is...We can't let this get out... If anyone asks: Rufus was old and sick... Could've been something he ate. So this goes no further than us. Even Beulah and Iris and the band must not know..."

Rory thought of this. *Could he keep anything from her? Especially when it pertains to the Electric Eel...* He thought with a sigh.

"You are dismissed," Carlotta told them.

"We can clean up tomorrow," Edgar informed them. "It's late."

He seems nice... Rory thought. *Just very unhappy...* He smiled warmly for a second in the young man's direction and then his expression dropped to its usual sadness. Edgar pushed passed him on his crutch. *He deserves someone nice...*

The air was cool but tolerable, so Rory decided to walk. His parents' home was modest and within walking distance. *What time is it?* He wondered. *Already after midnight...* He thought. *I can't go home...*

"Iris...I hope you are awake..." he called out to the darkness.

Even though it was well past dark, High Street was abuzz with activity. Two trolleys ran up and down the street carrying a group of tourists. Most of these people appeared intoxicated... *Probably coming from the University...* He thought.

A few prostitutes and homeless people stood on the corner as he turned to look for a cab. One of the vagrants held a tin cup as Rory passed, his leg a stump against the building.

"Homeless veteran..." his sign said.

The Electric Eel!

He thought of Edgar now. *How did he lose his leg?* He wondered. No one ever asked. And this man's leg was missing at the knee instead of at the hip where Edgar's had been truncated. He flagged a cab a second later.

"Old Towne East, please!"

To his relief, Iris's bedroom light was on when he arrived. Perhaps the doorman would let him in. He walked to the front where a sea of elegant hydrangeas stood waist high like popcorn balls. To his surprise some of the flowers were bright green like fresh pistachios.

"Miss Dupeon instructed me to let you in anytime..." the night watchman informed him.

Rory smiled. *He was in...*The building glinted as always; the stonework cool to the touch like a mausoleum. The doorman walked him to her front door and turned a long silver key in the lock.

"Miss Dupeon..." he called.

*She must be asleep...*He thought. Rory pushed the door open.

"Iris..." he called not wanting to interrupt something potentially embarrassing.

Peaches the dog ran to him growling at first and then he backed off in recognition. The dog sensed something was off somehow, the pale hairs on the back of his neck standing up. The hound's white teeth and dark eyes remained wary of the doorman but allowed Rory inside.

He found her lying on her back in the bedroom. They ran to her. Rory touched her face gently.

"Iris! It's me! Rory!"

A small hypodermic needle landed on the floor unceremoniously. To his horror he saw a circle of crimson inside her elbow. She let out of a gurgle as a small amount of foam exited her mouth.

"Call an ambulance!" he informed the doorman.

Five minutes later an ambulance arrived at Iris's uber rich apartment building. A few ultra-wealthy ladies in satin nightgowns appeared in the window of the neighboring penthouses to catch a peek of Iris being loaded on a stretcher. *Is that the Dupeon girl?* They wondered.

Finally, the gurney passed him in the hall, its wheel squeaking ominously as it exited the front of the building. Silently, Rory held onto her dog and prayed as his friend disappeared in the back of the ambulance a second later… On its way in the night to some unknown facility…

TWENTY-SIX

*N*o one seemed to notice as Edgar walked unaided into the Electric Eel Bar that weekend. He moved pretty much as he had done before the accident…*That was so long ago…*

He had forgotten how tall he was. *Taller than his brother…* His pelvis rubbed against the ball joint on his artificial right hip slightly. *The doctor said that would be normal for a while…*

Soon others began to notice his gait, Poppy first and then Lobelia. His mother rolled her eyes and dried a champagne flute on a towel. *She isn't going to ruin this day…* He thought biting his lip.

"I can even wear a shoe on the right side…" he informed the women as he took his place at the bar.

"And a pant!" Poppy noted.

"Not just a cut off on one side like a pirate…" Edgar quipped.

"Easy, everyone… It's still artificial…" Carlotta joked. "He didn't grow a new one like a reptile…"

But no one, including her son, found humor in her cruel wit. Poppy placed her palm in the middle of his back in support. He beamed and burned with anger and resentment at the same time.

"You look so handsome!"

"Thank you!" he said, unused to be compliented.

"Well don't forget it's *our* wealth from *this* place that allowed you to go to that specialist..." she said motioning her hands to the front door. "And you'll need to pull your weight around here...Not just hobbling around here drinking up our profits like you are used to doing...Or you're *out*!"

I know! I'm an accountant who does all the books for this place! He wanted to say. But he said nothing as usual and allowed it to fester like an unlanced boil on his soul. Then he felt his brother's hand on his shoulder, the smell of his aftershave thick and pungent like smog.

"You look great, bro!"

*I'm not sure what's worse...*Edgar mused. *The one who is honestly callous and cruel without remorse or provocation or the one who lies and tells me what he thinks I want to hear...*He looked to both of them, his brother's insincere smile and his mother's stone face. *And they get along perfectly...*

"You deserve some good news..." Poppy offered.

Edgar warmed at her genuine compassion. *And she's stuck with my brother and my mother too...*He thought with much regret. *She was pretty, in a wholesome kind of way...The girl your parents wanted you to marry...*He turned to look at her in a thin light purple wrap dress and scarf. *Maybe in another time and place...*

Just then the busboy approached him. *What was his name?* Edgar couldn't remember. He was short...*Even shorter than his brother...*He thought with a chuckle. His eyes and hair were dark in contrast to his light skin and reddish pink lips.

"Rory..." he said sparing Edgar the task of asking for his name again.

"Ah, Rory. Thank you...!"

An awkward pause ensued as Rory stood behind him. *He's nice enough I suppose... For*

The Electric Eel!

a guy...

"How is Iris doing?" Lobelia asked Rory with wide brown eyes.

Now it was Rory's time to get quiet. He thought of his friend and one time lover lying prostrate on the mattress with a needle under her arm...*How could a woman who has everything need that stuff?* A second later he realized they were waiting with impatience for him to answer.

"Still in the hospital..."

With most things regarding Iris's family he sensed it was all hush hush. *Will I ever meet them? Do I even want to? Will I ever see her again?*

"She's lucky to have a friend like you, Rory..." Poppy said.

By nine, a horde of people stormed the front door in search of alcohol and good times. It seemed to be more than they could accommodate as time went on. *We can't give them that bathtub stuff...*Lobelia said thinking of pouring the rest of it down the drain post haste the night before.

"What's the password?" Tiny asked humoring them.

"Monday!"

Several petite women in too much makeup stared up at him and giggled. The irony being that young attractive women intimated *him* and not the other way around was not lost on him. He was dressed in a tailored suit that made him look like a kid who had outgrown his brother's hand me downs. His neck was thick like copper piping underneath his collared shirt, a bead of perspiration forming on the nape.

"In the old days we could only legally accommodate a certain number of people at a time..." Orville said to the Sequoia-sized man with a slap on the back. "I'm so glad anything goes now!"

"Damn fire codes!"

"Yea! More covers for us!"

Carlotta shot them a glare. *She also scares me!* He thought as a swarm of people, mostly women entered the small space. *Only a few years ago it was almost all male...But look at all the women here now!*

"Tonight..." Orville called to them. "Without further ado: Filling in for Iris...Is the lovely Lobelia on vocals!"

While the audience was mostly white, Lobelia remained one of few black people in the establishment. Gone with Prohibition were the rules of racial segregation that marred most of the country. Here everyone was equal and allowed, unlike other clubs who were rumored to have brown bag rules where a paper bag was held up to someone's arm and if they were darker than the paper they had to enter through the back door...

*Even in black clubs...*Lobelia thought. *Funny how no one cares about that in here...Just as long as you pay and have a good time and leave without telling on them...*She straightened the flower in her hair and stepped into Iris's place, albeit temporarily. The piano, clarinet and string bassist played as usual. Soon she began her rendition of :"You Can't Keep a Good Man Down!" and the room suddenly went silent to listen.

Wallace the piano player, paused to listen for a second as well did the other musicians. Her voice dominated their instruments. Soon they moved onto another song and ad-libbed a few bars. The room full of people in various states of intoxication stood to cheer.

"And that is our newest talent Lobelia singing a Mamie Smith tune!"

Lobelia stepped down and caught her breath. All of sudden people were congratulating her. Recognizing her...She felt *alive...*

She spotted Carlotta by the back door and half-expected her to praise her; however, the older woman just gave her usual scowl. To her she was just another hired hand...Soon two large men joined her, and Carlotta forced an uncomfortable smile as if trying to buy her silence.

"We'll get you the stuff, Ms. Alfonso..." the heftier of the two informed her.

Lobelia blinked. Prior to Prohibition using a last name in social settings as a sign of respect was common, *now* it was never done...Anonymity was key now...Unless you had an unusual first name like her own where it really didn't matter.

"But we don't come cheap! Fifteen percent!"

But these men knew Carlotta professionally...And they weren't Electric Eel regulars. *No one ever comes to the back entrance...*

"That seems a little steep... Especially for a cut of the stuff you aren't bringing...Twelve on the stuff you bring and none of this rotgut shit... I won't have anyone dropping dead for that swill..."

"The good stuff is hard to find..."

Lobelia looked at her boss whose face was hard as stone. *Is she seriously bartering with mobsters?* The two men spoke to each other for a second and nodded.

"Nice doing business with you..." the other man said to Carlotta.

"Likewise."

"Say nothing," Carlotta ordered Lobelia as they walked back to the main room.

TWENTY-SEVEN

Detective Talbert's sole focus for the past year and a half had been solving the murder of Julius Alfonso. That and the disaster known as Prohibition had eaten up all his time. And he'd gotten nowhere...*On either....*

Crime was everywhere now as it hadn't been in 1919. *Sure we had murderers here and there and the occasional drunk and domestic...But nothing like this!*

"And the crime we saw before Prohibition was sporadic and rash and relatively easy to solve..." he said out loud. "This type is organized like a well-oiled machine. And *violent*! And nobody talks!"

None of us small town police forces are equipped to deal with it. *Us city police aren't faring much better...It all started with that bloody train robbery a year ago right before*

The Electric Eel!

this all started...And they didn't steal jewels, cash, or gold but whiskey! Whiskey! He thought.

"Now they're shooting each other left and right! Chicago typewriters as they're callin it...Sometimes they take a whole city block in the process! And they don't care who gets in their way!"

Talbert slammed his fist on the dashboard. He thought of Julius Alfonso again and pushed the bootleggers out of his mind. *Right around the corner he was stabbed! Did his family have anything to do with it?* Possibly. *Did Virginia?* No, he thought finally.

"I allowed myself to break the one rule of this line of police work: I allowed myself to get too close to a victim's family member..."

He pulled a small picture out of his glovebox of an attractive woman. He kissed the photo of Virginia Alfonso gently and looked for it. *In for a penny in for a pound...*

After months of courtship Talbert had finally decided that Virginia was the one for him...Sure there'd been other girls...Sycophants mostly who hung on the dangers of policework...Virginia had caught him a time or two...He had vowed that she was the only one for him.

He looked up at the Electric Eel, his mind drifting away from Virginia for a moment. *Finally somebody may talk about what happened!* He thought. One of them had agreed to meet him here near the spot where Julius had been stabbed. But only if he agreed to protect the individual's identity and privacy. Reluctantly, he had gone along with it.

The crime scene photos were seared in his mind as if burned in his subconscious by acid. He pictured Julius's face, the look of shock still frozen on his corpse. He remembered watching the coroner place the poor lifeless man in a body bag and then loading him in a mortuary van, carting him away to the morgue, his body sliced open like a spiral ham. *No one deserves that!* He thought.

He watched as the Electric Eel began to light up for the night. *Bakery my ass!* He thought wryly. It's one of the most popular speakeasies in town! *Everyone knows that!*

The Electric Eel!

"But I can't go in and just arrest people! I'd have to cuff half of the Columbus PD in the process! And now that Irene Wright's husband was a regular it would get most of the local politicians involved!"

Talbert looked at his watch and yawned. *I can't wait much longer...*He thought. *And Carlotta's bound to notice me sitting in a car outside the bar...Marked or unmarked. And throw a fit! And the last thing I need is a call into the station tomorrow morning having to explain why I'm sitting outside her place...*

All of a sudden the back door of the Electric Eel opened in the alley way, Detective Talbert turned and reached for his service revolver. Two large men in brown derby hats emerged and approached the car along with a figure he didn't instantly recognize...Before he could react, he was surrounded...

"Ambush!" he yelled ducking inside the car.

But it was too late. The sound of something similar to fireworks popped next. As if on cue, the two men opened fire in all directions, a cloud of smoke and gunpowder plumed grey in the gloaming night sky. The rat a tat sound of a machine gun peppered the police car with gunfire. Detective Talbert barely had time to feel the gunshots entering his body before everything went black...*He'd been set up...*

TWENTY-EIGHT

"Sorry about your brother..." a police dispatch woman informed her. "Unfortunately, I haven't seen Detective Talbert all day, Virginia..."

Virginia paused. *I should head over to the Electric Eel...*She thought pondering her next move. *They'll be thrilled to see me...*

Quickly Virginia showered and dressed, opting for a slinky black dress with a scoop neck and a string of opera length pearls that hung like a drape to her mid-section. As she fastened her strap heels she reached for a small spritzer bottle of perfume and sprayed her neck and wrists. The smell of something ladylike and floral dangled in the air and

The Electric Eel!

dissipated.

Her modest apartment glowed in the dim light of a small lamp in cool tones. Growing up her mother preferred putting her in pink and mauve; however, as an adult she preferred blue and grey. *Perhaps in spite of it...*Unlike many of the day who lived mainly on credit, she preferred to live simply and within her means.

She clicked off the small mission style gas lamp and allowed herself to sit in the near darkness for a moment and then slipped on a small slicker. *It's supposed to rain...*She mused looking out the small window.

"Better call a taxi while one's still available..." she said reaching for the phone.

Virginia thought of all that had transpired since Prohibition. Her brother's death had stuck with her six months earlier, an unhealed wound on the nucleus of her soul. And then they bought the Electric Eel with his money...

*Which they shut me out of...*She noted with much bitterness. Carlotta was greedy, and she taught her sons to be greedy...*They left Irene out of it too...Now that she wanted it...Soon as they got money they put the rest of us out...*

She thought of her niece and the cushy marriage she'd landed for herself. *I could have had that...*Virginia told herself. *But who wants to rely on a man?*

"Irene's a liability..." she told herself. "And so's her husband... Even if they say she's not..."

Five minutes later Virginia was in a taxi heading across town. Gritty sights of the less desirable Hilltop Neighborhood, west of downtown Columbus and Franklinton. The Columbus State Hospital for the Insane to the south loomed in her sideview like Dracula's palace. She shuddered. A few parcels of expansive farmland owned by wealthy black and Indian farmers came into view next alongside industrial buildings... Signs that the neighborhood was transitioning from agrarian to an urban suburb.

As she had predicted rain began to fall. First, a sprinkle and then a downpour. The Tin Lizzie quaked from the sudden onslaught. The driver didn't seem to notice as he weaved

The Electric Eel!

in and out of traffic toward Broad Street. The Model T's windshield wipers did their best to keep up as well.

"To the Electric Eel please..." she announced finally.

"The bakery?" he said with a sardonic look.

"Yes. The bakery..." she answered humoring him.

He winked at the inside joke that they were both in on. As visibility waned, traffic began to slow to a crawl. Up ahead a makeshift detour was set up as two black and white police cars with red and white bubble lights blocked the road.

"Can't go that way...Man's been shot..." an officer of the law informed the driver. "Whole street's a crime scene..."

Irene stuck her head out the window to gawk, her hair dampening from the inclement weather. The driver turned his head to look at her nervously, afraid she'd bolt without paying. *Wouldn't be the first time...*He thought.

"Driver! Let me out here..."

"You owe me a dollar seventy-five..." he ordered in a husky voice.

In haste, she fished in her purse and reached for two crisp dollar bills. The cabbie snatched it with much greed and hopped out in the rain to let her out. By the time she walked the few feet across the street she was soaked.

"Who is it?" she called.

"Miss! Get back!"

"I'm looking for Detective Talbert!" she shouted over the rain and the sirens.

"Are you friend or family?" the policeman bellowed back.

"I'm his girlfriend..."

"*Virginia...?*" he asked blinking away the dampness.

"Yes...!"

"Come with me..."

The officer led her across the street to an awning. Up ahead the fuzzy shape of the

The Electric Eel!

Electric Eel glowed in the miasma of the downpour. The smell of wet tobacco, Diesel fuel and rain hovered in her nostrils. He pointed to the detective's police car across the road.

"He was shot..."he said, his voice returning to a normal volume. "Multiple times..."

She gulped in realization. The awning bowed above them like a balloon ready to burst. He moved away from it and then he answered her next unspoken question.

"I'm sorry. He's dead..." he said. "There was nothing more we do..."

He studied her attractive oval face for a second and when he was satisfied that he had done his job, he walked away. Virginia stood in the rain for a moment processing it. *What do I do now?*

Then someone else approached her: A *woman*... She was wearing a drab olive-green calf-length dress that clung to her ankles. Her sensible haircut and shoes told her something immediately. *No way is she a customer of the Electric Eel or any of the other businesses nearby... She works for the police...*

"Miss! I know you were connected to the victim, but you'll need to go...We'll get your statement downtown tomorrow..."

*He's still in the car...*She thought. *They want me out of here so they can get his body out of the car...*

Virginia wanted to protest but instead she found herself nodding in agreement. The woman reached out and touched her shoulder, shooing her away from the sight. Rain continued to drip down her neck and shoulders as if she'd come from a sauna.

"Okay..." she said walking toward the only place she could think of.

Like the proverbial drowned rat, Virginia sloshed to her family's business. A few umbrellas in a stand were by the door, allowed to drip away from the inside of the establishment. Quietly she passed the bakery case, her shoes squishing on the parquet floor. Silently she rapped on the inside door. A second later, a large blue male eye peered through a small opening in the top of the door.

The Electric Eel!

"It's your aunt..." a deep voice informed someone else on the other side. "She's soaked..."

"Let her in..."

As the door opened with a creak, Tiny and Orville appeared. Orville was dressed smartly in a three-piece tweed suit, a cigarette in one hand and an amber hued cocktail in the other. He smiled brightly and then frowned. Tiny turned away at the sight of her.

"May I come in?"

"Of course...Got a little wet?"

"Detective Talbert is dead..." she exclaimed. "Shot multiple times in his police car outside..."

"Shh... Someone'll hear you...!"

"Can we talk about this later?" his mother's voice pleaded.

But it was too late... *The cat's out of the bag!* A few of the guests gasped...

TWENTY-NINE

A long silvery car with a blood red interior and chrome basket wheels was parked in front of Iris's building one afternoon when Rory arrived to check on his friend. As day waned the car's chrome rimmed headlights glowed like eyes and then faded. A driver in a tuxedo and white gloves emerged and opened the rear door for a stately man and woman. Rory's jaw dropped.

"It's a Duesenberg, my boy..." the man informed him as if used to being stared at. "Corinthian Leather... You can get it custom made with leopard, but I think that's a little gauche and my daughter would never go for that...She's okay with them killing cows for whatever reason but not a cat...The rest of the inside is Honduran Mahogany... My wife picked out the platinum color for her birthday even though I thought it looked too much like new money, you know..."

The woman blinked at the young man as if he were from another planet. Both were dressed like they should be standing on the red carpet of the premiere of a silent film. She was stout in a midnight blue, sequined gown, and expensive sapphire necklace, and he was tall in a light-colored linen suit and matching hat with a slight grey tinge to his dark perfectly coiffed hair. He pointed the end of a gold and ebony cane at the ground as his wife continued looking at Rory through vacant, hooded eyes as if he weren't there. Both smoked long cigarettes in pencil thin black holders. He straightened a teal silk ascot and then the matching pocket square on his left breast pocket out of habit as if posing for a photo.

"Veronica is our daughter..." she said finally.

Rory didn't immediately process what she was saying. She looked at her husband as if Rory were stupid. Her husband broke in to spare him further embarrassment.

"You probably know her as Iris...Her middle name...We're her parents..."

"Is she *okay?*" he stammered fearing the worst.

"Inside..." Iris's mother offered with a flat affect as if conversing with him was exhausting. "With the hound..."

It soon became apparent to Rory that even though the other people who lived in Iris's building were of privilege, that her parents far outdid them in affluence. The driver intercepted the doorknob with nimble gloved fingers as if preventing her from touching something hideous. She seemed not to notice, or care as if it were the most natural thing in the world to be catered to in this way...The driver then repeated this pattern with Iris's front door.

"It's that dreadful club, Arliss..." she said to her husband. "What did they call it? The *eel?*" she said with a mean deriding chuckle.

"The *Electric* Eel!" he corrected.

She made a cringey shrug as if being shocked with a thousand volts. "Excuse me!"

"Well, Rowena... We can't stop her...She's like me at that age!"

"You were never in the likes of a place like *that!* At least I *hope* not! Or else I would have never agreed to marry you!"

It seemed unnatural for Iris's parents to refer to each other by their first names...Rory thought. *As if they should always be referred to by some high-falutin title instead...Even by those closest to them...*

"*Electric* eel..." her daughter called from the other room.

Her mother gave her a dismissive wave and stood a few feet away from her daughter as if keeping a safe distance from a sketchy wild animal. Iris sat up on the bed, her eyes wide and completely sober for the first time in weeks. Then she looked at Rory and smiled afraid her parents would say something potentially embarrassing.

"The world has changed..." her father offered.

"But *we* haven't..."

"Maybe you should..." Iris mouthed.

Her mother shot her a haughty, icy stare. Peaches placed his muzzle in Iris's chest, and she held him. Mrs. Dupeon rolled her eyes at the spectacle between them.

"And keep that mutt off the bed linens! That's imported French silk damask!" she snapped. "I don't care if he is a purebred! It's sickening!"

"Hi, Rory!" Iris said ignoring her and cuddling the dog.

Rory smiled, glad to see his friend alive. Iris's mother boiled with rage like a very expensive, ornate pot ready to bubble over on the burner. Both of her parents turned to look in the young man's direction.

"Do you work at that place too?" she asked.

"I do..." he hesitated. "As a bus boy..."

"A *bus boy?!*" she repeated as if he'd said something dirty. "*A bus boy?* Did you hear that, Arliss our daughter is choosing to hang around with a bus boy? *The help!*! Tell me who else goes in there? Tramps? Drunkards? Women of ill repute?"

"Easy, dear! He saved our daughter's life!"

"He's probably the one who gave it to her in the first place..." she whispered to her husband as if he weren't there.

"I got it from the bass player…" Iris said candidly. "I injected it once…Never do *that* again…"

Mrs. Dupeon craned her neck like a bird of prey in her daughter's direction. But unlike most people, Iris did not seem intimidated by her mother. *Just nonplussed…*Iris gave a disinterested yawn.

"You see! *You see?*" her mother shrieked with the wag of a judgmental figure. "It's that place!"

Unlike Iris and her father, there was nothing attractive about Mrs. Dupeon other than her clothing and jewelry. Her face was somewhat plain and unassuming with hardened lines on the sides of her jowls. A large intricate braided topknot sat on her like a dark brown spool of yarn. *Like something he pictured in royal portraits…*

"How are you doing, kitten?" her father asked.

"Better…" she admitted.

"Glad you snapped out of it!" she said with the clap of her hands. "Cause your father is going to Monte Carlo on business and I have to be at the Metropolitan Opera in New York on Sunday! They're having a soiree/gala… You are welcome to come to one or the other! Or both!" she said brightening for a second. "I'm sure your friend can watch your dog while you are away…"

"No thanks…"

Rory blinked in disbelief at her refusal. *Why would anyone choose this place over Monte Carlo or the opera in New York City? Let alone the Electric Eel!* He wondered. *She seems to open up when they aren't here…*Reminding himself to ask later.

"Well your mother and I have dinner places at the Cosmopolitan…I assume you won't be joining us? Your friend is welcome to come…" he said thinking it may lure her out of her house.

His wife shot him an angry look. Iris put her hand up in refusal. Mrs. Dupeon felt

The Electric Eel!

relieved and headed for the door with doorman in tow like a puppy.

"Reservations are at seven..." she reminded them suddenly growing bored with the conversation. "Warm up the Duesenberg please..."

"Keep her out of trouble..." her father mouthed to Rory in the doorway.

Rory gulped. *Iris does what she wants...* He thought. *I'm not her keeper...I'm not even her boyfriend...*

"Can I ask you something?"

"Is it about them...?" she said placing a brocaded pillow over her head. "Then no..."

"Why would you choose the Electric Eel over opera at the Met or Monte Carlo?"

"I already told you... It's boring..."

"Your father doesn't seem boring..." he noted.

"It's a façade... It wears off...And don't even *ask* about mother..."

He couldn't argue with that. Rory bit his lip and tried to change the subject. Iris bounced off the bed a second later, her flitting fancy moving to something in the corner followed by Peaches the dog.

"What is it?"

"Clothes my mother sent over..." she said. "They always think they can buy me..."

Iris held up a long royal looking dress the color of ripe cherries with droopy lace bell sleeves. Rory nodded in approval. She placed it back on its place at the wardrobe.

"It's nice..." he said trying to be supportive.

"I guess...A little fussy..." she said reaching for the garment again and rotating it as if on a turnstile. Suddenly Iris gave an impish ornery smile.

"What?"

She held the dress up in front of Rory's body and eyeballed it. Rory's face reddened to the color of the dress. He held his hands up in protest as she disappeared in the vast walk-in closet for a moment and returned with something.

"Nah... Too brassy..." she said tossing something hair the color of hot dog mustard on the bed. "My mother's Sheitel wig…She only wore it once to temple on the high holy days anyway…." she mused throwing out another darker more subtle hairpiece this time. "Can't do it without falsies…"

"No that's all right…"

"You sure?" she said holding up a pair of high thick soled red shoes and a padded brassiere. "And I'll lend you my mother's ruby…We'll need to get you shaved.. Can't have you looking like a yeti on stage…"

Stage? 'You can't be serious!' the look on his face said. "Get your clothes off and try it on… Aint nothing I haven't seen before…"

Iris beamed and handed him the pieces of clothing. He took them reluctantly. For the first time in weeks, she felt happy.

"And you'll need makeup…I have *tons*…And we'll have to get you a new name… Rory just won't do!"

Iris looked at the dress again and then at her friend. She thought of her favorite dessert in front of her liked she'd had on her sixteenth birthday at Maxim's in Paris. She remembered the waiter lighting it and the room erupting in thunderous applause… A whoosh of reddish pink fire emanating off the sides. A la flambe…

"We'll call you Cherries Jubilee…" she squealed.

THIRTY

Mrs. Dupeon instructed the driver to pull toward the curb where the Electric Eel glowed like a lighthouse in the darkness that following Friday. She winced at the sight and almost told him to turn the car around but then thought better of it and handed him a fistful of money. *What's this for?* The look on his face said.

"Go…!"

"Whatever you like madam…"

He gripped the steering wheel as if ready to exit the car. Then he pulled on the parking brake. She touched his shoulder with abrupt indecision.

"No wait *I'll go*...No we'll *both* go!"

He let out a frustrated sigh. She put the money back in her beaded Hermes handbag and placed it under her arm. She pulled her long white gloves up to her bicep like a princess. The driver looked back at her as she patted the purse and held it by the bottom for support.

"Can never be too careful..."

He rolled his eyes. With the tip of her index finger she pointed to the establishment. He shrugged.

"Looks like a bakery..." he said dryly.

"That's what they *want* you to think...And who names a bakery the "Electric Eel" anyway? And besides, it was a bar *before* Prohibition started...It's a front!" she said. "Look at those stupid girls going in there! Do they *look* like they are going to a patisserie at nine o'clock on a Friday night?"

The aristocratic woman pointed to three twenty-something young women in cropped fringed skirts and Oxford shoes. She sneered at their choice of attire. He nodded appeasing her as the girls walked inside nervously and pulled out several dollar bills. Next, a door opened, and mountain sized man allowed them in.

"Probably not..." he offered.

"Right! And look at that short hair! Imagine that! Gams hanging out like a streetwalker and hair short like a six-year-old Dutch boy!" she snapped motioning to the bottoms of her earlobes. "Can you imagine Veronica going in a place like that?"

Actually I can... The driver thought. But per his usual, he said nothing and agreed with her. *It's easier that way...*

What do I do now? She thought approaching the door in the back of the bakery. *Sure we have champagne or a glass of wine with dinner now and then...*It's not a crime...*But to drink here...?* She'd heard of people dying from alcohol poisoning and thought better of it... *I'll stick with what I know*...She promised herself with a wrinkle of her nose.

On cue, her driver stepped in front of her and reached for the doorknob. She sighed in relief, not having to touch it. A man as large as a sycamore opened the door and widened his eyes. *As if Queen Victoria had suddenly decided to come back to life in their place and grace them with her presence...*

Unlike the other women in the establishment, she was completely covered save for her face and neck. Her black and white ball gown was tight at the bodice and flared out at the hem like an upside-down feather duster as she glided across the dance floor. All of a sudden all eyes were upon her.

Her white top hat studded driver looked equally out of place beside her...As if they had picked out matching outfits to correspond with each other like a the top on a ridiculous wedding cake... He straightened his red bow tie and gulped.

Carlotta froze at the sight of the other woman, unused to *not* feeling like the most well to do in the place. Unfazed, Orville stepped forward and greeted her. For a moment, his mother thought he'd kiss her hand.

"What will you have, madam?" he asked, drawn to her like a shark to a bleeding swimmer.

She pondered this a moment and scanned the bar. A glittering sea of glassware dangled above and below her along with a variety of alcoholic concoctions. *None she recognized except for their banality...*

"I'll have a snifter of Remy Martin..." she said if it were the most natural thing in the world to order a drink of this caliber. "Or a glass of Romanee Conti vintage 1900 if you have it..."

Orville blushed in embarrassment at first and then quickly recovered once he realized she was *not* trying to funny or arbitrary. *This was all she knew...Oh to be so lucky...*He daydreamed...

"How about a Napoleon Brandy?" he offered. "It's from Paris..."

The Electric Eel!

His mother glared at him and touched his forearm. *I'll replace it...* He mouthed. Mrs. Dupeon thought about it for a second as he reached under the counter and showed her the label. Unlike most of the other drinks he served this was unopened, the gold foil still intact on the neck of the bottle as if waiting for the right customer to come along and buy it. Her driver held up two fingers.

"Two..."

She shot him a look of surprise. They watched as the other man poured him a drink and laid it sideways on top of a glass of partially hot water. And then he repeated the process with another snifter and waited for it to warm.

"I'll have a Bee's Knees..." a girl about Iris's age inquired.

"What is that?"

"Honey and lemon... Sour and sweet...With just a hint of gin," she said coquettishly to the overly dressed man. "It's the cat's pajamas!"

He watched as Orville poured the drink in a wide glass with a narrow stem. There was something ladylike and dainty about it. Next, he reached for the two warmed brandies and placed them in front of them. *The perfect pour doesn't spill out...*

"Be careful...It'll sting you..." Orville said with a wink at the well-dressed man as he eyed the woman's yellow cocktail.

Across the room Iris was sequestered with her friend Rory behind the Shoji screen used by the musicians. Wallace the piano player peered in earlier, but she shooed him away. Rory shied away as if standing behind the dress like a valet.

"Play ragtime or something!"

Wallace gave a puzzled look and waved his bizarre prodigied hands and disappeared back to the piano. *I find lots of types of men attractive... Him I do not...* She thought wryly. *What a nebbish...!*

"He knows everything about everyone..." Freddy the clarinetist said. "Too smart for his own damned good...Want some dope later?" he whispered to Iris as if asking her if she wanted a hamburger.

Iris pondered it for a second. She thought of her near overdose and put her hand up. She frowned.

"No thanks…"

"Suit yourself. Are we still on for practice next week?"

"Yes…*Just* to practice…"

He soured and suddenly caught a look at the small man in the crimson ballgown. He watched as the man's bare hairy male shoulders disappeared under the mountain of fabric. Iris instructed him to breathe in as she zipped the back.

"Don't get makeup on it or we'll never hear the end of it…" she warned.

"Iris, I don't know about this…" he stammered trying to take it off.

"Don't you dare! I've heard you sing…You're probably better than I am…Lip sync it if you have to…Just do it like we practiced!"

"Hey! Get a load of Princess Margaret of Connaught in here!" Freddy told Jib the bassist.

"Hey little Bo Peep!" Jib shouted.

"*Scram!*" Iris ordered putting a wig and hat on Rory and securing it with a matching vermillion bow.

When satisfied that Rory was the best he was going to look, she stepped outside the screen and put her thumb up to signal Orvile at the bar. Orville adjusted his shirt collar nervously and looked around the room at the patrons, not realizing that Iris's mother was sitting in front of him. He spoke over the din.

"Without further hesitation filling in for Iris tonight is Miss Cherries Jubilee…"

Rory felt a push between his shoulder blades. Iris nodded to Wallace on the piano to begin playing the beginning of "April Showers" as he promenaded to the stage. Various men in the audience began to call to him.

"You're pretty! Nice chassis!"

Rory faltered a moment and began to sing...

"Life is not a highway strewn with flowers," he belted. "Still it holds a goodly share of bliss... When the sung gives way to April showers...Here's the point you should never miss..."

Rory walked past several long tables of mostly men and continued singing. Long white curtain-like fabric draped from the ceiling over them in the shapes of elongated vs and ws. A few of the men swoon. *Do they know I'm a man?* He wondered. *Does it even matter?*

"Who's the bearcat?" another one of them called.

Across the room Mrs. Dupeon turned and blinked in disbelief. She examined the performer and leaned in closer. *Surely I didn't drink that much...*

"...And where you see the clouds upon the hills..." Rory continued. "You soon will see crowds of daffodils..."

Rory passed Mrs. Dupeon without realizing her significance as Iris and others began to applaud. Instead of looking at his face the way others did, the stately woman focused on what he was wearing...A crimson gown brocaded in gold...*My royal gown!* She thought, festering with rage. Her driver, like the others, was applauding.

"Take me home!" she shouted over thunderous applause. "I've seen enough!"

THIRTY-ONE

Despite Tiny's imposing stature, most people found him surprisingly approachable. Many assumed he was older, in his forties instead of his actual twenty-three years old. In May of 1921, two formidable men in suits approached him by the back door.

"You've got a baby face..." Lobelia his closest friend at the place had quipped earlier that night.

"Could we have a word with you?" the spokesman for the two asked him.

"Yes..." he said in a polite voice.

The Electric Eel!

The other one motioned with his arm as he took away Tiny from the group. He touched the other man's arm and Tiny recoiled unused to be manhandled. But the two men didn't flinch at his considerable girth.

"Our boss, Mr. LaRocca, would like to talk your employee…"

"Tiny works for us…May I help you?"

At that moment Lobelia stepped between them, equally not intimidated by their presence. One of the men looked at her in half disbelief and half annoyance that a woman…A *black* woman, no less, would be questioning them…

"Pardon us, madam…" he said forcing himself to be politer than he would've preferred. "But this is a private business matter…"

Tiny gave a hardboiled stare and folded his arms across his chest. Lobelia looked at him. The two men smiled impressed with both of their resistance.

"Give me a minute, Lobelia…" he said turning back to the men. "She's copacetic… What were you saying about your boss?"

"We would like to speak with you about a job for Mr. LaRocca…"

"But I have a job-"

"Take it," he said cutting him off and forcing a business card in his direction. "We encourage you to keep this one…"

"I'll think it over…"

"Suit yourself. But I'll warn you we don't like to be kept waiting…"

Then another woman approached, this time in a skin tight green skirt with matching sharp fingernails. The two men grew annoyed. *What's with all these broads butting in?* Sensing being noticed they met Tiny's gaze and headed from the back door.

"We'll be back…"

Eugenia whom very few liked and even fewer trusted stood behind him sporting her usual trademark unpleasant expression. He held his breath unsure of how much to say which would not be repeated. She persisted.

The Electric Eel!

"What was that about?" she asked.

"Nothing, Eugenia..." he said with a sigh.

"Do Carlotta and Orville know about this?"

"Know about *what?*" Orville asked overhearing.

"Drop it..." he said glaring at Eugenia.

"Two men approached Tiny about a job..." Lobelia said, feeling protective of her friend again.

"He has a job..."Carlotta said repeating the earlier sentiment.

"If I could get out of here I would!" Eugenia whispered. "They don't pay me diddly..."

"They don't?" he asked half-listening.

"Nah! You see how much they make off that bootlegged watered down stuff? Versus what they pay us? You being the bouncer and me who takes care of their precious eels...We're irreplaceable...Not that Carlotta knows that! Remember what we're doing isn't even legal..." she said with a sarcastic click of the tongue. "Well! I gotta bounce! Hopefully, my ex got the kids to bed at a reasonable hour..."

What was that all about? Tiny thought. Edgar approached him a second later and placed his hand on his shoulder. Tiny turned half expecting it to be Eugenia again.

"You'll never make her happy..." he said trying to give the younger man a heads up. "Some people you can't...Stop trying to please everyone..."

For some reason he thought this piece of advice would stick with him as if Edgar were looking out for him somehow. Edgar walked away with only a slight limp this time unlike the way he had lumbered just a few months ago. *He just didn't seem to be used to it yet... Like a sailor on land...*

Outside Lobelia was waiting for Tiny. The smell of stale tobacco and human urine lingered in the alley way. The remnants of a few shattered green and brown beer bottles crunched under Tiny's feet like ice. Lobelia shivered and lit a cigarette.

"What does Eugenia want?" he asked her.

The Electric Eel!

"Who knows...We all try to avoid her..."

"Hard to avoid someone you work with..." he admitted.

"Okay. Suit yourself. Just don't tell her anything you don't wish repeated..."

Lobelia reached up to touch his arm as they spotted something moving in the distance. A rustling noise came camouflaged in the near distance by something unknown. Tiny hoped it wasn't Eugenia overhearing somehow. *But she was already gone*...He told himself.

Quietly they moved toward it. *Could it be a wounded or rabid animal? A skunk or raccoon perhaps?* Lobelia, always unsure about nature, paused as the sound continued. Tiny, the animal lover, approached it with caution.

"It's 's okay...I won't hurt you..." he promised whatever it was.

But as he got closer he could see that this was no animal. Two watery amber colored eyes stared back at him through the darkness. Tiny blinked in disbelief at if staring at a lowland gorilla at the zoo instead of a man like himself. The sour smell of alcohol and rotten teeth intensified as he got close.

"Who are you?" Lobelia called realizing.

The man stood on bowed wobbly legs and stared at them through double vision. The other people were both large; a young freakishly tall white man and a thick finely dressed black woman. The cool night air blew under his chin slightly as he moved away from them.

"Are you here to kill me?" he breathed searching for anything he could use to defend himself.

Tiny stifled a laugh causing the man to recoil more. Lobelia put her hand up toward Tiny instructing him to proceed with caution. The man suddenly seemed to sober up as he tried to get away.

"Why would you think we were here to kill you?" Lobelia asked the disenfranchised man.

The Electric Eel!

But the man did not respond. All of a sudden something whizzed by the side of tiny's cheek. Lobelia flinched as something else neared the bridge of her nose. *A beer can!* And then another!

"Murderers!" he said pointing to the Electric Eel.

"*Who?*"

Quickly the vagrant bolted further down the alley. As Tiny and Lobelia looked on, the darkness intensified to a lightless maw surrounded on all four sides by red brick.. *Is this even safe?* Tiny wondered.

Suddenly, like a charging Rhino, the homeless man knocked her down and disappeared somewhere up the street. As Tiny knelt to help her up he noticed something. A sea of fetid newspapers were spread out like an atlas.

"Are you okay?" he asked reaching for her.

"I think so..." she said.

But Tiny's focus was elsewhere. Lobelia stepped over the papers carefully as most of them were soiled and her shoes were opened toed. He continued to stare at the newsprint as if engaged in a page turning novel.

"What is it?" "They're all the same topic..." he noted.

"What topic is that?" she said feeling like an English teacher.

"Stuff that happened at *this* place... You know... Mr. Alfonso..."

"Coincidence..." she said walking away in disinterest. "Maybe those were just the ones he found all at once..."

"Normally I'd agree with you... But they're all from different days...Look! Here's one about that cop who was shot! What was his name?"

"The one with Virginia?"

"Uh-huh..."

But before they could respond further they felt the same set of eyes on them as before. This time the man kept his distance glowering at him as if they had invaded his living room. Lobelia had seen enough and walked away with her palm up to show the man she meant no him no ill will. Tiny followed a second later.

"What is going on?" she whispered to Tiny.

"I have no idea... But let's get out of here..."

Together they walked in chilly air to the front of the building. Both Tiny and Lobelia began to think in silence. Quietly, she grabbed his hand in hers a second later. He did not pull away. *Were they working for killers?* They both wondered.

With little hesitation Tiny and Lobelia embraced, which led to passionate kissing. Soon they were petting and making out at the same time. The forbidden attraction they'd been holding back unleashing in each other's arms.

"Well lookie here..." Eugenia said watching from across the street.

THIRTY-TWO

"*W*ake up!" someone shouted at Iris that following week.

Still partially hungover, Iris rolled over and opened her eyes to slits. Her mother's expensive perfume dangled in the air like smog; an intentional haughty floral-scented wall between her and the rest of the world. Iris cringed. *How do I get rid of her?*

"How did you get back here so fast?"

"That's not important! The important thing is your father, and I came! And just in time! To start: What's with this dressing up that busboy of yours like Mabel Normand in my crimson couture Hartnell coronation gown to parade all over High Street?"

Iris sat up and giggled in spite of herself. Soon her father also began to snicker. Mrs. Dupeon turned toward her husband in disgust.

"I'm glad you find this so entertaining, Artiss!" she snapped. "It's shameful! She's privileged! She should act like it! How can I ever show my face in that dress again! It's tainted!"

"She's just having fun..." he began.

The Electric Eel!

"Well! Let have her *fun* in someone else's gown...! With someone else bankrolling it! Anyway!" she said brightening. "We'll be back tonight at seven to take you to dinner and the symphony...Maybe there you can meet a suitable man or at least find some acceptable people," she informed her, turning before Iris or her father could deny or accept the invitation. "So be dressed appropriately and ready when driver picks you up..."

Iris nodded in agreement even though she had no intention of complying. *Not the first time I'd blown them off...*She thought wryly. *And it won't be the last...Works every time!*

With caution she craned her neck into the palatial sitting room to check for her parents but only saw Peaches. She smiled and kissed the dog on top of the head and walked to the kitchen. A nauseating headache stuck with her a little as the door opened again.

"In here..." she called, half expecting to see her parents again.

"Hi! Iris!" a male voice called.

Rory extended the laundered red dress in a bag in her direction. She smiled cordially and pointed to spare bedroom. Rory frowned a little as she reached for a small bottle.

"Are you okay?"

"Yes...Just a little hair of the dog..."

Quickly she poured a small amount of clear liquid in a shot glass and down it like medicine. She gulped and wretched at the taste as it warmed her esophagus. *Why do I do this to myself?* For a moment she thought she would regurgitate it, the thought of tasting it again repulsive.

With great care, Rory carried the dress to the spare bedroom and laid it on the substantial mattress. He examined the piece and smiled. Iris met his gaze in the doorway.

"You were spectacular!" she informed him. "Half of those men asked me for your phone number!

The Electric Eel!

He watched as his friend reached for a tube of reddish-pink lipstick and puckered. Next, she pulled a metal contraption with a cut out hole in the center, out of the drawer and placed it to her mouth to create the perfect cupid bow shape. Rory blinked studying her.

"You're beautiful…" he admired.

She waved her hand as if to say: Oh…*You*!

"I mean it…"

"You were not so bad yourself…"

"Why are you up so early?" he asked knowing her routine by heart now.

"My parents…" she breathed with frustration. "Mainly my mother… But it's okay… Jib and Wallace are coming over for practice…"

Rory looked into the spare bedroom again and then down at the red gown. Iris frowned reading him. He smiled awkwardly.

"What's wrong? Don't want to do it again?"

"No…That's not it…" he said trailing off.

"What is it?"

"The ball gown seems a little…*Stuffy*…" he stammered as if afraid of offending her.

"Oh! I totally agree!" she said surprising him. "What would *you* like?"

"I'm not sure…A little sexier…"

"Remind me to take you shopping! You know my mother saw you…" she said making direct eye contact with the young man. "In that thing…"

"No!"

"She *did*!"

"How'd that go over?"

"Not well! But it was *so* worth it to see the look on her face!"

They laughed together. Iris shuffled in her light pink chiffon nightgown to the ice box and reached for a small amount of food. Salmon cream cheese on rye toast… She sniffed it, still somewhat nauseated. Rory reached for more of the salmon in a bowl. Peaches wagged his tail in anticipation.

"What time are you practicing?" he asked placing the bowl of food on the floor.

"Two..." she said. "My parents will be here at seven..."

"So you *aren't* coming tonight?" he asked confused.

"I am..."

"But I thought your parents said..."

She smiled without saying anything further and reached for her toast. A half-moon shaped wedge stained the side of the bread like blood as she bit down. The taste of cream cheese and salmon lingered a second on her tongue and teeth as she swallowed and placed the remaining crust on a saucer.

"Want some coffee?" she asked placing two cups in front of him.

"Okay..." he said.

"Want a little Amaretto?" she whispered swinging a tiny bottle of something sweet back and forth like a pendulum.

"No thanks... Just black..."

"You're no fun!"

"Stuff makes me sick..." he said.

"Oh it does me too!"

Rory knitted his brows together not fully understanding her logic. But like always neither divulged their true feelings. *I think that's why we work...* He thought as she poured him a cup of the scalding brown liquid.

"I'm going to shower..." she informed him. "You're welcome to stay here if you like or take Peachy outside for a walk..."

Like everything in her penthouse suite the shower was luxurious. Rory craned his neck to catch a glimpse of her private bathroom. A recessed center steam shower with a back in the shape of a seashell was at the back of the room containing a white clawfoot tub, pedestal sink overtop a black and white diamond pattern tile floor. The smell of some expensive essential oil lingered a moment as she rubbed her palms together.

"Take a picture it'll last longer..."

Rory blushed in embarrassment. In spite of having already seen her unclothed on numerous occasions, he remained shy and unnerved. But this was different.

And then she began to sing. As always her voice was clear and perfectly on pitch but this time it was in a language he did not understand. *Hebrew!* And then French! *How many languages did she speak?* As she turned the shower off, steam billowed out like a locomotive.

"You sound amazing... How many languages do you speak?"

Iris thought for a moment as she reached for a towel to dry her hair and counted in her head. Her face was devoid of color save for her lipstick. She pulled a towel around her waist and walked to the wardrobe.

"Three...Four... I don't really *know* them...Hebrew...French...Yiddish... English, of course..."

Rory shrunk in embarrassment at his lack of education; however, she didn't seem to notice or care. Quickly she pulled on a pair of panties, skirt, and buttery white silk blouse and then reached for her shoes. Per her usual, her choice of heels was as high as possible giving her a height that she always desired.

"Are you coming to practice?" she asked him.

"Sure if you want me to..."

"Of course, silly...Otherwise I wouldn't've invited you..."

"Where do you rehearse?" he asked with wide innocent eyes.

"The building has a music room with a grand piano..." she informed him as if it were the most natural thing in the world to have access to something like that at her disposable. "We've practiced here a few times, but the acoustics are better on the third floor..."

The Electric Eel!

Despite living in the building, Iris arrived a few minutes later than she intended. *Fashionably late...*She noted with a swing of her hips. *With Rory and Peaches, her lapdogs, in tow...* The other musicians thought.

Jib rosined his walrus tusk-sized bow and then polished the instrument. *Does she realize how hard this is to get across town?* He thought. *Or does she not care? Not all of us have our owns means of private transport...*

Wallace, who was unfazed by most things, sat on the piano bench and ran his long fingers over the keys as if gently caressing a lover. The piano itself was finished in a crisp white and gleamed like dentures in the bright light. The room was surrounded on three sides by windows like a greenhouse. With little effort he played Beethoven's Fur Elise and listened to check its tune.

To further annoy Jib, Freddy arrived a few minutes later with his clarinet under his arm like a loaf of bread. Wallace stretched his fingers and continued to play without hesitation. Another classical piece Jib did not immediately recognize came forward through the piano.

"Can we get on with this?" the bass player hissed.

"St. Saens...The Swan..." he said answering the unspoken question. "Carnival of the Animals..."

"Sorry I'm late..." Freddie admitted.

"Sure! You only have an instrument you can carry under your arm..." Jib menaced under his breath.

"I think we should go a little more jazzy..." Iris informed them. "It's the way of the future... The now..."

"But we've always done blues..." Jib said raising his arms.

Why does it matter to you? Freddy thought shooting him a glare. *All you have to do is keep time either way...*

Iris hummed a melody and tapped her foot as they begun to play. *Why is everyone so tense?* Rory wondered from his place at the banquette seating.

"We should let Rory sing again..." Freddy said, furthering annoying Jib. "He's a natural..."

"Why are we even here?" Jib asked.

"Rory *will* sing..." Iris continued. "But we're all here now to practice as we planned..."

"I need a smoke..." Jib said placing the instrument down gently as if carrying an infant.

"You and me both..." Freddy said.

Iris sighed in frustration and joined them. Wallace paid them no mind and continued to play something random that he knew by heart. Soon they were all smoking. Once their nicotine habit was satiated, they snuffed out the butts and walked away.

Freddy reached into his pocket and showed the singer something. She flinched a second as if shown something obscene her mouth open partway. A small green, partially opened, tin with a pinup girls' picture embossed on the side was in his palm. A small amount of powdered substance was inside. Rory recoiled.

"What is it?" he asked.

"Nothing..."

"We'll be right back..."

"Watch Peachy for me..." she informed her friend.

"Can we get on with this?" Jib barked.

A visibly altered Iris and Freddy returned a second later. Rory held his breath in fear and approached his friend. Quickly she dismissed him, her words slightly off like a record player with a scratched needle.

"I'm fine...Just something to take the edge off is all..."

The corners of Freddy's eyes were reddish orange as if suddenly filled with pooling blood. As he reached for his clarinet and placed it up to his lips a strange vinegary smell tickled his nostrils. He tugged on his high-waisted pleated pants and began to play.

Iris moved between the others on shaky legs...*Like a newborn calf...*He thought. She put her arms out to steady herself.

"Can we get on with this…?"

Rory gulped.

THIRTY-THREE

*M*adame Beulah favored black and blue…Her eyebrows were drawn in two straight ebony bars with a grease pencil like Groucho Marx. Her thick raven-esque wig sat on her head and stuck out slightly at the corners like straw. The rest of her attire was a loud peacock blue, her sleeves drippy and patterned like a table cloth.

As always she requested that no one address her before the performance. Like a diva nearing her aria she considered herself the star of this place. The audience's connection to the great beyond…Quietly, she walked to the front of the stage and sat at a preplaced chair facing backwards from the audience.

"Is there a detective in the house?" she called. "Someone's whose last name starts with the letter T…"

Orville and Carlotta froze. *Where is she going with this?* The staff waited expectantly as she continued.

"Stop her…" Carlotta ordered with a menace.

Virginia, who was in the audience, too sat in shock. *Surely, she wasn't trying to contact Detective Talbert…*She thought. Her niece Irene crossed her ankle over her knee in nervous angst and pursed her lips together.

"Is there a detective here whose demise was recent?"

"This is tacky…" Virginia said standing in protest. "I have to go to the ladies' room…"

Then to make matters worse, Tiny spotted a petite bumptious woman standing under the peephole. *Do I let her in?* He wondered.

"Mrs. Dupeon…" he mouthed.

"Let her in…" Orville said bounding across the room to the door like a ballroom dancer.

Madame Beulah paused in irritation. Orville opened the door as if speaking to royalty. Two equally well-dressed men followed her.

"Madame Dupeon..."

Madame? Beulah thought with jealousy. *We'll see about that!* Quietly she pivoted and faced the audience directly and leaned over with her head between her knees and arms outstretched as if going downhill on a rollercoaster.

"This is my husband... And of course you know driver..."

"Mr. Dupeon! Charmed..."

"May the recently slain spirit of Detective Talbert be with us!" Beulah called shouting over them. "Along with the spirit of Mr. Alfonso and all those who have passed close by this place! Tell us who gunned you down... Tell us who stabbed you...Who took us from you too early?"

*She has us over a barrel...*Carlotta thought. *If we interrupt her it's an admission...If we don't she'll embarrass us...Maybe we should ask her not to return after tonight...*

"Fire her..." she warned Orville under her breath.

"She's our biggest act..."

Mr. and Mrs. Dupeon took their place at a table away from the rest of the audience. Orville opened a bottle of Remy Martin and showed it to her the label like a sommelier. She beamed, impressed. As Madame Beulah continued a few feet away Mr. and Mrs. Dupeon exchanged a curious glance.

"Murder and death are all around us! They go hand in hand!"

To their horror Beulah reached under the table with both hands and grabbed a hidden pack of theatrical red dye and held her hands up with closed fists and squeezed. They watched as red dye dripped down her hands and fingers like blood. Streaks of crimson oozed from between her fingers and thumb and ran down her arms.

"We all have their blood on our hands!" she shrieked. "The violent spirits are active

The Electric Eel!

tonight!"

Carlotta's jaw dropped like an unhinged drawer as Lobelia and Tiny paused, unsure of what was transpiring. All of a sudden Madame Beulah repeated the process with two more strategically placed dye packs between her toes. Another flood of rust flowed down the soles of her open-toed shoes and onto the floor.

"Get her out of here!" Carlotta whispered.

But to her amazement, the people in the audience sat enrapt. Like Romans in the Colosseum they clapped and cheered and pulled money from their pockets and placed it on the table at the bloody spectacle. Soon a huge pile of cash formed in a mound on the table.

But Beulah didn't stick around for the second act and disappeared somewhere in the dim light of the room. People continued to cheer and look for her like a demi god. Orville looked to Mrs. Dupeon who gave a confused look at what she had witnessed and stood.

Once they were sure that Beulah's performance was over, the musicians began to warm up. Wallace started playing without being prompted, the music coming forth like a waterfall. His huge fingers played most of the eighty-eight keys with ease. He looked up to see an elegant woman standing over him.

"Care to make a request?" he asked her without looking up at her.

She looked at a glass fish bowl that sat on the top of the instrument and for a second he thought she'd give him a gratuity... But then, to his disappointment, she spotted something in periphery and moved toward it. *The bass player...*

"What are you doing here?" Iris yipped.

"I could ask *you* the same thing! We were supposed to go to the symphony!" she snapped pushing past her daughter. "You're altered... Are you Mr. Jib?" she asked the bassist.

"Yes..."

Without saying anything else she reached for his palm and placed a huge amount of cash inside and closed it. The awkward feeling lingered for a second as her hands were icy and unused to contact with other people.

"Don't give my daughter anymore of that stuff you've been giving here and there's plenty more of that where it came from…"

Jib froze and palmed the money, unsure what to do next. Iris's cheeks reddened in surprise as her mother sashayed away nonchalantly. Her long green and gold gown swayed like the Liberty Bell as she moved.

"And tell your friend the clarinet player the same thing…" she called to him.

Artiss Dupeon froze at his place at the table. She gave him a demure smile, her dimples and expensive dental work showing. Her driver stood in haste and pulled her chair out for her.

"That wouldn't be necessary, driver…"

"What are you up to, dear?" her husband whispered.

"Nothing… Take me home…"

THIRTY-FOUR

As the weather warmed, a swarm of sketchy gentleman began hanging around on the street outside the Electric Eel at all hours of the night. Lobelia noticed them congregating outside the bakery window and called her boss. As he bounded to her, she pointed to the men.

"Who are they?" she asked him.

Orville paused unsure how much was proper to tell her. Then he gave her a wry ornery smile. Two more men gathered to the side of the front door.

"Are they feds?"

Orville laughed. She burned a little in indignation as if being left out of an inside joke. He spoke carefully.

The Electric Eel!

"No definitely not feds..." he informed her.

"Then who *are* they? They never come in here so they sure as Hell aren't customers..."

"Did you notice the business that opened up next door?" he asked pointing.

"What kind of business?"

Quietly he led her outside in the warm night air. Several young men in nondescript suits shuffled like spooked cattle and moved into the shadows. Lobelia looked around nervously.

"Excuse us, boys..."

Orville pointed to a store front window fifty feet away marked with a flashing pea green neon sign announcing: "Marie Toussad's Gallery..." She blinked not understanding. To further explain, he gestured inside to a series of halls and rooms that disappeared into the vanishing point of black light. Several waist high viewfinders with something that looked like binoculars sat inside the building. Lobelia reached for the door knob, but he reached up to stop her.

"It's pretty seedy... I wouldn't do that..."

"Who is Marie Toussad? What *is* this place? I never see any women go in there..."

"Eugenia went once...I don't even think Marie *exists!* It's owned by an old Chinese man, I think!" he informed her.

"What *is* it?"

"It's a peep show..." he said spelling it out for her. "You put a nickel in and look into those little viewfinders to see a lady in various shades of undress... Or it shows you an action reel..."

Lobelia recoiled. She looked back at the place to see a handful of folded white towels and lotions. She pointed to the items.

"What are those for?"

Orville dodged this question and smiled. Lobelia thought about it for a second and grimaced. When satisfied that it had sunk in, he walked back to the bakery in front of

The Electric Eel!

the Electric Eel. Lobelia was glad to be back inside familiar territory.

"I told my mother that most of them want a stiff drink anyway so it'll probably be good for business...If not, Tiny can take care of them for us! And none of us on this street wants the cops called...Didn't you notice the whole block? Mr. Houserman, the pharmacist two doors down, sells *everything*...You name it he's got it! Father Hanihan is legally allowed to have baptismal wine as is his freedom of religion... They'll never touch that one! I'm sure he sells a little on the side...The cosmetic lady... The Oriental Lotus Massage Parlor... The tattoo place down the street...It's all right there if you know what to look for!"

"How do you know so much about this?" she asked her boss. "Have you been in there?"

"To Marie Toussad's?" he asked with sharp pointy teeth. "I went once... Didn't do anything for me...Don't tell Poppy! I told Edgar to go...He's pretty hard up!" he said with a laugh. "Now that he has two legs again! But he refuses! I'd think he's afraid of getting arrested...I told him: Just don't sit down! I'd tell Rory to go but something tells me that's not his bag!" he chortled. "I told mother I'd put in a few booth myself at the back of the Eel but one of us would end up having to clean up after them..."

Lobelia swallowed hard at this tidbit of information. With his trademark flippancy, he turned on his heels and headed for the inside door. She stood aghast for a moment at his candor.

"Well! This place won't run itself!" he said smiling his permanent phony grin. "Did you see that Madame Beulah last night? Crazy!"

And in walked the soothsayer as if on cue...*Speak of the Devil...*He thought. *What's she doing here on a Friday?* They both wondered.

"May I speak with you?" she asked him, the normally theatrical timbre of her voice replaced instead by a flat business-like affect. "*Alone?*" she said avoiding Lobelia's gaze.

Lobelia shrunk away and began wiping down the bakery case. Madame Beulah pulled him close. Her eyes were wide behind thick lenses and framed by her token dark makeup. Orville maintained his cheery smile and placed his hands together behind his back.

"What can I do for you?" he asked.

"Increase my pay or I walk!" she whispered.

Orville bit his lip for fear of saying something he might regret later. He folded his arms across his chest, his patience growing thin. But Beulah persisted with her demands.

"Miss Beulah..."

"Madame..." she corrected.

"*Madame* Beulah..." he said choosing his words carefully. "You came dangerously close to embarrassing us last night with your accusations..."

"It was the spirits..."

"Spirits or not..." he said not believing her. "My father's death is still a sore spot among many around here...And there is an open investigation into the death of Detective Talbert..."

"I can't control the great beyond..."

"*Try...*" he mouthed drawing the word out for what seemed like an eternity.

"I'm the biggest cash cow here..." she said. "Be a shame if it all came crashing down...The whole street is one big racket..."

Had she heard his earlier conversation with Lobelia or was she truly psychic? He couldn't take the chance. *Maybe I can use it to my advantage though...*Orville thought, his wry devious smile returning.

"I'll give you the money..." he started.

"Good..."

"On one condition..." he said putting his hand up to prevent her from saying anything further.

"You never mention my father or the detective's murder again..."

The Electric Eel!

"Deal..."

THIRTY-FIVE

"*I* thought we were going shopping..." Rory called to Iris from the front seat of the luxury taxi cab.

"We *are!* Stop whining..." she chided, her normally fun mood growing contrary. "Driver, stop here...!"

"Okay..." the driver said turning his neck and parking in front of a store with a dark rx sign.

"Sorry..." she called. "I just don't feel right..."

*Now that my mother paid Jib and Freddy to not give me anymore of the junk...*She thought, biting her lip. *I have to find something else to take the edge off...And fast while my mother is in temple!* She thought, steadying herself so her hands didn't shake. *What was the guy's name Orville talked about? Houserman?*

Iris feigned confidence as Rory moved inside with obvious caution. A wall of mahogany display cabinets with bottles of questionable ingredients behind glass lay on either side of them as they walked in. A beautifully polished brass cash register with big black buttons and a man in a dark apron greeted them in the center of the room.

"May I help you?"

Rory looked up to see a sundry of pink and red stained-glass Tiffany-style lighting hanging from the ceiling like upside down tulips. More Art Nouveau inspired glass shaped like waterlilies sat around the flowers in shades of spring and Kelly green.

"We have belladonna for the beautiful eyes..." he called to her with a distinct Germanic accent by pointing to his eyes with his middle and index fingers. "Mercurochrome for the scrapes and bruises..."

"No thanks..."

She looked down at something that caught her eye and ran her finger over the top of

The Electric Eel!

two tins with black leaves painted on the side. The pharmacy beamed and handed her several. Iris nodded.

"Allen's Cocaine Tablets...For hay fever and cough..." Rory read out loud.

"The Heroin and Codeine Cough Drops *really* help with Rose Fever..." Mr. Houserman said with pride. "We have Heroin Hydrochloride as well over there that really help you relax..."

"I'll keep that in mind," she said smiling. "What *else* do you have for sale?"

"*Everything* is for sale..." he said like the serpent to Eve. "We have plenty of medicinal wines with all kinds of niceties in them..."

"How much?" she asked. "For all this?"

"Forty-five cents a dozen...You have three dozen...One dollar and thirty cents..."

*Chump change...*Iris thought handing him the money with glee. She thought of it for another second and placed another dollar on the counter. He returned the smile and reached for more product.

"Much obliged..." he said placing the items in a nondescript paper sack and handing to her. "You're very beautiful... And your friend is a gentleman and a scholar..."

"Thank you..."

"Come back some night and I'll show you the back room...You have to try our tonic wines..."

"Will do..." Iris said with a curtesy.

Rory turned to an ornate display of a red and green package of tobacco. *Dr. R. Schiffman's Ashtmador powdered Cigarettes...Inhale the relief! Contains belladonna...stramonium and potassium percholate...*Rory stepped away in uncertainty.

"Let's go..."

Iris's driver was waiting for her when they came back outside. Bright eleven o'clock sunlight blared overtop them. She turned to look at the Electric Eel in the daytime, a sad unassuming building like all the others on the street. Everything here seems have two

The Electric Eel!

sides... *Like Jekyll and Hyde...*

"Orville said that place is a peep show..." Rory said pointing to Marie Toussad's.

Iris raised one eyebrow. *He would know...*She thought shivering at the thought of the horde of creepy men who gathered on the street each night. Quickly, she turned to the driver, grateful to focus on something else.

"Lord and Taylor...Please..."

"Nice!" Rory smiled.

"If we *really* want to go shopping we'd go to their flagship store in Manhattan..." she said dryly.

"You miss New York don't you?"

"Mmm-hmmm..." she said with a little regret.

*But I'd never get away from my mother there...*She thought. *And I'd miss the Electric Eel...*

Once the driver opened the back door of the car, Iris swung her leg out onto the concrete in nonchalance. Next, she walked up to the fancy building in a disinterested way that only people who were accustomed to being around wealth did. The driver then hurried to the main entrance before she arrived to open it. She nodded politely.

"Shall I wait for you?" he asked.

Iris looked at the delicate diamond studded watch on her wrist and thought for a moment. Rory trailed behind her with the Aghan Hound. The driver looked at her with impatience.

"Come back here by 1:30..."

"Do they allow dogs in here...?" Rory asked stopping Peaches from going in the revolving door.

"I dunno...But they never say anything to *me*..." she said without looking at him.

If Iris was unimpressed by wealth, Rory looked up at the stained-glass ceiling of the store in ecstasy. She gave him a half-smile and pointed to the large fountain, escalator, and full-sized Steinway in the middle of the marbled first floor. She thought of Wallace sitting at the piano, as the tuxedo clad pianist tickled the ivories with white-gloved agile fingers.

"Moonlight Sonata..." he mouthed with the tip of his top hat.

"Lovely..." she said drawing the word out into two equal parts.

A swarm of women with overplucked high arched eyebrows standing by a glass counter in black dresses and matching shoes spotted Iris and began to point spritzers of perfume in her direction. Iris put her hand up to stop them as if thwarting paparazzi. A confusing, nauseating array of strong scents lingered in the air as they pushed their fare onto them.

"Perfume for that special someone?"

"No, thank you..."

"We also have men's colognes..." one of them shouted at Rory.

"Maybe later..." he promised, trying to keep up with his friend.

"Cute pooch..." one of them called.

"Jackals...All of them..." she mumbled.

"They smelled nice..."

"I *guess*...But for that we go to the *custom* cosmetics counter..."

As they walked she touched items with brand names that he only vaguely recognized or could comprehend buying. *Cartier...Rolex...Borghese...Does she even look at price tags?* She passed a piece of pinkish glass in the shape of a dancer and pointed.

"Lalique...Ruby glass... My parents have something like that on their roadster..."

"Beautiful..."

"It *is*... Mother was afraid to park it by the Electric Eel... Said somebody would swipe it..." she said with an eye roll.

Rory thought of her mother but was afraid of asking too much. He pictured Mrs. Dupeon walking in the bar with her driver as if she were royalty and then of his own parents, who were not upper class, who took no interest in his life...He sensed neither would be thrilled with their place of employment...

"Here we are..." she said approaching the high-end ladies' clothing.

Without hesitation she began sifting through the racks for something appropriate. Rory coaxed Peaches over to where he stood, and the dog looked at him with familiarity and wagged his tail. Iris motioned to a few dresses like a magician's assistant. He pointed to one.

"Eww no yellow on you..." said tossing a lemon-hued garment to one side. "Maybe gold...Gold is very now...But no yellow..."

"May I help you?"

They looked up to see a middle-aged saleswoman in a dark ankle-length dress standing with her hands folded over her navel. Unlike Iris, she was dowdy and unpleasant. They ignored her and continued looking.

"May I *help you?*" the woman repeated.

"Just looking..." Iris said finally acknowledging her.

What a shrew! She thought, reaching for another item of clothing, this time green. Iris picked it up and held it up to him.

"The red worked last time..."

"That's the thing... They *expect* you in red...Try the emerald..."

"I don't know..."

"If you don't *I'll* try *it on*..." she said growing frustrated.

Rory shifted nervously wondering what he had done. *Her moods change so fast...*He noted watching her reach for a royal blue dress with a slit up to the hip.

"We both should stick to the jewel tones... Tell you what: You try on the green and I'll try on this...!"

As Iris and Rory went into separate dressing rooms with their prospective garments, the saleswoman from before seared with displeasure. She watched as the blond dog peered its head out from underneath the curtain, its long back gracing the top of the fabric. Iris reached for a few pieces of expensive clothing like an actress changing between scenes in her own private dress room.

Once alone, Iris reached for her purse and fished for one of the items she had purchased from the pharmacy and down it. The pill was bitter for a moment as she swallowed, a slightly acidic aftertaste lingering in her throat. She gagged and reached for a small tin of snortable powder next.

"You all ready?" she called to Rory from the next room.

"Ready as I'll ever be…"

"One…Two…Three…"

They emerged together, he in the green and she in the blue. The top of his dress scalloped on each side like a seashell. She motioned with his finger for him to twirl around like a ballerina in a music box. She admired the backless garment and tugged on the top to pull it upward.

"You'll need to wax…But other than that, it's faboo," she informed him. "Now what do you think of mine?"

"You look wonderful…"

Iris turned and blushed at his genuine sweetness. *No man ever compliments me like that…Except for maybe my father…* She pushed her leg forward through the slit like a starlet.

"I think I'm too short for a dress like this… You need long legs…"

He pouted a little. She looked again in the full-length mirror. The sapphire dress sparkled in the light.

"Oh what the Hell? You only live once…"

Not wanting to see anymore, the saleswoman marched across the floor to where her boss stood and folded her arms over her bosom. The floor manager ignored her for a second, used to the other woman's histrionics and continued fiddling with an adding machine. Her employee; however, persisted and tapped her foot.

"What can I do for you?" the manager asked with only slight interest.

"There is a man in the ladies room!" she barked.

"A *man*?"

"Yes!" she said, the neurotic metallic tinge ringing in her voice. "And he's standing over there like a pervert admiring it in the mirror…"

"A *pervert*?" she repeated.

"Yes. A pervert. He must be a transvestite or something… And do we allow dogs here?"

Just then, Iris and Rory walked up to the cashier's stand with two dresses in hand. To her surprise, the saleswoman reached up and snatched the pinned sales tag from Rory's dress. She glowered at them and then at the dog

"Look at her eyes! She was doing something in that dressing room!" she snapped with the point of an accusatory index finger.

Iris's cheeks reddened. Rory turned to look at the corners of his friend's eyes. She blinked, admitting nothing.

"Mark my words! They aren't buying *anything!*" she menaced. "They'll wear it once and return it!"

The manager looked down at Iris's expensive watch and diamond tennis bracelet. She motioned to Rory to place both dresses on the counter. The saleswoman from before stood with her mouth open.

"Nice to see you, Miss Dupeon!" the floor manager cooed with more lilt than intended. "And who do we have here?"

"This is Peaches!" Rory informed her.

"I know! See if we have a treat for the puppy!"

"But he is a man…In the dressing room! Trying on clothes! *See?* I told you!"

"I said…" she began in impatience. "Go get Miss Dupeon's dog a treat…"

"But…But…"

"I apologize my salesgirl is a little eager and *high strung*..." she smoothed over. "Oh! I love the green! Is that silk? And the slit on that blue dress will make you look like a vamp!"

"He will be singing at the Electric Eel..." Iris promised.

"Wish I could wear a number like that!"

"You should come..."

And with that Iris turned and gave the saleswoman a little wave and a wink and headed for the door. A second later Rory and Peaches followed in tow. *I just might go to see them...* The sales manager thought...

THIRTY-SIX

*B*y July, Carlotta Alfonso's world began to unravel. Despite the copious amounts of money the speakeasy brought in, she grew bored with the drama night after night, day after day. Eugenia's eel shows and Madame Beulah's Thursday seances had long grown stale... But they couldn't terminate either of them as both continued to draw in crowds and fistfuls of income.

The looming threat of police raids hanging over the place made her uneasy as well. At first it was exciting, the constant peril adding a sense of mystery to the place, but now it was taxing. Outsiders wanted to stay on the wrong side of the law if only for the moment...But they *lived* it....

And there was the bickering, usually amongst Poppy and Orville, who were often at odds but also with Eugenia and the rest of the staff. Occasionally Orville would be openly hostile to his brother. *All of it is beginning to wear on me...*She thought.

Rumors of drug use soon surfaced too, mainly amongst the musicians...While Iris, Jib, Freddy, and Wallace continued to perform, many other bigger bands began to fill in as well that she did not always know. A few had been caught using heroin in the bathrooms and were immediately dismissed; however, they couldn't always vet them ahead of time. *And we can't always be sure if we fire them that they won't go to police...!*

"Welcome to the Electric Eel!" Orville called like the masters of ceremony, breaking her train of thought. "Where anything goes!"

And then there's the drinking...Carlotta thought with much regret. *I'm so tired of being around alcoholics...*She mused. *In the old days we could cut them off...We had to...But Orville never will! So they stay for hours!*

"Eat drink and be merry!" he called. "Lobelia! Get these nice people a round of our signature cocktails!"

To their surprise, someone walked in she hadn't seen in a long time...The elderly woman was dressed in a grey suit and thick Oxford shoes. Her gait was choppy and uneven like an old nag.

"Annamary!"

"She's gone senile from alcoholic dementia..." Orville whispered to his mother. "Ever since Rufus died..."

"How *are* you?" she said shouting over him to cut him off as if she were hard of hearing.

"All right," she slurred mashing the two words into a one syllable world salad.

"What's your pleasure, Annamary?" Orville asked.

"Beer..." she mustered. "And none of that stuff you gave Rufus the last time..."

Orville couldn't tell if she was kidding but he didn't take want to take the chance, so he ignored it and reached for a brown bottle of Pabst Blue Ribbon and opened it. He allowed the beer to foam a second over the sink and poured the ale into a pilsner glass. Annamary's eyes were hooded and dark as if fogged by cataracts. *Is she drunk? I can no longer tell...*

"I just need a drink..." she stammered like a broken record. "And none of that bathtub stuff like last time..."

The Electric Eel!

Annamary mumbled some other argle-bargle which he didn't comprehend as he placed the glass in front of her. She seemed to settle down as the hooch went down her gullet, the foam lingering on her lips for a second. When finished, she shrank down in her seat and requested another. Orville obliged.

Just then they looked up as Tiny let in a group of college kids, mostly boys into the establishment. Edgar looked over at the door. *They can't be twenty-one...*He noticed. *A year and a half ago we would have carded them...What's the point now?*

A handful of beefy midwestern young men stormed into the Electric Eel like linebackers and Lobelia and the rest of the staff rushed over to serve them. Most of the men sported brown and grey newsboy caps, collared shirts, and suspenders as if they'd just come from washing windows or working on the railroads. Their cheeks were rosy from the sunshine. Most of the young ladies sported fringed skirts. A small cloud of smoke formed as they passed around cigarettes and puffed.

"Hey are those real live eels?" one of the bellowed.

"They *are*!" Eugenia informed them with pride.

"Whoa! Neat-o!"

"That's why it's called The Electric Eel, dingus!" one of them guffawed.

"What's in a Sloe Gin fizz?" one of the young ladies in the group asked.

"Ever had strawberry jam? It's pretty sweet..."

They laughed again. Lobelia walked between them with caution as she always did amongst groups of men she did not know. A few of the boys looked up at her in awe.

"Hey, sister!"

"What can I do for you?" she asked ignoring his come on.

"I'll have a Tom Collins..."

"A round of Tom Collins..." her boyfriend piped in. "For all of us..."

"And none of that bathtub stuff!" another one of them called.

"You got it..."

The Electric Eel!

Eugenia counted the college kids at the table and reached for a silver tray and several clear vase-shaped glasses. Lobelia put her palm up to warn her. Eugenia gave her a sardonic frown.

"We only have a few of those and they are easily broken..."

Now what goes in a Tom Collins? She tried to remember...*Tom drinks gin...Simple syrup and lemon juice...And soda...*To her frustration, Lobelia checked the glasses for spots and laid them on the tray like a cairn and then poured in the gin.

Eugenia filled a spritzer bottle with water and pumped air inside. *Like one of the stooges in a slap stick vaudeville comedy...*She mused. Quickly she topped each glass with the soda as Lobelia placed a garnish neatly on top.

"Here you go, ladies and gentlemen..."Eugenia called.

Collectively they let out a gasp and reached for the cocktails. Instead of sipping them, as Lobelia would have preferred, they gulped the drinks. To her further dismay, Orville followed behind her with a glass pitcher, ready to refill their glasses.

"Maybe you should slow down..." Lobelia whispered. "I don't think any of them are used to drinking..."

"They're getting sloshed..." Eugenia whispered to Edgar with a chuckle.

"More of that giggle juice, please..." one of the girls called to Orville as she chugged her glass and slammed it on the table louder than she intended. "It's the berries!"

"Have you had our signature Electric Eel cocktail?" Orville asked egging them on.

"You mean eels like in the tank?"

"Kind of..." he said relishing the attention from the college kids. "Lobelia can you get our friends a round of electric eels on the house?"

"I guess..."

Soon the twenty-something kids began putting money on the counter. Lobelia and Carlotta began to make the drinks. A few of them swooned at the sight of the antifreeze-colored concoction.

The Electric Eel!

"Look at them giving him money hand over fist…"

"Quiet! The music is starting!" one of the young ladies announced.

As the group sunk deeper into inebriation, a couple of the girls stood and began to sway and hum in time with the music which made the less drunk in the room somewhat uneasy. Then the girls began to sing without knowing the words as if the midst of glossolalia. The sound of a horn and a clarinet wailed throughout the room.

"Is that a trombone?" one of the girls giggled.

"It's a clarinet!" her male friend answered with the snap of his fingers. "Waitress! More of those electric eel things, please!"

*Cut them off…*Lobelia pleaded with him in her mind. *Please cut them off…*

But Orville did no such thing and continued taking their money. Carlotta's eyes darted around the room nervously. *I would have never let my kids drink like that…*She thought. *And they're all at least ten years younger than Irene…*

Then, to make matters worse one of the young ladies stood on a chair and beckoned to the room with glazed dark pupils. Edgar dreaded what was coming next. *Oh no!* Quickly she pulled the top of her dress down and exposed her small breasts and turned to show the crowd.

"Get down!" Lobelia ordered. "You're cut off!"

But Orville ignored her and *still* continued handing out the lime green alcoholic beverages to the group. Anger rose in her as she had been undermined. Not to be outdone, one of her female friends stood on the chair and began to do the same with the top of her blouse.

"Nice rack!" an old codger shouted from across the room with an obscene gesture.

"Hey! That's my girl you're talking to…" a beefy young man in a pale-yellow shirt bellowed back.

"Then tell your *girl* to put her top back on!" a woman, most likely his wife, shouted with a laugh.

The Electric Eel!

"Shut up, kid!"

"And what are you gonna do bout it, old man?"

"*Old man?* I'll show you *old man*!"

And with that, the drunk older man descended upon on the table with the college kids and the room erupted in a collective brawl. A sea of drunken bodies and fists landed on the table, pulling the curtain down. Eugenia stood between them and the eel tank as the center table gave way and buckled under the weight.

"NO!" she said putting her hands up in panic as one of them landed on the side of the tank.

But it was too late. A small spray of water shot out of the side of the aquarium as if someone had hit an artery. The eels hissed in displeasure and settled to the bottom of the tank as the water gushed out one side.

"It's like the Titanic!" one of them shouted. *"Iceberg!"*

"Somebody get a bucket!" Eugenia ordered.

But water kept coming. Someone reached to hand Eugenia a bucket but was stopped by the mob. Meanwhile the group continued tussling, throwing things at each other as a spray of broken glass coated the floor.

"No! That's not big enough ! Get a washtub! *Hurry!*"

Then all of a sudden, the room *stank*! One of the girls who had removed her top wretched her nose up at the fishy aroma. A flood of brackish water filled the back of the room.

"What is that smell?"

"You see what you did?" Lobelia yelled at Orville unable to contain herself any longer.

"You're fired, Lobelia!"

"You can't fire her over that!" Tiny shouted in defense of his now girlfriend.

"Insubordination! I can and I *will!*" he yelled, his feet now in ankle deep disgusting water. "And you're fired *too!'*

"No one's getting fired!" Edgar soothed.

Carefully, Eugenia and Rory flopped the eels into a white enamel washtub. She inhaled and then turned to look at the tank in dismay. Rory recoiled as the eels buzzed like an unsafe electrical outlet as they placed the basin on the floor.

"No more of this fighting!" Carlotta yelled finally from her place at the bar. "Or you will not be welcomed back!"

But it was no use... The place is in shambles...They thought. *We're ruined!*

THIRTY-SEVEN

By the time every guest left, the Electric Eel was a soggy, broken mess...As someone turned out the lights the Electric Eels buzzed in their new temporary home. Eugenia put a tablecloth overtop of the keep them settled but they still did not seem thrilled at their relocation.

"We have to keep them warm..." she informed Rory.

*She really loves those stupid fish...*Edgar thought. But he said nothing for fear of setting her off.

"You should have someone come in to open the doors in the morning to get that smell out..." Eugenia advised.

"Well if you had kept those tanks clean we wouldn't have this kind of smell! It's like a sewer!" Orville snapped.

"Well! If you had cut those kids off when Lobelia told you to, they wouldn't have broken the tank, now would they?" she retorted without fear of reprisal. "We'll be lucky if they don't die!"

"No! *You'll* be lucky if they don't die! Next time you keep the tank spotless, understood? Or no more eels! Or so help me I'll fry them up myself!"

The Eugenia began to cry, big ugly unladylike tears. Orville bit his lip. Lobelia stepped in between them.

The Electric Eel!

"When's the soonest we can get the tank fixed...?"

"Mr. Houserman should have some sort of sealant until we can get a new one..." Orville said, his voice dropping a little. "Sorry..."

A second later his mother took he and his brother aside. Edgar stood, his prosthetic right leg not quite in step with his left. Orville felt like a school boy about to be scolded by the principal.

"I know it's a mess, but we'll get it cleaned up..."

"That's not *it*..."she began. "Or that's only part of it...We'll be lucky if those kids don't tell their parents and we don't get sued for everything we have...And I don't want to go to jail... *We* take all the risk selling it... *They* don't... You know the law...It's only illegal to sell it..."

"But..." Orville put his hand up to protest.

"I'm not finished..." she said. "We aren't even supposed to *be* here...As far as the world knows we're a bakery...The Lemon Drop down the street's front is a funeral home!"

"What are you saying?" Edgar asked.

"I'm done...'"

"Are you saying we should close?"

"I'm saying I am finished here... You can do what you like...Tonight was just the icing on the cake..." she said pushing passed her sons.

*She always does exactly what she wants...*Edgar thought. *Even if it affects everyone else around her...My brother's the same way...*

And without another word, Carlotta exited the Electric Eel one final time. Quietly, she turned and gave the place one last look, nodding that she did the right thing...The rest of the staff looked on in morbid fascination afraid to ask any more questions.

Outside Iris waited for Rory. The night temperature was stifling as a bead of sweat formed on the nape of her neck. She reached for a smoke and lit it but then quickly discarded it in disinterest. It glowed for a second and died under her foot, the ember turning orange and then fading in the darkness.

In haste, Carlotta passed quietly and walked to a square black carriage-like car. Iris pressed her lips together in forced silence. *Everyone is so on edge tonight...*

*Not that there is any love lost between us...*She thought. The older woman looked away pretending not to notice her standing there as the taxi pulled out... *What a bitch...*

"Mrs. Alfonso is leaving..." Rory said.

"I know. I saw her..."

"No, she's not coming back...*Ever*...She quit!"

"Good riddance..." Iris said under her breath.

"What?"

"Nothing. Sorry you didn't get to perform tonight...No one would have heard it anyway..."

"That's okay...We can always go on another night..."

*And probably not safe for you to be in a dress anyway give how raucous it has gotten...*But she did not want to tell him that. *No need to scare him off...*

Suddenly a horrific noise emanated from somewhere nearby. *Was it a sick animal?* She had heard of vagrants who inhabited the alley. Without asking she reached for Rory's hand. Her friend looked at her with confused dark eyes.

Another noise followed: The sound of someone spurting and choking. And then wretching...Iris led Rory to its source.

"Help..." someone whispered.

To their surprise, they spotted two of the college kids from inside. A young man stood over a girl, touching her on the side of the cheek. She gurgled a little, her eyes flopping open and closed.

"She passed out! C'mon wake up!"

At first, Rory wasn't sure if he was helping the young woman or if he was trying to take advantage of her; however, then it became apparent that he was genuinely concerned for her welfare. He tapped the woman again.

"Is this your girlfriend?"

"She's my sister..." the man said looking up at her in indignation with wide partially sober eyes.

"Oh..."

"Is she conscious?"

"I don't know!"

"We can't just leave her here..." Rory whispered to his friend.

Iris froze as if looking in a mirror. *I know what you're thinking...This is me...*She folded her arms across her chest and looked at Rory unsure how to proceed...

"Go inside and call an ambulance..." she said finally.

But before they could react Orville, Eugenia and Lobelia appeared outside. Eugenia, still partially damp with eel water, gave an exhausted sigh. Lobelia stepped over to the young people.

"I don't think she's breathing!" her brother pleaded.

"We'll get someone out here..." Lobelia said not waiting for Orville's response.

"Hurry!"

"Eugenia go back inside and call!"

Once again, Orville took her out of earshot of the kids. Lobelia wanted to walk away, for fear he would fire her...For *good* this time! He spoke to her.

"At least tell them that they were drunk college kids who *came* drunk from university... Make it up! Tell em it's a frat party or something..."

"I don't care anymore...People are getting hurt...The place is a mess...Everything we've worked for..."

"Everything *I've* worked for..."

"What's all this?" a male voice called.

"One of the college kids is passed out in the alley way... Eugenia went inside to call a bus..."

"My God!" Edgar said hobbling over to her.

"She's not breathing..." her brother called putting his ear to her mouth.

A second later, a siren wailed...

THIRTY-EIGHT

"Gather round everyone..." Orville called to the staff two nights later. "As you know, my mother is no longer working here at the Electric Eel..." he waited for any of them to express regret and then continued. "So without further ado, I'd like to present your new manager and my new best friend Sid Clark, or as I call him S.C...."

He motioned to a slender caramel-skinned man in a loud blue pinstriped suit with shoulder pads, high-waisted pants, and black and white shoes. Edgar put his head in his hands and looked down. *Don't do this, Orville...Please don't do this...* He thought recognizing the man he'd known since grade school.

"Nice to meet you, Sidney..." Lobelia said politely.

"No Sidney... Just Sid..." he corrected her with a haughty, arrogant, cat that ate the canary smile.

"Sid it is then..." she said walking away.

To Edgar's dismay Sid approached him and slapped him on the back with considerable strength. Edgar smelled his cheap aftershave and perspiration as he stood near him and winced. As always, Sid didn't seem to notice...Or care...

"Nice to see you got two new legs..." he quipped.

"I always *had* one..." Edgar said under his breath, not wishing to entertain him but feeling the need to defend himself at the same time.

"Oh. Well... No hard feelings, my man..." he said moving on with the conversation quickly as if nothing fazed him. "Tell me something..."

The Electric Eel!

"Yes...?"

"Is that uh lady over there...Uh... Seeing someone?"

Edgar looked to see Sid pointing to where Lobelia was standing. He stifled a laugh. *I've heard rumors about she and Tiny...Mainly from Eugenia...But I stay out of everyone else's personal lives...*

"Gee! I don't know...You'll have to ask her..."

With that, Sid marched away in bored frustration. *Same old Sid...*He thought with a smile.

Then something else caught his attention. Two burly men in work uniforms carried a large ornate tank inside the building. Eugenia clapped her hands together in glee. Orville pointed to a huge gold stand with four heavily decorated claw-footed legs.

"It's immense!"

"Guaranteed not to break!" Orville beamed.

We'll see about that! She thought. She called Rory and walked to where the eels resided.

Eugenia peered into the wash basin to see two live electric eels and felt relief at the sight of them swimming. Rory followed and then frowned at several linear scars on each fish. Eugenia winced.

"They fight when they don't have enough space...You don't realize how huge and strong they are...But they'll be okay...Get me that ladder in the corner, would you?"

Rory turned to see the men from before running hoses from the tap into the enormous aquarium. A reservoir of water soon filled the tank as Rory placed the ladder against the wall. Together they have hefted the eels into their new home.

"There you go..." she said talking to them.

With a look of surprise, the fish landed inside the water and swam for a moment their tails intertwining like a figure eight. They buzzed angrily like a swarm of perturbed bees or wasps, their unblinking beady emotionless eyes staring at them in the dim light. Rory

The Electric Eel!

tossed a few bites of fish inside the tank as Eugenia had taught him and while they normally pounced on it, it floated to the tank uneaten.

"They've just had a hard time... If they don't eat it in fifteen minutes fish it out so it doesn't rot..."

"What do you think of the new tank?" Orville asked his employee with a wide grin.

"It's lovely. I promise to keep it clean..."

"And nice to see Rory is helping you... Listen..." he said trailing off. "Maybe we can eventually get a tank large enough for you to swim with them..."

Eugenia looked up at Orville in disbelief and blinked to see if he was joking. He continued. She bit her tongue.

"Or at least give the *illusion* that you're swimming with them...Just a thought..."

Eugenia waited for her boss to walk away and then approached Rory. As usual Rory listened to her rant without speaking. *Don't tell her anything you don't want repeated...*Iris had warned.

"Did you hear that? He wants me to swim with eels...*Electric* eels! Is he insane? I'm no diver...Do I *look* like a diver? I mean, I put a finger in the tank occasionally and it hurts for a second...It does...But *swimming?* He *can't* be serious..."

"Yea it doesn't make sense..." he muttered trying to be supportive and say as little as possible at the same time.

"...And did you see that guy he brought in to replace Carlotta? Sheesh! What a strange bird! Probably he could never bring him in here as long as she was here..." she said under her breath. "Shh... Quiet here he comes..."

"Hey! You must be Eugenia! The eel lady!"

Eugenia paused as Sid leaned in painfully close. She instantly disliked the man but smiled anyway in his presence. Orville approached her again.

"How bout we get you a couple *more* eels?" he asked her.

"If we have room..."

The Electric Eel!

"Do we know if these two are male or female? Maybe have a few eel babies on the way..." Sid suggested motioning as if he were frying something in a skillet. "Could be a good little side business..."

Now we're in the eel breeding business? Does he realize how huge these things get? Is he stupid or does he just not care?

"Might be a good idea, my friend!" Orville said patting him on the back. "Keep thinking!"

Sid beamed in smug satisfaction and walked away. Eugenia blinked in disbelief at what had transpired. Then Iris walked up to Rory and touched his hand without looking at Eugenia, the dislike between the two women obvious.

"Hey sweetie! Wanna go get something to eat?" Iris called.

Rory turned to look at his friend who was surprisingly sober and chipper. Eugenia rolled her eyes at not being invited. *She still thinks she has a shot with him!* Rory gulped as Eugenia wandered away a second later in disgust.

"What's her problem?" she asked.

"I'm not sure..."

Then a few customers walked to one of the newly placed tables in the center of the room and sat down. Rory straightened their table linens and walked away as Eugenia pulled out a pen and began writing. To his shock, Eugenia began talking about him to strangers.

"He's the nicest guy *ever*...And one of the smartest people I know...But he has *no* common sense...! Sang in a dress here once! Wish *I* could wear that...But I don't feel like starving myself to fit into it the way he does..." she said looking in his direction to see if he could hear her. "And that one over there..." she said looking at Iris. "Claims to have all the money in the world...I have no idea if it's true and she sings *here*...Can you imagine? You could be on a yacht somewhere in the French Riviera and you come *here*? She's gotta be on something... She'd *have* to be... Or crazy...Her parents supposedly have beau coups of money...Her mother came here once to make her stop...Not that it worked cause she's still here..."

As he listened, Rory's cheeks reddened in embarrassment. Iris bit her lip and reached for him. The smell of her expensive perfume wafted against his cheek. *Told you...*

"I love you..."

"I love you too... Let's go..."

THIRTY-NINE

Tiny's tasks for Mr. LaRocca's goons were menial...*At first*....*Delivering a sandwich to an office or a bottle of beer to an address somewhere in the city*...And his goons always paid handsomely.. But then they seemed to demand more of this time...

"People are going to wonder where I am..." he said to no one in particular from the front seat of his car. "Especially Lobelia..."

The first meeting with the capos was extremely nerve wracking....*Like something out of a cheesy mobster film*...Most of the men were about sixty with heavily pomaded hair and white fedoras with dark bands and tailored pastel linen suits. A silent brown and black Doberman Pinscher sat by their side like a sculpture.

*That first meeting they asked my mother's last name... But not my first...*He remembered.

"To see if I was Italian..." he told himself.

Still he remained Tiny to everyone...*Cause no mother in her right mind would give a kid a Christian name of Tiny...*He thought.

Quickly he pulled his father's jalopy in front of a ubiquitous brick building. The car rattled and pinged like a shotgun a second after he turned it off. He studied the buildings trying to figure out where to go next...*They always find me...*

He reached for a small paper satchel. It was stapled shut so he couldn't look inside without tearing it. *Probably something innocuous again like a lunch...A pastrami*

The Electric Eel!

sandwich on rye...Again? He had been instructed to go to random butcher in the Italian Village and pick it up and bring it here...*But what they pay all this and have this much secrecy over deli meat?*

It all seemed so silly...He thought getting out of the car with a shrug. Like most things, he squeezed into as they were not made for a man of his girth. The automobile groaned a little as if in protest.

The monochromatic grey and earthtones of downtown Columbus were all around him. A small park with swans and ducks lay off to one side. The sound of a small fountain whirring inside the pond came next. But Tiny had no interest in a leisurely stroll or time even if he wanted to...

Quickly he walked up and down the sidewalk in front of a high rise building with stone facing. Unused to exercising he easily became winded from even a brief stint of brisk walking. As he caught his breath they found him.

"Easy, there, big fella..."

He took in two gulps of air, pretending that he was not winded in front of them. One of them laughed at his expense as the other snatched the bag. They looked at each other and nodded in approval. Despite the heat both men were in impeccable tweed suits and blazers. *How do they not roast...?* He wondered.

"Good job, Tiny..." the spokesman of the two said. "Mr. LaRocca will be mighty pleased..."

"Thank you...What do I do now?"

They laughed again. Like always: *They ask you...You don't ask them...*

"We'll be in touch..."

And they walked away. *Just enough time to get back to his night job at the eel...Another racket...* He thought. *How did I wind up with two gigs on the sly?* He asked himself.

The car groaned again as he climbed in. *Thank goodness this car has a self-starter...*He

The Electric Eel!

thought. *Or else I'd have to get out to crank it myself...* A small metal plaque reading: "Dodge Brothers Motor Cars" was secured to dash just below his left hand with two rivets. He put the car in neutral and eased it out of its parking space and drove the small distance back. He looked at the gas gauge... *Wish it wasn't such a hayburner...*

The lights were already on when he reached the Electric Eel. Hopefully, he arrived *before* the customers this time... *Otherwise that would be really hard to explain...* He straightened his tie and walked in through the back entrance only to find Lobelia waiting for him in the back room.

"*There* you are!" she called.

"Oh! Hi!"

"You were supposed to pick me up... I had to take a cab... What gives?"

He blanched in embarrassment. *She probably thinks I'm running around on her...* Tiny mused.

"Sorry. It's not what you think, Lobelia..."

"Oh! I know you aren't with another girl!"

"Good!"

"But that still doesn't mean I agree with what you're doing..." she added. "You're no gangster...You're just a big kid in a huge body..."

But she instantly touched a nerve. Tiny darkened a little with resentment. Soon he felt the need to defend himself.

"You do realize where I met those wise guys?" he prodded. "The place *you* run...Who do you think provides the booze for this place?"

"Oh, I know! They're all corrupt! That's why I'm just looking out for you!"

As usual, she caught him off guard with her candor. Her wide eyes were as if she were filled to the brim with strong coffee as she paused for effect and blinked. Lobelia reached for him, but he still seemed perturbed, somehow.

"Then what do you want from me?"

"I want you to be safe..." she said. "I care about you...Probably more than I should..."

"I care about you too..."

And she reached up and touched the soft skin on his cheek. He closed his eyes, savoring it. Just then Eugenia appeared in the doorway with hands on hips. Tiny ignored her for a second, no longer caring if anyone saw their affection.

"Ahem..." she hissed in two syllables.

"What is it, Eugenia?"

"Are you two done?"

"Yes... We're finished..." she said smiling. "What can I do for you, Eugenia?"

"Orville wants to open, and the bakery case needs filled..."

"Let's go..."

FORTY

*L*ater that night, rumors of a police raid began to surface around the place. While police officers and politicians on both sides of the law who frequented the place always kept them abreast of any pending actions, it always remained a possibility. The staff walked around nervously.

"We're always prepared..." Orville said not bothered by it in the least.

"They are losing control...That's why..." Eugenia informed Rory.

"Orville and the higher ups?"

"No, stupid... The *feds*...The *police*! They're all on the take! Everyone's saying Prohibition can't last much longer.."

"Who's *everyone*?" Iris asked overhearing.

"*Everyone!* Pick up a newspaper sometime! Do you read? At least we won't have to pretend anymore... Electric Eel Bakery, my ass!"

Iris resisted the urge to gag in the other woman's presence and instead turned her focus on her friend. She gave him a warm smile. He acquiesced and returned the

The Electric Eel!

pleasantry.

"Are you ready?"

"Yes. I'll be over in just a moment..." he informed her.

"What's this hold she has over you, Rory? It can't be because she's pretty, can it? You don't like girls, do you? Is it money? I know you like the dog and all..."

"She's my friend..." he said ignoring the third degree and heading in the direction of the stage.

Immediately Peaches leapt at him in recognition. He reached for the pooch and allowed the canine to place his pointy muzzle in his lap. Iris pulled him behind the shoji screen and showed him the green dress they had purchased before along with several similarly colored jewels.

"Isn't it stunning? You'll be such a hotsy-totsy in that..."

She handed him the garment and examined it in the light. It sparked like a piece of Tiffany glass, its shades of green subtly shimmering. Rory nodded in approval and pulled it over his head.

"Ready for our duet?"

"Ready as rain..."

"Get dressed and I'll let Wallace know...Psst...Wallace!"

Wallace looked up but did not stop playing till he found its source. Iris peeked her head out of the shoji screen. He played an octave and listened.

"Blue Danube Blues..."

"You got it!" he said flipping through music and playing at the same time. "And now from the musical Good Morning, Dearie... I present a lovely duet with Iris Dupeon and Rory Childs..."

"When a chap put out a word that made him stutter...To a girly sweet...At her state he's well aware that he has lots of hands and feet..." he began emerging in the green dress. "Then some kind musician... Seeing his position...Softly starts to play...His arm

The Electric Eel!

slips in haste, round her slender waste...I'll be the bluest of the blues...When I'm without you. The truest of the trues...I'll never doubt you. With all the world from which to choose, selected me to be the apple of your eye! I can't resist you and that's the reason why...I kissed you when the band was playing...The tune that sets me swaying...The Blue Danube Blues..."

"That sweet old strain... We hear again...The Blue Danube Blues..." Iris broke in.

"Raid!" someone interrupted. *"Get down!!"*

Then Wallace and the other members of the band immediately switched to another song without finishing the other piece. The tune of "Alcoholic Blues" whined from all three instruments as Iris and Rory were cut off on stage, signaling to the rest of the staff of the impending police presence.

Orville, Sid, and Lobelia at the bar tossed each other bottles of alcohol and placed them in the trap door beneath the bar while Eugenia and other staff members went around to the tables grabbing drinks. Customers, too, got the message and complied by downing their cocktails and hiding their glassware under the long tablecloths and drapes.

An old man at the end of one of the tables reached for his cane and unscrewed the top. Then he poured a small amount of alcohol from a silver flask and put the top back on the walking stick. Finally he placed the flask and his drinking glass under the table and sat quietly holding his cane.

All of a sudden the door burst open, and Tiny stepped back in surprise as if reacting to an explosion. The room was surprisingly free of the reminders of alcohol, save for the upside-down glassware. Three official looking men in bowler hats emerged with briefcases. Lobelia gulped as the rest of the room froze.

"Easy there, big guy! We're from the Office of President Herbert Hoover..." one of announced said handing Orville a stack of papers.

"May I help you, Officer?" Orville asked completely unrattled.

The Electric Eel!

"We have rumors that you are operating an illegal speakeasy!" he asked looking around the room for contraband.

All three of them looked at the tables on either side of the room. An elderly woman held a glass of something red between her fingernails. She looked at him without flinching. He narrowed his eyes like a bull ready to charge.

"What's that?"

"Pardon?"

"What's in your glass?" he yelled as if she were deaf or slow.

"Tomato juice... I have a heart problem..."

He picked up the drink and sniffed it like a bloodhound. When satisfied he set the drink down and moved on. Lobelia breathed a sigh. The older woman shrugged and continued staring ahead as if nothing had happened, her fingers never leaving the glass. Stealthily he looked at another glass...

"Ginger ale..." his partner said.

Then the lead officer turned to Rory who was still dressed in the emerald ensemble. The federal agent gave a mean humorless smile. *He's about my age...*Rory noted.

"Hey, Gray!" he said to other agent. "What's with the man in the dress?"

"Looks like a queer speakeasy performance to me..."

"It's not a crime to be in drag..." Iris mouthed in protest.

"It *may* be, my dear...I'll have to look into it," he said looking at the woman who unused to being told what to do. "This county does have Masquerade laws... Now whether we can enforce them is another story...We have a lot on our plate... Regardless it's in poor taste...You have a beautiful voice... We heard you...Next time try it in a suit! Makes more sense with the song that way. Is that clear?"

"Yes, sir."

"What's with all the glassware?" he asking turning to Lobelia.

"We cater!" Orville piped in with more enthusiasm than probably was necessary.

The Electric Eel!

The officer walked around the bar to examine the hanging champagne flutes and wine glasses and touched them. The glasses swung a little in the shape of a starfish. *Please don't break...*Lobelia thought not wishing to clean up another mess.

"Still damp..." he said. "And warm..."

"What *exactly* do you cater with those?" the other man asked.

Orville, a facile accomplished liar, gave him a smarmy grin. The lead agent chewed his lip, unsure what to make of the man's cockiness. Orville leaned in close as if letting him in on a secret.

"Whatever they like..."

"Shh.." Lobelia chided.

"It's only a crime to sell and distribute it...*You* know that...*I* know that...Whatever they put it in is up to them..." Orville continued. "We're a bakery, so I'd assume the little old ladies who buy our wares drink tea or coffee...But I really don't know...You'd have to ask my grandparents...All I know is that we sell a lot of scones and muffins...You're welcome to try one on your way out... They're delicious..."

"Orville...Stop..." Lobelia whispered.

And then the lead agent turned to Lobelia. She straightened her spine, unsure of what was coming next. He studied her for a second and then turned to her boss.

"Do you always let the colored help speak to you that way, Mr. Alfonso?"

Lobelia winced as if slapped. Then she placed her hands at her sides, willing herself not to say anything more. And he turned from the bar as if suddenly bored and looking at a covered table with something round in the center.

"And what, pretell is that?"

"We have a resident psychic who comes to do seances every Thursday..."

The agent lifted his hands afraid to touch it. *What goes on in this place?* He turned in disgust.

"Gives me the heebie-jeebies!" he said shivering. "What's with all these eels?"

The Electric Eel!

"It *is* the Electric Eel..." Eugenia informed him.

Oh no...Lobelia thought. *Eugenia be quiet...*

"Yes but why are they *here*...?"

"They're pets..."

"And speaking of pets...Do they allow dogs in here?"

"As long as no one is eating..." Orville added.

"But you run a bakery... You said so yourself..."

"Out *there*..."

"It's what you do *in here* that concerns me...So mister piano player..." he said turning to Wallace. "Do you always play "Alcoholic Blues" or just when I come to call?"

"I play a lot of things...Whatever they tell me..."

"I'm sure you do..."

Just then one of the officers beckoned to the lead agent on the case from the other side of the room. He pointed to something on the floor behind the Shoji screen. Both men examined it afraid to touch it. A small tin of something powdery lay in the shadows alongside a long handled silver spoon.

"Leave it! They probably got it next door! We're just here for the sauce!"

You can't be serious! The look on the other agent's face said. Iris and the other members of the band paused, fearing what was coming next. But then something else caught his eye.

"What's this, Mr. Alfonso?"

Orville bounded to him like a Springer Spaniel to examine it. A small partially full brown bottle lay propped up on its side. The officer picked it gingerly between a napkin and two fingers.

"Whose is *that*?"

"I have no idea..." Orville answered honestly.

"Come with me..."

The Electric Eel!

Lobelia and Eugenia tried to go with him, but he put his hand up to stop them. *Just us!* He mouthed. *Are they going to arrest him?* They wondered.

Then Orville watched as he moved away from the Electric Eel carrying the bottle away from his body as if would scald him. For a second, he thought the agent would down it; however, he turned to the storm drain and flipped the bottle upside down. It gurgled a little as it emptied and when satisfied, he tossed it at Orville's feet.

"Throw that out!"

"Will do…" Orville said picking up the litter.

"I think we're done here, boys…" he informed them. "For now…I may send my wife in to get muffins for her bridge club…"

"Anytime…"

Next, Orville watched as the three men got into a brown Plymouth and drove off. Members of the staff joined their boss a second later. The night outside was steamy in contrast to the cool temperature of the Electric Eel.

"Maybe we should close for the night…"

"Nah…It's all ceremonial.. Wait a few minutes and go back to what you were doing…Here! Throw this away…"

"When did we start catering?" Tiny asked picking up the discarded bottle.

"Maybe we should…What a rush, eh?!" Orville said heading back inside with glee. "Great job, everyone! Drink's on the house!"

FORTY-ONE

Edgar Alfonso heard about the raid the next day. It was *all* anyone could talk about…His mother sat at the end of the table as servants placed food in front of them. She reached for a platter of fruit and cheese and plucked a grape from a stem.

"Ugh. Sour…"

The Electric Eel!

Quickly she spit it out on a saucer and handed the plate to one of the help who hovered around her. Poppy always felt nervous in her mother-in-law's presence, an unhappy judgmental eye always upon her. Then she spotted Orville straightening his tie in the mirror.

"You look dapper!"

"Thank you! Now that that dreadful raid is behind us I can breathe a little…"

"I'm so glad to be out of there!" Carlotta added. "It might be good for you young people but not me…"

"Did you know your brother is lifting weights?" Poppy asked her husband. "He may even enter one of those strong man contests at the fair!"

"Least now he won't tip over…" he said with a callous laugh.

Poppy recoiled as Edgar looked down at the floor. Orville placed his hands in the air. As always his mother said nothing in her son's defense.

"What? He knows I kid… He's my little brother…" he said with a flippant little punch.

"Well I gotta go… No rest for the weary!"

"Are you going to jail, daddy?" Alistair called.

Now is my time to be offended… He thought. His son stared at him with innocent light eyes the color of his own.

"Where did you hear that?" he asked as the boy shifted his weight on his feet. "And no… I'm *not* going to jail…"

"Promise?"

"I promise… Now! Please no more talk of this… From *any* of you…"

"Can we go outside now?"

"Sure."

"He thinks of you as his playmate now…" Poppy informed Edgar.

"Good to know. You've kept the yard nice…"

Edgar knelt down carefully and examined her garden. Meanwhile Alistair sprinted across the backyard, jumping, and bouncing in the noon day sun. Poppy smiled as the warmth of day warmth her cheek.

"Are these Geraniums?" he asked.

He pinched a trumpet shaped bloom between his thumb and forefinger. What was once a silvery purple flower was now bleached translucent in the sun like rice paper. The center of the bloom remained dark and untouched by the light.

"Petunias..." she corrected.

"They're beautiful."

"I love them..." she said . "But they're sticky..."

He rubbed his fingers together to see what she meant. The texture was different but not unpleasant. Then he turned and looked up at her. She was wearing one of those gossamer ladylike scarves she favored that framed her face and trailed down her shoulders and fastened at the neck...*Like a petunia and its stem...*

Poppy, in turn, looked at her brother-in-law as he sat beside her on the bench. His thick mustache matched his sandy hair and a few freckles from being in the sun dotted the bridge of his perfectly straight nose. He was sweet and caring in a way that her husband never was...

Quickly, he cocked his head to one side.. She put her hand out to stop him from kissing her. He leaned in closer and looked into her eyes.

"We can't..." she whispered.

He leaned back dejected and thought about it. Alistair continued running somewhere in the yard, without stopping to notice. Poppy placed her hands in her lap as if nothing had happened.

"Mother will be leaving soon..." he informed her. "She goes to bridge on Wednesdays..."

"Mmm-hmm..." she said humoring him. "All right, Alistair! Five more minutes and then it's time for your nap!"

The Electric Eel!

"Aww! But-"

"No buts, mister..."

Once Alistair was asleep and out of earshot, Poppy sat down beside Edgar. He moved away from her in uncertainty. Then she spoke to him in that calm aloof ladylike way that made him want her even more.

"I have thought about it..."

"About what?"

"You and me..."

He grew silent for a moment. She patted him on the leg...*The prosthetic one*...And stood and walked across the room.

"And?" he said trying to follow her.

"But we can't..."

"Why?"

"*Why?*" she asked the normally calm timbre of her voice leaving for a second. "Because you're my husband's brother...The uncle of my son..."

But without warning, he kissed her anyway. Quickly, she put her hand up to initially protest; however, instead she found herself placing it between his pectoral muscles. Unlike her husband, Edgar's kiss was passionate and purposeful and left her reeling.

"Stop!" she said enjoying it a moment.

"Okay! l*Okay!*"

Poppy's heart raced in her chest. She chewed on her lip a little, still tasting his lips on hers. Edgar moved to embrace her, but she shrunk away from him and leaned against the floral wallpaper.

"I better go!"

"I think that's a very good idea!"

Edgar called a taxi, dressed in haste, and reached for his tie. Poppy gave him wide berth as they both felt a little guilty. A tension lingered between them that neither had felt before in each other's company.

"I'm leaving..."

Poppy bobbed her head in agreement and opened the front door...*I came on too strong...Can't say that I blame her...*

*Funny how they all still open the door for me like I'm still a cripple...*He noted. He shrunk down a little and waited outside a moment for his ride in the July heat. Ten minutes later he was on his way, the sun beating down on his right arm from the car's window. His mind began to wander.

"Everything a'right there, boy?" an old man in a derby hat inquired from the front seat.

"I think so... But once my brother finds out...I may be out on the street..."

"Finds out what exactly?..."

"Nothing..." he said fearing he'd already said too much.

*Not that it matters...*He thought. *What if she says I forced himself on her?* Edgar thought with a shudder. *No...She's not like that...She said she was curious about him in that way...It's only cause she is married to my brother...She's faithful which makes me want her more...*

And then he thought of his brother again. He thought of the rumors of infidelity that always followed Orville everywhere...*With men* and women...*No way he would tolerate his wife's cheating though...He's too egotistical to let that one go...!*

"Up here..." he said motioning to the familiar corner. "And thank you for listening..."

"Anytime..."

*I may learn to drive now...*He thought. *Everyone else does...Why not?* He thought getting out of the cab and paying the driver.

Inside his brother was surprisingly cheerful. A mass of people, mostly women were gathered in the right corner of the Electric Eel leaning over something. Orville beamed with pride.

"I present to you our newest edition...Genuine walrus ivory, rosewood and mahogany..."

A woman in a long coat dress reached for a white billiard size ball and tossed it in the center of a spinning wheel. A series of red and black numbers from 0-36 lined the perimeter of the outside of the circle. A large center heavy turret sat in the middle like a chess piece, a large cross on top like a weather vane.

"A roulette wheel?"

"Mmm-hmmm...All right, ladies...You heard what the man said: No metal buttons or purse latches that can scratch it... Gentlemen! Get those belt buckles back!"

The man sitting in front of the table reached for the ball with something that looked like a fireplace poker, his white gloved hands immaculate. Someone else called out a number. Edgar watched unable to keep up with fascination.

"Where'd you buy this?" he asked Orville.

"I *didn't*...It was a gift...To *Tiny*...From Mr. LaRocca..."

Tiny nodded proudly. *And now we have gambling...*Edgar thought.

FORTY-TWO

"*W*here do we hide this thing if we have a raid?" Eugenia asked putting a damper on the everyone's good mood.

"The table's on wheels! Eventually we'll knock out that back wall and have a VIP room with tables for Monte Carlo night but in the meantime we'll just say we are hosting a game night......But Mr. LaRocca promised there isn't going to *be* another raid..." her boss informed her.

Tiny stared at the high gloss polished wood wheel, unaware of what he had gotten them into. Lobelia came up behind him and looked at the table with uncertainty. All of those standing around it, including herself, remained in a trance as if hypnotized.

"Red seven..." the caller yelled. "Better luck next time...Remember the more the numbers you call the better your chance of winning, but it decreases your payout..."

The Electric Eel!

"We just pay Mr. LaRocca ten percent... *For now...*"

Just then someone tapped Orville on the shoulder. He turned to see the mysterious asymmetrical face of Madame Beulah. He shuddered a little at the realization of who was touching him, suddenly creeped out.

"May I help you?" he asked forcing pleasantries.

"Is that going to be going on during my performance?" shed barked pointing at the roulette wheel on the other side of the bar.

*Should have never introduced this on a Thursday...*He regretted. Madame Beulah looked up at him with hateful daggers.

"It's all new...Give it some time..."

"I go on in ten minutes! At least have them refrain when I'm on stage... It's distracting...The spirits are very sensitive to loud noises..."

Orville covered his mouth and stifled a laugh. Madame Beulah folded her arms across her chest in defiance. She set her jaw in a stony humorless grimace and looked at him as if staring through him.

"I doubt if they'll stop..." he informed her walking away. "You know that we always have things going on here simultaneously..."

We'll see about that! She watched as Eugenia and Rory grabbed the end of her table and moved it outward close to center stage. Madame Beulah held her breath afraid that the crystal ball would fall off and shatter.

"Careful..." she whispered. "That's priceless!"

Madame Beulah sat down, closed her eyes, and listened to the whirring sound of the wheel across the room. Quietly she raised her arms above her head like a Martha Graham protégé and brought her two thumbs and index fingers together in a diamond shape over her sternum. Then she began to chant.

"Oh, great, spirits! Speak through me! Come through me!"

She held up a black fountain pen with a pointed gold beveled tip and a piece of scrapbook paper to show the audience and placed the paper back on the table. As Beulah began to scribble, she threw her head back and allowed the pen to write automatically without looking at it. As the hypergraphia continued, her arm sped up like a pitcher throwing a fastball until a grainy image appeared on the paper.

"Tonight we remember the restless spirits who lost their lives to self-medication... Those restless spirits whose untimely demise from suicide, surfeiting, drunkenness, and gambling..." she said opening one eye with a wink and looking across the room. "Who cannot rest in death till they make peace with their choices in life...Repeat after me: Freedom from sin in life is freedom from sin in death..."

Orville burned at this slight but did not turn back to look at her. Madame Beulah continued, unfazed. Iris and the members of the band also heard this incantation and wondered where she was going with this. The audience continued reciting her mantra, forgetting about the gaming table for a moment.

"Oh great spirits of the beyond...!" her voice lorded over everyone, suddenly deepening.

Edgar shivered as the normal feminine tone of her voice broadened into a husky male pitch. Then she swayed from some unknown vertigo, her hands outstretched. *Is she drunk?* And then the words became a slurred mishmash of syllables.

"Make it stop!" a woman in the audience shrieked.

As the woman burst into tears, Madame Beulah shimmied a little, her body quaking like an aspen. As it continued she placed a hand over each ear in protest. Edgar studied her, trying to place where he'd seen her.

"My father died of alcohol poisoning..." she exclaimed. "But he also left us penniless with his gambling..."

"Go to the light... You are free of this affliction...No one can hurt you..." her normal peaceful voice beckoned and then shifted back to being male again. "No..."

Meanwhile the woman placed her head in her lap and continued to travail in despondence. Finally Madame Beulah swirled like a blender and opened her eyes. Rory jumped up to get her a glass of water as the room erupted in applause.

"What happened??" she called.

"Her father went to the light..."

Once finished Madame Beulah slunk away from the audience link a mink. Orville had to admit that she put on a good show although now he realized it was all fake. Still she had bested him twice and there was nothing he could do about it...*Which really sticks in my craw...*

He looked over at the throng of people around the roulette wheel and the bar. *That little spectacle of hers didn't even slow them down...*A tray of sparkly wide mouthed glassware filled with clear liquid and olives came next. *Don't mind if I do...*

"Make me a martini, would you?"

Once Eugenia made the drink, Lobelia stuffed the olive with cheese and placed a toothpick on each side and handed it to him. Orville thanked them with a thumbs up and sipped it. The salty taste of gorgonzola cheese lingered on his lips alongside the briny vinegary crunch of green olive. He shrugged realizing he liked it.

"Perfect..."

Edgar watched as the woman who had cried during Madame Beulah's performance walked across the room. *I can't place her, but I know her from somewhere...* Then it dawned on him.

"That's the woman with the pince-nez glasses..." he said out loud to whomever would listen.

"Huh?" a woman at the bar asked.

"You know... The glasses with no ear pieces...? She lost her mother last time she was here... Never mind..."

Then she leaned over to say something to Beulah. To his shock, he watched as the madame pulled out a few dollars bill with sleight of hand and passed it to her. With great discretion the woman took it, looked around to see if anyone was watching and pulled away. Edgar smiled in vindication.

"Bingo..."

FORTY-THREE

*M*arie Toussad's neon signed flashed in the near darkness. Sid Clark and other lonely men waited in the shadows like marsupials. Sid looked up to a see an arc of crimson light bouncing off his right shoulder. *Red light district...*It announced.

Edgar was there too. *Somewhere...*He thought. His brother had recommended this place but until now he had never even considered it...Now that he knew that the person he truly wanted was no longer an option he had nothing to lose...

With patience, Edgar waited until familiar faces from the Electric Eel exited for the night, and then emerged in the artificial light of the street lamps. Iris and Rory were the first to leave. The young woman's steps were uneven and careful like a toddler. Her feet teetered on unnaturally high strapped heels. *He's a good friend to her...*

As always the dog followed them closely. *The stupid hound with better hair than most adult women...*He thought as Rory grabbed the dog's leash and then reached for his friend to make sure both were safe inside the car.

*That day I caught Rory looking at me I briefly considered it...*He remembered. *Only one of a handful of truly good people around this place...But that wouldn't be fair...Regardless of how lonely we both were at the time...Guess I'm destined to be alone...Standing in line like a male opossum waiting for a lone female in heat...*

Then to his surprise, he watched as Rory and Iris stopped the car in front of the pharmacy. *What are they up to?* He wondered. *Whatever it is it has to be her idea...*He surmised. *Rory just goes along with it...*

For a second he watched as the woman, dog and young man disappeared around the

The Electric Eel!

back of the unlit sign marked RX Drugs. *And they aren't even going in the front door as one would expect...Is it even open at this hour?*

Next, he saw Madame Beulah exiting the Electric Eel. Even though it was hot outside, she was wearing a shawl...*Like a bat in the moonlight*...As she passed Marie Toussad's Gallery, she gave a judgmental, glare and then looked away. Quickly, she stepped away from the brick facade afraid to touch the building that would house such a place.

"Bad energy..." she whispered, the speed of her pace increasing.

Then the horde of unsatiated men shuffled a little as Sid and two others went inside. Despite the seedy purpose of the locale, the frilly Edwardian décor remained. Cheap girly pink and red glossy wallpaper lined three of the four walls inside covering several cracks in the horse hair plaster. *Like it's keeping the whole place from falling apart...*

Several ornate wooden boxes sat inside the front door on four curved convex Queen Anne style legs. An oculus for each eye lay on top connected by a black bar like a pair of upside-down binoculars. "Peep show! Five cents!" A tiny yellow sign over a slot announced. Sid fished in his pocket for change he had swiped from the Electric Eel and pushed it inside.

As he leaned over to peek, a cartoonish sepia toned image of a woman in lace began to form along with a woman kneeling. Both women were curvy and sported large Victorian sweeps of hair with small buns on top, their large chests heaving forward. Once satisfied another man who was looking at a viewfinder nearby asked Sid to switch.

The second image Sid looked at was of a pudgy woman with fair skin and blood red curly hair. While he found her alluring, the image seemed like a laughable letdown somehow. Her white puffy legs stuck out slightly as she lay on her stomach, her tiny shoes like hooves. Her huge chest spilled out of the bodice of her negligee. A smear of pink rouge was on each of her cheeks and Sid couldn't tell if it had been put on after the picture had been taken.

"The good stuff is *upstairs*..." he informed Sid.

The Electric Eel!

Sid nodded in gratitude and looked at a staircase that turned sharply at a ninety-degree angle blocking the view of the top floor. A sea of faded mint green carpet connected to wooden stairs leading him upward. As Sid went upstairs, Edgar entered with great caution.

"Whatever you do...Don't sit down..." his brother's voice warned in his head.

Edgar moved slowly into the front room of Marie Toussad's as a swarm of men pushed behind him. Since he'd received his artificial leg, he stepped carefully everywhere with his left not wishing to fall on his face... *Especially in here of all places...I'd never live that down...*

Though all the other men seemed to hurry inside, Edgar, on the other hand, took his time wanting to take it all in...As he pivoted he noticed a few curious items on the window sill. A series of lotions with pumps sat along with a few folded towels.

"You know what those are for?" he heard his brother's voice echo.

*Maybe I shouldn't have come here...*He thought trying to back out. Then something moved in the corner catching his eye. *Is that a rodent...?* But as it jumped onto the sill he saw it was an ordinary white housecat. He watched as the feline coiled its tail over the wood like an upside-down question mark and growled angrily. *Maybe he knows something about this place that we don't...*

Unlike Sid, Edgar decided to bypass the staircase and go to the rooms behind. A series of instantly recognizable noises emanated from behind the locked wooden doors. A few men stood in the hall, but he ignored them, moving carefully through the hall. A series of lewd pictures lined each wall. On several of the doors a few waist-high holes were drilled in each. Edgar shuddered, realizing their significance.

"This isn't for me..." he whispered.

And with surprising speed, he walked out. At the top of the stairs Sid spotted him and called to him. Edgar craned his neck and looked up in embarrassment. Quickly, he pushed through several young men and walked back outside into the stifling night.

For the second time in twenty-four hours he felt a rush. He looked around to see he was alone on the sidewalk and then took in a gulp of air. *Why did I leave?* He asked himself.

As he stood a rotund police officer with a night stick passed him. Edgar shrunk against the building hoping not to be noticed. *Will I go to jail?* He wondered.

"Move along..." the officer ordered. "Otherwise I'll give you a ticket for loitering...!"

But to his relief, the officer did not stop. Edgar gave a final look up at Marie Toussad's Gallery as he walked...His heart racing in his ears...And Edgar vowed to return...

FORTY-FOUR

"Come this way..." Mr. Houserman told Rory and Iris. "Your pooch is welcome to come as long as he doesn't bite...Or piddle on the rug..."

"Oh! He does neither..." Rory assured him a little confidence.

The pharmacy was different in the low light...*Creepier*...Like a mad scientist's lair...But the pharmacist was pleasant enough and smiled as if he had been expecting them. Once again he was wearing the same dark blue apron and work pants as before, his hard-soled shoes gripping the freshly polished floor.

"Is it just you working here?"

"Ever since my wife died..."

"Sorry..."

"Thank you..."

He led them to a set of basement stairs that creaked as he walked. While he was taller than Rory or Iris, he motioned to the low hanging light so they wouldn't hit their heads on it. A full basement lay beneath the pharmacy like a bomb shelter. The smell of mildew and dampness tickled Rory's nostrils.

"My wine cellar...My little version of a speakeasy..."

"Oh!" Iris said a little disappointed. "I have plenty of wine!"

The Electric Eel!

"Not *this* kind, I'm sure..." he said unfazed and clicking on a light with a string.

As Rory's eyes adjusted, he blinked to see the most incredible room he'd ever seen. Iris, too, was impressed by its grandeur. Bottles of rare alcohols encased sideways in four drilled stone walls greeted them from every angle.

"Stone keeps them at the perfect fifty-three degrees...This place is a natural built-in wine fridge...There's also a hearth and a fireplace which makes it feel more homey. You did purchase my heroin drops last time you were here..."

"Yes..." Iris stammered, not wanting to admit in front of Rory.

"No need to be ashamed...Takes the edge off...! That's why I keep a bottle of Laudanum handy..." he said branding a reddish-orange bottle. "Especially during the nippy Ohio months...Usually it's made from dissolving a tincture of Opium Poppy in ethanol...But I prefer it this way..."

He poured a small capful for Iris to taste and then offered some to Rory. Rory put his hand up to decline but the pharmacist had already moved on. Iris gagged a little.

"Bitter at first... I know... Ever read the book Frankenstein, my boy?"

"Yes..." he said unsure where he was going with this line of questioning.

"Victor Frankenstein took it to sleep and thus staved off a fever that would have killed him...Charles Dickens wrote about it in Oliver Twist....Anna Karenina became addicted to it before jumping in front of a train in Tolstoy's book... And it was in Silas Marner and Uncle Tom's Cabin...And the list goes on and on..."

"Your point?" Iris asked suddenly feeling a little high.

"My point is that it has historical significance...But no one really cares about that stuff anymore...Prohibition has taken over all of our lives... And it's only the start...And since then my most lucrative business has gone here...Underground..."

"It's a beautiful space..."

"Pity only a select few know about it..."

"What's *that* one?" Rory asked pointing to another.

The Electric Eel!

"Similar to the first one... But with a hint of Anise to take the acrid taste out of it...Care to taste?"

"Sure..." Rory said.

"Next I present to you a favorite of Pope Leo the XIII, Queen Victoria, Thomas Edison and more than a few U.S. presidents... Vin Mariani... Unlike this first one which will help you sleep... This one is designed to wake you up! Made from coca leaves... Some say it's the inspiration for our present-day Coca-Cola recipe..." he said offering them some. "But I warn not to take too much of them together...Your body won't know *what* to do!"

He turned the label to show her a woman with red hair pouring the drink in a bright yellow dress and shoes. "*French tonic wine!*" The bottle announced.

"It isn't as potent as snorting it, but it will give you a nice buzz...Pope Leo said he needed that when the prayers stopped working..."

Rory felt himself warming a little. Heat began to rise in his chest and back. Mr. Houserman smiled noticing.

"Warmth? Does that to everyone... Stimulates your heart! Gets your blood pumping!"

"What can I buy?" Iris said gung-ho on the idea.

"Well..." he said pretending to be coy. "I have tons of things down here that might tickle your fancy... Morphine...Methedrine... But most of that is medicinal and you two are young and healthy and are clearly not sick! So what I'd offer you is more for *recreational* purposes..."

"Do you make your own wine?" Rory asked with innocence.

"Heavens no, my boy! No that I *couldn't*...I'm a scientist...I just mix whatever is provided for me together to make something new..."

"I'll take bottles of that coca wine...And one of that anise...The first was a little too bitter for my taste..."

"Oh! Speaking of bitter! I almost forgot! I have Pernod... Made with the finest Wormwood!"

The Electric Eel!

He showed Rory a bottle marked "Green Fairy" and poured them each a spoonful. Rory looked down in vague familiarity. Mr. Houserman read his mind.

"It's in that Electric Eel Cocktail that your boss so favors...It's been banned in France since 1915. It looks like anti-freeze, which is supposedly sweet, but this has *no* sweetness," he said brightly. "Mrs. Alfonso used to come here all the time for it and now I never see her..."

"*Poppy?*" Iris asked.

"Oh no! Older lady with red hair..." he said, slightly confused by the name.

"*Carlotta?* Oh! I think she retired..."

"*Yes!* Excuse me... In my line of work, I don't always get first names...*Or remember!*" he said moving on with the conversation. "Said she was going to name the bar after it since it was her husband's favorite...And then he died *that* way...So sad...And here we are! Her son comes in here occasionally..."

"Well, it is getting late..." Iris said not processing what he was implying.

She pulled out a few bills and handed them to him. Mr. Houserman gave her a demure smile and motioned for the stairs like a docent. *Back this way...*

"Cash register's upstairs...I'll get you change..."

"Keep the change..." Iris slurred.

"Much obliged...Let me get you a paper sack..."

Mr. Houserman walked them outside and waved to their driver who was still waiting in the front seat of the car. Rory steadied her and reached for the dog at the same time. The pharmacist leaned over and whispered something to him.

"You know this street is full of vice...Half of the men who come out of your place just came from *there*...That guy with the one leg looked terrified! But truth be told, I think he enjoyed it..."

He pointed to Marie Toussad's Gallery. Rory shuddered. Iris plopped in the seat and reached for him. Rory waved.

"Talk later..." he said whispering to the young man. "Get home safe, Miss Dupeon!"

"Will do!" she called forcing the courtesy.

Rory closed the door and soon the car began to move forward. Peaches forced his way between the two adults so that both could offer him comfort at the same time. Iris's eyelids were leaden and icy as she touched Rory's hand.

"I love you..."

"I love you too..."

"Let's have a baby together..."

"What?" he asked suddenly awake.

"A baby...*A real* baby...You and me! Not just Peachy Poo Poo!" she said with a drunken guffaw.

Rory's eyes widened...

FORTY-FIVE

February, 1923

*J*rene Alfonso-Wright emerged from her black Cadillac limousine in an impeccable heavy-toothed ivory colored suit and matching pumps in front of her family's business at around nine o'clock at night. As she waved to her driver to park the car, a few male voices called to her from alongside the building. She turned, unaccustomed to the vulgar language.

"Hey! Classy lady!" one of them yelled.

"They keep getting rowdier and rowdier..." Lobelia said. "You know the rules! Stay back on your side! Or we'll have you for trespassing...!" she yelled out the door.

But they were unaffected by her threats and laughed. Lobelia herded Irene inside and apologized. But the men continued their cat calls.

"You aren't going to call the cops, big mama!"

"What's going on out there?" Irene asked Edgar and Poppy.

The Electric Eel!

"Just dirty old men…Don't pay them any mind…"

"Crass bastards! They're out of control!" Eugenia barked.

Orville smiled at his sister, pretending not to have overheard the drama. Instinctively he reached for a bottle of white wine and reached for a narrow goblet. She studied the place and all that had changed since the last time she'd come. A gambling station, a larger tank for eels and trays of food! He poured her a little.

"We have finger food now!" he said trying to impress his well to do sister. "Trixie! Show my sister our fare! Have a canape, Irene!"

A buxom blond brought in a beautiful tray of bite-sized bread topped with ham and a sprig of spring onion on top. Irene smiled, impressed, taking a piece. She tasted something creamy she couldn't place and smiled.

"Aioli…" he informed her. "Keeps the bread from getting soggy…They're bite-sized so guests can eat them in one bite while they're gambling or drinking cocktails…"

"Where do you *get* these?"

"The breads come in with the baked goods…The rest we add. Doesn't Lobelia do a lovely job? And we can sell them upfront without any ramifications! This is Trixie, one of our newest employees! Trixie, this is my baby sister Irene!"

A woman with nearly white spiral curls smiled a big toothy grin. She was wearing a short pink a-lined baby doll dress and Mary Jane shoes. Irene extended her hand with a gentile effect. Trixie took it gingerly.

"Charmed…"

"Trixie is our new cigarette girl…"

"What's with all the yelling earlier?" Rory asked taking Lobelia off to the side.

"I'll tell you…Those lecherous men from that place…At first it was cute but now it's just vile and pathetic…" Eugenia interrupted.

"Is there anyone actually running that place?" Lobelia asked with caution. "All I see are the same men standing there…"

The Electric Eel!

"There's a Chinese couple upstairs who run it..." Sid answered unapologetically. "Sometimes it's a man and sometimes it's his wife... But downstairs? No..."

Eugenia looked at Sid with disdain. *No wonder he's over there...He's just like them...I wish Orville would just get rid of him...*

"Cigars! Cigarettes!" a high-pitched voice emanated through the room like a piccolo.

And now we have Trixie! Eugenia thought. She took an hoers d oeuvres and popped it in her mouth. Lobelia shooed her away from the platter.

"He's gotta be sleeping with her..." she whispered to Lobelia and walked away before she could respond.

"So...Irene..." Edgar began. "How are things...?"

Things? The awkward pause obvious between them. She drummed her fingers on the counter nervously and looked away.

"Things... Are good. Mr. Wright and I are trying to have a baby..." she said ignoring him and speaking to Poppy who was sitting across from her. "Mother says I better get some rest... I haven't been sleeping much lately..."

"Congratulations! You'll be fine!"

Trixie passed again, this time with a change belt and several soft packs of smokes. Irene reached for her, and Trixie handed her one. Irene pulled a shiny silver lighter and lit the smoke.

"Thank you..." Irene said puffing. "Do you know how to make a negroni? We had one on our cruise to Tuscany last year..." she asked Orville.

"But of course..." he lied trying to remember its ingredients. "Do you know what's in a Negroni?"

"Campari... Sweet Vermouth and Gin..." Lobelia answered from memory.

As he stirred the drink, she placed a rocks glass in front of him without being asked. He smiled as she dropped a large ice cube inside and swirled the contents of the mixing glass inside. His sister continued smoking without noticing his angst in her presence.

The Electric Eel!

"Put an orange peel on top of it…"

"What would I do without you?"

She laughed and walked away. The reddish-orange drink resembled some sort of exotic tea or tincture. Irene balanced it between her fingers and sipped it. Sid hovered somewhere behind the bar fiddling with something under the bar.

"Which way to the ladies room? I have to powder my nose…" she asked Eugenia.

"Over there…" she said pointing to the far left.

"Thank you…"

When he thought no one was looking, Sid pulled a small vial of something powdery out of his pocket and deposited it in Irene's drink. Eugenia saw it and rushed over to it in a fury. The drink fizzed a second as its contents settled.

"Don't drink that!" Eugenia shouted to Irene as she walked back to her place at the bar.

Horrified Sid scurried away. Irene put her hands up, unused to being shouted at in such a manner. Eugenia searched for Lobelia and Orville…

"Don't move!" Eugenia bellowed like a traffic cop.

Sid dashed for the cocktail and poured it down the drain in haste. When a bit of the powder remained, he rinsed it and placed the glass upside down in the sink. Orville tried to hide his displeasure with a forced smile.

"What's going on?"

"He put something in her drink!"

"That's a ball-faced *lie!*" he shouted.

"Where's the drink now?"

"He dumped it…"

"Sid, is this true?" Lobelia asked.

"So why'd you dump it out?"

"There was a bug in it… So I figured I'd get her another one…"

The Electric Eel!

"A bug?"

Irene swung her legs over the barstool as if an insect might bite her. As she processed what had transpired the rest of the place began to take notice. Orville tried to get everyone to quiet down.

"He *did* put something in her drink..." Edgar broke in.

"He's lying! He never liked me..."

"He tried to Mickey Finn her..." Eugenia said.

"*Who?*"

"You know that saloon owner in Chicago they convicted a few years back who tried to knock out his customers to rob them...? *He Mickey-ed* her so he could have his way with her!"

"Keep your voice down...Sid, is this true?"

"Yea...But not to have my way with her...She said she wasn't sleeping...So I figured I'd help her out!"

"Where did you get it?" Eugenia asked growing hysterical. "So you mean to tell me you just magically had that in your pocket...? I don't buy that!"

"You could've killed her..." Lobelia mouthed. *And she's pregnant...*

But Sid went silent this time. A group of curious onlookers began to form around them. Most of the bar patrons pushed their drinks away as if they were now toxic.

"We'll get you all new drinks!" Orville informed them.

"Fire him, Orville..." Eugenia warned.

"I can't fire him. He's my best friend!" Orville protested like a school boy whose mate was now in trouble.

"Fire him or I walk..."

"I walk too..." Lobelia informed him.

"I guess I have no choice..." Orville said putting his hands out.

"Either he leaves, or we all walk..." Rory said speaking for the band as well.

And then Tiny approached. At almost three-hundred pounds, he leaned his weight close to Sid's smaller frame. Sid put his hands up in self-defense, the smell of his sweat intense.

"Okay… Okay! I'll go…!" his voice growing high and shrill like a girl's.

"Back door!" Tiny boomed.

Tiny strong-armed the man through the makeshift kitchen, past the roulette wheel to the back. Sid moved away from him as if engulfed in flames. Outside the place, the wind was chilly.

"Can't we talk about this?"

"No!"

"Why not?"

"Because I said so! And don't come back!" Tiny warned with the slam of the heavy door.

As Sid Clark stood in the dank alley, he vowed revenge…

FORTY-SIX

Rory Childs straightened up his small bedroom at his parents' home and folded a small comforter over the side of his bed. The tension between both he and his parents, growing steadily like a saucepan ready to boil over on the stove. Quickly, he hurried to get out the door, but his mother's voice echoed in the doorway.

"What's with all thee expensive gifts?" she asked. "She's an adult woman… You are barely out of your teens…"

"I'm twenty-three. We aren't a couple…"

"I know that…And you know that… But does *she* know that?"

"She knows that…"

"And I don't like this new dating thing you young people have started…Young women going out with young men without a chaperone just doesn't seem right…What

The Electric Eel!

happened to courtship?"

"Iris is different…"

"What does a woman with that much money want with *you*?" his mother asked.

"I'll tell you what she wants…" his father butted in. "She just isn't getting it from *him*! But if he plays his cards right…Oh, buddy! Did you see that Deusenberg her folks own?"

"We aren't together! And I don't want her money!" Rory yelled with surprising force.

"Don't talk to your mother like that, young man!"

And then Rory turned and reached for something under the small mattress. His mother gasped as he pulled out a faded brown boiled leather suitcase and placed it on top of the bed. Silently, he slammed a few items inside and buckled it haphazardly.

"Where are you going? Honey, tell him he can't leave!"

"To Iris's!"

"Honey, he's a grown man… He can do what he wants…! But if you come back you have to pull your own weight around here! Did you see that get up she dressed him in? Little rouge on his cheeks!" he taunted.

And without further ado, Rory stepped into the cold. Despite the frigid blast outside, he burned with rage and adrenalin. *Where do I go now?* He thought.

"Iris's…Of course…"

*We need to teach you to drive…*She kept reminding him. *Funny how she got her way on things… If I can't flag a taxi, I'll have to go back inside and call one…*

"Need a ride?"

Rory looked up to see a middle-aged man and woman in a black car slowing down. He turned and looked with apprehension as a cluster of feathery white snow began to landed on his scalp and eyebrows. He pondered it and got In the back seat.

"It's only about two miles…"

"Two miles is too far to walk in this weather, sugar…" the woman's raspy voice called to him.

The Electric Eel!

"Thank you for the ride...East Broad Street Olde Towne East please..."

The man let out a whistle. He turned in the driver's seat and looked at Rory and then turned to the woman and nodded in approval. Rory shifted uncomfortably in the small backseat of the car. He zoomed in on a gold bracelet on Rory's arm.

"Whoa! Gotta rich uncle?"

"Nah... Just a friend who works with me..."

"Where's your friend work? For the Rockefellers?" the woman laughed.

The backseat of the car smelled of stale cigarettes and something sour that he couldn't place. Rory shifted in unease as if he shouldn't have gotten in the car with them.

"I work for the Electric Eel downtown... he admitted and then instantly regretted it as soon as it came out of his mouth.

"The bakery?" the man said with an uncomfortable laugh.

"Stop giving him the third degree, dear..." the woman said.

But the man ignored her and said, "That whole street is a cesspool...!"

"How would you know?"

"Not that I *mind* cesspools..." he said with a chuckle. "After I got out of the navy that's all we had!"

"*You did not!*"

"It's right up here..." Rory said pointing to Iris's luxury complex.

"You weren't kidding!" the woman shouted.

The man waved his wrists as if they were on fire. A row of perfectly trimmed topiary bushes lined the front of the ornate taupe building. A fresh dusting of snow coated the tops of everything like cotton batting. A picturesque park and a pond lay behind the high rise with a few yellowish weeping willows.

"Does your friend know you are coming?" the woman called. "Maybe we should stop in to the Electric Eel sometime, dear? Would that be okay?"

The Electric Eel!

"She's home..." he said exiting quickly. "I think that'd be okay...And thank you for the ride..."

"Anytime, sweetheart..." the woman called out the window checking him out. "Anytime...Don't forget your suitcase! What'd you say your name was?"

"Rory..." he said walking away with luggage in tow.

And he felt their eyes upon him as he walked to the front of the building. *Maybe I shouldn't have told them where I worked...* He surmised. The doorman smiled.

"Is Miss Dupeon home?"

"She's inside her suite..."

Rory paused waiting for the car containing the man and woman to exit before going to Iris's apartment. *A little forward...But they seemed nice enough!* He rationalized. *Funny how their jalopy stood out in front of this place!* He noted as the doorman walked him down the hall.

"Miss Dupeon..." he called. "Mr. Childs is here..."

He looked down at Rory's casual clothing and cheap old suitcase compared to his own attire of epaulettes and velvet but said nothing. A fire glowed orange in the hearth on the far side of the room but the room remained cool. A thick red and white Persian rug was under his feet nearby. The doorman nodded and turned to exit with perfect posture.

"Thank you..."

"Iris?" Rory called. "It's me...Rory...I came to stay a little bit..."

Just then a low growl emanated from the hall. Peaches lowered his long muzzle, the fine hairs on the back of his neck rising. Then the dog stopped and hung his head as if ashamed in realization and walked slowly to Rory's arms.

"Peachy it's me..."

The hound wagged his curled tail and allowed Rory to embrace him. Rory began to panic, searching the palatial space for its owner. Peaches seemed relieved in his company, but his dark almond shaped eyes remained alert.

"Iris…"

Then he heard the sound of running water coming from somewhere in the apartment. The bathroom door was open with a crack, and he pushed in, not wanting to startle her. A pool of water sloshed on the marble floor as the tub overflowed.

"Iris!" he said running to her.

A sea of bubbles and the smell of something feminine and floral wafted out of the water. Her head was to one side, her ear against her shoulder. As he reached up to turn the tap off, she stirred.

"What the?"

"It's me…You left the water running…"

"I had too much wine… I thought you were a rapist…" she chuckled. "Or that Sid slipped me something…"

He couldn't tell if she was kidding but he found little humor in it. Gently he reached up and touched her face and then reached for a white towel to sop up the water on the floor. Peaches moved closer to nuzzle his master's navel.

"I'll be staying here for a few days… I had a big fight with my parents…" he explained.

"Peachy Poo Poo and Rory…" she whispered, still half out of it. "Here to take care of me…Don't leave me…"

"I won't. I promise…"

FORTY-SEVEN

*a*s winter settled on central Ohio, a new group gathered on the street outside the Electric Eel. Unlike the men they were not interested in carousing with buxom women or drinking and unlike the women who frequented this place they were older and dowdy with only their ankles and faces exposed. The two women in charge wore unflattering monochromatic two-piece dresses the color of steel wool, pea coats and chunky sensible square toed shoes.

"Intelligence knows no gender!" another woman in a floppy white hat shouted through an acoustic megaphone.

"Lips that touch liquor shall not touch ours!" a younger woman in a lavender cloche hat shrieked.

Orville who had been standing in the bakery, heard the commotion and went outside. A throng of matronly women spotted him and blocked the bakery window. He opened the door in dismay.

"Damn Protestant Teetotalers..."he muttered with no effort to keep his cool.

A group of people with no connection to any of the businesses on the street walked by. The women immediately bombarded them with literature. A few on the street took it while others walked away swiftly.

"Your husband..." a pamphlet announced with a picture of a penniless man holding a beer bottle..."Our husbands..." a second frame informed them of a wealthy man holding a Bible.

"The devil's orchard..." Orville read, ripping it up. "You got your right to vote! You got your Prohibition! What more do you dames want? Now! Off my property!"

"We *would*...But us dames want the treachery of the Devil's fire water to stop...And it continues!" the leader of the shouted at him. "Everyone knows this is a street is a den of inequity!"

As if on cue, two slender men slid through the door of Marie Toussad's and froze. Without hesitation the women pounced on them. Orville, too paused.

"Do your wives know where you've been?" one of them asked. "Do they know you could be bringing home social diseases? Do your *children* know where you are? Do you even *have* wives? Where's my camera?"

"And we can place all of this debauchery at the foot of places like *this!!*" she pointed to the Electric Eel. "All the social ills of domestic violence, poverty, fatherlessness, and pornography can all be laid at the feet of the consumption of alcohol!"

"We're a bakery..." Lobelia added.

"*Right!* As a woman you'd think she'd know better...But she too has been corrupted by the almighty dollar...And by the almighty lure of spirits!"

All of a sudden two police officers appeared on the street. Orville gulped and put his palms up to show them he was unarmed. One of the ringleaders gave a smug grin and folded her arms across her large bosom.

"Arrest them! Last I remember it is illegal to sell and distribute alcohol in this State of Ohio... The birthplace of the Temperance Movement! And last I remember pornography is *too*!"

"You are disturbing the peace!"

"We have the right to protest..."

"*Peacefully!* Now leave us to do our job or I'll haul all you worthless broads downtown!"

Orville returned the smug sentiment from before and walked back inside. He and Lobelia chuckled as they started their rounds for the night. Outside the women balked as they were shuttled off the property without further incident.

Inside manic music pulsed through the small space. Soon Trixie, Iris and other young women in short skirts grabbed their knees and performed a new peppy dance. A feather on Trixie's headband bounced up and down like a pompadour. Fringed vacillated off the backs of Iris's dress shimmering in the bright artificial lights as they performed the Charleston. Their eye make-up was dark and spidery, their lips petite and bright red.

"Beautiful girls! Beautiful job!"

And then Rory joined and soon did a lot of other men. A drum beat kept time along with a cymbal as the band had grown from four members to seven. Soon most everyone was dancing and those who remained seated at the bar applauded.

"Drinks on us!" Orville said reaching for a magnum of champagne and uncorking it.

The Electric Eel!

A long stream of champagne plumed in an arc over the sink as he poured the bubbly into several voluptuous flutes. To his delight Trixie approached him and tasted the champagne on the tips of his fingers. He tasted it too and smiled.

"Ahem..." Edgar warned as Poppy approached.

"Sorry..." he said with eyes blazing with wanderlust and inebriation.

Iris appeared, her cropped finger-waved hair plastered to her scalp with sweat. Orville handed her a small flute of the last of the champagne. She sipped it, the bubbles tickling her nostrils.

"Wish we could make mimosas!" Trixie called in a tipsy gratingly high voice.

"Let's put that on our list! They haven't banned orange juice yet have they?"

"Not yet..." Lobelia laughed sipping a rare taste of alcohol.

And then a banging noise broke through the festivities. And then another! Tiny took two steps back as the wood in the center door buckled in the middle.

"Raid..." he began.

But it soon became clear this was no raid. A large instrument with a ten-pound sledge came through, missing his knee by centimeters. *What the Hell?*

"Just a bakery, huh?" the voice on the other end of the tool called.

And then he watched through the hole in the door as she placed the hammer down and ran out the front. To their horror, a group of the same women as from earlier were standing in the street with a flatbed truck. Quickly they unrolled casks off the truck and rolled them into the streets and uncorked them.

Thirty seconds later a group from the Electric Eel gathered outside in the cold. Iris and many of the women in short skirts shivered as Orville stepped forward. A lake of hoppy liquid began to pour down the sewers like motor oil.

"Here's your bathtub gin!"

"Alcohol is poison! Don't drink poison!"

And then the young woman in the purple cloche hat ran inside and grabbed the sledge hammer and hefted it back outside. When satisfied that enough people were watching she swung it into the window of Marie Toussad's Gallery. Two men inside stepped back in horror as glass flew in from the street. Orville watched in horror as she aimed it toward the bakery window.

"Get down!" Tiny screamed, grabbing her forearm.

"Drink the Devil's crowbar and get smashed!"

But she was clearly out gunned as he took it away from her with ease. All of a sudden several men ran out of Marie Toussad's and scattered along with an elderly Chinese man and woman who stood firm. The Asian couple noticed the damage and began screaming at the women.

"What are you doing to our store?"

"You area peddling in filth!"

Then they watched as several women dashed inside the speakeasy and grabbed whatever bottles they could find and threw them in the street. The distinct smell of hops came next as the bottles exploded in the cold and fizzed. The street reeked of a distillery as broken glass covered everything.

Next, they unrolled two more oak barrels of brown liquid off the truck and uncorked them like a spring. *Where did they get those?* Someone wondered.

"Recognize these, Mr. Alfonso?"

Orville reddened in realization. *They took them out the back door!* He thought. But before he could react, two police sirens whirred in the street.

"Don't admit to anything…" he whispered to all from the Electric Eel.

"What's all the hubbub?" the police officer from before inquired. "I thought I asked you ladies *not* to come back here?"

"Mr. Alfonso is operating an illegal speak-easy! A blind pig! And that's just half of it! Gambling! Prostitution! Monstrous exotic fish! They've got a whole circus in there! And we won't stand for it!"

"We have no idea where all this alcohol came from! They brought it all in!"

"I'm sure! We'll get to you later..." he said turning to the women. "In the meantime, you ladies, can come with us downtown...!" he said forcing them into the back of the patrol cars. "Mr. Alfonso? Don't go anywhere and don't touch anything till we get back!"

FORTY-EIGHT

"You're lucky you got off with just a fine..." Carlotta reminded her son. "Why do you think *I* got out of there when I did?"

"Those women were savages!" he said pretending to swing a sledgehammer like a swashbuckler.

"When will you reopen again...Do you know?" Edgar asked his brother.

"I think we should just cut our losses and close... Now that they know where we are..." Poppy said to her husband.

Orville looked at his wife with clear annoyance. She stirred her coffee and said nothing further. *It's not that he hadn't thought of it...*

"In answer to your question...I can open anytime I want... They couldn't prove *we* provided the alcohol! The roulette wheel is on hiatus, unfortunately...Mr. LaRocca told Tiny he'd take care of it..." he said brightening. "And they told Lobelia we could still keep the bakery...We do need to get a new center door..."

"What about Mrs. Toussad's or whatever that place is called?"

"*Marie* Toussad's" he corrected.

"Closed... But that couple who owns it, Mr. and Mrs. Ping, is pretty unscrupulous...As of yesterday the Teetotalers' lawyers want them deported..."

"Typical..." Edgar mouthed. "I'm going out to get some air..."

Silently, Edgar fastened his pants over his artificial leg and then put on his boots. *Weird to have to put on two shoes now...* He thought thinking of the closet full of mismatched pair that lay on the other side of the wall.

"Do you want me to go with you?" Poppy called.

"No. I want to be alone..."

But secretly he yearned for her company. *Craved* it...Quickly his tied his snow shoes and pulled on his tan overcoat. Poppy gave a confused hurt little look. He smiled at her softening like room temperature butter. His brother bristled and waited for his brother to get out of earshot before he spoke.

"If you want to be with a cripple be with a cripple..." he said over his coffee with surprising calm.

"But-"

"And I don't care if he does have a new leg... he'll *always* be a cripple..."

Before he could say anything further, Poppy went into the other room and burst into tears. Orville pretended not to notice and disappeared somewhere in the house for his morning routine.

Outside, Edgar walked to the familiar open field behind the familial property. A thick coating of ice lined everything in sight, and the feeling beneath both his shoes was somewhat unfamiliar to him. As always the fear of falling stayed with him, the thought of landing on the ice like a scarecrow and the even bigger phobia of Orville finding him and laughing at his expense and begrudgingly helping him up lingering. And there was always Poppy...*Who doted on me more than she did her husband...*He stepped carefully.

A perfect blanket of winter snow painted the landscape. Out here the houses grew few, and the land widened. He knew it all too well...*Just a different season...*

His grandfather's Duryea sat frozen like a folly. *America's first gas-powered automobile...*Papi always bragged. Its four huge, disarticulated spoke wheels stuck out of the snow like Cinderella's carriage; the vehicle's front ankle connected like a chicken bone. The car's once elegant brocaded black interior had faded into obscurity, the wood and leather eroding quickly in the elements on the ground.

The Electric Eel!

"Get in!" his brother's voice prodded from his childhood. "Grandfather says it can go sixty-five miles per hour!"

"No, Orville..."

"Stop being a baby..." his friend Sid added in with a jeer.

And he felt the tug on his right arm, drawing him in, even though he knew it was wrong. The ride had been enjoyable...*At first...*He thought. Two brothers joyriding in the old car with a friend... The sun bright overhead.

"Isn't this fun, Edgar?"

"Slow down..."

*And then he lost control...*A nauseating spin as if he were in a clothes dryer hung in his eyes and sinuses. He recalled the look in his older brother's eyes, wild and unfeeling but clearly enjoying the rush...*Like a roller coaster instead of a tragedy enfolding...* And then the car flipped ejecting them both. Orville landed unscathed nearby; however, the car's axle rolled to the right pinning his right thigh against the ground...

A few hours later he woke up in the hospital with a nurse in crisp white pinafores and a stately doctor in a tie standing over him. As a kid he remembered looking down at where his right leg had been, a cute little ossified stub in its place...*Like a hotdog he'd seen a butcher shop window...*His mother looking away, unable or unwilling to process what her eldest son had done. His father and grandparents were in tears.

"You've had an amputation..."

The words echoed in his subconscious like the ring of an ominous bell. *I was too young to recognize their significance. My life would never be the same...*

"It was an accident..." his mother rationalized to Orville. "He shouldn't have gotten in there with him!"

"Orville shouldn't have been driving...He's lucky he wasn't decapitated!" his grandfather scolded her. "And we have to have a word with that Clark boy's mother!"

All of a sudden the sound of footsteps interrupted Edgar's stroll down memory lane.

But Edgar didn't have to turn to know who it was... The smell of rose soap and lavender lingered, giving its origin away immediately.

"He was going too fast, Poppy..." he said staring ahead. "I didn't want to go with him..."

"I know..." she said putting her hand on his shoulder.

Meanwhile Orville shaved his face and watched from the bathroom window as the distinct form of a tall man and a petite woman in a long coat came into view. Quickly he rinsed his razor and dried his face. A speck of blood began to form on his cheek and then dotted the towel.

"I'm sorry..." she said embracing her brother-in-law.

"Thanks..." he said leaning over and kissing her forehead.

FORTY-NINE

"*T*ime for work, Iris!" Rory called.

But she remained unmovable like a sullen teenager. Peaches the Afghan Hound looked at him with trepidation as if torn between his master and Rory. *Maybe if I start coffee...*Rory thought.

"I'm not going to the Electric Eel..." she moaned, her classic New York accent definite. "Ever..."

"You don't mean that..." he said babying her more than he intended.

"You're right. They need me...I just need a little pick me up..." she said opening one eye.

Rory gave her a look of horror as she sprang out of bed. Her pale nightgown flew behind her like a cape as she moved. She put her finger out and reached for the phone.

"I'll call Jib!' she said.

"You *can't* call Jib...*Remember?*"

She thought of her mother going into the club...And frowned...*Don't remind me...*

The Electric Eel!

"I'll just pay him more...Money talks, right?" she said stripping off her night clothes and changing into something smashing. "Oh! *Thank you*...Rory!"

"But you can't do that...Remember what the doctor said? Maybe it's best if you *do* stay here..."

And then her mood changed as if suddenly he was the worst thing on the planet. Her eyes darkened slowly like a panther. He stepped back afraid of her.

"Well! I'll just have the pharmacy deliver it to me!" she said pushing passed him to the phone. "Best part about being rich! Driver! Can you be here in ten minutes?"

Rory tried to redirect his friend's conversation to anything other than substance abuse; but, it was *all* she could talk about in the car. He motioned to the driver who was listening in on her conversation, but she prattled on. She lit a long cigarette to calm her nerves, but it did little to assuage her anxiety.

"What was that guy's name who worked for Mr. LaRocca? The young guy who had a thing for me..."

Rory shrugged and looked out the window. A cluster of feathery white snow began to fall and then blocked his view of the street. Iris looked over and him, suddenly self-aware.

"Are you mad at me?" she asked blowing a smoke ring out of her mouth.

"No..."

"I love you..." she mouthed.

He nodded, biting his tongue. Next, she reached for her compact and fixed her ashy hair and red lipstick. The stale taste of tobacco lingered in her mouth, and she stuck her tongue out gagging.

"Almost there..."

A dusting of snow coated the front of the Electric Eel as they got out. A large plywood board covered the front of Marie Toussad's gallery with a few ominous grey nails. A sad group of lonely men waited in the corner.

The Electric Eel!

The sound of music pulsing announced that they had started without her. Rory gulped but Iris was unfazed. Iris slithered in the front door passed the bakery case. Like the business next door, a large patch job was secured over the base of the door.

"Tiny it's me…"

"You're late!" Eugenia barked to Rory.

"Oh good! You're here! Get those tables bussed!" Lobelia told him.

"You know you don't *have* to work…" Iris whispered to him.

But he ignored her and started his usual routine. *Neither do you!* Lobelia handed him a white apron and he nodded in gratitude, thankful to be doing something with which he was familiar. Undaunted, Iris sauntered to the stage.

"Where were you?" Jib snapped.

"I know you don't *have* to work but the some of us *do*…" Freddy added turning away to polish his clarinet.

What's that supposed to mean? She recoiled. Only Wallace smiled and continued playing.

"Got any more of that stuff?" she whispered to Jib placing a handful of bills in front of him. "Is that enough? Did my mother give you more?"

"I don't want your money…" he said storming off. "I'm done with that stuff, and I'm done with you!"

"I'll take it!" Eugenia said listening in.

"Oh who asked you?" she snapped grabbing the money.

Iris spotted a customer at a corner table drinking something red. Quickly she sat down as if nothing had happened and motioned to Orville. Orville raised his eyebrow surprised.

"I'll have what she's having! On me!"

"Aren't you going to sing?" he whispered to her.

"They don't need me!" she said throwing her hands up.

The Electric Eel!

"Is she no longer with the band?" Lobelia asked.

"So it seems..." he said passing her by. "Bloody Marys all around...!"

Iris listened to the music and tapped her foot in time. Some of the songs she knew and hummed and others she did not. A second later the drinks arrived and the older lady at the table smiled as she sipped. The taste of acid coated her palette.

After a few minutes of getting tipsy she spotted someone in her periphery. A young man in suspenders and a flat cap. As Iris walked up to him, he straightened his spine and blushed. *Excuse me...*She whispered to the woman...

"Hi...Maynard...?"

"Heyward Robinon...But everyone calls me catfish," he corrected motioning to his curled mustache. "Iris, right?"

"You're remembered! Sorry about that *Heyward! Er catfish...*"

"That's okay..."

He gave her an awkward half smile. Iris waved her hands, pretending not to notice his mal ease. Then he stared at her beautiful oval baby doll face entranced.

"Do you think you could get me more of that stuff you got from Mr. LaRocca?"

"I don't know..." he said with a frown.

Iris gave him a little pout. Heyward bit his lip, feeling a little guilty. With gentle precision, she touched his chest with her palm.

"Why not?"

"Mr. LaRocca said we were out of that business..." he informed her. "And any of us who did could get in serious trouble..."

She stuck her lip out again. He felt bad for her. Effortlessly she batted her eyelashes again and looked into his eyes.

"I'll try..."

"Oh! *Thank you!*" she said with glee. "And I promise I won't say anything..."

Feeling better, Iris sat back down. By the time she returned, another round of the bright red drinks were in front of the table, a stalk of bright green celery in each. Iris sucked on a piece of ice and looked in Heyward's direction.

"Who's that?" Rory asked.

Is he jealous? Iris wondered. *Have I turned the corner with him?* Iris waved to the young man across the room.

"Heyward... The guy I told you about..."

"Well I'll leave you be..." he said turning from her.

"Where's Peachy?" she asked as if talking about their child.

"Sleeping behind the screen..." he said humoring her and walking away in frustration. "He's being a good boy..."

She looked at the old lady sipping the Bloody Mary next to her and chewed on a bite of celery. The woman sunk deeper into intoxication. Her words were a slurry hodgepodge as she talked to Iris.

"You're an attractive girl... Let me give you some advice...They never leave their wives..."

"Oh..." Iris said laughing. "I don't think I have to worry about that with Rory...But thank you..."

Iris stood, suddenly bored with the conversation. The woman closed her eyes and drifted a little, pretending not to notice as Iris walked back to the stage where the other musicians stood. Jibs and Freddy gave her the cold shoulder.

"I can sing again..."

"Good for you..."

*Rich, bitch...*He mouthed. When Freddy did not meet her gaze either Iris decided to sit on the piano bench next to Wallace.

"Hey there, sister!" he called without a hint of malice.

She watched as his long fingers stretched over most of the eighty-eight keys. With both pinkies he played keys on both sides of the keyboard. She hummed a little tune.

The Electric Eel!

"Very nice..." he said complimenting her voice.

As Iris stood she realized she was very drunk. Her knees bowed a little as she stood in the middle of the dance floor and for a moment she wasn't sure if they would hold her. Like a newborn calf she wobbled, searching for Rory. Up ahead two men snickered. *Are they laughing at me?* She couldn't tell.

"I'm going home..." she told him. "Where's Peachy?"

He looked up from the table in annoyance. *She's drunk and repeating herself...*He pointed to the stage. The dog stirred on his hind quarters and turned in her direction, the small hairs on the back of his neck and tail standing up.

"Will you call my driver?" she asked Tiny. "Let's go, Peaches..."

"Sure..."

"I'll be outside..."

As they walked outside, Iris noticed the drop in temperature instantly, the capricious nature of February Central Ohio weather. Despite the chill on her skin, her esophagus was hot with the taste of vodka, tomato juice and Tabasco. She felt the urge to wretch but stifled it. *I'll never drink tomato juice again...*She vowed.

As she moved she barely noticed the empty shell of Marie Toussad's Gallery. The red bulb was still in its place, but it had been unscrewed so its light had darkened to burgundy. Someone had scrawled *Keep out!* In red as if written in blood on the boarded-up sign.

Iris shivered and stumbled in the cold. Her precariously high shoes stuck out like stilts on her heels as she toppled. She reached for her dog, and he moved in her direction like a steed allowing her safe passage.

All of a sudden several opportunistic customers of the now defunct peep show were on her. Vaguely she recognized one of the faces as that of Sid Clark. Her heart sank as four sets of hands were on the top of her body holding her head into the snow. One of the men cupped her right breast and tugged at her shirt.

The Electric Eel!

Then, at lightning speed, Peaches was on them, snarling and growling with white pointed teeth. Sid recoiled at first at the sight of the beast but then pushed him off. Soon the dog was back on him biting at whatever he could latch onto.

"Don't hurt him!"" she shrieked.

Tiny and Eugenia heard the commotion and raced outside. Iris was on her back with several men tearing at her expensive clothing and her dog snapping his jaws down in protection. Tiny reached for two of the men and tossed them off her easily like rag dolls. Soon Lobelia and others from the bar joined outside.

"Get off her!" Eugenia shouted

"They tried to rape me..." she wailed.

"He bit me!" Sid exclaimed, picking himself off the concrete, nursing his hand.

As he looked down blood began to trickle down the side of his forearm. He winced as the other men, too, had sustained dog bites. Long streams of crimson began to form in the snow like a crime scene.

"Come on, Peachy!" Rory called to the hound with open arms.

Tiny helped Iris stand and led her back inside the bakery. The men's sweat and pheromones lingered on her clothing. Without ceremony she vomited into the wastebasket nearby, the acrid taste of tomato juice and spices heaving out of her mouth as she reached for the dog. Meanwhile Peaches kept watch out the window, barking and snapping at the men through the glass, his eyes nearly black with adrenalin.

"Mutt's probably rabid..." Sid stammered.

"I highly doubt it..."

"I'm calling the police..." Lobelia said looking to her boss.

But this time Orville did not resist and went back inside with a sigh. *Just another day at the Electric Eel...*He thought.

Rory caught her inside. His dark eyes were filled with worry. A few particles of snow were still in her hair, and he wiped them off. In the near distance a long black car appeared in front of the place and for a second he thought it may the police.

"Your driver's here..." Tiny informed her.

"Let's get you home..."

FIFTY

"All right, fellas!" a policeman barked at the rest of the men who were hanging around the street in front of Marie Toussad's. "Marie's is closed! And until it reopens you have no need to be here! And *if* it opens you won't be welcome to loiter at all hours! Now out! Or you'll be visiting Mr. Clark and the others in county lockup!"

"And now for you, Sid..." the other officer said.

"This place is a cesspool!" Sid Clark responded.

"Then why do you keep coming back?"

For this Sid had no answer...Pointing to the tops of his wrists instead at several angry welts. Blood began to form.

"Her dog bit me!"

"Good!"

"Take him downtown and book him. I'll head over to Miss Dupeon's to take a statement..."

Two miles away Iris recovered in her Olde Towne East penthouse. Rory wrung out a cool cloth and placed it on her forehead. Iris's eyes were heavy, the result of a sedative the pharmacist had sent in.

"I'll never drink tomato juice again..." she kept repeating.

"That's probably a good idea..."

The police officer stared up in awe at the building where Iris resided. *What's a woman like this doing hanging out at the Electric Eel?* He thought like everyone else who saw her life outside the auspices of the bar. *Everyone knows it's a speakeasy...*

The Electric Eel!

"I'm here to see Miss Veronica Iris Dupeon..." he informed the doorman. "I'm with the Franklin County Sheriff's Office..." he said removing his hat.

"I'm not sure she's taking visitors..." he said without moving.

"I'll make it quick. I just need to take a statement..."

The doorman sighed and led him down the hall with skepticism. As he opened the door a familiar Deusenberg appeared directly in front of the building. Quietly he hid his apprehension as the dog came forward to investigate them and the officer put his hand out to allow him to sniff.

"Miss Dupeon! You've got company!"

"Who is it?"

"An officer of the law to take a statement..." he said in that flat aristocratic way he always spoke. "And your parents are here it looks like..."

"Why are my parents here?" Iris called in a shrill voice. "*Who* called them?"

"They are your emergency contact..."

"Get *out!*"

Without getting out of bed, Iris threw a pillow across the room. The officer approached her with caution the way one might an animal in a trap. Rory stood between his friend and the door.

"They tried to rape me!"

"Can you identify the man who attacked you? Or any of the others...?"

"Sid Clark! Now out!"

Before she could expand further, her mother's contrary face appeared at the end of the bed. Like two bull moose they locked eyes from across the room. Iris's father broke the tension and stepped between them.

"So glad you're okay, kitten..." he said kissing her on the forehead.

"Thanks, daddy..."

"And your mother and Rory and all of us are here to help you..."

The Electric Eel!

Fearing he'd lost control, the policeman pulled out a pen and pad and began asking the young woman a few questions. *While I still have the chance...* He thought.

"How many of the men attacked you?"

"Three or four... It all happened so fast..."

"Did they force themselves on you, Miss Dupeon?"

"They tried..."

"It's not her fault... It's that awful place... It has an effect on all of us..." Mrs. Dupeon sat patting her daughter's hand. "But that part of her life is over...Now...Now... No more talk of that Eel place..."

Iris sprang up as if suddenly possessed. Her mother rolled her eyes nonplussed by her daughter's theatrics. Quickly she pulled the covers over her head in a childish way that made her father chuckle.

"Can we talk about this later? My daughter has been through a lot...Haven't you, kitten?" Mr. Dupeon asked with his usual condescension.

*He talks to her the way she talks to that dog...*The officer thought. *And she's having none of it...*

*They must be loaded...*He thought looking at a large white and blue Chinese porcelain vase that sat on an equally antiquated table in the hall alongside several other relics he couldn't price but guessed to be expensive... *Too rich for my blood...*

"Well, darling..." his wife said ignoring him. "You know we pay all your bills, and we can't continue to support you if you're going to be at places that are less than savory..."

"But I want to sing..." she said in a half whine/half declaration.

"You have a beautiful voice... Perhaps we can get you in at the Metropolitan? Your mother has connections there...Especially since our considerable donation last year...Of course you'd have to come back to New York with us..."

Iris snorted. Her temples pulsed as if a thousand trains ran between her ears. She looked at the other three and then reached for Rory...*The only person I can truly trust...*

The Electric Eel!

"We'll let you rest... Officer, could we see you in the hallway for a moment?"

The officer moved with hesitation as they led him out of earshot. *I get the feeling that no one tells them no...And Iris is the same way...*

"What can I do for you?"

"It's that dreadful stuff she's been on..." Rory heard Iris's mother whisper.

"*Stuff?* You mean like alcohol...?"

*Everyone takes a sip now and then...*He noted with a nod. *I don't care how illegal it is...*

"Not that kind of stuff...*Worse*..."

She touched her nostrils furtively and then the inside of her arms as if injecting something. The officer pressed his lips together understanding. Rory burned with rage as they were talking about her as if she weren't in the next room.

"She was attacked..." he offered. "But if what you're saying is true: There are places now to help people get *over* things..." he suggested.

"Hospitals?"

"Uh-huh..."

"They have good places right here in Columbus..."

"That guy in there with her is the only friend she has..."

"Is *he* okay? What's his role in all this?"

"He seems to be..." Mr. Dupeon admitted. "But you can never tell with people these days...And he's a part of that vile place too!"

"I see! Well...The hospital thing was just a suggestion..."

"We'll keep that in mind..."

"Thank you, officer..." Mr. Dupeon said extending his hand gentlemanly. "Get some rest, dear... We'll stop in and see you soon..."

Rory decided *not* to relay to Iris what her parents had talked about and instead focused on helping her remain calm. Without thinking she grabbed his hand and kissed it. He allowed the affection and squeezed. While Iris's eyes were heavy, Rory's were wide and alert. *I have to protect her he thought...From all of them...*

And Iris Dupeon fell into a troubled, medically induced sleep...

FIFTY-ONE

Carlotta Alfonso's dreams were anything but serene. Despite medication and copious amounts of wine, prescribed by her physician, something bothered her. *Perhaps it was the heat...?* She wondered, kicking the thick rose-colored comforter off the bed.

But the room was cool now...And it was still there like an incubus. Waiting for her to let her guard down...Like a viper waiting to strike...

As she drifted, a familiar face came into her mind's eye. *Her husband Julius...* Face down the way she'd seen him in the newspaper headline. Multiple stab wounds from several unknown assailants littering his back and arms.

Someone from the Medical Examiner's office had even asked her to come identify him...She'd sent Orville...*Like a coward...But he wasn't fazed by it...Seeing his own father that way...Just inconvenienced to have to go downtown...*

"Your husband is deceased, ma'am..." a serious-faced police officer informed her at her house with reverence reserved for these moments.

She remembered wailing. *The way they had done in the old days...*Her face in her hands...Falling on the ground...*They had sedated her then too...*

"I never wanted that bar anyway..." she muttered in her sleep. "But the prospect of that much money was just too much of a temptation... The idea of becoming wealthy...Too great...And then people were paying for alcohol hand over fist...*Even rock gut!*"

She thought of the elder Mrs. Dupeon now. *She walked everywhere like she owned the place...And maybe she did...*She smiled in her sleep. *And she never had to do anything to earn it...Never had to get her hands dirty by breaking any laws...*

"What's this cocktail, dear?" Julius's voice called to her once she was asleep again.

The Electric Eel!

"It's called an Electric Eel... They served it on the Titanic..."

"Why is it *green?*"

"That's the Pernod... It's French... Mr. Houserman says it's banned in Europe now..." she said growing frustrated. "Are you going to drink it or not?"

He studied it and downed it and then another. Carlotta smirked, satisfied to have gotten her way. Julius's eyes began to get cloudy.

"I was contemplating meeting a few friends on High Street..." he said growing drunker by the moment. "But now I'm tired..."

"You *should* go..."

"It's late...And I can't drive..."

"Nonsense..." she reassured him. "There are plenty of taxis near the university...It'll be good for you to get out...I'll call you one!"

"Okay..."

And then I watched him exit the house... None the wiser... I'd debated stopping him... Like a gangster with a change of heart... But didn't... Never to see him again...

Carlotta's eyes flew open. Her hair was mussed like a discarded bird's nest. The room was stifling. A silver tray of tea and crackers sat nearby.

He was always so gullible! She thought now in her woke state. She pushed it out of her mind and walked to the bathroom to rinse her mouth.

"Maria!" she bellowed to the housekeeper. "Come get this tray!"

"Yes, ma'am..." she called, never questioning her authority.

*None of us are innocent...*She thought rationalizing. *Even Julius...*

She thought of her immediate family now. Her eldest son Orville...The cocky one who can take on anything with a smile on his face...Edgar the sensitive, damaged soul who didn't want people to *think* he was frail...And Irene, her daughter the socialite...

Then she thought of Electric Eel bar that was now raking in tax free cash! *It's never enough...I want more!*

Carlotta's face began to get hot again, a sickening nausea rising in her like toxic fog. Perhaps she had Spanish influenza...Was that still a thing? Her mind trailed off, unsure. But I can't take that chance!

"Maria!" she bellowed into the other room.

"Yes, Ms. Alfonso?" the woman said peeking in the doorway.

"Please call a doctor...And please no more interruptions for today..."

"Yes, ma'am..."

FIFTY-TWO

May, 1923

"Why don't you come to Martha's Vineyard with us?" Mr. Dupeon asked his daughter on the phone early one morning. "That way we can yacht and brunch..."

*There was something phony about people who use the words yacht and brunch as verbs...*Rory thought overhearing the conversation, his interest piqued. Iris didn't seem to notice as she was used to the way her father spoke.

"Too far... And I can't leave Peachy that long..."

"Bring your pooch with you and that friend of yours..."

"No thanks..."

Rory hated to admit that what Mr. Dupeon was proposing *did* sound intriguing. The idea of *yachting* in New England with the wealthiest people he'd ever met sticking with him a moment, the salty air blowing in his hair on the deck of a swanky sea pad. Iris hesitated, but her father prodded, used to getting his way.

"Well then! Come to your aunt's property in Bexley! Now that the snow is melted!"

"Okay..." she said finally agreeing. "We'll have to plan something..." she said trying to get out of it.

*Not so fast...*Her father thought on the other end of the phone. He proceeded as if procuring a business deal.

The Electric Eel!

"We'll see you at noon at your aunt's...I'll send driver..."

Iris placed the phone down slowly as if the phone were leaden and weighing her wrist down. Rory figured she was just being dramatic and watched out of the corner of his eye. She collapsed on her side on the bed a moment as if paralyzed.

"Feed Peachy, would you?"

He nodded, not telling her he had fed the dog *hours* ago...*I'm always one step ahead of her*...She snored a little, still partially hungover.

"Better get ready!" he called an hour later, assuming she was still sleeping.

"I'm up..." she said making her way to the bathroom.

Rory stepped into her spacious walk-in closet. A sea of hats, shoes, jewelry, purses, and seasonal clothing greeted him on all sides. He caught a glimpse of himself in the three-hundred-and-sixty-degree mirror at the end. A petite young man with a receding hairline and a narrow waist and athletic forearms from two years of lifting trays at the Electric Eel stood at the end. He flexed a little.

"What are you doing?" she called.

"I love this color..." he said reaching for a silk aqua blouse and handing it to her.

"It's pretty..." she admitted. "But I'm not going..."

She fell back on the bed again. Rory put the blouse back in the closet and walked to her. She grabbed his hand and pulled him close to her in a ludic way.

"Why not?" he said falling on the bed.

"Because it's dull..." she said. "But you're welcome to go..."

Rory thought of showing up alone at their mansion in Bexley and chuckled. Iris looked at him as if to say: *What's so funny?*

"Nothing...I just can't go by myself."

"Fine!" she said slapping her thighs. "I have no choice!"

Quickly she showered and pulled on the blouse he had picked out earlier. He motioned to a pair of seersucker slacks. Her eyes widened.

The Electric Eel!

"I can't wear those..."

"Why?"

"Cause my mother would flip her wig if I wore pants..."

She reached for a black poplin a-lined skirt with two distinct pockets on each side and a pair of pointed thick Pilgrim-inspired calfskin shoes with a buckle and placed them on the mattress. She pulled on the blouse over her head and stood in front of him in her panties for a minute.

"What are *you* wearing?"

"Your mother's red dress is still in there..." he offered. "You wear the pants and we'll both go in drag..."

Iris pondered it for a moment and then pulled on the skirt and buckled the shoes. She looked down at the skirt and straightened it. The hem of the garment cut off at the top of her calf. Next, she pointed to a lightweight suit of her father's that he left in the back of the closet in case he needed to change.

"He won't mind... Now you can say you wore *both* my parents' clothes..." she said cutting off his next question.

"It's way too long...." he informed her holding it up to his legs.

"Wear your suit from before..." she bossed. "The olive one..."

"All right..."

"Does this look okay? Does it make me look *fat*?"

He shook his head. She stared at him with incredulity. She held up a small bottle of bright red pills.

"You look fine..."

"Fine? No... I need to know... My mother always comments..."

"You look great..."

"Thank you... Any other guy would lie to me to get into my pants..."

A second later a Deusenberg pulled up in front of the building, its hood stretched out

The Electric Eel!

like a panther. Rory held his breath carefully afraid to mar the car. The familiar driver smiled coolly and opened the door. Rory and Iris and the dog climbed inside the back. *It's like a huge leather sofa...* He noticed.

"Ahem..." the driver motioned, eyeing the dog. "Claws..."

Iris reached for a small blanket that was on the floor and placed it under Peaches' feet. The driver smiled in smug satisfaction. *Careful what you say...* She mouthed to her friend.

"The missus said to make sure to tell you *not* to eat before you arrive..." the driver spoke in a surprising amount of words. "She's providing Beluga Caviar and lox...And fresh salmon for the poochie..."

Caviar? Rory thought, growing excited. She placed her hand on his leg, telling him to calm down as if talking to the dog. Rory held his knees in anticipation of what was to come. Iris looked out the window in disinterest.

The air inside the car began to warm slightly as they drove. Signs of spring lined the main boulevard of Olde Towne East...Stubby pastel crocuses with dark green pointed leaves and white and yellow daffodils with flowers like brass instruments blew in the breeze; however, despite the wind, the flowers remained erect, their posture perfect. Delicate bright spring yellow-green leaves darted out the tops of most of the trees indicating new growth.

"Beautiful day...hmm?" the driver said.

"Yep..." she said reaching for her compact and fixing her makeup.

Why is she so chilly with him? Rory wondered. *She's never like that with me...She just says what she wants...What about them makes her so guarded?*

"I love spring..." the driver said forcing conversation.

Figuring it was futile, he got quiet and turned the car north toward Bexley. Here the homes grew far apart, bucolic, and opulent. Most of the estates were behind long serpentine driveways and substantial wrought iron gates. Some of the gates had family names or crests scrawled in iron or gold plating on the front. *Whoa!*

"Almost there..."

The driver pulled the car up the pristine road. Both sides were lined with Hydrangeas, Japanese maples, and fire engine red burning bushes. The ditch in front of the family property came into view along with the largest gate Rory had ever seen. *It has to be twelve feet high!*

In the near distance a palatial estate loomed ahead like something out of a silent movie set. Iris held her breath as the gate opened with a creak. The driver beamed.

"Here we are..."

FIFTY-THREE

They pulled up to the circular driveway in front of the house after what seemed like an eternity. A wide Neoclassical white marble fountain greeted them in the middle of the circle, two Greco-Roman athletic figures holding cups of perpetually filled water in each hand like a tarot card. A series of deep purple petunias ran along the perimeter of the fountain blowing slightly in the slight breeze.

The mansion itself was also white with a roof the color of tomato paste and as wide as a city block. It towered in several tiers over immense ornate Corinthian columns. *How many stories is this place?*

"This is her aunt's *summer* home..." the driver informed them with a wink.

"Thank you, driver..." Iris said politely, swinging her legs out of the car.

"And now for you, sir..."

"Oh, I can get it..." Rory said reaching for the door.

But the driver held it anyway, perhaps out of habit, and then beckoned for the dog. Peaches waited, looked down at the ground and then jumped out of the automobile. Rory looked at the dog and gave him a pat. The smell of clean country air and floral gardens greeted his senses.

"This is beautiful..."

The Electric Eel!

*You aint seen nothing yet...*Iris thought, giving him a coy reserved smile. Up ahead a young man in a blue velvet suit and matching hat held the door. *Why my mother dresses him like an organ grinder monkey I'll never know...*Iris thought.

"This way..." he informed them.

Quickly, they walked up the considerable steps to the massive front double door. The door was also reddish, matching the roof and trim of the house. An enormous Oriental rug and footed antique table met them in the foyer along with Iris's father. Behind him a staircase balanced on either side connected by a grand white and gold landing at the top and a rolled banister on both sides at the bottom. Two arched doorways leading to the rest of the house greeted him to the left and right.

"Welcome..." Mr. Dupeon called.

Just then Rory looked up to see an automobile sized crystal chandelier hanging in the center of the recessed ceiling. The lighting pointed upward at different intervals, glinting in shades of silver, white and gold. A few hints of ruby and sapphire glinted throughout. A series of gold piping ran around the chandelier and the outside perimeter of the room.

"I see you notice our electrolier..." her father informed him. "Been in my wife's family for generations... We just had it shipped here from New York and it seems to work better in here...Originally from France... Hi, kitten..." he said reaching for his daughter.

"Hi, daddy!" she said allowing the embrace for a second.

Rory blushed at his observance. Like his daughter, he was unfazed by wealth or by those impressed by it. As Iris spotted her mother in the entryway she gave a cordial, cavalier smile.

"So glad you came..."

But unlike Iris's father there was not even a *pretense* of affection between mother and daughter. Rory looked up at them. Though Iris resembled her father, she was short in stature like Mrs. Dupeon. Her mother was dressed in a royal purple embroidered gown that gave her a regal majestic look.

The Electric Eel!

"Your brother's here..." her father informed her.

Iris frowned and then tried to hide it. Rory caught her glance. As they stepped up the step to where her mother stood, Rory got the vibe *not* to approach her mother physically. *Like a dignitary or royalty...*

"We may take a dip in the pool later if you'd like to join us..." her father said. "You can borrow one of my suits..."

"Is it warm enough to swim...?" Rory whispered to his friend.

Both of her parents chuckled awkwardly. Rory blushed in embarrassment unsure of what he had said incorrectly. Iris touched the top of his wrist and explained.

"The pool is indoors..." she whispered.

"Oh..."

"Didn't make sense to have an outdoor one in Ohio... But we had one in Saint Tropez!" her father said. "Ah! Who knows! Maybe we'll tell your aunt to put one in! Have you been to Saint Tropez?"

"No..."

"We'll have to take you..."

"Where *is* Auntie?" Iris asked.

"In Sante Fe with her new beau..." he said with a dismissive wave. "You know her! Husband number three..." he said putting up the appropriate amount of fingers.

Iris and her dad are similar... Rory noticed. Just then an athletic man a little older than Iris appeared behind Mrs. Dupeon.

"Gerard Dupeon..." he said extending his hand to him.

"Rory Childs..."

Gerard withdrew his hand and pushed his perfect golden hair back away from his brow. He stuck his cleft chin stuck out a little as if pondering something but said nothing further. Iris rolled her eyes.

"Hi, kid!" he said reaching for his sister.

The Electric Eel!

"Hi..." she said shying away.

"Before we swim your mother has had a feast prepared!" her father informed them with a clap of his hands. "I know you're supposed to wait an hour after eating...But..."

"I am a little hungry..."

They led them into a dining room that was, in actuality, the size of a banquet hall. Long silk drapes the color of caramel candy hung from the top of the huge bay windows behind a long white carved inlay table with silver platters of seafood on ice and small three-tined forks. Rory waited for Iris's lead before approaching anything.

"Driver will take pup while we eat..."

"I promise to bring him back in one piece..." he said grabbing the leash and walking away.

"This all looks amazing... Thank you!" Rory said with genuine gratitude.

Iris studied the various decapods and fish that were placed neatly on each platter. *I'm surprised cause most of this isn't kosher...*She thought reaching for a piece of shrimp.

"Try the caviar, dear boy!" Mr. Dupeon said.

With great care Rory reached for a small silver plate and examined the fare. The eggs were nestled in a ceramic bowl inside another receptacle filled with ice. He reached for a small spoon made of bone lined in gold and dipped a small amount of the delicacy on his bone China plate.

"Great with the toast points..." Gerard leaned over to inform him.

He tasted the salty roe and savored it. He held his breath, allowing it to linger on his palette a minute. He decided he did like it though it was a little fishy.

"Do you like it?"

"I do... It's cold!"

"You *should* like it... It's beluga...And it doesn't freeze if kept above twenty-degrees," her father said.

Meanwhile Iris pointed to a strips of something fishy and charred with lemon. The

The Electric Eel!

seafood was long and fileted thin as if with a long knife. Iris hesitated.

"What is *that*?" she asked not recognizing the meat.

Her mother dodged her as the valet from before handed her a small plate. She smiled politely. Iris persisted with her line of questioning.

"Anguilla..." she said finally. "With wild rice..."

"*Eel?*"

She nodded and walked away. Iris turned her nose up and burned with rage at this obvious slight and wandered away from the fish. Rory felt the tension immediately.

"She's never served this stuff *before*..." her brother said.

There's a reason for that... Iris thought. She put her seafood plate down and walked to the other side of the room to get a slice of fresh bread and cheese. Her father reached for a small portion of the eel and picked at it.

"You can't serve it raw like sushi cause the eel blood is toxic if not cooked..." her father told Rory. "But it's delicious grilled! The eat it in Italy all the time!"

Just then Rory spotted a blond blur in the window. He looked up in panic as Peachy bolted in ecstasy across the yard, his tongue and hair flying. Mr. Dupeon put his hand on his shoulder.

"Oh he can't get out if that's what you're worried about... It's all fenced in... And driver is watching him! He watches Rowena's Papillons all the time!"

"Oh! He'll chase anything so be careful!"

"Most sight hounds have a high prey drive... Thankfully I had him put her dogs inside before you came... I have him bring him in shortly before it gets too hot..."

"Thanks..."

"Now! Shall we commence to the pool?" Gerard asked.

"Absolutely..."

"I have a suit that will fit you, young man..." her father said. "Valet, will you pick one out for Mr. Childs?"

The Electric Eel!

The man servant nodded. Together they followed her father down the corridor. Several niches in the shapes of seashells lined the wall containing small sculptures, vases, and other various pieces of art. Rory walked carefully as if in a museum, afraid to touch anything.

Together they passed quickly through two sitting rooms and a music room. *One formal and one informal...*Iris remembered. A row of striped Parisian inspired one armed chairs with bowed legs sat on either side of the room. A few enormous family portraits in heavy gold frames hung above them.

As they reached the back of the house the smell of chlorinated water hovered somewhere. An Olympic sized swimming pool with teal and white majolica tile came into view underneath a large glass ceiling and a diving board. Several gardens surrounded the outside of the pool room along with a few horse stables. The sky above was a brilliant blue.

"Truly beautiful, daddy..." Iris said.

"Sometimes the horses come right up to the screen. If the glass gets too hot we can put up the shade. It's truly amazing to be in here and watch the rain... Or the stars..."

A second later the servant from before held up two one-piece bathing suits with something like skirts that came down mid-thigh, the kind that looked ridiculous on men in later decades. Rory examined a black and white striped piece and selected it. The valet nodded and motioned to a room behind the pool.

"Back there is a hot tub and a sauna..." Mr. Dupeon said. "You all are welcome to change in either of them."

Once they changed, Iris's father fiddled with a golf club as swinging it. His wife remained on a chaise lounge and said something to her daughter. She looked up slightly as if lifting her head was too much effort.

"Your father *loves* to golf...I told him most country clubs forbid Jews from joining...But at least he can play with the Rothschilds..."

The Electric Eel!

"Are you getting in, dear?"

"No…" she said in a clipped tone.

Gerard hopped in the pool and splashed his sister. His permanently tanned body and bright eyes glistened, the corners of his eyes reddening a little from the chlorine. Iris inched away from him in the shallow end of the pool.

"We're short…Remember?" Iris said referring to her and Rory. "And I don't want my hair wet…"

But her brother persisted like annoying teenager. Just then driver appeared alongside the pool with Peaches in tow. The Afghan Hound immediately ran to Iris and Rory at the end of the pool and wagged his tail. Iris brightened.

"There's my boy!" Rory called.

"So how long have you worked at this Electric Eel place my mother talks about?" Gerard asked the other man.

"A couple years…Iris is a singer…"

"So I've heard…"

"Mind if I pop in sometime?" he asked.

"Sure!" Rory said answering for her.

Iris shot him a look. He shrugged. Next he tugged on his suit a little, pulling it down close to his knees.

"Gerard just graduated from West Point…" his mother broke in from her place beside the pool.

"Congratulations…"

"But his *real* passion is film…" Mr. Dupeon added. "Wants to be the next Cecil B. DeMille…"

"And knowing him… He'll get there!"

*So let me get this straight…*Iris thought getting out of the pool. *He can pursue the film industry and they praise it…But I pursue music and they hate it?*

The Electric Eel!

"Where are you going?" Gerard asked.

"Out..."

The valet handed her a towel and she nodded gratefully and placed it to her forehead. A second later she disappeared into the back room. Rory craned his neck as if checking up on her but did not get out of the water. Iris went inside the unisex bathroom and locked the door.

In near tears, she searched for her clutch. A sea of elaborate black and white marble lined the wash room. Her hands shook a little as she reached inside the purse for a small bottle of pills and a vial of something. Quickly she downed a little bit of each as she listened to the others talking outside the door.

"Speaking of the Electric Eel..." Rowena Dupeon broke in. "I talked to the lady who owns it... She's *lovely*...Alfonso something...Carla...Carlita?"

"Carlotta..." Iris said opening the door, her voice echoing off the tile of the pool house.

"Whatever...It's nice to meet a smart successful business woman...To bad it's in a blind tiger like that!"

"Are you ready to go?" Iris asked Rory cutting her mother off.

"But we just got here..." he mouthed.

"Fine..." Iris said sitting in a chaise a few feet away from her mother.

She folded her arms across her chest and reclined. As the pills began to take effect she dozed. Sensing he had overstepped, Rory got out of the pool and dried off. As he walked to the changing room he thought he spotted the valet eyeing him. He smiled curiously and went inside.

Once he dressed, Rory spotted something red and oval on the floor of the changing room. He picked it up and examined it. *One of Iris's pills...!*

"You ready?" he said waking her.

"Sure... If you want to..."

"You'll have to come back and see the horses..." Gerard informed him.

"Deal..."

"Thank you for having us..." Iris told her family as they got in the car.

"That was lovely..." Rory admitted once inside the car.

"It's a beautiful place..."

Ten minutes later they were back inside Iris's penthouse. Iris began to peel her clothes off in relief.

"Thank you for taking me... Your family seems nice... Especially your brother..."

"He molested me..." she said flatly.

FIFTY-FOUR

Iris was thrilled to be back at the Electric Eel that following Thursday away from the prying eyes of her family. The room was unusually crowded, she noticed. Orville approached her and explained.

"Ever since Mr. LaRocca got the roulette wheel and gaming table back we've been in the weeds..."

Just then Iris spotted someone and walked away from her boss. Catfish, the guy she'd met before. He looked away nervously, shifting the weight on the balls of his feet.

"Did you get the stuff?" she whispered.

"Yes, but just this once..." he whispered. "Please don't ask me again... I could get in real trouble..."

"I promise..." she said putting her palm out of if taking an oath.

With great caution he moved his head and motioned for her to meet him by the restroom. She followed intrigued, waiting for him to give her the contraband. In the dim light, he reached for her palm and slipped her the dope. His hands were damp with sweat.

In return Iris reached for several large bills and exchanged it with him. He nodded as she placed the junk in her handbag. He smiled, relieved the transaction was over. She

The Electric Eel!

kissed him on the cheek.

"So do you want to go out with me sometime?" he asked.

"We'll see..." she said. Sensing his disappointment she added. "Sure..."

"Neato..." he said moving from her.

*But I have no intention of going out with him...*She thought heading for the ladies room. For a second she remembered the changing room at her parents' pool house and then looked up at the low rent bathroom of the Electric Eel. As she snorted the drugs, she wondered: *How did I wind up here?*

The high felt good for a moment but then she realized eventually she'd have to go back out to the main room...*Or someone would have to use the restroom*...A whoosh of blood rushed through her head and for a moment she was afraid she'd teeter backward and hit her head. Then came the inevitable knock at the door...

"One second..." she called in the most natural voice she could muster.

Quickly she flushed the toilet and walked to the small sink to wash her hands. As she opened the door a heavily made-up face peered through. *Ugh! Eugenia!*

"What were you doing in there?" she barked.

But Iris pushed past her without answering. *She probably knows anyhow...* She mused, now high as a kite. She breezed past Rory without stopping.

"Where are you going? You're on in three minutes!" he called.

Iris processed the words slowly as if in a dream. In haste most of the staff zoomed past her with trays and glassware as she walked to the stage. Suddenly a familiar face greeted her at the door. Suddenly she felt sober again.

"Gerard!"

But there was no time to think about her brother...Jib pushed her in the direction of the stage. She faltered on her feet and threw her arms out to steady herself. Wallace began to play but suddenly she forgot the words.

"I've got you..." she improved. "Under my skin..."

The Electric Eel!

But then the audience began to glare at her. Then someone *booed*...Where was that beautiful voice they'd all come to hear? Wallace started over giving her a second chance...But she froze again and hobbled off stage...

"Boo...Get her off the stage!"

"What happened?" Orvile asked.

But she didn't answer and sauntered over to the table, afraid her knees would buckle beneath her. The room began to spin as she sat down. Soon another figure she recognized sat close to her at the end of the table. *Her parent's valet!* What's *he* doing here?

"Did you come with Gerard?" she asked him.

"Nope..." he said. "Here on my own..."

She noticed he was wearing normal clothes and not the goofy get up her mother had preferred. He looked around the room and her eyes fixed to where his gaze was headed. *Rory!*

"What happened?" Rory asked repeating his boss's words to her.

"I forgot the words is all...Could happen to anyone..."

"Hey Rory!" a chipper voice called.

He turned, unused to his name being called here and looked for its source. He blinked, not recognizing the face at first. The man was about his age with dark hair and goatee and blue eyes.

"It's me Scotty...The valet from Bexley...We met at the Dupeon's!"

"Oh!" he said in surprise. "What are you doing here?"

"I came to see *you*, silly!"

Before he could react, a couple sat down on the other side of the table. They, too, stared in Rory's direction. But he couldn't place them either.

"Hi...Rory...Remember us?"

He blinked and then looked at the valet and shook his head. *They do seem vaguely*

The Electric Eel!

familiar... He thought.

"We gave you a ride home!"

Oh no! He thought, remembering. He wanted to die! Iris got up in frustration and he followed her. He put his finger up to the table signaling them to wait.

"Nice that you gotta fucking fan club!" Iris snapped. "What am I? Chopped liver?"

"Now, Iris. You know that's not true..."

"Just need my money and a place to stay? Is that it?" she hissed, loud enough to be heard over the music.

"Iris..."

"Well! You can find your own place! I'm done with you! All of you! Go be with your fucking valet!"

Meanwhile, her brother ordered a few drinks and made himself comfortable. Orville approached him next, not realizing the connection. He handed him a gimlet with a twist of lime.

"My sister is a little...Shall we say? High strung?"

"Ah..." he said. "Nice to meet you...I'm Orville... I own this place..."

"Charmed...I'm Gerard... Iris is my sister..."

"And don't follow me!" Iris shouted.

Quickly she grabbed Peaches' leash and walked out the door. For a second Rory turned, afraid he'd never see her again *or worse*...Something would happen to her...But then he spotted her driver. *At least she's safe...*

"Let her cool off..." her brother advised. "Have a seat..."

"I can't. I'm working..."

"Nonsense!" he said drinking his cocktail. "Why Scotty! What are *you* doing here?"

But the valet shrunk away in search of the reason he'd come. Gerard looked up at where he was heading and motioned to Orville. Orville nodded.

Precisely on time, Madame Beulah approached her usual table. Today she was dressed

The Electric Eel!

in all black with long drippy sleeves and jet buttons. *Like a bat...*

"Tonight the energy is electric...Or shall I say *electric eel?*"

Next, Beulah pulled out a sketchbook and a piece of vine charcoal. All of a sudden people began to chatter. She put her hand up in insistence.

"For this next part I must have absolute quiet!"

To Gerard's amazement, the audience listened. At lightning speed, Madame Beulah began to sketch. Soon her fingers were smeared with black dust. Once she held the drawing up, someone in the audience shrieked.

"That's my sister's face!" a man shouted.

She ripped off the drawing and handed it to him. When they were sure it was safe to make noise, they began to clap. Soon she regained her composure and began to draw again. She closed her eyes and drew from memory.

Outside the Electric Eel, Heyward aka Catfish remained. He had watched as Iris...Or Miss Dupeon, as he had known her walked away with her driver without acknowledging him. He rubbed the toe of his shoe into the ground feeling like he'd been had. *She had gotten what she wanted...*He'd seen it all before... The fractured gait... the slurred words...*Just a junkie with money and expensive clothes!*

"You coming?" one of his buddies from Mr. LaRocca's group called.

"What'd you give that girl?" one of the others demanded as soon as he was out of earshot.

"Nothing! I swear!"

"Didn't look like nothin! We told you we were out of that business!"

"But I didn't..."

"Okay...We believe you!" one of them said patting him on the back walking away.

Catfish held his chest in relief. All of a sudden a car buzzed down the alleyway followed by the sound of fireworks that lit up the night with a bright orange flash. And Heyward was filled with lead...

The Electric Eel!

FIFTY-FIVE

*O*rville Alfonso got out of Trixie's bed at two o'clock in the morning.

Uncertainly he buttoned his pants and pulled his shirt over his shoulders. She sat up on the bed expecting more... *How do you tell someone that's all you want?*

*Thankfully she only lives a hundred yards from the Electric Eel...*He mused. *A great lay but dumb as a bag of hammers...*

"Did you hear gunshots?" she had piped up earlier.

"It's just a car backfiring..."

But he *had* heard them...He just didn't tell *her...She'd be the type who'd keep asking...Or worse make him stay...*

Crime has gotten so bad recently...This never happened before Prohibition...And everyone's in bed with it...

Now there were rumors that *his* employees were dabbling in organized crime...*Tiny working for Mr. LaRocca for example...*He himself had been swayed by the prospect of a roulette wheel...*It was the only way we could reopen after those Temperance Women raided us...We're all up to our neck in it...*

*They'd first approached my own mother...*He gulped. Orville looked out the window at the familiar street where his father had been brutally slain. *Used to be when crimes like that happened people were excited to jump in and help police...Now no one says anything... They're all afraid...*

"Can't you stay?" Trixie whined.

*You know I'm married...*He wanted to say. But once he saw her reflection in the mirror as he tied his tie he couldn't be cruel. *She's sweet...Just naïve...*

"No..." he found himself saying. "I gotta get home, Trix..."

The Electric Eel!

"Okay..." she said drawing the word into two long syllables.

Another now familiar sight appeared on the street in front of the Electric Eel...*A cop car...*He thought wryly. *The alley is cordoned off again...*

"What are you looking at?"

"Nothing... See you tomorrow, babe..."

"Sure..." she said with a sigh.

Quickly he raced down the stairs of her two-story walkup to the street. Trixie waited in the partially open doorway like a forlorn family pet. Orville paused, not wanting to look back at her.

"Take care of yourself, Trixie..."

Orville felt like a heel. *Maybe I should break it off...*He thought. *But I suspect she wouldn't take it well...Once Eugenia and all of them get a hold of this tidbit I'll be the laughing stock...She may even go to Poppy...*

But per Orville's usual, he ran. *Get on with your life, Trixie...*He might tell her. *I'm no good for you...You'll find someone else...You deserve someone who loves you...*He'd said it all before...

"And she'll believe it..." he said to himself.

Just then a police officer he recognized tipped his hat in Orville's direction. Orville gave him wide berth and tiptoed around what was now a crime scene. A large white sheet on two tent poles was placed between the body and the street like a flag of surrender.

"May I ask who it was?" he asked the lawman.

"Heyward somebody... People say he called himself Catfish..."

*Catfish... Catfish...*He said rolling the name over in his head. And then it dawned on him...*The guy Iris was talking to...*

"Another mob hit..."the officer said unimpressed. "Guy never saw it coming...Least they're only killing their own this time...Not my fellow officers..."

Orville winced at this last sentence. Up ahead the building containing Marie Toussad's

The Electric Eel!

loomed... *Now renamed The Peking Massage Parlor...*

"What did you say your name was, young man?" another officer barked at Orville.

"Orville..." he said scurrying away.

As he walked down the street he spotted the other businesses who remained one step of the law like his own...*Mr. Houserman's pharmacy and drugs...The cosmetic counter... A house of ill repute...The Catholic Church across the street that peddled in communion wine and bingo...*He stopped to examine the last building on the corner.

"*Waverly Brothers Funeral Home...*" a sign announced.

*Another speakeasy...*He remembered. *What a perfect front for bootlegging...If the feds ever go in there you could always say they were disturbing the dead...*He'd heard rumors they were transporting bottles of hooch in the bottom of caskets and the back of hearses in broad daylight right under everyone's nose...*And no one thinks twice about a funeral home getting deliveries at all hours of the night...*

"If you see more pallbearers than usual you know it's a bootleg..." one of his customers had told him.

"Why?"

"Cause that way you know the caskets are too heavy to carry and the bottle doesn't fall out the bottom!"

*There must be a million places like this in the United States right now...All with the purpose of catering to illegal vice...*He thought. He'd heard of cars getting stuck on Lake Erie as they tried to drive to Canada thinking it was frozen...Only to find it wasn't...

"For every prohibition there is an underground..." someone had once informed him.

In the silence of the black night he scanned the corner for his automobile. His parent's black Model T sat where he had parked it several hours earlier...*Technically my father's car...*He thought with some regret. *Not as flashy as the Buick I totaled...But it'll get me home...*

Orville pulled the choke on the car, and it started with some protest. The car's headlamps glowed a second later like two full moons. Soon he was bouncing up the main drag near the State Capitol.

"Almost home…"

At three o'clock he pulled into the driveway and shut the car off. Quietly he pulled the parking brake and walked to the front. Poppy's pristine flower beds rested in the darkness on either side of the walk, waiting for daybreak to come alive again. *I hope everyone is asleep…*

*Poppy never asks where I am anymore…*He noticed, putting the key in the door. His brother was snoozing on the sofa, his artificial leg and a crutch propped up beside him. *Besides…She doesn't want me asking questions either…*He thought with a smile.

A second later he peered in his son's room. But like the others, Alistair was out like a light. Orville pressed his lips together in regret.

He found his wife laying on her side on the mattress. With much effort he reached for her and kissed her on the cheek, not realizing her eyes were wide open. Quickly he removed his clothes to his undershorts and lay beside her. The smell of another woman's perfume lingered in the room.

"Night night…"

FIFTY-SIX

*I*t was four-thirty in the morning by the time Rory graced Iris's penthouse. He sat in the taxi for a moment, pondering his next move. *On one hand, I really enjoyed my time with Scotty…On the other, I want to preserve my friendship with Iris…*

They'd gone to all night café. One of those swanky places that had *no* interest in alcohol. To his surprise, there were many people like he and Scotty…Intellectual young men and women who favored things like poetry and the works of Gertrude Stein and Alice B. Toklas and German Expressionism…

The Electric Eel!

Seems we have a lot in common...We both work similar jobs...With the same types of people...I with Iris and he with Iris's mother...We both love dogs and art...

"The meter is running..." the cabbie said breaking his train of thought with impatience.

"Can you wait? I'll pay you..."

"Five minutes..." he growled.

Rory bounded up to the grand entryway of the building. The usually jovial doorman put his hand up in frigidity and looked up at him. *Uh oh! This can't be good!*

"Nothing personal, Mr. Childs, but Miss Dupeon does *not* want you here..."

"Tell her I need to get my things..." he said beginning to panic.

"Come back later..."

"No...I have nowhere to go... Ask her..."

"Come this way..." he uttered, his voice dropping.

What if she's asleep...Or passed out? Rory wondered as he walked. The doorman rapped on her door gently.

"Go away!" a sharp lucid voice answered through the door.

"Miss Dupeon..." he said. "Mr. Childs is here to collect his things!"

"It's four thirty in the morning! Tell him this not a hotel..."

"She says this is not a hotel..."

"I heard her!' he said pushing past him. "Iris! I just want to talk to you!"

As the door flew open, the dark part of Iris's eyes blazed like a lit coal furnace. She was still in the dress she had worn to the Electric Eel...*A crazy woman in a cocktail dress...*

"What do you want from me?"

"I just want my things..."

Peaches ran to him, but Iris shot him a look. He sunk back on his haunches in confusion, unsure of whose loyalty to which he should remain. Rory encouraged the dog to remain inside.

To their horror, Iris began pitching items of his clothing out the front door. Her mother's red dress and expensive wig came next along with the shoes he had worn on stage the first night.

"You're out of control!" he shouted.

Rory turned to the doorman who put his hands up signaling that he wanted to stay out of it. *He's scared of her!* He thought. *And she's paying his bills!*

"No! You used me! I took you shopping and to my parents to go swimming! I paid for everything you needed on stage! And now you throw me over for my mother's valet?"

"What are you *on*?"

This question only seemed to incense her more. The apples of her cheeks reddened a little. She settled a little.

"I'm not on *anything!*" she lied.

"I saved your life!" Rory reminded her.

"Get out! And don't come back!"

With that she grabbed the items of clothing in her arms and handed them to him. Next she reached for a sack and stuffed them inside. Then she turned to the doorman ignoring Rory.

"Take these and put Mr. Childs back in his taxi..." she said. "And don't let him back on the property..."

"Yes, ma'am..."

Soon after Rory found himself back in the cab, now with a bagful of clothing he'd probably never wear again. The driver turned and exchanged a wry look with the doorman.

"Please don't bring him back!" he told him with a slam of the door. "Mis Dupeon is not well!"

"Where to?"

With much reluctance, he gave the man his parent's address. *I hope I have enough...And they let me in!*

The Electric Eel!

By the time he arrived dawn was beginning to break. *What a night!* Rory reached for the remnants of his belongings that Iris had given him and walked outside. He handed the driver a small amount of money and he nodded. Wait! He mouthed.

Rory's mother appeared in the doorway with arms folded. He let out a sigh of exasperation and walked like the prodigal son up to his familial home. She said nothing and allowed him back inside.

"Tough night?" his father called from the bedroom.

"Thank you for letting me come back…"

"Your father says that this is it… You can't just come and go as you please…" she said storming off but remaining in earshot. "Now keep it down and let him get ready for work in the morning!"

When he was sure she was gone, he reached in his pocket for something crinkled. A series of numbers had been scrawled on the paper. He reached for the phone in the hall and dialed.

"Operator? This is Rory Childs…Trying to reach Scotty…"

"Hold please…" a nasally woman's voice said.

Rory paused, holding his breath in anticipation. A male voice came on the other line a second later. He felt a little better.

"Scotty? It's Rory…From the Electric Eel…Sorry to call you so early…"

"Hi, Rory…" he said with a flat affect.

"What's wrong?"

"Mrs. Dupeon called and told me not to come in today…"

"What?"

"Iris got me fired!"

FIFTY-SEVEN

The next day Rory found himself at The Electric Eel with no Iris *or* Scotty. *I don't even* have Peaches to keep me company anymore...He mused. *Maybe I should get a dog...*

"Has anyone seen Iris?" he asked around.

"Not all day..." Lobelia said.

Who cares? Eugenia thought. *Good riddance...*

"She didn't treat you very well..." Eugenia opined. "And that guy who got shot out there? What was his name? *Catfish?* Rumor is he got killed for selling her that stuff..."

"I'm not sure that's true..."

Rory walked away in annoyance. She shrugged. *Suit yourself...*

Why do I still feel protective of Iris? He wondered. *She ditched me without a place to stay and threw clothes at me.* He yawned. *And then I had to go crawling back to my parents...Perhaps it hasn't sunk in yet...*He rationalized.

Up ahead he saw another woman standing at the stage. Jib and Freddy whispered something as if afraid to say it in his presence. A thin light skinned black woman in a shimmering white gown and matching pearl earrings was in her place.

"Malka will be filling in for Iris..."Jib informed him finally.

"Oh? Is Iris coming back?"

But they said nothing and walked away. Rory looked up the woman who towered over him. *Is she a model? She must be almost six feet tall!*

"Rory..."

"Malka..."

Unlike Iris's speaking voice, hers was deep and soothing...Like a man...*But feminine...*While she was polite, Rory didn't feel camaraderie between them or any humor...She looked up at the ceiling, examining her surroundings and simultaneously avoiding his gaze.

"You're on next!"

"Wish me luck!"

"And now without further ado... We present Malka singing a rendition of Bessie

The Electric Eel!

Smith's 'Downhearted Blues!' with Wallace on piano!"

"Where's Iris?" someone shouted. "And the dog?"

He ignored him and motioned for her to step on stage. As she broke into the first few notes, the room went silent; some began to cry. When she finished, most stood and applauded.

"I think we found Iris's replacement..." Orville whispered to Lobelia with a grin.

Rory frowned. *It hasn't been very long...They must have decided this a while ago...*

"Would you like something to drink?" Lobelia asked the other woman.

"Ginger ale..." she said.

"How about a Presbyterian? Whiskey and ginger ale...Or a ginger ale mojito?"

"*Just* ginger ale..."

"You got it..." she said backing off.

"What's that all about?" Eugenia prodded.

"A teetotaler in a place like this..."

"Maybe she just didn't want alcohol *right now*?" Orville offered.

"I don't think so..." she mouthed reaching for a rocks glass and a cup full of gold sparkling water.

Lobelia grabbed the drink between two fingers, careful not to get fingerprints on the glass, and handed it to her. Malka examined it and nodded. As she sipped the soda, a red half-moon shaped mark of lipstick formed on both sides of the glass. The other woman watched as she pulled out a compact and checked her hair, a do resembling a high intricate soft loaf of braided whole wheat bread.

"Seems like she's a hit..." Edgar said to his brother.

*Not much in the personality department...*Lobelia pondered. *Let's hope she's dependable and drama free!*

"At least we know she's sober..." Orville whispered.

Rory burned a little in embarrassment for his friend at this slight. The room went silent again as Malka started her next tune. When she finished they applauded.

"So...Uh Malka... Where are you from?" Wallace asked once the song concluded.

"Philadelphia..." she answered in a clipped tone.

"Well! We're glad to have you here in Ohio!" he said wandering back to the piano.

"Cold fish..." he whispered to someone close by.

"Bunch of people just went to the roulette wheel..." Lobelia whispered to Rory and Trixie. "Go sell them drinks and cigarettes...I'll get the food..."

"Okay..."

Trixie reached for a high lipped tray with a u-shaped leather strap and pulled it over her head. Rory handed her a tiny pillbox hat and cocked it on one side of her head. Per Orville's instructions she had donned an above the knee red and black saloon style skirt and patent leather Mary Jane shoes.

"Orville says: All the cigarette girls are wearing them!"

Rory reached for a handful of cigars, cigarettes and hard candy and placed them on the center of the tray. Trixie steadied the tray with both hands over her voluptuous chest and walked to the gamblers.

"Gotta have strong neck muscles for this! *Cigars! Cigarettes!*" she shouted in a high-pitched voice.

A woman in a pale blue cloche hat and jacket pulled out a long cigarette and looked at Trixie. She scanned the tray and then looked at Rory. He looked up at her.

"Got a light?"

"Sure," he said reaching for a lighter and handing it to her.

As the woman puffed, she put the lighter back on the tray along with a handful of change. Lobelia appeared next beside the gamblers with a tray of appetizers.

"Canape? Care for an amuse bouche?"

"Don't mind if I do..." the woman with the pale hat said transferring the smoke to the other hand and reaching for a piece of crusty bread.

The Electric Eel!

"Red seven..." the caller yelled

"Damn!" one of the gamblers yelled.

"Nice to see everything going so smoothly..." Orville said to Eugenia.

"So far..."

Eugenia walked to the eel tank on the far left and demonstrated to a group of twenty-something onlookers. As the fish buzzed their angry tune, the group asked her the usual questions. *Are they real? What do you feed them? Can they hurt you? How big will they get?*

"I think they're used to me... They'll grow to the tank..."

The group of mostly college kids watched in awe as she reached under the bar for a small bowl of something fishy. With nimble fingers she torn the hunk of fish into two equal pieces and tossed it in the tank. Instantly both eels raced to the top to pounce on it, their tails interlocking in a heart shape.

"Cool place you got here!" one of the students yelled.

"Thanks!" Orville said taking credit.

Eugenia bit her lip in hurt. Orville froze a moment as she stormed off. As usual Eugenia complained to anyone who would listen...

"He always takes credit for everything...Even though he doesn't *do* anything...Let him try to keep these things alive without me...Let's face it if his old man hadn't croaked that way we wouldn't *be* here!"

Orville moved close behind her without making a sound. Eugenia turned to look up at him. *To her credit she doesn't back down...*He thought. Instead, she shrugged and walked away as if nothing happened.

"Excuse me! What was all that?"

"The truth!" she said, her voice growing loud and shrill.

"Keep it up, Eugenia..." he mumbled.

"Or what?' she shouted loud enough for everyone in the bar to hear.

Orville chewed his lip and froze. He motioned to her with one finger, beckoning her away from the group. She smiled with smug satisfaction.

"So what can I do for you?" he asked of her with a less than pleasant smile.

"I want a raise..."

He stifled a laugh, "A *raise*?"

"I know everything..." she whispered. "Your old man...Carlotta...*electric eels*..."

She pantomimed as if playing a game of charades. Eugenia pretended she was drinking a cocktail and then raised a knife over her head as if stabbing someone. Orville's eyes widened.

He gulped, unused to being bested. A second later his voice squeaked. He put his index finger up to his Adam's apple as if it were happening to him.

"How much?"

"As much as Lobelia makes..." she said. "Tax free under the table..."

"You got it..."

FIFTY-EIGHT

Irene's house in the suburbs was far removed from the gritty sights and smells of the state capital. Unlike many of the flashy homes that were going up in other neighborhoods, theirs was conservative and classically designed with a white picket fence. A large white porch swing dangled lazily in the breeze.

"The crazy twenties..." her husband commented. "So glad we have our lives out here..."

"And our baby..." she cooed.

She motioned to a chubby cherub in a wooden Victorian high chair with a scoop attached tray. Playfully he pounded his sizeable fists on the tray and shouted something indecipherable. Irene walked around him proudly as if examining a sculpture in the round.

The Electric Eel!

"Baby Wright..." she called. "Gonna grow up to be Mr. Wright junior..."

"I have to go to a luncheon with the governor..." her husband said kissing her on the cheek. "Say hello to the fam for me...Bye, baby..." he waved.

"I will..." she promised.

As he exited, Orville and Carlotta entered. The baby reached for his grandmother and uncle; however, only Orville acknowledged him. He waved his middle and index fingers in front of his nephew's face. The baby giggled.

"Looks just like Alistair at that age..."

"He does *not*!" Carlotta argued. "That baby is chubby... Alistair was a twig!"

Irene did her deedy job of putting out rectangular platters of food and reached for a sippet of crusty bread. Her mother looked at all of the food with suspicion. Irene bit into the bread and blinked, unused to be criticized.

"Something wrong?"

"Do you have any *real* food? I swear if I ever have to see another canape or green cocktail again, it'll be too soon..."

But before she could respond, someone knocked at the door. *It's Virginia...*She whispered in a less than thrilled tone of voice...

"Let me show you around..." Irene called. "We have the grand foyer on the right...And the powder room on the left..."

"It's lovely..."

"Thank you...Orville and mother are in the kitchen..."

She looked around the very ladylike kitchenette. It was decorated, per her family's Spanish ancestry, in shades of pale yellow, white, and blue. Fine flowers adorned most of the tile behind the appliances. An enormous bay window with shelves of African Violets and Gloxinias in cheery sun yellow pots bathed the plants in diffused light.

"Why am I here?" Virginia finally.

*Testy...*Irene thought motioning to the tray and offering them some. Virginia reached for a rectangular slice of cheese with reluctance. The women looked to Orville.

"It's about Eugenia..." he said finally, his normally chipper timbre of his voice flat and unfeeling.

"*Eugenia*? The girl from the club?" Virginia thought in confusion.

"What about her?" Carlotta asked, reaching for a small amount of food.

Irene passed her a white and silver plate and a cocktail napkin. Carlotta chewed and spat it out in a napkin, realizing she wasn't hungry. She pictured Eugenia in her mind...The heavyset girl in fishnet stockings and too much makeup...

"She knows everything..."

"Who cares?" Virginia retorted, in a nasty tone. "She's a nut..."

"She's becoming *more* than just a kook..." he said. "She's an albatross..."

"I told you not to hire her..." his mother began. "But you had to have those damn eels..."

Orville ignored Carlotta and poured himself a glass of Chardonnay. The wine was dry and oaky as it breathed. He sipped it, allowing it to warm his esophagus a second and then spoke.

"You're right..."

*But now I'm stuck with her...*He thought. *We all are...*

"What are you going to do about her?"

"I gave her a raise to keep her quiet..."

"A *raise?*"

"Only as hush money, mother...And only temporarily..."

*I should have just given them the money when I had the chance...*Irene thought. *But we just didn't have it at the time...Then we'd be free of this nonsense, and she wouldn't have had to rely on the inheritance to open that God-awful place...And father would be alive...*

Irene let out a breath of exasperation and reached for her child. *My source of joy...*She smiled. *We all have plenty of money now...*She mused. *And this looming over our* heads...Mr. Wright would leave me a heartbeat if he found out! And who could blame him? We'd be mired in scandal.*

Orville and the women stood for a minute in silence. Virginia began to seethe inside and then explode. Carlotta looked up at the ceiling, unimpressed by her former sister-in-law's antics.

"It was *my* boyfriend they killed!"

"You set him up-"

"I had no choice!"

"I wish I never knew Mr. LaRocca's name!" Carlotta spat. "I should've never called him in the first place..."

"What'd you *think* they were going to do? Invite him in for tea?"

"I had no idea they were going to *do* that! They just told me to get him a little tipsy is all!"

But even *she* didn't buy the words that were coming out of her mouth...Orville bit his lip hard wanting to be anywhere in the world but where he was at the moment. He placed the wine glass back on the counter, suddenly wanting nothing to do with alcohol. The white wine left a vinegary aftertaste on the roof of his mouth.

"The Electric Eel is a smashing success..."

"That place is a pit..." Carlotta said with little candor. "Definitely not what I had in mind..."

"That place..." he repeated. "Is making money hand over fist..." Orville said smiling. "For *all* of us!"

"That it is..."

But at what cost? Carlotta wondered. *Will we go to jail? Maybe they'd even give us the chair...I'm too old to die!*

Irene reached for the used plates and placed them in the sink. Next she dried her hands on a tea towel. She chose her words carefully and spoke.

The Electric Eel!

"Let's get back to the matter at hand...What are you going to do about that girl?"

"Eugenia...?"

"If she keeps it up...We'll have Mr. LaRocca get rid of her..." Carlotta spoke without hesitating. *In for a penny...In for a pound...*

Before they could discuss it further, a mustached face peeked in the front door. Carlotta reached out to stop them from saying anything further. Edgar's familiar uneven gait and sandy hair came into view followed by Poppy and Alistair.

"Say no more..."

"Sorry we're late..." Poppy said looking at all of them.

Her smile dropped at the sight of the others. Edgar pretended not to notice the tension, as had been his usual since this whole thing had started...*I miss my father...*He thought looking at his relatives.

"Why the long face?" Orville said, recovering his upbeat bravado.

"Oh, nothing..."

He reached up to embrace his wife, son, and brother. Poppy allowed it for a second like a feline and then grew tired of him. The stink of his cologne hung in the air for a second. Alistair ran to his dad and hugged him.

"Hey, kid! Do anything fun today?"

"Uncle Edgar and I played baseball!"

"Neat!"

"Nani and Papi are taking us out for ice cream..."

"They *are*?" he said looking around for his grandparents, whom he had not seen in ages. "Where are they?"

"In the car..." Poppy informed him.

Are they coming in? The look on Carlotta's face said. Alistair waved outside to where his great-grandparents sat. *They don't even want to come inside...*Irene thought, a little hurt.

"Well! I better get to work! I'll say hi on my way out!"

And without further fanfare, Orville walked outside and flashed his grandparents his trademark Rudolph Valentino smile. His grandfather reached through the window and grabbed his hand. His grandmother smiled coolly as if she knew something about him she wasn't supposed to but said nothing.

"Good to see you, my boy!" Papi called.

"You too, grandpa! I'm on my way to work! Stop in sometime!"

But he knew the invitation was futile. *They'll never come...*He thought. Once in the car, Orville's cheery demeanor dropped. *Everything is coming unraveled...*He thought looking back at his sister's house and his grandparent's car. A second later he turned the car and drove back to the Electric Eel.

FIFTY-NINE

October 31, 1924

*W*ith great care, Rory and Eugenia and the others hung warm-colored Chinese paper lanterns inside the bar and around the outside perimeter of the Electric Eel. Most of the decorations were orange but several other autumn-hued ephemera dotted the room in shades of burgundy and gold. Rory placed two pumpkins on the porch and stepped back to examine them.

"Looking good!" Lobelia said.

"Should we be hanging things outside?" Eugenia barked sullenly.

"Why not?"

"Cause we're a speakeasy..."

"Pretend it's for the bakery..." Orville said, examining the festivities.

*She's not going to spoil my good mood...*He told himself. Eugenia looked over at the massage parlor next...*Formerly known as Marie Toussad's...*

The Electric Eel!

"Let's hope they don't piss in them..." she whispered to Rory.

Eugenia was dressed in green and yellow sequins and snake skinned boots. She fastened her long tail to the back and twirled. Rory studied her

"What's your costume?" Rory asked pleasantly.

"An electric eel, of course!"

I should've known! The sky was beginning to darken above the Electric Eel. A large lucent moon was coming into view. *Perfect!*

"You better go change, Rory..." Lobelia told him.

Lobelia had opted for a dark blue floral headpiece and matching dress with large petal like points that radiated out from the circumference of the garment. She stepped into a pair of blue peep toed shoes with corresponding blue toenail polish and walked across the room.

"You look beautiful!" Rory exclaimed.

"Thank you!"

*He's so sweet...*She thought. *Genuinely...*

Orville went into the men's room and reached for a garment bag with a zipper. He pulled out a black cape, wide brimmed hat, and mask. Then he pulled on a pair of black pants and thigh high boots and reached for a Samurai sword.

"Who are you?" Rory asked his boss.

"Don Diego De La Vega..." he said with a giggle. "Zorro, silly..."

Rory blushed, suddenly titillated by the sight of him. Orville sliced the sword through the air like a swashbuckler. Orville's light eyes sparkled through the mask like aquamarine.

"Orro..." he whispered.

"Orro... I like it..."

"Oro means gold in Spanish..."

"Even better..."

The Electric Eel!

Next, Rory donned a pair of floppy dog ears and reached for a little of Lobelia's makeup she'd let him borrow to create a makeshift nose and muzzle. Then he safety pinned a tail on his rear end and moved to make sure it was secured to his knickers. He looked in the mirror and smiled.

"Woof!"

He spotted Trixie on the other side of the room. They had become friends…Though not as close as he had been with Iris… Trixie was wearing fuzzy pink and white ears and a bob tail on the back of her skimpy outfit. Several whiskers stuck out of her face like straws along with two buck teeth she had drawn in with an eyeliner pencil.

"I'm a bunny… Hop…*Hop!*" she informed him putting her wrists out as if riding a horse.

"I see that…"

"Orville helped me pick it out…" she said giggling uncomfortably.

"You two have grown fond of each other…"

"Uh-huh…He says you should come over sometime again," she said donning the cigarette tray. "Hard to get this over my long ears… But I'll manage! See ya, Rory!"

And with that she spotted the first guests and hopped away. He shook his head at the sight of her. Orville smiled.

"The guests love her!" he said to him. "I guess you heard my offer…"

Rory blushed. He thought of the night he had spent with Orvile and Iris and now Trixie…But Orville had already walked away… Impressing the guests with his epee.

"I'm Zorro!"

As the band began to start, a group of people stood around a pit to bob for apples. Iris walked in the door and looked at the spectacle. Eugenia gagged.

"So gross…" she said as someone stepped up in line to catch a red delicious apple with his teeth.

"Iris!" Rory shouted in glee.

Eugenia tasted bile. *I thought we got rid of her…*She mused.

The Electric Eel:

Rory leaned down to greet Peaches. The dog ran his nose over Rory's unfamiliar extra set of dangly ears with suspicion. Iris was wearing a headband with triangular ears and a long, curled tail and a cheetah printed catsuit. Like his master, he was in a lion costume with a fuzzy mane at the collar.

"Peachy!" she exclaimed.

"Yes! What are you?"

"I'm a Leo!" she said growling with pointed nails outstretched, her meow coming out as more kitten than lion. "Rarr!"

"Long time no see..." Orville said in familiarity.

"Love the Zorro costume!"

"Thank you..." he said stepping forward. "As many of you know our resident soothsayer is normally here on Thursday; however, I am pleased to announce she will be Friday, Saturday and Sunday through All Soul's Day...Without further ado...Madame Beulah..."

They clapped as Beulah stepped forward. For this occasion she donned orange and a black pointed hat. *Like a witch...*

"The spirits are always especially active on All Hallow's Eve...Or Samhain," she called. "Or as most of you call it...Halloween...As we move into the height of Scorpio season...When everything dies...Plants die... Animals go into hibernation... Crops go dormant..."

As Beulah prattled on, a woman walked in whom they had not seen in the Electric Eel for a while...Carlotta Alfonso appeared in a Carmen Miranda inspired fruit hat that attached with a red and gold turban behind her ears. She wore a long low-cut yellow and red floral dress with lacy collar and thick red heels.

"Carlotta!" Lobelia said, trying to hide her surprise.

"What are you?"

"A lobelia..."

The Electric Eel!

"Oh! Like the flower! I get it!" Trixie laughed.

"Ahem!" Madame Beulah bellowed.

"Sorry..." Trixie whispered.

"Tonight we call on the God of Horn and Hoof to put us in touch with the spirits...I asked that you grab hands with the person closest to you and form a circle and close your eyes..."

Several people looked around but did as they were told. Then one of her assistants rolled something out on a stand. Madame Beulah began to chant in glossolalia.

"God of Horn and Hoof... Goddess of the Moon..." she chanted. "Show us the great spirits all around!"

All of a sudden the legs of the table she was sitting at slammed on the ground, forcing everyone to look up. Then the sound of something metallic banged. *A gong!*

As the group looked around a flash of something orange and blue blazed in the middle of the cauldron in front of her. And then it died...*She's going to burn the place down!* Orville thought from his vantage point as smoke fizzled.

And then her voice changed to gravelly. An oppressive ominous groan. Rory's eyes widened.

"Death is all around..." she moaned.

"All around who?" Iris shouted humoring her.

"*You...!*" the voice hissed.

And as suddenly as it came, it was gone. Madame Beulah began to sway as if in time with music and then she opened her eyes. Everyone in the room looked around in apprehension.

"What happened?" she called as if returning from a far-off place.

"A fire came out of the cauldron..." someone informed.

"And the gong sounded..."

"Madame Beulah will be here reading tea leaves and palms all week for a nominal

The Electric Eel!

fee..." Orville said. "Give her a hand..."

Madame Beulah nodded as if expecting it and stood to walk off stage. When they were sure she was finished, people got up and started milling around the Electric Eel. Iris grabbed a cocktail from the bar and wandered over to the stage where an unfamiliar woman stood.

*The only person in the place without a costume...*She mused. *Beautiful...But no sense of humor...*

"Iris Dupeon... I used to sing here..."

"Oh," she said as if she was afraid of saying too much.

She's heard things about me...I've been replaced! The next thought came.

"And you *are*?" Iris said forcing conversation the way her father did when he wanted pertinent information.

"Malka..."

And the statuesque woman walked away in disinterest. The back of her beehive hairdo was pulled up with bobby bins as if knitted together intentionally like an Afghan. Her dress was silvery and backless and cut to her sacrum.

Iris spotted her former band members next. Jib and Freddy snubbed her, smiling uncomfortably. Wallace beamed at the sight of her but as Malka began to sing he turned his attention back to the piano. Iris blanched a little at the slight and walked back to the bar.

"My music career is finished..." she whispered to Rory.

"What music career? You sang at a sleazy speakeasy and then you got canned..." Eugenia chimed in under her breath. "Seriously... You're loaded... Go home..."

"Excuse me?"

"You heard me..."

"I don't think I did..." Iris said turning, her almond-colored eyes flaring.

Before Iris could confront the other woman Eugenia was gone. Just then Tiny let two

The Electric Eel!

adults and a child into the place. The man was dressed like a pirate with a plum frilly vest and wide legged pants. The woman was dressed in ivory lace.

"We went trick or treating, daddy!" the son called to Orville from behind a ghost costume.

"Cool!"

"He got tons of candy…" Edgar explained with a wry smile.

"And he isn't allowed to eat it all at one time.." his mother chimed in.

"Nice costume, brother…" Orville admired. "Way to use the peg leg…"

"I figured one day a year wouldn't hurt without the prosthesis…"

"Well you wear it well…"

"And look at you with your Zorro get up!"

"Thanks…"

"Well! We got a few more houses to get before it gets too late…"

"On *this* street?" Orville said with gritted teeth.

He thought of the fares that people were peddling nearby. Poppy placed her hands on her son's shoulders. The boy looked up from behind his ghost costume.

"No… Not on this street…"

"Have fun!" he waved.

Lobelia watched as two well to do young ladies walked in The Electric Eel, their arms, and hands pale but their faces were deep brown as if coated with mud. Another of the women's face was coated in charcoal. *Blackface!* She mouthed to Orville.

Orville nodded as if it were the most natural thing in the world to see this and took their order. *I think she was supposed to be Josephine Baker…* He thought reaching for a cocktail napkin and a straw.

"Let's just hope they don't get charcoal everywhere.."

Just then Iris noticed an attractive man about her age that she found intriguing. Before she could approach him, he walked to Eugenia and handed her a slip of paper. Eugenia took it and put it down her bra... Then she turned and focused her gaze on the other woman with smug satisfaction.

Iris stormed to the bathroom and locked the door. Peaches paced nervously inside the small room as if trapped as she dug through her purse for whatever she could use. *How many times have I gotten high here?*

She emerged from the water closet with more confidence than she had gone in with. She stumbled a little. Rory knew the look all too well...But said nothing. She walked away leaving her silver engraved compact on the counter.

"Could you call my driver?"

"Absolutely..." Orville said with genuine concern.

And she and Peaches walked outside the Electric Eel never to see them or the place again...

SIXTY

November 1, 1924

Iris arrived home after two with Peaches. The driver nodded as she emerged from the car with as much nonchalance as she could muster. The tail on her Halloween costume swung slightly as she walked. Her steps were careful with substance abuse.

"Don't tell my parents where I was..." she said handing him a wad of cash.

"You got it, Miss Dupeon..."

Above them the moon glowed like a beacon. Iris looked up and swooned, waxing sentimental. Peaches looked up at her and wagged his tail, unsure what had caught her attention.

In her haze of addiction, she led him to the side entrance up to the roof as she and the hound climbed the stairs, bypassing the doorman at the front, leaving the door ajar slightly. A large pool was on the top floor of the building. Like most things about this place it was opulent and ornate in shades of teal and silvery white. She thought of her

The Electric Eel!

parents and Rory and the day they had spent swimming and felt a little regret. *And I had that valet who liked him fired...*She remembered. *Out of spite...*

Peaches sniffed the edge of the pool with caution, but she tugged him away. What water remained in the pool glimmered like fine crystal in the moonlight. Chilly air blew against the backs of her knees. A row of deck chairs lined the wall, unused till the next summer.

"Isn't it beautiful, Peachy?" she said looking up.

The dog smiled a little, trying to please her. He was on alert for some reason but was unsure why...Iris didn't seem to notice his angst...

"C'mon, Peachy..." she called.

But he resisted. She tugged on his leash a little. He attempted to dig his feet into the ground, sliding a little on the concrete. Iris looked up at a billion twinkling stars. *Maybe I can get a closer look...*She thought.

Quickly, Iris released her dog's lead and motioned for him to stay while she reached for a high backed white wooden Adirondack chair. With some effort she pushed the chair against the far edge of the building and climbed on top.

Iris's legs were wobbly as she climbed. Once on the chair the stars seemed to get closer, and she went up the ledge to get a closer look. A haze of white drifted through the nearly black sky.

"Is it beautiful up here, Peachy?" she called. "Everything is wonderful up here..."

Suddenly everything began to spin as if she were in the midst of a typhoon...A lucid moment of regret at the bad decision she had made filling her with dread. And then she felt herself falling...

SIXTY-ONE

𝒫eaches the Afghan Hound raced down the stairs in panic. The stairwell echoed with his footsteps as he barked. In haste he jumped up at the door pushing it open enough to exit into the night, his large fuzzy paws like women's slippers against the wood. Once outside he sprinted like a gazelle.

He looked around unsure of his next move. His long, parted blond hair flopped in and out of his eyes, his tongue hanging out part way as he caught his breath. *What now?*

And then he found her...Face down on the pavement, her arms, and legs out like a discarded child's toy...The smell of her perfume and cigarettes familiar to his senses but unfamiliar at the same time. Peaches circled her trying to figure out how to save her. But she wasn't moving... He sniffed her palm and began to bark.

Suddenly the night doorman heard something...*Is that howling...?* He thought of the holiday... *Perhaps some kids playing a Halloween prank...*He mused. But the sound continued, this time with more urgency. The doorman walked outside...

Then he spotted it. A tall wheat-colored dog raced around him, a long spittle of saliva forming in the corners of the dog's mouth. But the dog wouldn't let him approach, instead bouncing on his haunches, biting, and snarling. *What the?*

"Peaches? What's wrong boy?"

The dog whined. To his horror he found the source of the dog's panic. A young blond woman in a cat suit was on the ground, her chin turned in an unnatural position. Quickly, he dashed inside and dialed the authorities.

Across town Rory held his friend's compact in his palm. He pondered his next move. *I haven't been back to her penthouse since our last fight...*He thought. *And she killed my relationship with Scotty and got him fired...But she was pleasant to me tonight...So...*

"She was clearly altered when she left..." he said to himself.

But he decided to be the bigger person and head over to bring it to her. Before he could get into the taxi, he spotted the stairs to Trixie's walkup apartment. He had briefly pondered joining them, as they had done before, but then thought better of it. *He's*

The Electric Eel!

married...And I like Poppy...

"But now everyone is saying Poppy and Edgar are together..." he said to himself.

"Huh?" the driver said overhearing.

"Nothing... Olde Towne East, please..."

As they drove in silence across town something felt off...Rory couldn't place it...He looked at his watch...*Almost four o'clock in the morning...*

And then he saw it: Two huge cars...One black and one silver...And a van... The street was blocked off ahead. Rory reached for the door handle before the car had a chance to stop. The driver turned to look at him.

"I'll get out here..." he said. "Keep the change..."

"Do you want me to wait...?"

"If you want..." he said racing forward. "What's going on?" he asked an officer.

"There's been an accident...Stay back..."

And then he saw it. A large sheet covering a body with high heeled shoes sticking out. A set of manicured red fingernails were out on the concrete like claws. Rory's stomach dropped. *Like a baby bird that had fallen out of the nest...*

"It's Miss Dupeon..." the doorman informed him.

He pointed to a hound with a long muzzle, snarling and barking at investigators. Occasionally the dog would circle the body, the hairs on the back of his neck standing straight up, his tail in an unnatural curl. Rory looked away from the body and focused on the dog.

"We can't get the dog away from her..." the officer whispered to Iris's father. "Not the dog's fault but we may have to euthanize it..."

Rory's eyes widened in horror and then he stepped in. All of a sudden one of the officers raised the muzzle of his gun and aimed. Rory put his hand up and walked between his scope.

"*Stop!*" one of them shouted.

The Electric Eel!

"Move away, young man!"

"Don't kill the dog...I'll get him..."

"That's my daughter's friend..." Mr. Dupeon told him.

And the officer placed the weapon by his side and paused. He breathed, his heart pounding in his ears as Rory approached the dog, hovering over Iris's body like a helicopter. *It's what Iris would have wanted...*He and her father thought.

"Come here, Peachy..."

Peaches looked up in confusion at the sound of his own name. Then he dropped his nose to ground in submission as Rory inched closer to him. The young man focused completely on the dog, avoiding the sight of Iris's lifeless body. The other men who had tried to coax the dog for hours watched in awe. The dog remained out of reach as if he would bolt at any second.

"Go to him, Peaches..." Mr. Dupeon called.

"Shh..." the police officer warned, afraid he would spook the dog.

"Come on, boy..." he said. "It's okay..."

*But it doesn't feel okay...*The hound allowed him to come close but remained at a distance. His almond-shaped eyes were dark and weary with exhaustion, his normally placid, compliant demeanor replaced with panicked aggression. Rory was afraid for a second that he would bite him. Before the dog could react, Rory grabbed his collar and pulled him away from the body.

"Thank God..." Mrs. Dupeon breathed from a short distance away.

At lightning speed the officers rushed to Iris's body. *If there had been any hope that she had been alive we would have taken it...*One of them thought. Her skin had cooled slightly to the touch, her limbs stiffening with rigor mortis. Mrs. Dupeon looked away in tears.

Tears also welled up in Rory's eyes as he embraced the dog. He held onto him carefully, afraid he would bolt back to where her body lay. The dog opened his mouth and gave a labored breath, his muzzle pointed in the direction of where Iris was slain.

"Good job, my boy!"

"What happened?" Rory asked them finally.

"Looks like she fell…"

"We aren't sure yet…" the officer said focusing his attention back on Rory and the dog. With expertise, the police officer turned Rory away from the sight of them removing Iris's body. As the sun began to rise behind him, a salmon-orange light hovered on the horizon. Quickly, they removed Iris from where had laid for the past two hours, placing her in a body bag and transferring it to a non-descript black windowless van.

"What do I do with him?" he whispered to the officer.

"Keep him… For the time being…"

"He was our daughter's pet…" Mr. Dupeon offered and for a second Rory thought he would take the dog away. "But given the circumstance it might be best if *you* cared for him…I'm sure there's food upstairs for him and we'll gladly play for his care for the rest of his life… It's the least we can do…"

"Okay…" Rory said processing all that had transpired.

As they led him away from the death scene, Rory felt something metallic and weighty against his thigh. *Her silver compact…The reason I came…*He thought. *Maybe I should give it to them later…*

Rory looked up where the taxi had been and wondered how he would get home…Iris's father read his mind as they walked. Peaches kept moving his head in the direction of where Iris had fallen.

"One of us can give you a ride home…"

"Thank you…"

As Rory exited, he thought of the lavish funeral they would have for Iris. He thought of her parent's religion and wondered what that would entail…He pictured fringe and a gold ornate casket and tons of mourners…Maybe even a Rabbi or a Shiva…? Perhaps people from the Electric Eel would mingle with her parent's high society friends? *Would they even be invited?*

Then another thought crossed his mind. *Would they even have a funeral at all, or would it be all hush hush?* He wondered. *Surely this was a scandalous way to die...A sad ending for such a glamorous woman in the prime of her life...*

In the confusion, someone pushed he and the dog in the back of a police car...Peaches hopped in reluctantly keeping his gaze out the window where his master had taken her last breath. As the car began to move, Rory gave her penthouse complex one final glimpse... Never to see his friend or her home again...

He thought of the painting on her wall of the girl who jumped out the window after finding her lover dead...Still in shock, he couldn't recall the artist *or* the girl's name...

"She jumped out the window to off herself...About my age..." he heard her voice echo in his mind.

Had Iris taken her own life?

SIXTY-TWO

Despite Rory's absence the next day, word spread quickly at the Electric Eel of Iris Dupeon's sudden demise. In haste, Lobelia and Eugenia took down the Halloween decorations, leaving up only a few reminders of autumn. Eugenia said very little...*Out of guilt...*

Outside, the wind howled as if it knew something they didn't... Madame Beulah appeared precisely at nine p.m.. Quickly, Orville filled her in on what had transpired with Iris...

"You remember her..." he said. "Short, blond, sang with the band...Always had a dog with her...I think she was originally from New York City..."

*Vaguely...*She thought. *There's been so much death around here recently...I can't keep* *track!* Then she remembered the dog and nodded, forming a picture in her mind as if looking at a blurry photograph. *Maybe I can use this...?*

"How did she die?"

"She fell off a balcony last night..."

"How tragic!"

Jib and Freddy were also quiet...They pondered a tribute to her...*But what would they play?* Wallace smiled his usual pleasant smile, remembering Iris fondly. *He never has a bad word to say about anyone...*They noticed.

Tiny, too, was somber over Iris's death. On this particular night he chose to stay by the door, quiet as a tomb, not feeling the festivities that the place usually fostered. At five after nine Edgar and Poppy appeared in the doorway and looked to Orville.

"Alistair's with mother..." Edgar said.

"What happened to Iris?" Poppy asked her husband.

"They aren't sure, but it looks like she went home and went up on the balcony and either fell or jumped..."

*She didn't seem like the suicidal type...*Edgar thought. *Unless she was on something...*

"Rory went over last night. The doorman found her..."

"Oh, poor Rory! How *is* he?"

"In shock... But okay... He has the dog..."

Orville looked up with the realization that others at the bar were listening...He wondered how many of them actually knew Iris or whether they were just curious gossips... But he walked away with the shake of his head, not wanting to speak about the matter further...

At around ten Madame went behind a small curtain and pulled on a long black hooded robe over her clothing... She emerged looking like a druid or the grim reaper...The hood was dark, masking her face, giving her an eerie silhouette. A few in the audience gasped at the sight of her. Several white partially melted candles burned in a circle in the center

The Electric Eel!

of her table ominously, the only light in the room...

*Maybe I should have cancelled her for tonight...*Orville thought. *But how would I have known?*

"I ask for complete silence!" she shouted as she put both hands up like a sorcerer.

Usually, a few people in the audience would continue to talk or mill around during her act; however, on this night they did as they were told...Possibly out of fear...and remained quiet...

"In the past few years this place has seen its fair share of untimely *death*!" she said spitting out the last word like a serpent. "First the death of Mr. Julius Alfonso..."

Uh-oh... Orville thought. But he said nothing, wanting to see where she was going with this before he chastised her for it.

"As many of you know, Mr. Alfonso was slain on the very street this place was built on... Stabbed by several unknown assailants! His body right over there! His death which we were forbidden to speak on! But we will not be silenced!"

Orville opened his mouth to speak but she cut him off. Quickly she turned away from him, the long black robe like a shadow. She moved on to her next point without stopping to notice his anxiety.

"Next, we had Detective Talbert...Felled by an assassin's bullet! His spirit lingers outside! Right where he was murdered!"

Beulah pointed to the far-right alley and waved her arms as mimicking being hit by gunshots. Her head bobbed up and down like she was trying to dodge something. Quickly she fell backwards.

"And then Heyward...Or as many of you know him as Catfish... Also taken by gunshot...Which proves knowing too much can be deadly..."

She put her hand up in front of her chin to demonstrate a catfish's whiskers. Tiny looked around the room at Mr. LaRocca's associates, but they didn't seem to notice...Also, too enrapt by Madame Beulah to care...She put her hands over her head as if trying to protect herself, the heavy fabric of the robe dripping like curtains.

"And now Iris...Our dear friend...The songstress for the band..." she said, her accent changing into something distinctly east coast and high pitched. "Her dog *mourns*...Iris, who less than twenty-four hours ago was here on All Hallow's Eve! Iris who many of you died an untimely death from a fall...Or was it untimely? Or was it just her time? She too is here...With us..."

And she began to hum something...The tune Rory and Iris had sung to on the night they were raided...All of a sudden, Madame Beulah toppled backwards as if she had tripped on a rock. As she fell to the floor, someone in the audience reached for her to help her up. She swirled a little as if regaining consciousness.

"Oh great spirits! Let us communicate with you! With *all* of you who have crossed over! Show us tonight where you are!"

And with that, the candles went out with a whoosh, darkening the room completely. Madame Beulah backed away from the table slowly, the oval shape of her great hood remaining in their vision, until she disappeared behind the screen. The audience applauded. But before the lights came on...Madame Beulah was gone...

"Quite a show!" someone whispered to Orville.

I'm surprised he allowed it! Eugenia thought. An eerie calm filled the room. Orville looked around the bar for her as she appeared back in her normal jeweled toned clothes.

"As promised, Madame Beulah will be reading tarot cards and palms for the rest of the night and tomorrow and every Thursday as always. Isn't she fabulous? Madame Beulah, everyone!"

As the group went back to whatever they were doing before the performance, Madame Beulah sat back down at her table. A red and yellow tarot deck lay in front of her in a pile; a line of people formed waiting for a reading as she shuffled the cards. Two young lovers walked up to her first. The woman turned over a card.

The Electric Eel!

"Queen of Cups..." Beulah informed them. "Loving, tenderhearted and intuitive..."

The young woman looked at the young man, swooning. When they were satisfied that she had told them what they wanted to hear, they put a couple dollars in her bowl and walked away. Another young man followed...And then another...Until it was well past midnight.

"You were quite a hit tonight, Beulah!"

"*Madame* Beulah..." she corrected.

*And I'm a hit every night...*She told herself proudly. Orville forked over a generous amount of cash, and she placed it in her robe pocket for safe keeping. Outside a clear shift in weather from moderate October to chilly November was evident...But something else had changed just in the few short hours she'd been inside that she just couldn't place...

And then something caught her eye: a shape of someone lying on the concrete. *Maybe a vagrant or a hobo...?* She'd seen them before...Unhoused and living on the streets of Columbus, cuddled up with newspapers or boxes or whatever else they could find to keep warm. But this individual didn't move...Suddenly a pool of something rust colored spilled out around him...*Was he hurt? Was he even alive?*

"Help...Me..." the man whispered.

Madame Beulah blinked and as suddenly as it appeared it was gone. *Balderdash!* She thought. *You're scaring yourself! Starting to believe your own schtick!* She thought with a chuckle as she moved down the street.

Then her ears picked up a sound...*Gunshots!* She ducked as if they were popping in her own ears...Like a Chinese fire drill! The image of a man in a car came first, riddled with bullets and then another standing by the alley...His curled whiskers were like a walrus...*Or a catfish!* Both men were bleeding profusely, their bodies peppered with bullet holes...Their final moments played out in front of her like a movie reel...

"This *can't* be..."

The Electric Eel!

And then, like the man before, they vanished. In all the years Beulah had been performing as a psychic she realized she never really *believed* her own story...It had always been an act...*Till now...*

As she moved away from the Electric Eel another figure lay on the ground... This time of a woman, face down on the ground... Her hands were extended like talons as if she were trying to catch herself from a nasty fall...The woman's neck was contorted in a gruesome way like the renditions of saints she'd seen in Renaissance Cathedrals...As if the proportions of her body were intentionally *off*, her knees were bent like snapped tree limbs, her shoes strapped on her heels as if in bondage...

Beulah stared as a large flaxen haired dog circled the woman's body, its eyes were bloodshot and menacing like a hell hound. With ferocity it snapped and barked a warning. *Stay away!* Madame Beulah stifled a scream...A white sheet levitated over her lifeless body and settled over her, but the dog remained frozen, its eyes fixed on Beulah.

And then all the bodies reappeared together in unison...First, the knifed man on the concrete followed by the two who had been shot and the young woman... Their eyes turned in her direction in accusation... A second later they disappeared...

In haste Madame Beulah dropped the robe as she sprinted in absolute unabashed terror... Quickly, she gave the Electric Eel one final quick glance...As she turned into the night, she vowed never to return to this place again...

SIXTY-THREE

November 2, 1924

*L*obelia was the first to arrive at the speakeasy the next day. Something felt different but she couldn't place it...Though it was still light out, the temperature was dropping steadily by the hour...The sky was darkening from silver to a dark ominous grey...

"It's November in Ohio..." she reminded herself.

The Electric Eel!

As she opened the bakery door her eyes picked up on something...An item of clothing she didn't immediately recognize...She picked it up to examine it...*A robe*...

"Where have I seen this before?" she asked herself.

At first she was afraid to touch it, thinking it might be one of the bums on High Street who had dropped it...*I don't want to take someone's only means of warmth*... But as she inspected it, she realized it was too expensive...Too elaborate for any of the homeless people to have left it behind...

She held it up by the hood and rifled through it, hoping to find some sort of indication of who owned it...With great care she sifted through the pockets and felt something folded... *A considerable amount of cash...!*

Lobelia briefly considered keeping it but thought better of it...She was not a thief and whomever owned this robe would surely want it back...Quietly she draped the dressing gown over her arm and carried it inside. *Orville may know who it belongs to...*

Carefully she placed it on a chair and removed the money and placed it in the drawer...*For safe keeping*...Orville and Eugenia arrived in the door next.

"Hey, Orville..."

"*Yes*?"

"Do you know who this belongs to?"

Eugenia stood on a step stool to feed the eels but continued listened intently. Orville nodded at the fabric in recognition. Lobelia took him aside. Behind her the eels splashed and pounced on the seafood with ravenous intent. Once satiated they settle back to the bottom of the tank, their tails touching slightly. One of the serpentine fish let out a buzz like a hive full of bumblebees.

"It's Madame Beulah's..." he said in half confusion. "Where'd you find it?"

"Outside. There was a ton of money in the pocket..."

"Hmm...Put it away so someone doesn't take it..."

"*I did*..."

The Electric Eel!

"Good...She'll be here tonight...She's always early..."

Madame Beulah doesn't seem like the type to just leave her things lying around...And she certainly would never leave money...! He put it out of his mind and walked away, promising to ask her later when he saw her...

But Madame Beulah *didn't* show...They noticed. Her table remained empty, its usual contents of Ouija board, crystal ball and spirit trumpet untouched and still wrapped up in the black lace tablecloth as she preferred...

By ten thirty Lobelia began to grow worried. She approached Orville again. To her surprise he was pensive, with genuine concern for the other woman.

"Maybe she thinks she doesn't have to be here on a Sunday..." he said to Lobelia. "Get her on the horn!"

Lobelia searched for whatever contact information she could find on Beulah and walked to the bakery the only portion of the business allowed to have a phone and dialed the operator. She waited a second as a ubiquitous female voice came on the line.

"Number please..."

"Franklin County, Ohio please...From the Electric Eel Bakery," she said looking down and reading off the numbers.

"One moment please..."

The line buzzed a moment like one of Eugenia's eels. The sound pulsed back and forth in her ear...*Beep...Beep...*

"Call from The Electric Eel Bakery..." the nasally monotone female voice informed the other caller. "Go ahead please..."

"Beulah? This is Lobelia-"

"This is her sister...Beulah's not here..."

"Do you know when she will be back?"

"What is this in regards?"

"She left her stuff here last night...And she was supposed to be here at nine...She left money and-"

"I'll tell her..." the voice said cutting her off upon hearing the word money.

"Okay but..."

"Your caller has hung up..." the operator said returning.

"Thank you..."

She hung up...Lobelia mouthed to her boss, somewhat confused. Finally, she placed the phone back on its clip and looked at him.

"Was it Beulah?"

"No, her sister...She's gone."

It dawned on Lobelia at that moment that she didn't really *know* Madame Beulah or *anyone* really for that matter here even though she saw them every day...*I don't even know most of their last names nor have I ever been to any of their homes socially... My only connection to all of them being the auspices of the Electric Eel...I suspect that's true of everyone here...*

She thought of the laissez-fair culture of the decade...*Speak easy if you will...So no one will hear you...*

Then a loud crash like a bomb going off in the other room broke her train of thought. She and Orville rushed to bar, their steps quickening as they moved. Several people looked at them in stunned silence.

"What happened?" he asked one of his employees.

One of the customers pointed to a sundry of shattered glass. For a moment Orville thought maybe someone had thrown glassware or a fight had broken out but then dismissed it. Rory reached for a dustpan as Orville knelt to examine it.

"It must've fallen off the table..."

"Looks like someone hurdled it..." Orville said. "It practically dented the floor..."

Rory shuddered. His boss walked away in unease. Lobelia began to pick up the large shards with her fingers, careful not to slice herself and placed them in the wastebasket.

The Electric Eel!

"Get this cleaned up..."

Eugenia walked over to inspect Madame Beulah's table further. It was as if a strong wind had blown the tightly secured runner off the table and catapulted the crystal ball where it landed. As she leaned over the table she spotted something wooden and triangular. She hesitated and leaned over to pick it up.

"Madame Beulah's spirit board..." she informed Lobelia.

Lobelia recoiled afraid to touch it. Eugenia placed it on the table like the proverbial hot potato. The planchette on the board was cockeyed as if bent by some unknown force, its gold lettering twisted as if ready to fall off the plywood. Figuring it was busted, Rory placed it in the receptacle with the broken crystal.

"Everyone! I know you were expecting a show tonight, but I apologize for Madame Beulah's absence tonight..." Orville informed the crowd. "Drinks are on the house!"

As the horde received their libations they seemed satiated for the time being...*If you can't beat em...Join em!* He thought reaching for a Manhattan and raising his glass.

"Bottoms up!" someone called.

Orville tasted sweet vermouth and maraschino cherry and crunched on a bit of ice. He looked over at Madame Beulah's table wondering if she'd ever return...*Even though I couldn't stand her...How can I replace her?*

He closed his eyes and listened to the band, the whiskey warming his esophagus. As Malka sang the blues, the clarinet emanated its soulful whine while Wallace played a few effortless cords on the piano...Jib's fingers bounced over the bridge of the string bass causing a few low notes to reverberate.

When everyone's attention was on the band, Eugenia walked to the bar and stood for a moment. With watchful eyes she scanned the room to see if anyone was looking. When she sure it was safe, she slipped Madame Beulah's wad of money in her pocket and walked away as if nothing happened...

SIXTY-FOUR

*O*ver the next week, no word came from Madame Beulah. When Thursday rolled around, and she still didn't show, Orville had to decide what to do with the rest of her stuff. He scratched his chin and stared at her table.

"We can always bring it back out if she comes back..."

But she wasn't coming back...Something told him. *So who do we get to fill in for her?* He wondered. *Where's a spiritist when we need one?* He looked around the room. *Only musicians, drunks, and eels...*He noted.

Before Orville could ponder it further, Tiny opened the door to throng of people. As they descended on the Electric Eel. he hesitated. They all seem to have one thing in common...*Alcohol...*

Orville looked around the room and touched Lobelia on the shoulder. He scanned the crowd... *Politicians...Detectives and other law enforcement agents...As well as religious people and prominent members of the community...*

"Shh!" one of them whispered.

Lobelia slid a whiskey sour across the bar, and he caught it as if waiting for a fly ball. A confusing mass of cocktail glasses, both full and in various stages of empty collected on the bar. As a group of young people began to line up to do shots, Eugenia stepped in to pour as if operating an assembly line. A sea of cash collected in mason jars placed at different intervals.

"We can't keep up..." Lobelia said.

"Yes we can..." Orville said snatching up some of the money. "If you leave a *small* amount in the jar people feel sorry for you and tip better..."

"I'll remember that..."

Orville's face soured. Lobelia cocked her neck and looked at him. Quietly she placed the bottle she had been pouring from back on the counter.

The Electric Eel!

"Madame Beulah's money..." he said looking back.

"What about it?"

"It's gone..."

"Gone?"

But Orville wandered away in annoyance before she could question it further. *I hope he doesn't think I took it...*She mused. Silently he prayed that Madame Beulah wouldn't return so that he wouldn't have to repay her or explain why her stuff had been stolen...

Rory looked up at his boss, with hollow wan dark eyes. *How old is he anyway? He looks like he's aged twenty years...*After the crowd had their drinks Lobelia joined him.

"When's Iris's funeral?" she asked.

"It's over...She had to be buried within forty-eight hours..." he said dryly. "But her family is accepting visits all week...Something called a Shiva call..."

"Maybe we should go..."Orville said.

But his motives in going weren't completely altruistic...He pictured Mr. and Mrs. Dupeon's residences in his mind...Images of palatial estates in the Hamptons and Bexley and the tropics flooded his thoughts...*Mother goes on and on about how much money they have...Maybe she will want to go?*

"How's the dog doing?" Lobelia asked.

Rory brightened at the thought of the hound. For the first time since Iris's death, he smiled. Lobelia waited.

"He's good...With my parents... They *adore* him..."

*Funny how they never wanted a dog...Now they let him on the furniture...*He mused.

Next, Eugenia interrupted them in her usual impolite manner. Orville rolled his eyes. She motioned to the back of the room.

"What is it, Eugenia?"

She pointed to Madame Beulah's table. He shrugged as if she were wasting his time. Again she gestured to it.

The Electric Eel!

"So...?"

"Her spirit board..."

"What about it?"

"I threw it in the trash last night..."

"So?" he repeated, growing bored with the conversation.

"Outside..." she said spelling her words out as if talking to a slow child. "And they picked up the trash this morning...And it's *back!*"

*Surely this is a joke...*He thought, his eyes darting around the room. *She's screwing with me...* The look on his face said.

"Burn it..." he said finally.

"Nuh-uh..."

Eugenia backed away from the table. *She's serious!* He looked at his other employees who in turn took two steps back. He turned to Rory who put his hands up in protest. Finally, Lobelia stepped forward and took the board.

"We used to see stuff like this in the Caribbean all the time..."

"She's brave..." Rory whispered.

With great care, Lobelia reached for the board and a cigarette lighter and carried it to the back door. She looked down at how innocuous it seemed...She shrugged and tossed it on top of the metal trash receptacle and lit a small amount of newsprint beneath it. The flame sputtered at first in the cold and then flashed as if coated with gasoline.

Feeling like cowards for sticking Lobelia with the task, Rory and Orville joined her outside. Orville turned to the fire as if looking at a bonfire, his normally blue irises reflecting blaze orange. Rory placed his palms out to warm them.

Suddenly, someone else came up behind them without their realization. Rory's nose picked up on something acrid and fetid. A shadowy figure moved in the light of the fire, like a nocturnal rodent.

"Murderers..." it whispered.

The Electric Eel!

"Who are you?" Rory called.

But the individual had disappeared. They shuddered as the blaze died down, the piece disintegrating into only a few filigreed strands. Rory could make out a few scripted letters. He shivered.

"Let's get back inside..."

"Well! Thanks for leaving me with all these people while you all go galivant in the night!" Eugenia snapped.

"You didn't want any part of it..." Orville muttered with gritted teeth.

Lobelia stepped in and began making cocktails without acknowledging her. Two drunk men chortled something obscene in her direction. While she smiled, inwardly she had grown sick of it...*So tired of drunk men...*

"Leave her be! You came here with me!" a young woman shrieked.

And drunk women too...! The man blanched and sipped his drink as she got up in his face, her arms folded. *In the old days we would have cut them off...*

"Have you seen Trixie?" Rory asked his boss.

Orville took him aside, his light eyes looking around with caution. He flashed him an uncomfortable great white shark smile...He touched Rory's shoulder as the younger man looked down unsure of what it meant.

"Not all night...*Why?*"

"Cause we have a bunch of people wanting to buy cigarettes and she's not here...!"

Just then a familiar blond rushed in the back door. *Speak of the Devil!* Orville thought, smiling.

"Where have you been?" Rory asked

"Sorry..." she stammered. "But I need to talk to Orville..."

"Can it wait?" Rory asked, somewhat frazzled.

"No..." she hesitated.

Orville took her aside. *What is it?* He blinked in a thoughtful bravado.

"I'm pregnant!"

With these words, Trixie chortled and covered her mouth with the back of her hand... Orville's eyes widened. Eugenia stifled a laugh, overhearing...

SIXTY-FIVE

"We don't even know if the baby is *his*..." Carlotta bristled to Irene. "Have you *seen* that girl?"

As Poppy passed in the hall, Irene reached over and touched her mother's arm to silence her. Edgar came into the kitchen next and both women glared at him.
Well this is awkward... He thought reaching for a piece of rye bread and placing it in the toaster.

"What'd I do?" he said to both of them.

"Nothing, Edgar...It's not always about you..." his mother quipped with a sigh, thrusting her usual proverbial projection upon him.

They giggled a little at his expense. He reached for the spring-loaded door that hinged on either side of the toaster and fished out the bread to butter it. An Art-Deco swirl pattern was seared on either side of the toast like cattle branding. He felt the warm bread in his hands as he put another piece inside the appliance.

"Making breakfast for your brother's wife?" Carlotta snickered.

"She's not my wife for long..." Orville said breaking in to defend his brother and himself... "Stop causing trouble...*Both* of you..."

His mother sneered, unused to being chastised. A second later Alistair, now ten years old, bounded up to the dining room table. They looked to Orville for direction.

"May I have some eggs?" Alistair asked.

"Sure. Have your mother fix you some..."

"I can fry my own..."

Edgar blinked at his brother's ignorance in not knowing that his son could not cook his own breakfast...Alistair seemed not to notice his father's faux pas and reached in the ice box for a small carton of eggs. Then he slid a stepstool close to the stove and reached for a small skillet.

"Should he cooking by himself?" Orville asked, trying to cover for his gaffe in not knowing.

"We watch him... He's fine..."

With fastidious precision, Alistair reached for a pat of butter and placed it in the skillet to sizzle. Next, he reached for the small skillet and turned it with the flick of his wrists as the butter melted and darkened. Once it was bubbly he broke the egg into two equilateral parts and placed it in the skillet to fry. When finished, he turned the burner off, flipped the egg on a plate and walked to the table.

"Boy should be a chef..." Edgar said with pride.

"Or an engineer..."

Alistair ate carefully and looked up to see the adults watching him. As he chewed the last bit of egg, he carried the plate to the sink to rinse it. Once finished he placed the dish upside down. Finally he washed his hands and walked back to the table.

"Am I going to have a brother or sister?" he asked his father.

Orville froze. The other adults held their breath in anticipation of his answer. Edgar constrained a laugh at his nephew's naïve candor.

"We don't know yet..." Orville said, trying to match his kid's honesty.

Just then Poppy stopped in the doorframe, overhearing. She shot her husband a smoldering look, an uncharacteristic contrast to her usual even temper. With loving arms she reached for her son to redirect him away from his father, aunt, and grandmother.

"Almost time for school, Alistair..."

Orville touched his wife's shoulder the way one might an acquaintance or a family pet. A chill ran up Poppy's spine. Orville craned his neck to make sure his son was out of earshot.

"Poppy and I have agreed to go our separate ways..." he said dryly.

"Orville has agreed to sign for a line of credit for me so I can get my own place...Since I can't do it legally on my own..."

"It's the least I can do..."

*I thought so...*She thought looking up at him. *Now that he's loaded...*

"And I'm Catholic and don't want a divorce on my record..." he said quietly.

*They'll make her prove infidelity in court...*He thought with a shudder. *And she has plenty of evidence now with my baby growing inside Trixie...I'd be humiliated...And they'd surely bring the Electric Eel and father's murder into it...We'd be ruined...*

He looked at Edgar and Poppy. As his brother exchanged a sidelong glance with his wife something dawned on him. *I don't think she's innocent either...Perhaps I was too rash...*

"What about you two?" he asked with forced polite intonation.

Irene shifted as if watching an intriguing talking picture. Edgar twitched his mustache like a rabbit. But Poppy was unfazed by this question as if waiting for a flyball.

"Our relationship is proper..."

"So far..." Edgar added.

Orville burned in embarrassment. *Are they playing me?* He wondered. His mother and sister looked on in bemused condescension at the spectacle that had begun their lives...Irene sipped her tea.

"How's the baby, Irene?" he asked changing the subject.

"Fine..." she said in a calm voice. "Mr. Wright says he's growing like a weed... With the governess at the moment...Lord knows I need a break..."

She pulled out an emery board and buffed her nails. Somehow Edgar couldn't picture his sister as a doting housewife. But he said nothing for fear of his mother and sister's wrath.

The Electric Eel!

"Did I tell you Madame Beulah disappeared?" Orville asked his mother.

"*Good!*" his mother snapped. "She always scared the Bee-Jesus out of me!"

"But she left all her stuff... And it gives us all the Willies!"

"Pitch it..."

"We *tried...*!"

Carlotta cringed and placed her coffee cup back on the table. The thought of Madame Beulah and all her spiritual paraphernalia filled her...Like a horror movie...

"Maybe you should try to contact her on one of her spirit boards..." Irene added, in half interest.

"But she isn't dead..." Edgar pointed out. "They talked to her sister..."

"Does that really matter?" Irene asked with a sly smile.

*It's a thought...*Orville offered. *Maybe we should conduct a séance of our own...*

Ten hours later, Orville arrived at an empty bar. Truth be told he enjoyed the quiet moments before everyone in town showed up. The bakery, too, which had been open for most of the morning was also quiet...*A hit in its own right!* He thought with much pride, flipping on a light. As usual the bakery was pristine, the floors and glass gleaming and immaculate. *Ala Rory and Lobelia!*

He noticed a leftover cruller and reached for it with a piece of wax paper. It's texture was crisp and sticky at the same time, its outside patterns like a wheel in reverse. It smelled of cinnamon sugar as he bit into it...*A little stale but still good...*He thought chewing.

The Electric Eel Bar was as it had always been...Glassware hanging upside in the center above the bar... Wallace's piano and the stage nearby... As he opened the speakeasy door, something else hit his senses...He spit out the remainder of the pastry in the paper, nearly gagging at the smell. *What is that?*

"What is that smell?" a low female voice shrieked from somewhere behind.

"Dead fish!" he exclaimed nearly choking on the words.

"It's coming from the back corner, Eugenia..."

Near the eel tank... He observed covering his mouth. *They usually buzz when I open the door...She's going to flip...*

As Lobelia turned on the overhead lights, Orville spotted something floating like driftwood on the top of the water. The eels were belly up; their mouths open as if gasping for air. The serpentine fish's once vivid orange eyes were now open and devoid of color and shrunken in their sockets. Eugenia let out a scream.

Lobelia turned to the look at Madame Beulah's table a few feet away. The Ouija board was where it always sat, burnt at the edges but intact, alongside her spirit trumpet and the shattered remains of a crystal ball...Orville gulped at the realization.

"Is this a joke?"

"*Look!*" one of the women shouted.

To their horror, they watched as the spade-shaped planchette began to move on its casters...Slowly at first...As it spun it spelled out something cryptic in three distinct letters...

"E-E-L...."

SIXTY-SIX

"We can't get you anymore electric eels at the moment..." Mr. Mark from the zoological society informed Orville on the phone the next day. "All we have are Morays... And those are far and few between...But we have two and they're tame... Well... As tame as an eel *can* be..." he said with a laugh. "We've been calling them Jezebel and Ahab...My wife names all the animals and she's a big fan of Moby Dick...And the Bible...But you can name them whatever you like..."

"Whatever you want to call them is fine..."

"It's gonna cost you extra since it's cold and we'll have to send a heated truck..."

The Electric Eel!

"That's fine...Whenever you can get here." Orville said hanging up with a defeated sigh. "They don't have any electric eels..." he informed Eugenia.

He held his breath, waiting for the gnashing of teeth and histrionics. Eugenia's green eyes flashed temper. Orville placed the phone back on its hook and wandered over to the bakery case. *Here it comes...*

"What are we going till then?"

"We'll have moray eels..." he said growing tired of the whole mess.

"But we're the *electric* eel..." she said spelling it out to him as if he weren't all there...

"Then we'll just be the eel...Or the moray eel..." he joked. "Maybe invent a new cocktail in their honor..."

"What a dunce! I should run this place..." Eugenia whispered to Lobelia. "How am I going to do my show?"

"The same way you always did..." Orville whispered. "We have to get this all emptied before they get here... It has to be converted into salt water anyway..."

Though they cleaned thoroughly, the smell of deceased, rotting eel remained. Eugenia held her nose as the tank emptied the rest of the way and then refilled. An hour later someone arrived from the zoo to measure the salinity of the aquarium.

"They're here..." Orville announced.

An official looking man walked in and shook Orville's hand. He was dressed in all khaki and matching hat as if going on Safari. *Must be from the zoo...*

Four burly men carried in something covered in thick wool blankets. Like pall bearers they walked across the room, past the guests who had already arrived. A few people turned away from their drinks and vice to watch. Silently they removed the blanket unveiling the fish.

Unlike the electric eels, these creatures were long and sinewy and brightly colored. One of the fish was the color of a weeping willow with a long snout, an underbite and a top fin like a crown while the other was smaller and torpedo shaped, spotted like a

The Electric Eel!

Dalmatian with two predominate nostrils...They looked up in omniscience at the people around them.

"Meet Jezebel and Ahab..."

"Which one's which?"

"Ahab is the green...Bigger one...He'll grow to be about six feet long...Jezebel's will only get about four and a half feet..."

"I *knew* it!" Eugenia clapped, warming up to the idea.

"She may be smaller but she's the real hunter...Both of them can give you a nasty bite... And they have teeth like hooks and a second set of jaws that come forward so they can't release easily...So if they bite you, your thumb is as good as gone...They have to swallow to release. Their eyes are small, so they rely on smell to hunt their prey...Ahab is covered in mucous to protect his skin..."

Lobelia shuddered. *May this wasn't such a good idea...*She watched as the men stood on a ladder and hefted the vessel upward to release the fish into the water. A second later the fish slithered down the side of the tank, adjusting to their new home.

Once he was sure they were situated, the group walked to the tank to examine them. Jezebel immediately hid behind a small rock, but Ahab stared at them intensely, his jaw dropping as if wishing to say something.

"The nice thing is he isn't afraid of anyone...So people can walk right up and greet the tank...People call them the gangsters of the sea...So they should work well round this place," he said with a wink.

*I can see why...*Lobelia thought staring at the fish's sickly green eyes. He gazed back at her and gave a ghastly pointed toothed smile. Then his mate joined him and turned her neck around his as if beckoning him away from the crowd of onlookers. She faded into the background like camouflage, satisfied with getting her way.

"Sign here..." the man from the zoo said to Orville. "Sorry we didn't have an electric eels..."

The Electric Eel!

"That's okay... I think these will work out nicely..."

"And if they have babies let me know and I'll take them off your hands..." he said. "That way they don't eat them...And you won't have 60,000 eggs on your hands..."

Sixty thousand? Orville thought. The man from the zoo moved on and checked the tank.

"Do we feed them the same way as the others?" Eugenia asked with hands on hips. "Since I'll be the one doing it..."

"Always with a stick or pliers...Never with your fingers! That way they don't associate your hands with food..."

"Got it..."

"Well. I better be going...It keeps getting dark earlier and earlier..."

"Want a nip for the road?" Orville asked, unconcerned with the prospect of the man driving while intoxicated.

The man pondered it. He looked at the two men he had come in with. They nodded. Orville poured them each a beer. As they reached in their wallets, he put his hand up to stop them.

"On the house..."

"Don't mind if I do..."

Once they consumed the ales, they ordered another and another...And once they ran out of beer they drank whiskey. After drinking for an hour and a half, they got off the bar stools, sloshing like eels in the tank, their torsos swaying back and forth...Though far less gracefully than the morays who resided in the back of the room...

Finally the three men walked to the front of the room and gave a tip of their hats to Tiny who stood by at his usual post at the door like a Centurian. He nodded and let them pass into the bakery and out the front door without asking any questions.

While the temperature outside hovered at freezing, the three men's bodies remained warm with an abundance of alcohol. One of them even took off his jacket as his shoulders and throat heated up like a furnace with cheap liquor.

The older of the two pointed to the building which *used* to contain Marie Toussad's but now housed something equally as reprehensible...*A massage parlor*...One of them noticed standing under a glaring red-light.

"Good way to get v.d.!" the older man guffawed with the slap of his knees.

"No thanks!"

After a few minutes of searching, they found the delivery truck. It was an electric kind with a wooden bed like two vertical palettes that was popular in the decade for door-to-door deliveries. The vehicle was high off the ground, towering over most of the cars on the road with a heavy two-ton chassis and spoke wagon wheels. "Columbus, Ohio Zoological Society" was stenciled in a white, elegant font between the cab and the bed of the vehicle.

"Get in! The wife's gonna kill me for bein so late..."

The interior of the truck was simple with a steering wheel on a diagonal beam sticking out if the floor and a small oak panel separating them from the engine. Three pedals sat on the floor alongside a black and brass corkscrew shaped horn. The men piled in and began their bumpy, inebriated ride back to other side of town.

"The original zoo closed in 1905 after being open only a few months..." Mr. Mark informed them with slurred speech. "They're supposed to open the new one in Powell in twenty-seven...Turn here..." he told the driver.

As the truck bounced with turbulence, none of them realized he turned the *wrong* way down a one-way street...A few blares emanated warnings from several car's horns as they careened down a red cobblestone street, the wheels of the vehicle flying off the pavement and landing back on the ground. The weight of the truck came down on the suspension nearly breaking the wheels as it came back down.

All of a sudden the driver gave a swift turn to the right, causing the truck to falter and lean to one side like ship taking on water. As the sights and sounds of High Street came into view, he overcorrected the wheel, causing the car to take a sharp left up the sidewalk. At great speed, the delivery truck flew and pivoted in a spiral, flipping like a tilt-o-whirl at a county fair.

As the cab of the truck inverted, all three men jostled in their seats like ragdolls, their heads hitting the interior. A nano-second later the driver was nearly impaled as the center of the steering wheel hit his sternum, heart, lungs, and ribcage and bounced off his chin and face. The clear impression of the "Ford" logo would later be found by the medical examiner etched in his chest like a moniker.

Meanwhile, the others flopped to the side, their arms and legs bending like gelatin as they crashed against the door jam, ejected facedown onto the pavement. Before they could react, the truck came down on top of them, killing them instantly...The truck's lights flickered a moment as the wheels continued to spin upside down...

And died...

SIXTY-SEVEN

Jezebel and Ahab waited patiently for the last of the onlookers to disappear before moving around their new home. In the dim light Jezebel scanned the room outside the tank, her eyesight not as great as her sense of smell. Her tankmate laid the side of his shovel-shaped head on a rock as if resting on a pillow and opened his mouth to take in air as salty water washed over his gills and exited through two holes on either side of his cheeks. Then in unison they rose to the top of the tank where they could see everything clearly...

Fifty feet away something long and wooden sat. On it rested something else wooden, elevated slightly with strange unfamiliar alphabet characters. In the middle of the board something leaf-shaped and trimmed in gold rested. All of a sudden it began to quiver and then spin. The two eels not far away watched as it moved in a purposeful path and then returned as if on invisible racetrack...*It knows where it's going...*

The Electric Eel!

As the wooden thing moved, something else slid across the table. Large sharp shards of glass reflected like prisms as they crept back and forth. A moment later they came to a halt in a circle as if forming the shape of a perfect sphere.

A silver triangular shaped object rose and pointed at the ceiling held by an unknown, invisible hand. A woman's voice began to chant in a language they didn't understand...Calling them...*Pleading* for whatever resided here to make its presence known...

Even though the doors were locked, figures entered the room...*Somehow*...First, came a petite woman with a cigarette in her left hand and a dog lead in the right...But her body was off somehow...Broken as if her bones were brittle and aged despite being in her prime. She moved across the room and lingered at the stage for a second...And vanished...

Strange noises Jezebel and Ahab had heard but couldn't place came next...Melodious whines of some unknown instrument hung in the air followed by human voices strung together in various chords and notes...*Music*... Another instrument came, fluid like running water, its tones going up and down...*Pianoforte...!*

The second figure to enter the room was a man...Unlike the woman with the dog, who felt comfortable in the space, he hesitated near the front door. As he turned they spotted puncture wounds dotting his back...*Like a giant cheese grater!* Before he exited, he gave the bar a long, vacant, mournful, melancholy look of regret...

With little effort, Jezebel pivoted, her striped serpentine tail slithering across the floor of the aquarium like a garden hose. Her right eye focused on three vaguely familiar male humans in matching clothing sitting on stools in front of the bar. Over time their bodies began to sink as if overcome with some unknown malady. After a while, the men stood on shaky legs and headed for the door. Someone else looked at them in hesitation as if wanting to stop them from going where they were going in the state they were in...But said nothing that would have prevented them from leaving...

The Electric Eel!

All of a sudden a loud crash came from somewhere...A vision of the men falling unceremoniously came next in the middle of the room as if they were acting out a violent game of charades or pantomime...A large wheel on a pike flew upward out of nowhere, knocking the wind out of one of the men, the sound of his ribcage cracking and popping from the force.

Before the others could react, the other two men landed facedown with their fingers spread. A large weight from above landed between their shoulder blades, crushing them with the sound of bones breaking as the men expired...And left...

The sounds of more violence came from elsewhere around the building. Sounds of weapons firing and people breathing their final breaths came and went...All of it replayed ad nauseum in this place like scenes from a b horror movie...

In the aquarium, Jezebel and Ahab intertwined and while they didn't really *like* each other, they had bonded. At the other place when he had consumed live octopus, Ahab would tie his body in a knot to prevent the tentacles from latching onto his body; however, the food he had consumed here was *easy*, requiring no forethought of the hunt...*Especially* not like pursuing something as cunning as a mollusk...

Soon, the day would begin again...The actual living beings would return again to replace those who only popped in from time to time...A few small bars of lemon yellow morning sun danced through the blinds in the only window in the place, signaling that day had broken...

As light flooded in, the two newest residents of the Electric Eel sank back to the bottom of the tank unnoticed. Jezebel's black and white exterior blended into the rocks perfectly as she swam backward and hid. Ahab's neon green skin suddenly disappeared like camouflage against the bottom. A second later, only the sight of his milky, left Peridot-colored eye remained, blurred like a cataract on a person of advanced age.

By the time morning came, the deceased individuals who inhabited this place, faded. The nocturnal eels rested now, their bodies rocking back and forth as if snoring or having a bad dream. The snakelike fish's mouth opened and closed rhythmically as they breathed in deep, labored breaths...

Elsewhere in the room, the pointed end of Madame Beulah's heart shaped planchette spelled out something illegible. Like a music box winding down, the nightly noises that had become routine around this place quieted down and then stopped altogether. A moment later, the Electric Eel was silent...

SIXTY-EIGHT

January, 1925

*N*o one had heard from Trixie in *months*...Partially out of guilt and partially out of obligation, Orville had sent money and the occasional delivery of flowers and groceries...But over the weeks, she had dropped out of sight from everyone at the Electric Eel...Even though her apartment was less than one hundred yards away...

Before the bar opened, Rory suggested to Orville that they go visit her. *Why he never thought to go see her on his own, I'll never know...*He thought expecting an argument. But to his surprise, Orville went along with it...

"She *is* carrying my kid..." Orville said with trademark flippancy.

"That she is..."

Earlier in the month, the city had been inundated with freezing rain which in turn created a crystalline undertow of ice beneath a dusting of morning snow. The steps to Trixie's walkup glistened with wintry silver and white particles, the sides of which dripped with icicles in various stages of frozen paralysis.

"Careful..." he warned Rory.

Rory had an eerie feeling. *What if she died?* He thought of Iris now anytime he had to climb even a moderate height, his new acrophobia a constant side effect of his memories.

The Electric Eel!

"Does she have heat...?" he asked his boss.

Orville looked up as if it had never crossed his mind...*He's not malicious...Just oblivious...*He pointed to smoke rising out of the chimney that attached to the west side of her building....*That's a relief...*

As if trekking the Arctic, the two men moved up the stairs. Before work they had donned thick fur-lined gloves and heavy soled shoes. Orville had chosen a long coat over his usual three-piece tweed suit that belted at the waist. Rory wore a toboggan with a silly fuzzy ball on the top and a wool jacket that came up to his chin.

*It's a stupid hat...*Orville thought looking at him. The ice crunched beneath their feet like eggshells as they reached the top step. Rory steadied himself, his fear of falling returning.

"Remember the night we spent here with her?" Orville whispered with a wry smile.

"Don't remind me..."

"Trixie!" Orville yelled as loudly as he could muster.

He reached for the door handle and jiggled it. It moved a little. Rory began to panic.

"Open it!" he said with growing impatience.

Orville did as he was told and pushed the door in. A layer of crusty snow stuck to his shoes, and he kicked it off in the door jam. Rory peered in the apartment with caution.

In contrast to the frigidity outside, Trixie's apartment was *stifling*... Orville stepped over piles of clothing in the entryway. *What a mess!*

"Trixie..." Rory called with much caution.

Is she dead? Then they spotted her. Slumped over in the couch...Orville blinked not recognizing her at first... She was hugely fat like the carcass of a beached sea creature. *Is she alive?*

"Trixie..."

To his relief, she stirred, her eyes wide in surprise. Her now round face was pleasant as always. She patted her stomach like a shelf.

The Electric Eel!

"We came to check up on you…" Rory called as if she were infirmed.

"That's sweet…" she said still groggy from her nap.

"When are you due?" Orville asked.

He looked around the apartment as if he wished to be anywhere else in the world but here…. Trixie didn't seem to mind, her eyes closing again. Rory poked her shoulder, and she awoke.

"The doctor says April First, but mother doesn't think they'll wait that long…"

"*They?*" Orville repeated as if he'd heard incorrectly.

"Twins!" Rory said reading between the lines.

Rory clapped his hands together in glee. Orville gulped and turned on his heels. *What else could go wrong?*

"Uh-huh. Sorry to hear about your friend Iris…" Trixie said reaching for him. "I know you loved her…"

Unexpected tears welled up in the corners of Rory's lids. *She's sweet…*He thought. In his mind he compared Iris's penthouse to the dump Trixie was living in and then stopped himself…*Iris had someone to do everything for her…Trixie is poor and all alone…*

"Do you need me to send someone here to clean, Trix?" Orville hinted.

He looked at a sink stacked with dirty pots and pans filled with sudsy water and the remnants of a red sauce that had separated. A few gnats hovered around the top of the heap. *How'd they get in here?* More dishes were stacked haphazardly on the kitchen table along with food that was beginning to rot at room temperature and congeal on the plates.

Rory looked at something cluttering the kitchen table….A vase of ancient cut flowers that were rotten inside the water but dried and withered at the tips…The detritus of the petals were shriveled like dead skin around the glass in a pile of dust… *I sent those…*Orville recalled.

Trixie noticed his gaze on her slovenly housekeeping…*Or lack thereof…*And said,

The Electric Eel!

"Sure... If you want to...But it'll just get dirty again!"

She laughed that bawdy, uncomfortable laugh of hers again...Rory tried to pay attention to her face and *not* the mess around him...He patted hand the way one might a pet or distant relative...

Orville thought of his child...*Or children*...Living in this squalor...*My mother would flip her wig!*

"We'll get someone up here to help you..."

"Okay," she said with only slight interest. "I appreciate the groceries..."

Some of them are still on the counter I see... Orville noticed. Trixie looked down in the direction of the Electric Eel. A tinge of regret filled her.

"I miss all you guys..."

"We miss you..."

"I couldn't fit into my cigarette girl uniform anyway..."

"You will..." Rory promised.

Orville studied her as she tried to stand up on bowed legs. *I'm not so sure about that*...Suddenly growing bored he looked back at the stairs.

"Well we better be going...Do you have a phone?"

She looked around the room sheepishly. With some embarrassment she reached through a pile of women's undergarments that lay on an end table. Then she reached through another, tossing the clothing at her feet...A few minutes later a phone appeared.

"We'll send someone up..." Orville said, with disgust.

Once the two men were on the ledge Orville looked at Rory and shook his head. Rory pulled his hat down over his ears again and backed down the stairs as if descending a mountain. In the distance the wind howled, buffeting the side of the wooden stairs with a shake.

"I didn't recognize her..."

"Me either..." he said making a sour face. "But I can't let my kid grow up in that..."

"She didn't seem bothered by it..."

"True...But I *am*..."

Near the bottom of the stairs Lobelia stood in brilliant purple coat. As the cold escalated she rubbed her gloved palms together as if starting a campfire. She looked up at Trixie's second floor apartment and then at her boss.

"How is she?"

"Fine..."

"Having twins!"

"Congratulations, papa!"

Thanks! I think... He thought passing her into the open the door to the warmth of the Electric Eel. Rory walked in and started a pot of coffee.

"Want some?"

"Definitely!"

An hour later a throng of people were waiting outside the door to get in. Despite being glad to be back in the familiarity of the bar, Orville couldn't concentrate on the task at hand. His initial thought had been that the freezing temperature would deter people from coming in, giving him a relatively easy night; however, it only seemed to give them more reason to be there...

"Cold enough out there for ya?" an old man said forcing small talk with Tiny.

"Brutal..."

"Hot toddies for all of us!" the leader of the group shouted.

"You got it!"

Lobelia heated the water to near boiling on a small electric burner and stirred in a little honey and lemon juice. Eugenia reached for a bottle of whiskey and handed it to her. Next, she rinsed several clear mugs and dried them with a tea towel. Lobelia held the glasses up to the light to examine them.

The Electric Eel!

I hate when she does that! She thought, pouring the hot toddy mixture into the glassware. A group of middle-aged men in cherry red flannel shirts and ridiculous hats with earflaps sat at the bar, waiting. *Not our usual clientele...*

"At least it's not illegal to *drink* these!" one of them chimed.

"Not yet... If they pass that Jones Act it will be!"

"They just now figured out there is a loophole...I heard they will be arrest you for just *witnessing* someone drinking! Up to three years!"

"It'll never pass...At least not till twenty-nine..."

*They said that about Prohibition...*Orville thought handing them the scalding drinks. *Still it would be an awful prospect to enforce...Even though we all kind of think of it as a big joke...*

One of the men looked at the toddies as they steamed. A wedge of lemon floated in each...*A tough commodity to get in Ohio in winter...*

All of a sudden, the sound of something jarring came as if someone had detonated a bomb...Everyone began to look around...*Was it another raid? Had those temperance women returned?* Panic ensued.

"I don't think it's a raid..." someone said.

The sound of someone shouting came next...

SIXTY-NINE

"*W*e are just enforcing the law!" a male voice bellowed.

A group from the Electric Eel gathered with trepidation in the bakery front of the establishment. The men in the flannel walked out next, some of them still holding their beverages...Orville looked at them in horror... *Put that away!*

Quickly Lobelia grabbed the glasses and placed them under the bakery counter. But no one seemed to care about the alcohol anymore...Their gaze focused instead on the spectacle outside...

The Electric Eel!

"We are taking back our streets from the debauchery of the Jew, the Catholic and the Negro..." someone projected up and down the street as if preaching a sermon.

Lobelia looked up at the sea of ghostly figures in all white and gulped. Their pointed hoods were like giant gnomes as they marched in sync. *There have to be dozens of them!*

"It's everywhere if you pay attention...The Chinese den of inequity calling itself a massage parlor...The Jewish Pharmacist selling hallucinogens...The priest down the street peddling in gambling and illegal wine...The feminists demanding the right to vote and organized labor! The queers on High Street playing checkers with each other right under our noses...What do you boys call it these days? Basketeering? The flappers who are turning their backs on motherhood to flaunt being whores who drink and smoke," the leader screamed from atop a white horse, pulling his hood down to be heard further.

The man on the horse's gold tooth glinted in the moonlight, the rest of the group's eyes were only visible through small peepholes cut into the fabric of their hoods. Like elementary school trick-or-treaters dressed as ghosts they stood firm. A few of the select members had red sashes or red and white crosses embroidered on their lapel. Rory blinked not realizing any of its significance, unsure of any of their symbolism.

Though Orville was small in stature, he wasn't intimidated. As he walked closer to the street, the ice crunched under his feet in protest. The leader stopped his steed, shocked by his audacity.

"And who might you be?"

"Orville Alfonso... I own this place..." he said with pride. "I thought we got rid of you after the Civil War?"

"A Catholic with an illegal speakeasy? Who would have thought? And to answer your question we never went anywhere..."

"We're a bakery..."he informed them. "And why are you here?"

The Electric Eel!

"We, as good Protestants, Mr. Alfonso, are here to bring law and order *back* to streets of Columbus, Ohio! Despite your will to stop us! Prohibition is the law, and we will not tolerate inebriation!"

Lobelia attempted to move back inside the bar; however, the man noticed her. Rory touched her arm in protection. The night sky loomed above them, dark with a hint of silver clouds.

"And who do we have here?" he said calling Lobelia.

"Leave her alone!" Rory shouted in a surprisingly strong voice.

He looked up and down at the young man and gave him a wry, unwelcoming smile, his tooth glinting again. Rory gulped. *They're gonna lynch us...*

"What's wrong there, nance? Don't have your Jewess with the dog to protect you anymore?"

"But how did...?"

"We know *everything*..."

Lobelia reached back and touched Rory in gratitude. Tiny moved closer to her in a protective stance. She distanced herself from him out of fear of him triangulating their relationship...

"This your girlfriend, big fella?" he said without waiting for an answer. "What are you doing slumming it with the likes of them?"

But to Lobelia's relief, he did not answer the man on the horse. Suddenly, the man pulled his hood back down over his eyes and turned the animal away from the Electric Eel, its front legs raring up on its haunches. Rory bit his lip in anticipation of what was coming next...

He signaled something to those in white who stood in three single file lines. Collectively they turned facing the other end of the street. Their crisp white sheets glowed in clear contrast to the blackness of the now pitch-colored sky.

A few of the group lit torches on long wooden sticks, the flames reflecting orange in their eyes as they marched. Despite the bitter cold, sweat began to pour down their faces through the heavy satin fabric of the hoods. A few in the group lifted American flags on poles above the torches so they would not catch fire while others made the letter k with their index, ring, and middle fingers.

With morbid fascination, a few from the bar followed the callithump as it whooped up the street. Eugenia and Orville were in awe as a sea of flames rose above the pointed hoods. *Are they going to torch the whole block?*

Rory and Lobelia, the most vulnerable of the group, paused at the other end of the street. Rory pondered bolting but feared being viewed as a coward…He thought of Iris now…Unable to defend her honor…

*She could buy and sell them…*Something whispered. *How on Earth did they know about my relationship with her?* He thought of Peaches as well…*Protecting her to the end…Most likely lying on the bed at my parent's house right now…*

From their vantage point, they watched as the mob lit something wooden at the end of street. The man on the horse galloped toward it; a cross wrapped in burlap now engulfed in flames. Lobelia smelled something sulfuric that she didn't instantly recognize.

"Kerosene…" someone informed them. "It's soaked in it…"

Her eyes widened as the flames leapt up the cross and sideways in the shape of a letter T, consuming the structure and some of the partially frozen grass on the ground. A second later they watched as the scores of Ku Klux Klan members made a circle around the cross, still holding their dwindling torches like fizzling matchsticks…As they disappeared, the points of their white hoods stood like elongated triangles, moving in perfect unison as they disappeared into the night…

The Electric Eel!

SEVENTY

𝒯hough the damage the next day was minimal, the disquieting fear, particularly among Lobelia and Rory, remained...*Maybe that was the point*...They rationalized.

"Let's get this picked up before it gets dark..." Orville informed them.

They were targeting your business...Eugenia thought. *Why don't you clean it up?*

Several piles of garbage had been pitched alongside the sidewalk and later pushed against the windows by the street sweeper....The refuse was thrown in a heap as an afterthought. To their chagrin, Orville was his usual chipper self.

"Not near as much damage as those Temperance broads, eh?" he quipped. "Hopefully it doesn't freeze against the walk..."

But none of his employees were laughing...The smell of burnt wood and petroleum hung in the air as a reminder. Across the street a door slid opened on the ice, and a high-pitched voice called to Rory.

"What happened? You have a party?"

"No, Trixie..." Eugenia mumbled in exasperation.

"The KKK was here for a march..."

"Oh," she said, her humor flattening.

"Congratulations on the twins, Trix!" Lobelia called looking up in her direction.

"Thanks, Lo!"

"Can we get on with this...?" Eugenia hissed.

Lobelia bit her lip. Eugenia looked up at the sight of the once petite woman. *She's gotten fat!* She thought feeling a little better about herself...

Rory reached for a broom and dustpan and began sweeping the discarded papers and food stuffs. He shook his head, not understanding why anyone would choose to target them in the way that they had. *Still it could have been worse...Much worse...*

A group of bar regulars and onlookers stood patiently as if waiting for a bus with their

The Electric Eel!

hands folded over their navel. Most of the young women sported abbreviated skirts, their legs hanging out in the cold.

"Electric Eel..." one of them whispered to Eugenia.

"Not open yet!" she barked. "Jesus! Back off would ya?"

"Thanks everyone..." Orville said heading inside.

Up ahead a long familiar car turned and parked. Three women got out, their expensive suits and high heels giving them an air of elegance not usually seen on this street. Irene, Virginia, and Carlotta walked into the cold and examined their surroundings.

"The Ku Klux Klan burned a cross here last night..."

"Technically they call it a cross-*lighting*..." Irene corrected.

*Not sure why you have the need to defend them...*Rory wondered. The women moved past them into the front of the facility. Carlotta stepped over the pile of swept trash as if were radioactive....*Menial cleaning was now beneath her...*

Only Virginia was congenial. But something told Lobelia to be wary. A light snow began to fall as the group moved inside.

Inside the building several other classy ladies were waiting at a back table. Most of these women were in their thirties and forties and married as compared to their usual female clientele who were younger and single. Not long after Tiny let in a cluster of men he presumed to be their significant others.

"Are those *real* eels?" one of the women asked them.

"They are..." Eugenia piped in. "Our newest additions Jezebel and Ahab..." she informed her.

The gaggle of women craned their necks in unison like a flock of birds toward the eel tank. The large green serpentine fish lifted his torpedo-shaped head and eyed them from across the room as his tankmate intertwined her black and white body against his... The pattern on her skin like a Holstein cow...Irene shuddered and looked away in disgust.

The Electric Eel!

"Welcome, ladies..." Orville said making a beeline for their table. "What can I get for you?"

"Well..." one of the women said clapping her hands together. "The Mr. and I were in England last year and we had something called and Aviation...And it was *purple*...!"

Orville pressed his lips together and pretended to know the reference...She sensed his unease. They looked at her intrigued.

"It had something called Crème de Violette in it and maraschino liqueur and gin..." she said. "If I recall..."

"I'll try that..."

"Me too..."

As women often do, they ordered the same things as their friends...Orville scanned the room for Rory and motioned to him with utmost discretion. They gave the women the universal sign to wait by putting one finger up.

"Go down to the pharmacy and see if Mr. Houserman has Crème de Violette and Maraschino Liqueur...Take money out of the till and give him whatever he wants for it...And pronto..."

Orville wrote it on a piece of paper and handed it to him. Rory nodded, trying to remember it. Then he reached for a wad of cash.

"Got it!"

"I vaguely remember that drink *before* Prohibition..." Carlotta said.

As Rory pulled on his coat, he noticed two people coming in the door...Mrs. Dupeon and Iris's brother Gerard...He stifled a little bit of rage at the sight of her brother, remembering what Iris had told him in confidence...

"Hi!" he said forcing pleasantries. "I'll be right back!"

Rory puffed a breath of air outside, glad to be away from the Electric Eel for the moment. He walked the block to the pharmacy, praying that it was open... His heart dropped seeing the lights were out.

The Electric Eel!

"Oh, hello, young man..." a voice called.

Mr. Houserman looked up with a little embarrassment. He held a bucket of hot, soapy water and a sponge and washed the remnants of something blue off his windows. Rory's eyes focused on it.

"Seems I got a little vandalism last night..." he said. "Hoodlums...Not the first time...At least they didn't break anything this time...But you didn't come to talk about that...What can I do for you?"

"My boss sent me to see if you had any Crème de Violette?" he said looking down at the piece of paper. "And Maraschino Liqueur..."

"Maraschino I'm not so sure... But the Violette Liqueur...I'm pretty sure I have one bottle somewhere...Becoming rare nowadays...Say! How's your lady friend doing? The one with the pretty pooch..."

"She passed away a few weeks ago suddenly..."

"*Oh...*"he said, feeling like a heel for putting his foot in his mouth.

"No...It's okay... She died accidentally... Her pooch is doing well!" he said trying to make him feel better. "He stays at my parents' house...!"

"That's good, at least!" he offered. "Here you go! My last bottle!"

Rory reached in his pocket for the money, but Mr. Houserman put his hand up. The young man looked at him curiously. He handed him the light purple bottle and scanned the shelves for the Maraschino Liqueur...

"Thank you..."

"Crème de Violette is nice...Floral...Very delicate and ladylike...Turns the drink purple...A real showstopper for the ladies...." He said trailing off. "Maraschino is a little sweet for my taste, but they go nicely together...Cut it with a little acid from lemon juice..." he told him.

"I'll remember that..."

"Here you go...That'll be five dollars, my dear boy..."

The Electric Eel!

Gladly, Rory fished in his pocket and handed him the crisp bill. Mr. Houserman nodded in gratitude and placed the note in his breast pocket. Then he reached for a discreet brown paper sack and flattened the bottom like a grocer.

"That won't be necessary…"

"No…I insist… This place is being surveilled all the time now! They won't bother you this way…"

"Oh, okay…Thanks…"

"I may be moving out here myself…If I can afford it…Too many memories…"

"Where would you go?"

"Florida maybe…I've heard Miami is nice this time of year…" he said heading for the door. "Until then, don't be a stranger…And again, sorry about your friend…"

"Thank you…"

"And serve those drinks up with something sweet like a cherry…!" he called.

This guy knows everything! He mused. Rory buttoned his coat and nodded.

"Will do!"

Rory returned to the Electric Eel a few minutes later. Orville reached for both bottles and began making the cocktails. *Just in time…* He reached for the remainder of the expensive gin beneath the counter he'd been saving for an event such as this… *No way rock gut liquor would pass with this group…!*

"Serve it up with a cherry…" he repeated.

He improvised the drinks, placed them on a silver tray and studied them like a sculptor examining his craft. The cocktails sparkled like amethyst in their glasses as Lobelia speared a cherry with a toothpick and placed it on top of each beverage.

"Here you go, ladies…"

"Bout time…" his mother chided.

He shot her a look, but the others didn't seem to notice, instead focusing on the violet concoctions. Iris's mother sat close by nodding in approval. *Tough crowd…* He thought.

"Evening, Mrs. Dupeon..." he called in a cool, erudite voice.

"Evening..."

When they finished, Rory reached for the tray of empty glassware. As he moved toward the bar he reached for the discarded toothpicks and put them in the waste receptacle. Then he noticed a few of the men standing around Irene and Orville's mother. One of the men smiled politely, the hint of a gold tooth catching the light like jewelry...

*The man on the horse...*He thought. Before he could respond, someone called his name.

"Rory? Rory Childs!"

Who here knows my last name? He turned to meet the handsome gaze of Gerard Dupeon. Gerard gave him a disarming grin, his cleft chin coming forward a little in a pout. Rory found himself unable to speak, like a scream that would not come out yet oddly intrigued at the same time...

"Thank you for being so kind to my sister..." his persisted. "If you ever need anything please don't hesitate to find me..."

And without waiting for a response, Iris's brother walked away...

SEVENTY-ONE

April 1, 1925

a crew of housecleaners arrived at Trixie's apartment for the second time in two months on the morning of March First, 1925. Trixie had moved to the mattress, on bed rest at her doctor's request. She slept often, getting up only to use the bathroom or get something to eat...

Many of those who came to clean her home she recognized from the Electric Eel. One of the women looked at her as if she should be ashamed of the mess...*Especially* given her condition...

The Electric Eel!

Still others judged her based on the fact that she was single and pregnant. Though they never said anything she sensed it...One of them scanned the room for any sign of a father...*Or a man at all...*

She'd heard it all...Her own mother had outright said it...Calling the babies...*Her babies*...Bastards...

"But we'll love them just the same..." her father had uttered as an afterthought.

But they rarely visited. Unlike her sister, who was happily married, whose children they spoke of in glowing terms....*To everyone...*

"Such a pretty face..." her grandmother had said. "What a shame she let her body go..."

While most things didn't bother Trixie, *this* did...She remembered smiling outwardly at this comment, but the backhanded compliment stung inwardly as if she'd slapped her. *Does everyone view me this way now?* Trixie wondered, suddenly experiencing self-consciousness in a way she'd never felt before...

Around fall of the following year, she'd begun to feel changes in her body. She began to experience hunger and weight gain simultaneously as well as mood swings. By the time her mother convinced her to go to the doctor the truth was painfully obvious.

"And here we are!" she said talking to the babies who resided inside her for the time being.

"Who is she talking to?" one of the cleaners asked the other.

"Who knows? The babies, I think..." the other one said.

All of a sudden, Trixie felt a sharp pain in her abdomen followed by a popping sensation. Then she felt a trickle. For a moment she feared she'd wet herself.

"Call the doctor!" she called to one of them.

"Is everything okay?"

"I think my water just broke!"

An hour later she found herself at the hospital on a gurney with her mother and the doctor standing over her. Her mother reached for her hand as her knees were placed

The Electric Eel!

up. The doctor spoke calmly.

"Since you are giving birth to twins we are going to administer something called Twilight Sleep..."he informed her in a knowledgeable voice.

"What is that?"

"It's an amnesic state to reduce pain during childbirth...By mixing a combination of morphine and scopolamine..." he said. "It didn't really catch on in the United States, but it was all the rage in Germany a few years ago... I assure you. You'll be perfectly fine...The only side effect is that you won't remember your birth..."

"But I *want* to remember giving birth to my babies..." she protested.

But her objections were ignored as they wheeled her into the birthing room. Before she could protest further, someone injected something into her arm and placed a towel smelling of bleach and chloroform over her face. A nurse grabbed her wrists and ankles and tethered her ankles to the bed.

"It's to keep her from thrashing..." the nurse said.

"Administer the memory test, nurse!"

"Do you know where you are?"

Trixie began to giggle like a fool. She wiggled her fingers since her legs and arms were now tied to four corners of the hospital bed, unable to move. Her eyes were heavy and weighted down with the cloth.

"The hospital?" she said as if questioning it herself.

"Let's proceed..."

Outside the hospital room, Rory and Orville waited. At this time in history, men were segregated from women during the birthing process. A man, Rory presumed to be Trixie's father, fidgeted with a newspaper.

Inside the room they heard banging as if someone were throwing around pots and pans. After thirty minutes or so it grew silent...Rory tapped his foot nervously.

"Lobelia's taking care of the things at the Electric Eel..." he told him. "Alistair's excited

The Electric Eel!

to have a brother or sister...Or *both*..."

Rory had forgotten that Orville had another child for the moment...*A polite little boy*... He recalled now. In the hospital door he noticed Edgar, Poppy, and Carlotta...*I want to hide*...

"How is she?" Poppy asked first.

"In labor now... They're giving her something called Twilight Sleep..."

Poppy wrinkled her nose, having heard of this practice. Edgar nodded, not completely understanding the procedure but wanting to be supportive. Carlotta held her handbag in her lap and sat down nonplussed.

After a few more hours the sound of a baby crying came. Then the sound of a second infant...A funny cry, that sounded off and unnatural as if they were competing with each other for attention.

"Would you like to see the babies?" the nurse said entering the lobby. "Two baby girls..."

The nurse led all of them to the maternity ward that separating them by plate glass. Rory froze instantly at the sight of the children. They were not light eyed and fair like Trixie or Orville, for that matter, their hair dark and fuzzy. One of the twins opened her nearly black eyes. Orville beamed and elbowed him.

"They're beautiful..." Poppy admitted. "Their eyes and hair always lighten..."

But none of them thought this was true...*They're not mine*...Orville thought with glee. Edgar and Carlotta stared wide eyed as well at the sight of them. Both babies were small and dark complected... *Like Rory*...

"Congratulations, dad..." Orville joked.

Rory gulped. The nurse returned again. Trixie's father looked up at her.

"When can we hold them?" Poppy asked.

"In a few... They're resting..."

"How's my daughter?" Trixie's father asked.

"Her vitals are dropping...They are trying to get her stabilized," she said sadly. "I'm afraid we might lose her..."

SEVENTY-TWO

"You may see Beatrix now..." a head nurse in white pinafores told the group after what seemed like an eternity. "But keep it down...Others are trying to rest..."

Beatrix...? They all wondered. They paused, unsure what had transpired. *Had she died? Maybe they had the wrong person...*

"How is Trixie, nurse?" Poppy asked, figuring she may tell a woman.

But the nurse put the clipboard down at her waist as if protecting the sensitivity of the information. All of them gleaned this was not good news, including Trixie's father... Rory feared the worst.

"What if she dies before she could even meet her babies?" Rory whispered.

My babies...Our babies... He corrected himself in his head. Carlotta shushed him as they were herded in one by one.

Trixie lay flat on her back on the mattress with her head still bandaged. Her wrists and ankles were stark white and turning reddish-purple with swelling. Her head flopped to one side. The expression on her face was as if she'd stepped on a landmine.

"Is she alive?" Edgar asked as if preparing for calling hours.

"Very much so..." the doctor said dryly without looking in their direction. "Was touch and go there for a moment...She's still under anesthesia so keep it brief..."

"Hi, Trix!" Poppy called, visibly relieved.

Trixie's eyes moved a little and she let out a groan. She twirled her fingers again in Rory's direction and then at her father. He reached for her hand.

Then two nurses came in each carrying a newborn. Both girls were the size of a small housecat with dark brows and lashes, mirror images of each other. Trixie's mother, who

The Electric Eel!

had been quiet through most of the ordeal, swooned taking one of the babies.

Trixie's parents looked at Rory as if addressing the elephant in the room...But they said nothing. Then someone handed Rory one of the girls and then the other. Rory, too, felt an instant kinship with the girls.

"You have twin girls, Trix..." Poppy told her.

"Twin girls..." she muttered. "Who's are they?"

The group looked to Rory again. One of the nurses took the babies and offered to let Carlotta hold them. *Not my grandchild...!* She wanted to say, putting both her hands up. Quietly the nurse took the babies out of the room. Trixie fell into a deep slumber.

Once visiting hours were over they were shuffled out of the hospital. Though Rory and Orville had taken the night off, they decided to go to the Electric Eel on the way home. The moonless sky was black as they climbed into his car.

"Guess that night we all spent together *did* mean something...Eh, Rory?"

Orville reached for one of the cigars that they passed out to men at the maternity ward and placed it in his teeth to chew on it. As he lit it smoke blew out the sides of his mouth like a dragon. Rory looked out the window forlornly.

"We did it with Iris too..."

"I *remember* that night! She was wild! Bet you wish they were *her* kids...! Then you'd be loaded..."

Rory shot him a look. *She wanted to have a baby with me...* Realizing he'd overstepped, Orville backtracked. *He's on cloud nine now that he knows he's not the father...!*

"That Trixie was quite the dish too...Then she got *huge*!"

As they approached the familiar block, Rory reached for the car's door handle. Orville looked at him in shock. *Is he going to jump out?*

"Stop the car..."

"Almost there..."

"I said: Stop the car!"

The Electric Eel!

"What's *your* problem?"

Unused to being told what to do, Orville stopped the car. A light rain became to form as Rory hopped out of the car, ignoring him. In a fury he slammed the car door.

"Oh! Stop being such a girl!" Orville shouted. "If only I'd met Iris first before you I would've picked her!"

Rory burned with ire at this insult and dashed away from the curb. Lobelia and Eugenia were waiting as he entered the bar. Tears mixed with freezing rain streamed down Rory's face as he processed what had transpired.

"How's Trixie?" Lobelia asked with genuine cocoa-colored eyes.

"Fine... She had twin girls..."

"Well! You don't seem very happy about it!" Eugenia barked. "How's Orville taking it?"

"They're my kids, Eugenia..." he admitted, walking away.

Orville emerged a minute later. He straightened his tie and vest, pretending as if nothing had happened between he and the other man, the remnants of the cigar still in his mouth. The women looked at him in disbelief.

"What's with him?" Eugenia said.

"Oh, he's just being emotional..."

Before Orville could say anything further to his employee, Rory stormed out of the Electric Eel...Into the pouring rain... Tiny shrugged as he breezed past him.

SEVENTY-THREE

Sid Clark had had plenty of time in jail to think about his plan for when he got out. The chaplain, whom he'd grown to like, had suggested forgiveness and while he'd considered it, jail only seemed to make him angrier as time went on...By the time the jailer came around to release him earlier that morning, he was furious...

He thought of Orville Alfonso, with whom he'd grown up. They had been friends in a time when white and black kids did *not* intermix...Even if they lived on the same

The Electric Eel!

street...And for that he'd always been grateful.

As he returned to the familiar street where his former friend's business sat, he pondered his next move. Like a jackal he lay in the shadows watching people coming and going from under the eave...*You're not even supposed to be here...*He thought, dodging the oncoming rain.

"What to do...? What to do?" he muttered to himself.

Sid watched as a tipsy middle-aged woman wandered up the street *One of Orville's customers most likely....*Briefly, he pondered having his way with her but then dismissed it...*No need to be arrested for that again...*Up the street she staggered like a newborn calf...Most likely in search of a vehicle...*She probably shouldn't be driving...*

Hastily, he dashed up the street toward her. At first she thought he was friendly...Just another vagrant in need...But as he grabbed her, she screamed.

"Don't make another sound...Or I'll kill you right here! Give me the keys!"

The woman did as she was told. Sid gave her an unnecessary shove causing her to fall on the cold concrete as he commandeered her automobile. The car rattled as it started. She stood, glad to be alive.

Sid aimed the car in the direction of the Electric Eel and gave an unsettling laugh. The owner of the car slinked away from the sidewalk; afraid he might intentionally run over her. He rolled down the window and gave her an obscene gesture.

As the rain died down he saw someone walking...A man this time but short of stature and fine boned like a woman...*Why does he look familiar?* Sid wandered, slowly down to get a closer look. *It's that guy from the Electric Eel... The one in the dress who sang with the girl with the dog...*

"Need a ride?"

"Thank you..." the young man said reaching for the car door.

But as Sid's face came into the light, something spooked him. Rory recoiled, backing away from the car. Before he could react, Sid grabbed his arm and strongarmed him into

The Electric Eel!

the jalopy.

"Long time no see!"

To Rory's horror, Sid sped up the car with him in it. *Now I have a hostage...!* Sid thought.

"What do you want with me, Sid?"

"You remembered! Funny I don't recall your name!"

"Rory..." he stammered.

"Rory...That's right!"

"Where are you taking me?"

"That's for me to know and you to find out..."

Sid drove out of town in silence. Open fields and farmland greeted them. He suddenly became talkative.

"Do you know Orville's brother Edgar?"

"Yes..." he answered wondering where he was going with this.

"Did Orville tell you *how* his brother lost his leg?"

"No..."

"I was there..." he said with pride, pulling over to the side of the farmland. "Their old house is up there..."

"Really?" Rory said humoring him, looking for a way to jump out of the car.

"He drug him onto his grandpa's old farm equipment...And told him he was going to take us for a ride...And he kept speeding up... Edgar was screaming...Begging him to stop...But Orville didn't stop... He never stops...And it fell on Edgar's leg... *Poor Edgar...*Orville's always been reckless..." he said, his hot breath heading in Rory's direction... "Like me...Can you believe Edgar's mother blames *him* for it...? We always knew she was a bitch...But that's just cruel, man..."

Rory swallowed hard. *I'm a dead man...He'll leave me here and no one will be the wiser...*

The Electric Eel!

"Don't worry...I'm not going to kill you..." Sid said reading his mind.

*He can smell fear...*Rory noticed. *And he's getting off on it...*

"You aren't?"

"No...I need you... You're gonna be my leverage..."

*This just keeps getting worse...*The rain began again, this time harder in a downpour. Sid grew bored with the farmland and sped the car up again, heading back in the direction of downtown.

Sid looked at Rory again with that insane smile of his. A haze formed as they got closer to High Street, the smell of rain mixed with petroleum and pollution stayed in the air as he drove. *Keep him talking...*Rory thought.

"Where are you taking me?"

"Back to your favorite place...The Eel...Or whatever that place is called..."

"Why?"

"Cause the last thing Orville Alfonso wants there is police! Now will you shut up?!" he said cutting him off in a volcanic mercurial shift.

Rory was suddenly afraid of him again. *He has nothing to lose...*Sid pulled the car to a crawl as if not wanting to be spotted in the city, turning the cars headlamps off as he drove.

"Wanna know where I got the car?" he bragged.

"Tell me..."

"Some broad was leaving from that place...Drunk as a skunk...So I took it...Shouldn't've been driving anyway!"

"Did you kill her?"

He turned to look at the other man incredulously. Rory watched as his mood shifted again. Sid felt a little hurt and rage.

"No! Why do you always think I'm a killer? I *threatened* to kill her if she didn't give me the wheels..." he said with a chuckle. "She gave it up right quick! Now no more

The Electric Eel!

talk...Almost there..."

With that he pulled the car alongside the street and brandished a weapon. Rory held his breath as he felt something poking him in the side. *What time is it?* He wondered, suddenly exhausted.

"Make a sound and I'll blow a hole in your side!" he menaced Rory with a shove.

But Rory gave in easily as they walked, his knees like gelatin. Sid's bad breath, stale cigarettes and body odor stank behind him as he pushed the gun closer into Rory's kidneys. *Closer...Closer...*

"Almost there...Let's just hope they're still open otherwise I don't know what I'll do with you..."

*There's a sobering thought...*They moved as one toward the door of the bakery. A large male eye appeared in the slat above the center door. Sid banged on it with his fist.

"Let me in! It's Sid!"

The person on the other side of the door was silent for a moment. He reached in the bakery case for a cookie and put it between his teeth like a dog. The taste of cinnamon sugar stuck to the roof of his mouth as he pounded again.

Customers and staff alike began to panic inside the Electric Eel. Quickly, they hid their glassware and contraband. *It's Sid!* Tiny mouthed.

"We told you never to come back here!" a voice called through a crack in the door.

Sid seized the moment and forced it open. Rory followed in tow like a ragdoll, still remaining on the other side of the wall. The other man pointed the muzzle of the weapon in the room like a cartoon character.

"Tell em, Rory!"

"Let him in or he'll kill me..." Rory pleaded.

Tiny opened the door without hesitation. They rushed in, the gun still pointed at the young man's internal organs. Orville gave Sid a mortified look.

"Let him go, Sid..." Lobelia ordered.

"Not so fast..."

SEVENTY-FOUR

"What do you want, Sid?" Orville asked from across the room.

"Vengeance..." Sid answered.

A lump formed in Orville's throat. They looked at the young man who Sid held captive with the butt end of the gun. Rory struggled against him like a fish on a hook.

"C'mon, Sid! We can talk about this! Let Rory go!"

While still holding onto Rory, Sid turned the gun on the rest of those in the speakeasy. A few panicked customers gasped. Orville put his hand up as if deflecting a bullet.

"Do you know you're working for murderers?" Sid shrieked.

"It's not true...Everyone go back to your drinks and gambling... Drinks are on the house..." Orville said, pretending to be unrattled by what was transpiring in his place of business. "He's out of his mind...Lobelia? You remember!"

"Then his girlfriend here..." Sid shouted. "Got me arrested. Said I tried to rape her! Did almost a year for that one! *Where is she?* The blond with the dog!"

But no one said anything, their silence only seeming to incense Sid further. Then he grabbed the gun and placed it at Rory's temple. Rory began to cry and plead.

"Please don't kill me..."

"I want the police here!"

"The police?" Orville said, trying to hide his quavering voice.

Sid pushed the gun further into Rory's face and placed his finger on the trigger. Sid's perspiration and hot breath hovered in his ear again. Lobelia and Tiny stepped forward as if ready to snatch the weapon.

"Just call them..."

"We don't have a phone in here..." Orville told him. "So we'll have to go out in the

The Electric Eel!

bakery...But let Rory go... He hasn't hurt anyone..."

Once at the bakery door, Sid gave Rory a hard push. Rory felt his feet go out from underneath him as he toppled...His fear of falling returning in an instant. Lobelia reached for him and pulled him inside.

"You okay?"

"I think so..." Rory said, the words sounding flat and uncertain.

Lobelia embraced him and released him. *She always cares about me...*He noted.

As promised, Orville reached for the phone in the bakery. Sid turned the weapon on his former friend, pointing it squarely between his chest. Orville seemed unfazed as if he were planning something.

*Get him outside...*He told himself. *Mother always said he was crazy...They told me not to hire him...*

"Operator..."

"I need the police..." he said. "Electric Eel Bakery near High Street...*Hurry!*"

"What is the nature of your emergency?"

"There is a man with a gun in the bakery..."

"Has anyone been hurt?"

"No..."

"The police are on their way, sir..."

Sid's eyes were wild as if he'd gone feral. He blinked unsure what to do next... *They'll probably arrest me too...If they have to take me down to take them down, then so be it...* He rationalized.

While still distracted by the phone, Lobelia and Tiny moved into the bakery without Sid noticing. Like a man half his size, Tiny pounced on Sid and pushed him toward the front door. Sid's arm flailed, the gun moving like the barrel on a cannon.

"Be careful!" Lobelia shouted.

But the gun went off, hitting Tiny squarely...

SEVENTY-FIVE

Over the next week, Rory began to process the operose task of being a father...*To twins!* His mother kept reminding him.

While Trixie remained in the hospital, the babies were allowed to come home with Rory. With the guidance of Trixie's mother, his own mother and the nurses, Rory learned the ins and outs of taking care of infants. He touched the bottoms of one of the girl's foot.

"Has Trixie settled on names yet?" his mother asked.

"Not yet but she was calling them Molly and Dolly..." he said.

"It was going to be Trixie and Dixie..." his father whispered.

His mother rolled her eyes and reached for a cloth diaper. One of the girls squirmed and kicked her legs in her crib as she folded the cloth over her arm and changed them both.

"They are beautiful..."

"Do these girls seem *off* to you?" Rory's mother whispered to her husband in the hall.

He knitted his brows together in confusion as if she had noticed something he hadn't... *Women always know more about this than I do...*He mused, trying to be supportive.

"*Off?*" he repeated.

Off? He rolled over in his mind. *This whole thing is off...My son has somehow gotten a girl pregnant with twins even though he doesn't even like her! Or girls for that matter!*

He went to speak again but she silenced him before she could explain further as Rory and Trixie's mother entered the room. He walked away, silently confused, examining the twins closer in their crib.

Just then Peaches, their now family pet, wandered over to the babies and gave them a sniff. Trixie's mother hesitated at the sight of the large dog; however, Rory put his hand up to indicate that the hound wouldn't harm them. The Afghan Hound wagged with curled tail inquisitively.

"When is Trixie coming home?" he asked.

"Today hopefully..."

"But I think he's taking the babies over tonight to the Electric Eel..."

"To a bar? *A speakeasy?*"

"Just to show them off... Lobelia really wants to meet them..."

"Can't they just come here?"

"They'll have to get used to it sooner or later... Trixie lives right above it..."

"I s'pose..." his mother accepted.

After the twins had their nap, Rory's father reached for two aluminum car seats with an attached burlap sack with two holes cut in the bottom and placed them in the back of his automobile. Two hooked bars sat on the top of each seat that secured to the top of the automobile's rear seat.

"Will that hold?" Rory's mother asked. "Looks too big for them..."

"It'll hold..." he promised. "They're only going a mile and a half...See? It just dangles from the headrest..."

With much hesitation she handed him each girl and he placed them down in the makeshift nest, allowing their feet to stick out the bottom. Both girls cooed contently. Trixie's mother looked on longingly as well. *Funny how we're already so attached...* They all thought.

"I just called the hospital...Trixie is coming home tonight!"

"That's wonderful!"

Rory's father drove them to the Electric Eel and parked in the side street. Before the car could stop, Rory turned and looked at the girls...*His girls...*His father beamed. *Funny in all the years I've passed this I've never been here before...*His father thought.

The Electric Eel!

They never invited me... He looked at his son wandering what to expect...

He'd heard tales of raucous behavior...Of loose women getting arrested for dancing on taxi cabs...And drunkenness...He wondered how much of it was true...*And now I'm taking my grandchildren there...Maybe my wife was right...*

"It'll be fine..." Rory promised.

To his surprise, Lobelia, Eugenia, and others came out to the car as if they'd been waiting for them. Orville waved from the doorway, puffing on a pipe...His new found addiction to calm his nerves...

"Hold on one second!" Lobelia said.

Eugenia wheeled out a weighty white stroller with four high spoked wheels and cornflower blue trimmed interior out onto the walk. A large divider sat in the center allowing for two convertible tops to cover each child simultaneously. Rory beamed.

"It's beautiful!" he exclaimed. "But I can't accept this!"

"We got it second hand..." Lobelia informed him with a demure smile.

"Can we get it in the car?" Rory asked his father, who was much more mechanical than he was.

"It may come apart..." he said. "If not we'll get the truck back..."

"Super hard to get it up Trixie's stairs, I'm afraid..."

"How is Trixie anyway?"

"Fine. I think..."

"It's a beaut..." Orville noted. "I think I saw them helping her up the stairs about an hour ago..."

"We'll just leave this here and you can come pick it up whenever you like..." Lobelia said kneeling down to wheel it.

As she wheeled it away, Rory thought of something. She turned to look at him. He chose his words carefully.

"How is Tiny?" he asked.

The Electric Eel!

Lobelia held her breath. Eugenia chewed her lip and went inside with Orville. She turned and met his gaze.

"Okay…Just a shoulder wound… He's very lucky…He'll be in a lot of pain for a while…Thanks for asking…"

Rory nodded in relief. Lobelia pivoted and wheeled the pram back inside. He felt gratitude in that moment.

"Let's head upstairs before it rains…" his father said reaching for one of the girls. "Which one is which?"

"That's Dolly!" he pointed.

If you say so… His father cradling her sister in one arm. Together they climbed the stairs and his father knocked on the door. A second later, a nurse opened the apartment door.

"We got company…!"

"Now! Miss Trixie is just resting…" a black nurse in a white skirt and matching shoes and blouse told him with hands on hips.

"I'm sure she can spare a moment to see her babies…" Rory's father pressed.

"My babies…" Trixie called in a meek uncharacteristic voice.

"Is she all right?" Rory whispered.

"She's fine…She's just been through a lot…" the nurse assured her with perfect hearing.

Each man placed an infant on her thigh like a package. Trixie brightened, her effervescence returning a little. One of the girls yawned a little as she reached for them.

"Thank you…" she mouthed.

"You're welcome…"

SEVENTY-SIX

The Electric Eel!

𝒟ownstairs at the Electric Eel a hellacious celebration began. Though neither Rory nor Trixie were yet in attendance, Orville passed out cigars with pink ribbons. The men, many of whom were fathers themselves, chewed on the sticks as lighters were passed around, causing the room to fill with cigar smoke. Eugenia stifled a cough.

"To family!" Orville shouted.

"To family!" a cacophony of male voices bellowed.

"To wives and children!"

"To wives and children!" they recited.

Many of the women in attendance, held pink ladies and daiquiris and smoked flavored cigarettes...One of them pointed to a pinkish-red drink and inquired. Eugenia smiled with a rare tidbit of graciousness...

"It's called a Clover Club...Gin, raspberry syrup, lemon and egg white..." she said.

"Would you like to try one?"

"I'll take one!"

"Me too!" another lady said.

"On me!" a partially tipsy well to do man in a tweed suit said with the wave of his hand.

Orville noticed a brass chain attached from a pocket watch to his breast pocket. He nodded as the drinks came to fruition. The egg white frothed a little as it emulsified. Expertly, Eugenia dropped in a few fresh raspberries on top as garnish, the fruit floating a little before it sank to the middle of the glass.

Someone handed Orville one of the cocktails and he too, began to imbibe. The bitter hint of lemon and sweet fruit juice coupled with tart fresh fruit and gin lingered on his palette. Foamy egg white tickled the roof of his mouth.

"Interesting..." he thought.

Rory and his father emerged later. Orville waved his arms to embrace him like a bird flapping its wings. Rory's father looked at him with skepticism... *Why do I have a feeling*

The Electric Eel!

he's only celebrating cause he found out the babies weren't his?

"Where are the little ones?" one of the women, a regular customer asked.

"Upstairs with their mother and the nurse…" his father said, clearly uncomfortable in a place like this. "Rory needed a break…"

Orville slapped him on the back. His usually buttoned up collared shirt was open at the neck, a side effect of the alcohol warming his upper body. Rory's father prayed he wouldn't hug him…

"Aww! We wanna see the babies! Babies! Babies!" he chanted as others around the bar joined in.

"Maybe you should slow down…" Lobelia advised.

"Okay…Okay…I'll slow down…" he promised. "Did you know this place is haunted?" he asked. Mr. Childs. "People see my father…And the detective who was shot…And Catfish… And even Rory's friend Iris…Madame Beulah's stuff is still here… We stopped taking her Ouija board out to the trash cause it keeps coming back…Nobody'll touch it now…"

Rory's father wondered who Catfish and Madame Beulah were but did not ask…Orville downed another cocktail and passed a brown bottle down the table and two cigars with pale pink labels. Mr. Childs looked at it with trepidation.

"Congratulations, grandpa!"

His burned a little, unsure if he liked this new moniker. Not wanting to be rude, he took the ale and held it. *Would I get in trouble if I get caught with this?*

"Don't worry… No one's going to arrest you…"

"That's a relief…" he mumbled.

"Say… Have you all seen *my* boy…?" Orville said having an idea. "Where's my wallet?"

Clumsily, he fumbled through the bar for his billfold. *Do I not have any pictures?* Eugenia backed up, frozen allowing him to rifle through it.

"Ahem…"

The Electric Eel!

"I know what I'll do!" he said. "I'll get *my* baby in here!"

Like a Clydesdale, Orville clomped to the bakery phone. The operator, too, seemed nonplussed as he dialed. *Wonder if she remembers me?*

"Poppy Alfonso please…" he said trying to sound sober.

"One moment please…"

"Hey…"

"Orville it's getting late…What's wrong?"

"Everyone down here wants to meet Alistair…"

"*Tonight?*" she asked.

"Yes *tonight!*"

"It's a school night…"

"I'm tired…"

"Well then have Edgar bring him…*Please!*" as she paused he began to grow angry. "Listen! I am his father. I have rights too, you know!"

"I never said you didn't…" she said in a flat, disinterested voice. "I'll see if Edgar can stop by with him…"

"Oh, Poppy…Thank you! *Thank you!* You are a good woman!"

Before she could hang up, Orville dropped the phone and bounded back to the bar with the energy of a gazelle. He clapped his hands in celebration and reached for another cocktail that was sitting on the bar. Eugenia *glared*!

"That was for a guest…"

"Oh…Sorry… I'll buy the next one… Everyone hear that music? Isn't Malka spectacular? Give her a round of applause… Did everyone see our new eel tank?" he said heading over to the massive tank. "We are the electric eel, but we can't get electric eels, no more…" he said slurring to the point of unintelligible words. "Jezebel and Ahab…From the Bible…"

"Orville, maybe you should sit down…" Lobelia prodded.

The Electric Eel!

"Nah, I'm okay…"

Then the roulette wheel caught his attention on the other side of the room, and he dashed to those sitting around it. Unlike those at the bar who were rowdy, these people were serious and tight-lipped. They watched the center of the wheel hypnotized as another number was called out.

"Red! Eleven!"

"Damn!" a man yelled, turning away in frustration.

As the ivory ball spun and landed, Orville began to feel a little nauseated from its rotation. He looked away and sat down, the alcohol sloshing in his gullet. He held his stomach as if queasy.

"We're here…" his brother called from the front of the room.

Suddenly energized, Orville leapt from the chair and ran to Edgar and Alistair. Edgar was dressed smartly in an overcoat. His nephew wore short pants and dark coat. He looked up at his father, unsure what to make of his altered state.

"Hey there, kid! Hey everyone! Gather round! This is my boy Alistair…"

Though a few acknowledged him, the others ignored Orville…*Maybe they were afraid of seeing a kid in an illegal speakeasy…*He surmised.

To everyone's surprise, Orville picked up his son with surprising strength. Alistair squirmed as the scent of alcohol and his father's perspiration hovered from his pores. Orville toted his son like a handbag and held him up to show the crowd.

"Put me down!" Alistair ordered in an adult voice,

"I will…I will…"

To everyone's horror Orville climbed on top of the bar like the gorilla in a b horror movie…Next he hoisted his son up and allowed him to stand toe to toe with him. He steadied himself as the boy's slippery shoes slid on the shiny polished bar…

"Careful…!" a woman shouted in two distinct syllables.

"Orville get down!" Edgar shouted.

"Put the kid down!" someone else yelled in clear annoyance.

"Jesus! Get your feet off the bar! You're a mess!"

But Orville did *not* listen... Instead climbing higher into the center, lifting his son up by the waist to show everyone. Edgar watched helplessly as a sea of glassware dangled precariously above and below his brother like stalagmites and stalactites. Alistair gave a panicked look and flailed his arms as his father stumbled...

All of a sudden, the boy slipped from his grasp like an eel... Edgar looked on in fright as his nephew fell...Careening from the top of the bar like a cannon ball...

SEVENTY-SEVEN

*They're all giving me dirty looks...*Orville thought as he paced around the lobby of the hospital, smoking...He puffed cigarette after cigarette, snuffing them out in haste before he was even finished with them...A celebratory pink cigar was still in his pocket as he realized he was at the same hospital he'd been in a few hours earlier with Rory, welcoming the new lives of twins.

As Poppy entered the doorway, he wanted to disappear. *Like a puppy that had piddled on the carpet...*The look on her face was of scorn, and betrayal. He wanted her to scream at him but what she did was *worse*...She ignored him! *Say something!*

"Where's my baby?" she said at the hospital lobby desk, the usual, pleasant, calm timbre of her voice gone.

"He's had a serious accident, ma'am..."

She looked at Orville again. His brother and mother entered the facility next. *More bad news...*

His brother looked down at his artificial appendage, the spot where his real hip met leather and metal. Orville placed his hands behind his back as if reading him telepathically. The bottoms of Edgar's eyes were red where salty tears had settled like drain reservoirs, his irises a funny color he was not used to seeing...

The Electric Eel!

"Alistair didn't deserve that..." he muttered.

I didn't deserve that... Edgar's expression said. Orville returned his gaze with a pugnacious look. While Edgar was taller and muscular, his older brother balled his fists together and dug his heels in a truculent display like an angry rooster in a barnyard. His younger brother looked at him with an apoplectic glare. *Wanna hit me? Go ahead and try it!*

But like Poppy, he said nothing and turned from Orville. Orville looked at his mother next. His mother who had always made excuses for everything he said and did...Even at the detriment of her other son, who was now stone faced and silent in judgment... Carlotta's expression was chilly...*She's ashamed of me!*

"Let's hope he pulls through..." Edgar offered Poppy.

I don't understand any of this... Poppy thought. *Who lifts a ten-year-old up on a bar? What kind of mother am I for letting him talk me into taking him there...?*

"You had no way of knowing he'd do this..." Edgar whispered.

Poppy wept. Edgar walked around his brother the way one might pass a bum on High Street. He sniffed something foul.

"You reek like a brewery..."

Orville watched as his brother comforted Poppy with an embrace. *His wife...* All of a sudden something bubbled in him like a pot left on the stove to boil too long...Or a volcano...

"You think you're better than me?" Orville shouted, loud enough for everyone in the hospital to hear.

But instead of fighting, Edgar gave him a dismissive wave. Orville's eyes watered like a tea kettle filled to the brim with too much steamy water. Suddenly, sober Orville began to weep.

"Nurse!" Edgar called. "Is there any news on my nephew?"

"What is his name, sir?"

The Electric Eel!

"Alistair Alfonso..."

As Orville bawled in a corner chair, two more familiar people entered the lobby. He gulped at the sight of them...His grandparents...*Nani and Papi...*

"How did this happen?" his normally stoic grandfather asked.

*More importantly...*Edgar wondered. *Why did this happen?*

"Orville was drunk and lifted Alistair up on the bar..." Edgar said with shocking candor.

Their grandmother blinked as if she were being told a falsehood. She squeezed her husband's hand. Orville looked away and continued to travail in despondence.

"Pull yourself together!" Papi ordered.

"How is Alistair?" Edgar repeated to the head nurse.

"The same, sir! If there is any update I will tell you!" she barked.

And without further communication she turned on her heels and walked behind a swinging door. *She's tired of listening to me and I don't blame her!* Edgar thought, remaining frozen at the nurse's stand, his feet made of clay.

"How did he land?" their grandfather pressed. "I mean... Did he land on his side? His arm?"

They turned to look at the older man as if he were joking. Poppy thought about this for a moment, pondering it. *It's a fair question!*

"He landed on his right side and hit his head..." Edgar began as if telling a somber tale. "There was glass everywhere..."

Their eyes widened. Carlotta spotted her former in-laws in her periphery and stepped away from them. They pretended not to notice her standing beside them, but the message was clear. *Murderer!*

To Orville's surprise, his wife pulled an official looking paper from her pocket and handed it to him. Orville rotated and stared ahead. He dropped the paper on the floor and examined it.

"What is it?"

The Electric Eel!

"It's a summons..."

Orville's blue eyes were horrified. *You're giving me this now?* He began to read.

"From the family of Mr. Mark..." he read out loud.

He blinked, not instantly recognizing the name. Poppy picked up the paper with smug satisfaction. Orville shrugged.

"Mr. Mark ! From the zoological society! *Remember?* He and two others were killed driving drunk from the Electric Eel a few months ago...They're *suing* you for negligence! And since alcohol is illegal they have a good chance of winning!"

The color drained from Orville's face. A canary yellow piece of onion skinner paper with imprinted writing fell on the floor next. Orville looked at his feet, examining it.

"Three hundred dollars?"

"Oh and I think they excluded the bill...*For the eels!*"

Carlotta raised an eyebrow, overhearing. *We're finished!* The look on her face said. *No one will ever come back to the Electric Eel now!*

Before Carlotta couldn't finish her thought, the night nurse stepped forward alongside a physician. The doctor pressed his lips together like an undertaker trying to be professional to the grieving and respectful at the same time. All eyes were on him as he spoke.

"I'm sorry, Mr. and Mrs. Alfonso but Alistair may not make it through the night...It may be time for you to say your goodbyes..."

SEVENTY-EIGHT

*B*ut Alistair *did* pull through the night...*Somehow*...The boy stirred a little in his hospital bed the next morning, his large bovine lashes fluttering.

"Kids are amazingly resilient..." the doctor had to admit. "That being said, he has a long way to go. He's not out of the water yet...Keep it brief and upbeat... He needs his rest..." he said in a clipped tone that reminded them of a somber newspaper headline.

The Electric Eel!

This may be worse... Orville thought, with selfish ideation. *Now I have to live with the guilt from him too...*

His sister and aunt arrived next in the hospital. Irene walked over to the bed as if visiting an acquaintance in the morgue and gave him a little pat on the hand. *He looks like one of those vets who got back from the Great War...* Virginia thought not wanting to meet his gaze.

The boy's once flawless face was now marred with an ugly bandage wrapped three quarters of the way around his head. His right eye was completely obscured as only a small slit ran through it like a vertical blind leaving a deep shadow on his forehead. His right arm was also mummified and immobilized, his hand elevated and wrapped like a mitten.

"His right side has a lot of cuts..." the doctor said making an intentional arc around Orville. "Right where he landed..."

The others glared at him again. *Broken glass...* They all thought as a nurse changed his bandages rousing him.

"Where's grandpa?" Alistair whispered in his lucid state.

Now was Orville's turn to look at *them...* Carlotta who had barely spoken gestured to her in laws. Nani and Papi reached for him simultaneously.

"They're right here..." she said sweetly.

"No..." Alistair hesitated. "Grandpa *Julius*..."

Edgar felt a knot in the pit of his stomach. Carlotta left the room. *My cue to exit...* When they were alone Poppy walked to where her son lay. A nurse discarded a bandage with a reddish yellow stain on one side and stepped away to retrieve a clean gauze. An angry gash caught Poppy's attention.

"His big hurdle now is the risk of infection..." the doctor told the nurse quietly.

Orville reached for Poppy, but she shied away. Edgar's stomach growled a little. He looked longingly at the uneaten tray of food that had been left for his nephew.

The Electric Eel!

"Did you eat anything?" Edgar asked her.

Poppy shook her head. But food was the furthest thing from her mind. Edgar walked to the lobby with peckish intent and spotted the women in his family. He walked quietly, careful not to let his right leg make its token squeak on the floor.

"Did you see the looks they gave us?" Carlotta whispered to her daughter.

"Just ignore it..." Virginia said lighting a cigarette.

"No...They were too busy looking at *Orville*..."

The women laughed in agreement at this truth as a cloud of smoke rose above them like a trio of dragons. Edgar walked to a vending machine in the corner and placed a nickel in the slot and then another...Two cream-colored vanilla cookies in a clear wrapper landed on the bottom of the machine with a *thunk*...Carlotta, Irene and Virginia looked up at him with sudden quiet as he reached for them.

Edgar bit into one of the treats and carried the other to Poppy in the next room. She looked at the fare for a second and took it in her teeth with much reluctance. *He's so thoughtful...*

"She's not a dog...It's not a biscuit..." Orville mouthed.

"You just don't get it. Do you?" Edgar said reading his lips.

*Nice family...*The head nurse thought. She reached for a rag and dipped it in cool water to wring it out. Alistair began to stir and mumble again.

"How are you feeling?" Poppy asked her son.

But Alistair mumbled something unintelligible again. *I'm so used to talking to him like a grown-up...*She thought. *And to think we almost lost him...How can I ever talk to Orville again? I can tolerate anything but this...*

"He lifted me up...And I fell...I didn't wanna go up there..."

"Just rest..."

*I asked him how he was doing and then when he answers me I shush him...*She thought. Alistair blinked as if feeling the need to explain. As she kissed him on the head,

The Electric Eel!

he closed his eyes. Orville appeared a few seconds later and touched his son's forehead.

"Sorry..." he muttered.

*It's a start...*Poppy thought looking up at him. *Still I can never tell if Orville's genuine...Or if he's just saving face...As always...*

Alistair drifted in and out of sleep again. He let out an uncomfortable cough in his sleep. His Uncle Edgar joined them at his bedside. But then the boy began to sputter as if trying to breathe in his sleep.

"Nurse! *Nurse!*"

The nurse tried to hide her panic and returned with an ominous looking hypodermic needle. Without hesitation she reached for Alistair's left hand...His *good* arm...And injected him. Edgar watched with wide eyes as his nephew, who had been well less than twenty-four-hours ago was reduced to this.

"He's in a lot of pain," she said with a tinge of sadness. "It'll help him rest."

Poppy gulped. *Like a horse with a broken leg...*She blinked back tears and patted him near the spot where he'd just injected. *Be strong...You know he can hear you...*

"Get some sleep, sweetie!"

Orville seemed to have a clarion moment at what had transpired. All of a sudden he wanted to be anywhere but where he was now...A roller coaster of emotion filled him.

"I'm going to go now..." he said finally.

Poppy and Edgar continued their focus on the boy. Without looking at him she gave Orville an indifferent, dismissive, disinterested wave. *I no longer matter...*Orville thought.

SEVENTY-NINE

The Electric Eel!

*L*ater that night, Orville readied for work, grateful to be away from Alistair, the hospital, and his family. He shaved, showered, and searched his closet for his best Italian suit, a pewter grey ensemble with a turquoise ascot. *My mother says it brings out my eyes...*

Lobelia knows I'll be coming in late... He said to himself tucking the cloth into his collar in the full-length mirror. When satisfied that it was straight, he reached for his shoes, also grey, with dark laces and pulled them on.

Why am I so excited to go back to work? He thought suddenly. *None of them are thrilled with me right now...* He pictured the look on everyone's faces as they rescued his son from his fall on the bar. *The fall he caused...*

"It wasn't like Alistair climbed up there himself..." he said to himself. "He has too much good sense for that!"

He thought of Lobelia and Eugenia pulling his son out of the broken glass on the bottom of the bar. Blood *poured* out of his son's arm and face as Lobelia carried him in her arms out to the waiting ambulance...*Alistair the martyr...Orville the terrible...And Lobelia the hero!*

"You're lucky he wasn't blinded!" one of the bar regulars had scolded.

Another customer who will probably never come back! He mused. *Good riddance!*

"What were you thinking, Orville?" Eugenia had barked.

But he didn't owe her an explanation. *Or anyone for that matter...* He remembered thinking.

It was dark by the time he exited the house. Instinctively he looked around, expecting to see someone familiar but even his mother had gone home. *I am truly alone in this world...By my own choosing...*

Quietly he drove across town in solace. The night was perfect. Neither too hot nor too cold. A bright platinum moon hung in the sky like a street lamp as he pulled on the parking brake and walked the familiar street to his place of business.

The Electric Eel!

"What day is it?" he asked a cagey man on the street between the Electric Eel and the massage parlor. *Aka Madame Toussad's Gallery...*

"June First..." he said walking away, not wanting to be recognized.

Six years! He thought stepping over the spot where his father had been slain. *More regret...*

As if anticipating his arrival, Tiny opened the speakeasy door without being prompted. Tiny's left sleeve was rolled up, revealing a large square bandage. Reminded of Alistair, Orville looked away. Tiny bit his lip and nodded coolly allowing his boss to pass.

He wasn't here when Alistair fell...He must have heard...They all heard...

"How's your arm?" he asked forcing small talk.

"Okay, I guess. I'm a big target," he said in a half jest.

He saw Lobelia next, dressed this night in all red. *As if she's reminding him of the blood that was shed...* He thought and then immediately dismissing it. *No, she's not that passive-aggressive...*

"How is he?"

"He had a rough night," Orville said, grateful that she was still talking to him. "But he's going to be okay..."

He's very lucky... The unspoken thought hung in the air between them. *I'm lucky*, he corrected himself.

Orville walked to Rory next. The young man raised an eyebrow, his veiled dark eyes unreadable. Rory draped a white towel over his arm and straightened his spine.

I've only been a parent for a short time... The look on his face said. *But I can't imagine doing what you did...*

"How's your son?" he found himself inquiring.

"Still in the hospital but okay..."

Just then Eugenia shot him a searing scowl from across the room. *Here we go...* He thought, walking toward her. *Let's get this firing squad over with...* She looked down at

The Electric Eel!

the floor.

"We're short on glassware..." she said making no attempt at sparing his feelings. "So what we have left will have to be rewashed till we get some more..."

"Understood," he said placing his hands on his bellybutton as if in reverent humility. "Thankfully it doesn't look that busy..."

"Oh and I'm giving you notice...I'm only here till I find something else..."

"Also understood. Who will tend the eels?" he said flashing her a jocoserious smile.

She looked up, caught off guard. Growing quiet, she turned to look at the giant tank in the corner, the nocturnal fish starting to rise for the night. Ahab's languid body glided with ease across the bottom while Jezebel slumbered a little behind a rock. *I hadn't thought of them...*

A dozen or so upper middle class forty-somethings arrived at the bar next. Tiny shrugged. *They all seem to know the password...* He noticed.

"Eel..." one of the women giggled as if saying something naughty.

While most of the group sipped their drinks casually, this woman began to pound alcohol at a much faster rate. A few of them hummed to the band, the sounds of Malka's voice, the clarinet and piano in sync.

"Nother whiskey neat please..."

"A lot of the places are moving to bigger bands..." Orville informed Lobelia.

"I think it'd get too loud in here and draw a lot of attention..." Lobelia whispered pouring the spirit.

"Can't get more attention than what we've had recently..." Eugenia said under her breath.

As most of the group swayed to "Sweet Georgia Brown" the one woman who was drinking heavily wandered away from the herd. Something caught her attention at the back of the place, drawing her like a moth to a flame. As the music concluded, only the sounds of a few people gambling and talking quietly remained.

The Electric Eel!

No one noticed the skinny woman heading in the direct of the eel tank. With an intoxicated chuckle she spotted the wheeled ladder used for cleaning the tank and feeding the fish and steadied herself on the rail. It wobbled a little as she climbed the first two steps.

Instantly, Ahab rose to the top of the tank intrigued. His tankmate held back in aloof reservation, her black and white tail shaking back and forth like a rattlesnake. The electric green eel opened his mouth in a grin, beckoning her.

With the twirl of her index finger she stuck her digit in the top of the tank. The water was warm and inviting like a hot tub...*Or a day at the beach...* Unafraid, Ahab floated to the top to greet her, his bottle shaped nose moving pointed upward close enough for her to stroke him.

"Oh! You're slimy!" she said with a snigger.

To her delight, the yellow-green eel allowed this affection. He opened his eyes to reveal what looked like cataracts. A small amount of water exited the sides of his cheeks as he breathed. He opened his mouth further in ecstasy.

Just then Lobelia noticed the drunk woman on the ladder leaning over the aquarium. She elbowed Eugenia and Orville who stood aghast. Quickly Lobelia pushed through the crowd at the bar.

"Excuse us! Pardon me!"

"It's an emergency..."

As she stroked the top of Ahab's crown, Jezebel slithered to the center of the tank to inspect what was going on. A crowd of onlookers also began to watch it enfold as Jezebel inched closer to the woman, hovering centimeters below Ahab. The woman leaned in further to touch the fish's dorsal fin.

"Get down from there!" Lobelia shouted, startling her.

But before she could react, Jezebel leapt upward in a protective posture toward the tip of the woman's finger and bit with strong pharyngeal jaws. Caught off guard, Ahab

The Electric Eel!

flopped and floated to the bottom like a lead bobber. Lobelia reached for the woman's scant waist and pulled her away.

"What do you think you're doing?"

The woman brushed her off and rotated on the ladder to look at her. Orville, Rory, and others watched in morbid fascination as the woman froze. Suddenly, she looked down as blood gushed down the side of hand, the tip of her finger nearly sheared off from the impact. She shrieked as salty water ran in the wound.

"That one bit me!" she screamed.

"You're lucky you didn't fall in, darling!"

As she stood over the tank, a trickle of blood dripped into the side of the tank. Ahab saw something floating at the top and moved toward it. The woman smiled in glee as the now familiar eel came back to see her like the family dog. But Ahab's focus was on the smell of blood. With nostrils flaring and incredible strength he jumped to the top of the tank and lunged at her. She screamed again as someone grabbed her, pulling her to safety.

"You scared him!" she bellowed. "The other one should be put down...She's vicious!"

Without asking, Rory grabbed the woman's bleeding hand and applied a cold compress. She winced.

"You need to see a doctor!" Orville ordered.

"I'll sue you!"

*Get in line...*They thought. She writhed in agony as an angry wound began to form and pulse beneath the towel as the cloth soaked and turned crimson.

"You're lucky you have a finger *at all!*" Eugenia shouted.

Meanwhile, Ahab settled down into the tank as if nothing happened, the smell of coppery blood lingering on his nose a second and then dissipating. Jezebel flicked her tail in an angry warning waiting for the woman to return. Then both fish intwined finding security together.

The Electric Eel!

"Get her to the hospital, Tiny..." Lobelia told him.

"Nothing to see here, folks..." Orville called. "Just another day at the Electric Eel..."

EIGHTY

"So..." the detective began with some disbelief. "Let me get this straight? You are saying you participated in the murder of Julius Alfonso on the night of June 1, 1919... Is that correct, Mr. Clark?"

"Uh-huh..." Sid answered, his voice bereft of any hit of guilt or remorse.

One of the police officers handed him a pack of smokes and a bottle of soda. He exchanged glances with the lead detective. *Keep him talking...*

The detective scratched his head, unsure how to proceed. The other law man fiddled with a pencil, a nervous habit that drove his partner crazy. He looked to Sid again as his partner put his hand up to stop him from saying anything further.

"What do you want, Sid?" he asked, figuring there must be an angle.

"Time served..."

Sid gave a shameless smile and lit another smoke. The room was austere in shades of brown and olive with a high walnut table utilized as a desk and a hot, white light under an aluminum shade with a long black cord running down the side. The officers too light cigarettes and tapped them on a tin ashtray.

"Tell us the truth," the lead officer said with a shrug. "And we'll think about it..."

The younger police officer took his partner outside the room, away from the prying ears of Sid Clark. Sid sat unfazed, knowing exactly what they were saying. He twiddled his thumbs as they talked.

"Are you kidding? We're gonna let a murderer out on the streets?"

"In six years we got nothing else! Besides... He has serious charges pending... He won't be out long!"

Without waiting for more discussion, the lead detective brushed past the other man and reached for a piece of paper and stuck a pen in an inkhorn on the desk. Next, he handed it to the other man. A sickening feeling rose in both of them as he reached for several piles of crime photos.

"From the looks of these pictures there was more than one attacker..." the younger man said.

Sid said nothing. The image of Julius Alfonso caught his eye; however, he did not flinch. The other man looked up at the ceiling pleasantly.

"You know what I think? I think you and your friends fileted Mr. Alfonso like a Christmas goose and left him to bleed to death on the sidewalk...And I want names of those friends...And I wanna know who hired you?"

"Carla..."

Carla? He blinked, looking through the file. The other officer put his finger up allowing Sid to clarify. Sid spoke again.

"Carmina...Carmella..." he stammered trying to form the word in his mind. "Mrs. Alfonso... Whatever she goes by..."

"Carlotta?" he suggested trying to make it not to appear as if he were leading the man into a confession.

Sid brightened. *Yea!* He breathed through the smoke.

"How much did she give you?"

"Three hundred dollars...And she didn't pay me...His *sister* did..."

"How do you know her?"

"I went to school with her brother..."

"Was *he* involved...?"

Sid shifted in his chair. *Pay dirt...*He thought. But what the man said next surprised him.

"No..."

"*No?*"

The Electric Eel!

"I said no..."

"Okay. Okay...So he just found out *after* the fact?"

"Yes."

"Who else was involved...? What about his *other* brother?" he asked processing all of it.

"Just the women...*And us*..." he said growing bored with the conversation and getting up. "Can I go?"

"Not so fast!" he said pushing him back on the chair. "We're going to need some *corroboration* of your story..."

"Like what?"

"A receipt...A deposit..."

"Where'd the other guys come from?" the other one asked.

"Mr. LaRocca found them..."

To their dismay a man in a navy-blue suit appeared in the doorway, his large belly sticking over the brim of his high-waisted trousers. In his hand he held a boiled leather valise with a thick handle.

"I'm Mr. Clark's attorney..." the portly man introduced himself. "This interrogation is finished, gentleman..."

"Not so fast! Mr. Clark here wants time served for a murder he says he was hired to do!"

The attorney pulled out a chair and adjusted his shirt collar as if suddenly too warm. He stared at the floor, avoiding contact with all of them. Mutual disdain remained. *Everyone hate attorneys...Till they need them...*

"So... Your call, Mr. Clark... Either you give me some evidence, or we put you back in your cell and throw away the key!"

"That detective..."

"Which one?"

The Electric Eel!

"Not him...The *other* one...They one who died..."

They leaned closer. His attorney reached out to stop his client from saying something incriminating. Sid began to get bored again.

"Detective Talbert? Did you kill him *too*?"

"No...But I know who *did*..."

"Who?"

"Take me there and I'll show you..."

An hour later, they piled into a car and drove to the front of the Electric Eel. The place looked different in the bright light; the roof overshadowed by the overhead sun. Sid pointed to the sidewalk where the event had taken place.

"So tell me how did you know Mr. Alfonso would be *here*?"

"She told me he'd be wandering down High Street...Told me not to worry that he would be easy to take down..."

"Why?" the officer asked, sensing there was more.

"She said she drugged him with some kind of drink..."

The officer thought of his visit to his place...He breezed through the cocktails in his mind, searching for a right answer. The heat beat down on his neck and shoulders as he stood with the other men.

"Can you recall what the drink was called?"

"The Electric Eel..."

Then attorney and officer alike looked up at the sign in unison. *It's over...* He thought, realizing that his client was telling the truth.

"So what did you do when you saw him?"

"We all jumped out from the alley and..."

He motioned as if raising a knife over his head. Then with the other hand he raised his fist as if stabbing with more than blade. His long arms flailed in a theatrical manner. The group watched hypnotized.

The Electric Eel!

"How can we be sure?" he asked.

Sid pointed to the alley where the bum usually lay. A few sheets of soggy cardboard clung to the concrete like mud. The younger officer squinted as if trying to figure out he was looking at.

"The bum... Saw the whole thing... We probably scared him away by being here..."

"You told us you knew who killed Detective Talbert?"

"Yea..." he said. "Mr. LaRocca said the detective's girlfriend would set him up..."

"How do you know this?"

Sid shrugged, revealing nothing. Just then Tiny and Lobelia walked into the bakery carrying a tray of canapes and pastries. Like a bird of prey, Sid craned his neck.

"So who killed the detective?"

He pointed to Tiny...

EIGHTY-ONE

The day started like any other at the Electric Eel...Eugenia took it as an opportunity to clean the aquarium. She sprayed a small amount of ammonia on a small white cloth and polished the outside of the tank. A small amount of pink came off on the rag as Ahab came up to examine her.

"You got the taste of blood...You little vampire!"

He opened his triangular mouth to reveal a row of hooked teeth as if laughing at her. Eugenia touched the outside the glass where he hovered, unafraid. Jezebel came up next, her black and white skin vacillating like camouflage. She gave Eugenia a look of scorn and sank back to the bottom. *What a bitch!* Eugenia thought.

Rory appeared in the doorway with Trixie and the babies, with Peaches trailing behind. The pram that Lobelia had given them shined like a movie photo, the girls moved a little inside. Lobelia and Eugenia ran to them.

The Electric Eel!

"Nice to see you guys out and about! Hello Molly and Dolly! How are you doing, Trix?"

"Great!" Trixie said fixing her hair. "Still getting my figure back..."

Aren't we all? Lobelia thought. She turned her attention away as a group of customers entered earlier than expected.

"What can I get you?" she asked.

"Daiquiris...All around..."

"You got it!"

Just then a young man with dark hair stood in the corner looking around the room. Rory noticed him immediately, the valet who worked for Iris's parents...*Scotty...*

"Hello," he said coolly.

"Hi!"

Just then Scotty spotted the pram and Trixie and looked up in embarrassment. Rory put his hand up as Trixie let out a giggle. Scotty reddened as if they were laughing at him.

"No...I think you misunderstand...They're mine *but*..."

"We aren't together..." Trixie said taking the hint and walking away with the pram. "We just had babies together...*On accident!*"

"She's great!" Rory said. "I'm happy being a father..."

"That's good...Mrs. Dupeon gave me my job back!"

"That's great!"

"Well, I just wanted to say I was sorry..." he said turning from him.

"Can I call you sometime...?"

"Sure..." Scotty said exiting.

Orville arrived next. While they smiled at him, he sensed that tension remained. Out of the corner of his eye he saw Rory and Trixie and the baby carriage.

"They look healthy!" he said bending down to their level.

"How's Alistair?" Rory asked, addressing the elephant in the room.

The Electric Eel!

"Better. Thank you. Should be coming home next week..."

"Wonderful!"

"Big crowd coming tonight..." Lobelia whispered to her boss.

"Oh?!"

Carlotta, Irene, and Virginia arrived next along with Edgar. Edgar looked around the room, thinking. *Poppy will probably never come back to this place again...*

"Evening, brother..." Orville said.

"Evening..."

As the night progressed, a large group of people gathered around the bar and at every chair in the building. Some people even gathered by the stage, taking up precious space for the band. Malka walked on stage and began to serenade them, suddenly overwhelmed by the crowd.

"It's hopping tonight!"

"Here's hoping no one goes into the eel tank tonight..." he said clinking a glass with her.

"Let's hope..."

At a quarter till ten, a large sound emanated from the bakery. Figuring it was a raid, they began to put their alcohol away, stashing bottles in their usual hiding places. *We're getting better at this...* Lobelia thought. The band switched to its usual warning song as Malka was caught off guard mid-sentence. Wallace continued playing at the piano as if nothing happened.

"That won't be necessary..." a uniformed man informed them with the flash of a badge.

"We aren't here for hooch..." the other man said.

"What?" Orville said in confusion.

"We're here about the murder of Julius Alfonso..."

Carlotta reddened and tried to stand. One of the officers thwarted her with the point of a weapon. She clutched her chest as if having a coronary. Irene reached for her mother in defense.

"Not so fast, Mrs. Alfonso! Mrs. Wright! Miss Alfonso, we're all going downtown!"

"What is this?" Carlotta barked.

"You're under arrest for the murder of Julius Alfonso..."

"This is absurd! I have rights!" she barked.

"You are correct! We have a female officer waiting outside to take you downtown...!"

"Well. I never!"

The officer chuckled to himself in spite of it all. Orville approached him, trying to hide his anxiety. A bead of sweat formed on the back of his neck and dripped down his back.

"Officer, can't we settle this like gentlemen?"

"I'll deal with you later..." he warned. "Don't go anywhere!"

"Well then I'm coming!"

"Me too," Edgar said.

She is my mother after all... He thought. *And I wouldn't miss this for the world...*

"Suit yourself. You can meet us downtown, even though most of it doesn't concern you...Anyone else feel the need to see the police precinct?"

As always, Orville looked to Lobelia and reached for his keys. Then he looked at his brother. *You coming?*

"One more thing..." the officer informed the group.

"Emilio LaRocca, you are under arrest for the murder of Detective Talbert..."

Emilio? They all thought. *LaRocca?* Others looked for Mr. LaRocca in the crowd. His partner turned and handcuffed Tiny.

"Sorry to have to do this...And you are suspected in the murder of Heyward "Catfish" Robinson...."

Lobelia lost her usual cool and ran to him. Tiny's shoulders drooped as if expecting it. Tears welled up in her eyes, causing the corners to redden slightly.

The Electric Eel!

"Is this true? Did you kill that detective? Did you kill Catfish too? Please tell me it's not true!" she pleaded. "Tiny say something!"

"It's best if he doesn't say anything incriminating, ma'am..." the officer warned. "At least not without a lawyer present..."

"This way, Mr. LaRocca..."

But Tiny exited in shackles without answering her. Lobelia continued to cry as an officer led the man she loved outside to a separate police car. She watched as he tucked Tiny's huge body in the back of a squad car, careful not to bang his head on the door in the process and disappeared inside.

"Ladies?" the lead detective said to the three women.

Carlotta pulled her arm away in indignance and reached for bright red purse as all three women stood. Irene gave the officer a haughty look as if he were wasting her time. Virginia bit her lip and followed them like a lost puppy...

Orville and Edgar met them outside at his car. Edgar shifted his weight into his brother's automobile moving his artificial leg carefully inside and closing the door with his right hand.

"Were you in on this?" he asked his brother directly.

Orville ignored him for a second as his sister, mother and aunt were led into a patrol car. He blinked, thinking about his brother's question, and turned to him in the passenger seat. Edgar's eyes widened in anticipation of the answer.

"No..." Orville said affirmatively.

*Well that's a relief...*Edgar thought facing forward. Orville followed the police car.

"But you knew..."

Orville gripped the wheel in hesitation. Edgar took his silence as an admission of guilt...*How could he not tell anyone?*

"She's my mother, okay?"

She's my mom too! Edgar thought, shooting him a look. *And he was our father!*

As Orville sped up, they turned to give the Electric Eel one final glance. *It's all built on lies!* Edgar thought.

EIGHTY-TWO

Virginia Alfonso sat patiently away from the rest of the family with her hands in her lap...Immediately, the police had separated her from her niece and sister-in-law at the precinct once they arrived. The room they had put her in was miniscule... *A five by nine cell...*

*I set him up...*She thought. *And Carlotta set up my brother...And truth be told I miss them both tremendously...And Irene put up the money to pay for it!* She thought, weeping.

She watched as her niece and sister-in-law, both unused to being manhandled, were segregated. Irene's husband appeared next, doting on his wife as always. One of the officers recognized him and placed his palm on his face in frustration.

"Evening, Congressman Wright..." he said. "Dear God, what have we opened up?"

Mr. Wright pushed past him and made a beeline for his wife. Irene made a pouty baby face and hugged him meekly as if she lacked strength to stand. She touched his shoulder gently and reached for her compact to fix her lipstick.

"There...There..."

"Oh, Alvin it was awful! They took my picture! They fingerprinted me! They took my purse!"

"We'll get you out of here..."

"I didn't kill my father..."

"I believe you..." he whispered.

"All I did was loan my mother money... How was I to know what she'd do with it? I never wanted anything to do with that place, anyway..."

"Shh..." he chided.

The Electric Eel!

Not wanting to spend anymore time on this and to save face, Mr. Wright stood and walked to the desk. The woman at the desk looked at him as he reached in his pocket for a wad of bills. She blinked.

"I can't take a bribe, sir..."

"No..." he said. "I'm paying my wife's bail...How much is it?"

"Your wife is being charged as an accessory to homicide...Her bail is set at one hundred dollars..." the police officer informed him. "You are free to go so long as you surrender your wife's passport...Don't go anywhere..."

Irene began to cry. Mr. Wright reached in his briefcase and handed him the appropriate dark blue document along with the cash. *There goes our trip to Europe...*He thought.

"You're free to go..."

The officers watched as the well to do couple walked to the front. Before they could exit, Carlotta realized her daughter was leaving in her periphery and dove for her. Carlotta began to wail and then shriek at her youngest child.

"Irene! Don't leave me here! Irene! *Irene!* I'm innocent... You were as in on it as I was...! And now you're leaving me here to rot! I don't wanna die in this place! They'll give me the chair for sure! Irene! Say something..."

Irene, however, brushed her mother off and walked toward a long black car that was waiting outside, her pale satin heels clicking on the bare floor. Carlotta put her head in her hands and continued to bawl. Mr. Wright embraced his wife but did not look at his mother-in-law as if afraid of admitting something...

"She'll probably get off with a slap on the wrist..." the older officer told his partner. "Still, because of who he is it'll be all over the papers by morning..."

Orville and Edgar arrived as their sister's limousine was pulling out of the precinct. *Irene always gets off easy...*They thought as their baby sister ducked down in the seat to avoid their gaze. Next, they watched as their brother-in law pulled down his visor to shield his face, despite the fact that the sun had not yet risen.

"What a mess!" Edgar told his brother.

"Are my mother, aunt and sister under arrest?" Orville said ignoring his brother and speaking for the family.

"Your sister posted bail and has been released on her own recognizance…"

Before they could react to this news, Tiny was led across the floor in handcuffs. His large feet shuffled as he walked the walk of a condemned man…*Like Jacob Marley in a Christmas Carol…*

Tiny mustered a smile at the sight of Edgar and Orville…He hung his head slightly again, dwarfing the police officer in front of him. Orville opened his mouth to address him but Tiny cut him off.

"LaRocca is my grandfather…" he informed them. "Say goodbye to Lobelia for me…And tell her I'm sorry…"

They nodded as Tiny was led away…To be booked, most likely…*What is happening to all of us?* Orville asked.

Then all eyes turned to Virginia as she was led out of her small room to be processed, next. Her pretty face was marred by tears and exhaustion, the constant reminder of the bad choices she had made now on her wrists and ankles.

"Did you do this?" Edgar asked point blank.

"I set up Tal, yea…" she said.

"Why?"

"They told me to…"

"*Who* told you to?"

She ignored the question and continued, "And I was mad cause he was with another girl…But I didn't kill your dad…Tell Nani and Papi bye for me…"

*I guess that's some relief…*Edgar thought. *That poor detective…* He knitted his brows in confusion as his aunt disappeared somewhere into the jail amongst other similarly well-

The Electric Eel!

dressed, incarcerated women.

Next, a slovenly man was led inside the precinct. His eyes darted around the room as if it were a trick...A ploy to get him off the streets...Despite allowing him to shower, he reeked of alcohol. *From the cellular level!*

"It's okay..." one of the police women called as if beckoning to a frightened animal. "We just want you to identify whom you saw hurt Mr. Alfonso...They can't hurt you...It's a two-way mirror...They can't *see* you!"

The indigent man inched forward as if not believing them. Unlike the others he was not shackled, his hands free at his side. A kind woman reached for him and pulled him in front of a long window where several men of similar build, age and complexion stood holding sequential numbers.

"Turn to the right..." a man ordered them.

"Number three..." the man pointed in near tears.

"Turn to the front..."

"Number three!" he repeated, louder.

"Witness has identified number three...Mr. Clark!"

The officers cheered. Sid gave a defeated look as if losing a championship ball game and was led away in handcuffs. The man began to weep at the memory.

"We really appreciate you and we're going to help you get off the street..." one of the whispered. "Once we find the others we'll have you help identify them as well... You're free to go..."

Carlotta sat alone in a hard chair as the homeless man was led outside. Her red and black outfit reminded him of the devil...*She craned her neck, not processing what had transpired...*

One of the officers reached for her but she resisted, like a willful child. Then she fell over on her left side in despondence... *Get up!*

"I want my lawyer!" she shrieked.

"You'll be provided one…"

"I'm innocent!" she proclaimed.

"Tell it to the judge!" he said calmly but fearing he was losing control. "Let's go quietly…"

But what Carlotta did next was *horrifying*. With considerable speed she reached for the officer's service pistol and put it up to her left temple…The gun slipped out of the lawman's grasp as they wrestled with it.

"*NO!*" Edgar yelled from across the room.

As if in slow motion, Carlotta squeezed the trigger. With quick reflexes, the officer pushed the gun upward with the heel of his hand redirecting its trajectory to a one-hundred-and-thirty-degree angle. The bullet missed her temple by millimeters, the sound buzzing in her ear like an angry hornet. A fraction of a second later a plume of smoke and gunpowder came as the bullet ricocheted off the plaster ceiling. Finally, Carlotta fell to the floor.

"I wanna die!!" she screamed. "Let me *die!*"

Unimpressed with her theatrics but glad she was unharmed, the officer secured his gun in its holster and reached for the older woman's wrist. She cried in a pathetic, despondent heap as Orville and Edgar looked on at the spectacle that was now their mother. Another officer came to help her off the floor.

"C'mon, Mrs. Alfonso…Let's go…"

EPILOGUE

1927

Sid Clark found himself on a familiar street… Between the Electric Eel and the

The Electric Eel!

seedy joints he used to frequent leading up to High Street... Marie Toussad's Gallery now sat behind him, rebranded as another sleezy joint with the attempt at a classy, exotic name... *The Oriental Lotus Massage! But still under the same management!* He thought with a chuckle, lighting up a smoke. *They're just too dumb to notice the difference!*

Sid had been let out on good behavior between court dates...*Free for now!* All the rest had either been killed or sent up the river...*Except me!* He thought with much arrogance.

He flicked the cigarette out on the concrete as something caught his attention. The orange end of the smoke lingered for a second and then died, fading into the obscurity of the darkness as he walked to the shell of the Electric Eel, now abandoned, and forgotten. Sid reached for the door, and it gave way easily...And went inside.

The bakery, too, was vacant; the pastry case empty and dust covered. Its glass was broken in several places from vandals as if struck with a hammer. Sid remembered the baked goods that used to fill this place...*The front for the illegal activity going on behind...The first place I tried canapes...*

The center door which used to divide the center room from outsiders, also was busted and swung open with a light push. He pictured the huge man with the baby face who used to guard this place like a watchdog. *What was his name? Tiny? Didn't he go to jail?*

The bar was now also dilapidated. Its once beautiful, exotic wood splintered in pieces and sticky with something green like antifreeze. The luxurious glassware that used to hang above the bar in the shape of a starfish was now smashed to smithereens as evident by shards of broken glass everywhere. Pieces of green and brown bottles crunched up his feet as he moved further into what was once a spectacular speakeasy.

The roulette wheel was also gone. Carted away most likely, to another establishment where it would continue to generate revenue...*Legally and illegally...*The plush chairs where gamblers would sit around the wheel were now torn and reduced to matchsticks along with their shattered glassware. A few cigarette butts remained nearby in ashtrays along with the permanent, residual stink of second-hand smoke as if the smokers had simply vanished into thin air...

The stage and grand piano were also missing. He pictured the strange guy with the long fingers playing effortlessly alongside the woman with the dog as they serenaded the crowd with their soulful tunes...*Did she die?* He couldn't recall...

Particles of broken glass continued to protest under his weight as he walked to the far-left side of the room. Chips of wine glasses and bottle caps stuck to the soles of his shoes as he walked.

Outside two of Mr. LaRocca's associates, who had just come from the massage parlor next door, spotted Sid going inside what used to be the Electric Eel. One of them scratched his head, wanting to make sure it was who they saw. He nudged his partner.

"It's him..." the other one reassured him.

Unaware that had anyone had seen him inside, Sid approached what used to be the eel tank. A once spectacular aquarium sat empty like a sunken ship, its occupants vacated to some unknown place. A thick carpet of deep green moss coated the center of the tank leaving a disgusting, opaque teal film that blocked the view inside the glass. *Where had they gone?* He wondered.

As Sid came to the back of the facility, two men entered quietly, careful not to make a sound with their shoes on the detritus of glassware that lay everywhere. One of them put his fingers up to his lips. *Shh!*

What Sid saw next made him feel disquieted. A large ornate table with pieces of what looked like a crystal ball along with something stiff and papery. *Tarot cards!* He recognized the imagery as someone had brought a deck into prison. A large instrument of some kind sat on the chair. *A silver horn of some kind! What's that for?*

As he continued to peruse, he touched nothing. One of the men scanned the premises behind him as Sid leaned over what used to be Madame Beulah's table and reached for

The Electric Eel!

something long handled and weighty. *A snow shovel someone had tried to clean up the mess with that had been discarded in a corner...The perfect weapon of opportunity!*

Then something else on the table caught Sid's attention...A board with gold and black letters and a leaf-shaped planchette with a hole in the center...*A Ouija Board as his grandmother would have called it! Why is it here?*

But before Sid could ponder it further, he was struck with something. *Hard!* And then he was hit again with something else...This time with a more cylindrical end... Like the sharp end of a fireplace poker...

Before everything went dark, Sid found himself being dragged by the shoulders like a prisoner of war...He gave little resistance as blood poured from the center of his skull like a burst pipe, down his chest, his hands going limp at his side. Through the broken glass, they drug his lifeless body outside into the night...Never to be seen again...

Inside a few spirits began to emerge for their nightly rounds as if nothing had transpired...A blond woman in a catsuit with a dog moved in and out of where the stage used to be...A young man with a handlebar mustache...And man cut open like a ham...And several others...Soon a man in a blue pin-striped suit and spats would join them...His face dented in with a garden tool...

Points of cloudy bits of crystal spun in a circle forming the shape of a sphere in the center of the table. The silver spirit horn raised slightly, announcing something unintelligible. Spun by some unknown hand, the spade-shaped planchette moved one-hundred and eighty degrees and began to spell something...

"E-E-L!"

THE END

Cocktails featured in this book

Electric Eel

15 ml Pernod

15 ml Crème De Menthe

Lemonade

Add half of Pernod and half of Crème de Menthe so it layers to a tall glass. Fill with lemonade

Punch A la Romaine

1 egg white

1 oz. white rum

½ oz. simple syrup

½ oz. fresh lemon juice

1 oz. fresh orange juice

Champagne

Orange peel

Combine egg white, rum, simple syrup, lemon juice and orange juice in a cocktail shaker. Shake without ice, then add ice to the shaker, and shake again until chilled. Strain into a snifter filled with crushed ice, and top with Champagne. Garnish with orange peel.

Aviation

2 ounces gin

The Electric Eel!

¼ ounce Crème de Violette

½ ounce Maraschino Liqueur

¾ ounce lemon juice squeezed

cherry or dried cherry garnish

Add the gin, maraschino liqueur, Creme de Violette and lemon juice to shaker with ice and shake until well-chilled. Strain into a cocktail glass. Garnish with a brandied cherry.

Negroni

1-ounce gin

1-ounce Sweet Vermouth

1-ounce Campari

Orange Twist for Garnish. Fill old-fashioned glass. Pour gin, Vermouth and Campari. Stir. Squeeze orange twist over glass. Top with orange

Clover Club

2 ounces gin

3/4-ounce lemon juice

1/4 ounce raspberry syrup

1 large egg white

1 teaspoon granulated sugar

Fresh raspberries, for garnish

In a cocktail shaker with ice cubes, pour the gin, lemon juice, raspberry syrup, egg white, and sugar. Shake vigorously (more than normal to mix egg white and sugar). Strain into a chilled cocktail glass. Garnish with a skewer of fresh raspberries.

Classic Bloody Mary

Celery salt

The Electric Eel!

1 lemon wedge

1 lime wedge

2 ounce vodka

4 ounces tomato juice

1 tsp horseradish

2 tsp Tabasco

1 tsp Worchester sauce

Paprika

Olives

Salt

Parsley

Celery Stalk

Pour celery salt on a plate. Rub the juice side of a lemon and lime on the outside of a pint glass. Rub outside of glass with celery salt. Wipe inside with paper towel. Squeeze lemon and lime in shaker and drop them in. Add all ingredients except garnishes with a handful of ice. Strain into prepared glass. Top with celery, olives, lime wedge and parsley.

Made in the USA
Columbia, SC
29 November 2023